A Second Chance for the Millionaire

LUCY GORDON
NICOLA MARSH
BARBARA WALLACE

MILLS

First Published in Great Britain 2016
By Mills & Boon, an imprint of HarperCollins*Publishers*
1 London Bridge Street, London, SE1 9GF

Fixed up with Mr Right?, *Who Wants To Marry a Millionaire?* and *The Billionaire's Fair Lady* were first published in Great Britain by Harlequin (UK) Limited.

ISBN: 978-0-263-92050-5

05-0116

Our policy is to use papers that are natural, renewable and recyclable products and made from wood grown in sustainable forests.The logging and manufacturing processes conform to the legal environmental regulations of the country of origin.

Printed and bound in Spain
by CPI, Barcelona

RESCUED BY THE BROODING TYCOON

BY

LUCY GORDON

Lucy Gordon cut her writing teeth on magazine journalism, interviewing many of the world's most interesting men, including Warren Beatty, Charlton Heston and Sir Roger Moore. She also camped out with lions in Africa and had many other unusual experiences which have often provided the background for her books. Several years ago, while staying Venice, she met a Venetian who proposed in two days. They have been married ever since. Naturally this has affected her writing, where romantic Italian men tend to feature strongly.

Two of her books have won the Romance Writers of America RITA® Award.

You can visit her website at www.lucy-gordon.com.

I should like to dedicate this book to the Royal National Lifeboat Institution, without whose help my heroine could never have been as spunky as she is.

CHAPTER ONE

IT WAS the burst of beauty that caught Darius unaware. He didn't regard himself as a man vulnerable to beauty. Efficiency, ruthlessness, financial acumen, these things could be counted on.

He'd been driven to hire a helicopter on the English mainland and fly five miles across the sea to the little island of Herringdean. Since it was now his property, it made good sense to inspect it briefly on his way to an even more important meeting.

Good sense. Cling to that, since everything else had failed him.

But the sudden vision of sunlit sea, the waves glittering as they broke against the sand, stunned him and made him press closer to the window.

'Go lower,' he commanded, and watched as the helicopter descended, sweeping along the coast of Herringdean Island. From here he could study the place with a critical eye.

Or so he believed. But there was no criticism in the glance he turned on the lush green cliffs, the golden beaches; only astonished pleasure.

The cliffs were sinking until they were only a few feet higher than the beach. He could see a large house that must once have been elegant, but was now fast falling into disrepair. In front of it stretched a garden leading to a plain lawn, close to the sand.

In the far distance were buildings that must be Ellarick, the largest town on the island: population twenty thousand.

'Land here,' he said, 'on that lawn.'

'I thought you wanted to fly over the town,' the pilot protested.

But suddenly he yearned to avoid towns, cars, crowds. The beach seemed to call to him. It was an unfamiliar sensation for a man who wasn't normally impulsive. In the financial world impulsiveness could be dangerous, yet now he yielded with pleasure to the need to explore below.

'Go lower,' he repeated urgently.

Slowly the machine sank onto the lawn. Darius leapt out, a lithe figure whose fitness and agility belied the desk-bound businessman he usually was, and hurried down to the beach. The sand was slightly damp, but smooth and hard, presenting little threat to his expensive appearance.

That appearance had been carefully calculated to inform the world that here was a successful man who could afford to pay top prices for his clothes. A few grains of sand might linger on his handmade shoes but they could be easily brushed off, and it was a small price to pay for what the beach offered him.

Peace.

After the devastating events that had buffeted him recently there was nothing more blessed than to stand here in the sunlight, throw his head back, close his eyes, feel the soft breeze on his face, and relish the silence.

So many years spent fighting, conspiring, manoeuvring, while all the time this simple perfection had been waiting, and he hadn't realised.

Outwardly, Darius seemed too young for such thoughts;

in his mid-thirties, tall, strong, attractive, ready to take on the world. Inwardly, he knew otherwise. He had already taken on the world, won some battles, lost others, and was weary to his depths.

But here there could be a chance to regain strength for the struggles that lay ahead. He breathed in slowly, yielding himself to the quiet, longing for it to last.

Then it ended.

A shriek of laughter tore the silence, destroying the peace. With a groan he opened his eyes and saw two figures in the sea, heading for the shore. As they emerged from the water he realised that one of them was a large dog. The other was a young woman in her late twenties with a lean, athletic build, not voluptuous but dashingly slender, with long elegant legs. Her costume was a modest black one-piece, functional rather than enticing, and her brown hair was pinned severely back out of the way.

As a man much pursued by women, Darius knew they commonly used swimming as a chance to parade their beauty. But if this girl was sending out any message to men it was, *I wear what's useful, so don't kid yourself that I'm flaunting my body to attract you.*

'Can I help you?' she cried merrily as she bounced up the beach.

'I'm just looking round, getting the feel of the place.'

'Yes, it's wonderful, isn't it? Sometimes I think if I ever get to heaven it'll be just like this. Not that I expect to go to heaven. They slam the gates on characters like me.'

Although he would have died before admitting it, the reference to heaven so exactly echoed his own thoughts that now he found he could forgive her for interrupting him.

'Characters like what?' he asked.

'Awkward,' she said cheerfully. 'Lots of other things too, but chiefly awkward. That's what my friends say.'

'Those friends who haven't been driven away by your awkwardness?'

'Right.'

He indicated the house behind him. 'I believe that belongs to Morgan Rancing.'

'Yes, but if you've come to see him you've had a wasted journey. Nobody knows where he is.'

Rancing was on the far side of the world, hiding from his creditors, including himself, but Darius saw no need to mention that.

She stepped back to survey him, a curious look in her eyes. Then it vanished as though an idea had occurred to her, only to be dismissed as impossible.

'You're lucky Rancing isn't here,' she observed. 'He'd hit the roof at you bringing down your machine on his land. Nobody's allowed on his property.'

'Does that include this beach?' he asked, regarding the fences that enclosed the stretch of sand.

'It certainly does.' She gave a chuckle. 'Be a sport. If you see him, don't say you caught me on his private beach. He disapproves of my swimming here.'

'But you do it anyway,' he observed wryly.

'It's so lovely that I can't resist. The other beaches are full of holidaymakers but here you can have it all to yourself; just you and the sun and the sky.' She flung out her arms in a dramatic gesture, smiling up at him. 'The world is yours.'

Darius nodded, feeling a curious sense of ease at the way her thoughts chimed with his own, and looked at her with renewed interest. Despite her boyish air, she wasn't lacking in feminine charm. There was real beauty in her eyes, that were large and deep blue, full of life, seeming to invite him into a teasing conspiracy.

'That's very true,' he said.

'So you won't tell him that you saw me on his private beach?'

'Actually, it's my private beach.'

Her smile vanished. 'What do you mean?'

'This island is mine now.'

'Rancing sold it to you?' she gasped.

Without knowing it, she'd said the fatal word. Rancing hadn't sold him the island, he'd tricked him into it. In a flash, his goodwill towards her vanished, and a stubborn expression overtook his face. 'I told you it's mine,' he said harshly. 'That's all that matters. My name is Darius Falcon.'

She drew a quick breath. 'I thought I'd seen your face before, in the newspaper. Weren't you the guy who—?'

'Never mind that,' he interrupted curtly. He knew his life, both private and business, had been all over the papers, and he didn't like being reminded of it. 'Perhaps now you'll tell me who you are.'

'Harriet Connor,' she said. 'I have an antique shop in Ellarick.'

'I shouldn't think you get much trade in this place,' he said, looking around at the isolation.

'On the contrary, Herringdean attracts a lot of tourists. Surely you knew that?'

The question, *How could you buy it without knowing about it?* hung in the air. Since he wasn't prepared to discuss the ignominious way he'd been fooled, he merely shrugged.

From behind Harriet came a loud yelp. The dog was charging up the beach, spraying water everywhere, heading straight for Darius.

'Steady, Phantom,' she called, trying to block his way.

'Keep him off me,' Darius snapped.

But it was too late. Gleeful at the sight of a stranger to

investigate, the dog hurled himself the last few feet, reared up on his hind legs and slammed his wet, sandy paws down on Darius's shoulders. He was a mighty beast, able to meet a tall man face to face, and lick him enthusiastically.

'Get him off me. He's soaking.'

'Phantom, get down!' Harriet cried.

He did so but only briefly, hurling himself at Darius again, this time with a force that took them both down to the ground. As he lay helplessly on the sand, Phantom loomed over him, licking his face and generally trying to show friendliness. He looked aggrieved as his mistress hauled him off.

'Bad dog! I'm very cross with you.'

Darius got to his feet, cursing at the wreck of his suit.

'He wasn't attacking you,' Harriet said in a pleading voice. 'He just likes people.'

'Whatever his intentions, he's made a mess,' Darius said in an icy voice.

'I'll pay to have your suit cleaned.'

'Cleaned?' he snapped. 'I'll send you a bill for a new one. Keep away from me, you crazy animal.'

He put up his arm to ward off another encounter, but Harriet threw her arms protectively around the dog.

'You'd better go,' she said in a voice that was now as icy as his own. 'I can't hold him for ever.'

'You should know better than to let a creature that size run free.'

'And you should know better than to wear a suit like that on the beach,' she cried.

The undeniable truth of this soured his temper further, leaving him no choice but to storm off in the direction of the helicopter. He guessed his pilot had seen everything, but the man was too wise to comment.

As they lifted off, Darius looked down and saw Harriet

gazing at the machine, one hand shielding her eyes. Then Phantom reared up again, enclosing her in his great paws, and at once she forgot the helicopter to cuddle the dog, while he licked her face. So much for being cross with that stupid mutt, Darius thought furiously. Clearly, he was all she cared about.

He thought of how he'd stood on the beach, alone, peaceful for the first time in months, and how clumsily she had destroyed that moment. He wouldn't forgive her for that.

From this high point on the hill overlooking Monte Carlo, Amos Falcon could see the bay but, unlike his son, he failed to notice the beauty of the sea. His attention was all for the buildings on the slope, tall, magnificent, speaking of money, though none spoke so loudly as his own house, a sprawling, three-storey edifice, bought because it dominated its surroundings.

It was money and the need to protect it that had first brought him to this tax haven years ago. He'd started life poor in a rundown mining town in the north of England, and got out fast. Working night and day, he'd built up a fortune of his own, helped by marrying a woman with wealth, and he'd left England for a more friendly tax regimen as soon as he could, determined that no government would be allowed to rob him of his gains.

'Where the devil is he?' he muttered crossly. 'It's not like Darius to be late. He knows I want him here before the others.'

Janine, his third wife, a well-preserved woman in her fifties with a kind face and a gentle manner, laid a hand on his arm.

'He's a busy man,' she said. 'His company is in trouble—'

'Everyone's company is in trouble,' Amos growled. 'He should be able to deal with it. I've taught him well.'

'Perhaps you spent too much time teaching him,' she suggested. 'He's your son, not just a business associate to be instructed.'

'He's no business associate of mine,' Amos said. 'I said I'd taught him well, but he never quite learned how to take the final, necessary step.'

'Because he has a conscience,' she suggested. 'He can be ruthless, but only up to a point.'

'Exactly. I could never quite make him see… Ah, well, maybe his recent troubles will have taught him a lesson.'

'You mean his wife leaving him?'

'I mean that damn fool divorce settlement he gave her. Much too generous. He just let her have whatever she demanded.'

Janine sighed. She'd heard him ranting on this subject so often, and there was no end to it.

'He did it for the children's sake,' she pointed out.

'He could have got his children back if he'd played hard, but he wouldn't do it.'

'Good for him,' Janine murmured.

Amos scowled. He could forgive her sentimental view of life. After all, she was a woman. But sometimes it exasperated him.

'That's all very well,' he growled, 'but then the world imploded.'

'Only the financial world,' she ventured.

His caustic look questioned whether there was any other kind, but he didn't rise to the bait.

'And suddenly he had a pittance compared to what he'd had before,' he continued. 'So he had to go back to that woman and try to persuade her to accept less. Naturally, she refused, and since the money had already been transferred to her he couldn't touch it.'

'You'd never have made that mistake,' Janine observed

wryly, perhaps thinking of the pre-nuptial agreement she'd had to sign before their wedding five years earlier. 'Never give anything you can't take back, that's your motto.'

'I never said that.'

'No, you've never actually said it,' she agreed quietly.

'Where the devil is he?'

'Don't upset yourself,' she pleaded. 'It's bad for you to get agitated after your heart attack.'

'I'm over that,' he growled.

'Until the next time. And don't say there won't be a next time because the doctor said a massive attack like that is always a warning.'

'I'm not an invalid,' he said firmly. 'Look at me. Do I look frail?'

He rose and stood against the backdrop of the sky, challenging her with his pose and his expression, and she had to concede the point. Amos was a big man, over six foot, broad-shouldered and heavy. All his life he'd been fiercely attractive, luring any woman he wanted, moving from marriage to affairs and on to marriage as the mood took him. Along the way, he'd fathered five sons by four mothers in different countries, thus spreading his tentacles across the world.

Recently, there had been an unexpected family reunion. Struck down by a heart attack, he'd lain close to death while his sons gathered at his bedside. But, against all the odds, he'd survived, and at last they had returned to their different countries.

Now he had summoned them back for a reason. Amos was making plans for the future. He'd regained much of his strength, although less than he claimed.

To the casual eye, he was a fine, healthy specimen, still handsome beneath a head of thick white hair. Only two people knew of the breathless attacks that followed exertion. One of them was Janine, his wife, who regarded him with a mixture of love and exasperation.

The other was Freya, Janine's daughter by an earlier marriage. A trained nurse, she'd recently come to stay at her mother's request.

'He doesn't want a nurse there in case it makes him look weak,' Janine pleaded, 'but if I invite my daughter he can't refuse.'

'But he knows I'm a nurse,' Freya had pointed out.

'Yes, but we don't have to talk about it, and you can keep an eye on him discreetly. It helps that you don't look like a nurse.'

This was an understatement. Freya was delicately built with elegant movements, a pretty face and a cheeky demeanour. She might have been a dancer, a nightclub hostess, or anything except a medical expert with an impressive list of letters after her name.

An adventurous spirit had made her leave her last job in response to her mother's request.

'I was getting bored,' she said. 'Same thing day after day.'

'You certainly won't get that with Amos,' Janine had remarked.

She was right. After only a few days Freya remarked, 'It's like dealing with a spoilt child. Don't worry. I can do what's necessary.'

Luckily, Amos liked his stepdaughter and under her care his health improved. It was she who now came bouncing out onto the balcony and said, 'Time for your nap.'

'Not for another ten minutes,' he growled.

She smiled. 'No, it's now. No argument.'

He grinned. 'You're a bully, you know that?'

'Of course I know that. I work at it. Get going.'

He shrugged, resigned and good-natured, and let her

escort him as far as his bedroom door. Janine would have gone in with him, but he waved her away.

'I can manage without supervision. Just keep your eyes open for Darius. I can't think what's keeping him.' He closed the door.

'What's going on?' Freya asked as the two women walked away.

'Goodness knows. He was supposed to arrive this morning but he called to say there'd been an unexpected delay.'

'And then all the other sons, Leonid, Marcel, Travis, Jackson, just a few days apart. Why is Amos suddenly doing this?'

'I can only guess,' Janine said sadly. 'He puts on this big act of being fully recovered, but he had a scare. He's seen that his life could end at any time, and he's…getting things sorted out, is how he puts it, starting with changes to his will.'

'Funny, he's so organised that you'd think he'd have fixed that ages ago.'

'He did, but I believe he's taking another look at all of his lads and deciding—I don't know—which one will manage best—'

'Which one is most like him,' Freya said shrewdly.

'You're very hard on him,' Janine protested.

'No more than he deserves. Of all the arrogant—'

'But he's very fond of you. You're the daughter he never had and he'd love you to be really part of the family.' She paused delicately.

'You mean he wants me to be his daughter-in-law?' Freya demanded, aghast. 'The cheeky crook.'

'Don't call him a crook,' Janine protested.

'Why not? No man builds up the kind of fortune he did by honest means. And he's taught his sons to be the same.

Anything for money, that's how they all think. So if one of them can talk me into marriage he'll cop the lot. Was Amos mad when he thought of that? Nothing on this earth would persuade me—there isn't one of them I'd ever dream of—ye gods and little fishes!'

'Don't tell him I told you,' Janine begged.

'Don't worry. Not a word.' Suddenly her temper faded, replaced by wicked mischief. 'But I might enjoy a good laugh. Yes, I think it deserves that.'

As she hurried away her mother heard the laughter echoing back, and sighed. She couldn't blame Freya one bit. She, of all people, knew what madness it was to marry into this family.

Darius arrived the next day, apologising with a fictional tale of business dealings. Not for the world would he have admitted that he'd been forced to leave Herringdean, return to the mainland and check into a hotel to put on a fresh suit. Normally, no power on earth could force him to change his plans and he resented it. Another thing for which Harriet Connor was to blame.

He found her mysteriously disturbing because she seemed to haunt him as two people. There was the girl who'd briefly charmed him with her instinctive empathy for his feelings about the isolated place. And there was the other one who'd interfered with his plans, destroyed his dignity with her stupid hound, and committed the unforgivable crime of seeing him at a disadvantage. He had dismissed her from his mind but she seemed unaware of that fact and popped up repeatedly in one guise or another.

A fanciful man might have defined her two aspects as the Good Fairy and the Bad Fairy. Darius, who wasn't fanciful, simply called her 'that wretched female'.

His father greeted him in typical fashion. 'So there you are at last. About time too.'

'An unexpected matter that required my attention.'

Amos grunted. 'As long as you sorted it out to your advantage.'

'Naturally,' Darius said, brushing aside the memory of lying on the sand. 'Then I got here as soon as I could. I'm glad to see you looking better, Father.'

'I *am* better. I keep saying so but my womenfolk won't believe me. I suppose Freya talked a lot when she collected you from the airport.'

'I asked her questions and, like a good nurse, she answered them.'

'Nurse be damned. She's here as my stepdaughter.'

'If you say so.'

'What do you think of her?'

'She seems a nice girl, what little I've seen of her.'

'She cheers the place up. And she's a good cook. Better than that so-called professional I employ. She's doing supper for us tonight. You'll enjoy it.'

He did enjoy it. Freya produced excellent food, and could crack jokes that lightened the atmosphere. She was pleasant to have around, and Darius found himself wondering why more women couldn't be like her instead of invading other people's private property with their sharp remarks and their dangerous dogs.

Awkward. She'd said it herself, and that was exactly right.

After supper, in his father's study, the two men confronted each other.

'I gather things aren't too good?' Amos grunted.

'Not for me or anyone else,' Darius retorted. 'There's a global crisis, hadn't you heard?'

'Yes, and some are weathering it better than others. That

contract you had the big fight over, I warned you how to word the get-out clause, and if you'd listened to me you could have told them where to stuff their legal action.'

'But they're decent people,' Darius protested. 'They knew very little about business—'

'All the better. You could have done as you liked and they wouldn't have found out until too late. You're soft, that's your trouble.'

Darius grimaced. In the financial world, his reputation was far from soft. Cold, unyielding, power-hungry, that was what people said of him. But he drew the line at taking advantage of helpless innocence, and he'd paid the price for it; a price his father would never have paid.

'But it's not too late,' Amos conceded in a milder tone. 'Now you're here there are ways I can help.'

'That's what I hoped,' Darius said quietly.

'You haven't always taken my advice, but perhaps you've got the sense to take it now. And the first problem is how you're going to deal with Morgan Rancing.'

'I must tell you—'

'I've heard disturbing rumours about some island he owns off the south coast of England. They say he'll try to use it to cover his debts, and I'm warning you to have no truck with that. Don't give it a thought. What you must do—'

'It's too late,' Darius growled. 'Herringdean is already mine.'

'What? You agreed to take it?'

'No, I wasn't given the chance,' Darius snapped. 'Rancing has vanished. Next thing, I received papers that transferred ownership of Herringdean to me. His cellphone is dead, his house is empty. Nobody knows where he is, or if they do they're not talking. I can either accept the island or go without anything.'

'But it'll be more trouble than it's worth,' Amos spluttered.

'I'm inclined to agree with you,' Darius murmured.

'So you know something about it?'

'A little. I need to go back and inspect it further.'

'And you're counting on it to pay your debts?'

'I don't know. But in the meantime I could do with an investor to make a one-time injection of cash and help me out.'

'Meaning me?'

'Well, as you're always telling me, you've survived the credit crunch better than anyone.'

'Yes, because I knew how to treat money.'

'Like a prisoner who's always trying to escape,' Darius recalled.

'Exactly. That's why I came to live here.'

He pushed open the door that led out onto the balcony overlooking the view over the bay that now glittered with lights against the darkness.

'I talked to a journalist once,' Amos recalled. 'She asked me all sorts of tom-fool questions. Why had I chosen to live in Monte Carlo? Was it just the tax relief or was there something else? I brought her out here and became lyrical about the view.'

'That I would have loved to hear,' Darius said.

Amos grinned. 'Yeah, you'd have been proud of me. The silly woman swallowed it hook, line and sinker. Then she wrote some trash about my being a man who appreciated peace and beauty. As though I gave a damn about that stuff.'

'Some people think it has value,' Darius murmured.

'Some people are fools,' Amos said firmly. 'I'd be sorry to think you were one of them. You've got yourself into a mess and you need me to get you out.'

'Two firms I did business with went bankrupt, owing me money,' Darius said grimly. 'I hardly created the mess myself.'

'But you made it worse by giving Mary everything she asked for in the divorce settlement.'

'That was before the crisis. I could afford it then.'

'But you didn't leave yourself any room for manoeuvre, no way to claw any of it back. You forgot every lesson I ever taught you. Now you want me to pour good money after bad.'

'So you won't help me?'

'I didn't say that, but we need to talk further. Not now. Later.'

Darius spoke through gritted teeth. 'Will my father invest in me, or will he not?'

'Don't rush me.'

'I have to. I need to make my decisions quickly.'

'All right, here's a way forward for you to consider. A rich wife, that's what you need, one who'll bring you a thumping great dowry.'

'What the hell are you talking about?'

'Freya. She's already my stepdaughter, and I want her properly in the family as my daughter-in-law.'

Darius stared. His ears were buzzing, and somewhere there was the memory of Freya, on the drive from the airport, saying, 'Your father's got some really mad ideas. Someone needs to tell him to forget them.'

She'd refused to elaborate, but now he understood.

'Why not?' Amos asked genially. 'You like the girl, you were laughing together at dinner—'

'Yes, I like her—far too much to do her such an injury, even if she'd agree, which she wouldn't, thank goodness. Do you really think you could make me crawl to do your bidding? If I have one thing left it's my independence, and I won't part with that.'

'Then you'll buy it at a high price. Don't blame me when you go bankrupt.'

Darius gave a cold smile. 'I'll remember.'

He turned and walked away, resisting the temptation to slam the door. Within an hour he'd left the house.

CHAPTER TWO

THE storm that swept over Herringdean had been violent, and nobody was surprised when the lifeboat was called out to an emergency. A small crowd had watched the boat plunge down the slipway into the sea, and a larger one gathered to see it return later that night.

Soon the rescued victims had been taken ashore into the waiting ambulance and the crew were free to exhale with relief and remove their life jackets.

Harriet took out her cellphone, dialled and spoke quickly. 'Is he all right? Good. I'll be home soon.'

When they had all finished making their report she slipped away and was followed by Walter and Simon, fellow crew members and friends.

'Hey, Harry,' Walter called. 'You sounded worried on the phone. Is someone ill?'

'No, I was just checking on Phantom. I left my neighbour looking after him. She promised to keep him safe.'

'Safe? Why suddenly? You never worried before.'

'I never had cause before. But now I worry. He's a very powerful man.'

'Who?'

From her pocket she took a newspaper cutting with a photograph and passed it to Walter.

'"Darius Falcon,"' he read. '"Giant of commerce, skilled

manipulator, the financial world is agog to know if he will avert disaster—'" He lowered the paper. 'How does a big shot come to know Phantom?'

'Because he's bought the island,' she said. 'Rancing had money troubles and he solved them by selling this place.'

Simon swore. 'And not a word to the people who live here, of course.'

'Of course. What do we matter to men like that, up there on their lofty perch? If you could have seen him as I did, arrogant and sure of himself—'

'You've met him?' Simon demanded.

'He came here a couple of days ago and I saw him on the beach. Phantom made a mess of his suit and he got mad, said he'd make me pay for a new one, and Phantom shouldn't be allowed out. So tonight, I asked my neighbour to watch over him while I was away, in case…well, just in case.'

'Hell!' Walter said. 'But is he really as bad as you say? If you two had a dust-up he probably just got a bit peeved—'

'You didn't see his face. He was more than a bit peeved. Now, I must get home.'

She hurried away, leaving the two men gazing after her, frowning with concern.

'Surely she's overreacting?' Simon mused. 'A bodyguard for a dog? A bit melodramatic, surely?'

'She's been that way for the last year,' Walter sighed. 'Ever since her husband died. Remember how good she and Brad were together? The perfect marriage. Now all she has left is his dog.'

'Hmm,' Simon grunted. 'Personally, I never liked Brad.'

'You say that because you fancied her rotten.'

'Sure, me and every other man on the island. Let's go for a drink.'

* * *

Harriet's car made quick time from the harbour to Ellarick, then to the little shop that she owned, and above which she lived. As she looked up the window opened and Phantom's head appeared, followed by that of a cheerful middle-aged woman. A moment later she was climbing the stairs to throw her arms about the dog.

'Mmm,' she cooed, and he responded with a throaty growl that sounded much the same.

'No problems?' she asked Mrs Bates, the neighbour who'd kept watch in her home.

'No sign of anyone.'

'Let me make you a cup of tea,' Harriet offered gratefully.

But Mrs Bates refused and departed. She was a kindly soul and she knew Harriet wanted to be alone with Phantom, although how she could bear the loneliness of the apartment Mrs Bates couldn't imagine.

But to Harriet it would never be lonely while Phantom was there. She hugged him fiercely before saying, 'Come on, let's take a walk. You need space to go mad in.'

They slipped out together into the darkness and walked down through the streets of the town, heading for the shore.

'But not "the ogre's" private beach,' she said. 'From now on, that's out of bounds.'

They found a place on the public sands where they could chase each other up and down in the moonlight.

'That's enough,' she gasped at last. 'Yes, I know you could go on till morning, but I'm out of puff.'

She threw herself down on the sand and stretched out on her back. Phantom immediately put a heavy paw on her chest, looking down into her face while she ruffled his fur.

'That's better,' she sighed. 'How could he not like you

when you were trying so hard to be friendly? Being hurled to the ground by you is a real privilege. You don't do it for everyone.' She gave a soft grunt of laughter. 'Just people with expensive clothes. If he really does send me the bill you'll be on plain rations for a long time. So will I, come to think of it.'

He woofed.

'The funny thing is, when I first saw him…he seemed decent, as if he really loved the sun and the fresh air; like someone who'd found himself in heaven. But when I discovered who he was he looked different. And then he was so rotten to you—'

Suddenly she sat up and threw her arms around the dog.

'You must be careful,' she said fiercely. 'You must, you *must*! If anything happened to you I couldn't bear it.'

Harriet buried her face against him. Phantom made a gentle sound, but he didn't try to move. This often happened, and he knew what he must do: keep still, stay warm and gentle, just be there for her. Instinct told him what she needed, and his heart told him how to give it.

'They think I'm crazy,' she whispered, 'getting paranoid over your safety. Well, perhaps I really am crazy, but you're all I've got—without you, there's no love or happiness in the world…only you…'

She kissed him and gave a shaky laugh.

'I expect you think I'm crazy too. Poor old boy. Come on, let's get home and you can have something special to eat.'

They left the beach, climbing the gently sloping road that led to the town. Suddenly she stopped. Far away, she could just make out the house where Rancing had lived before he fled, and where 'the ogre' would soon appear. It went by the grandiose name of Giant's Beacon, which might have been justified in its great days, but seemed rather over-the-top now that it was in a state of disrepair. At this distance it was tiny, but it stood out against the moonlit sky, and she could just make out that lights were coming on.

'He's here,' she breathed. 'Oh, heavens, let's get home, fast.'

They ran all the way, and as soon as they were safely inside Harriet locked the door.

Within hours of Darius's arrival the news had spread throughout the island. Kate, who'd kept house for Rancing, had a ready audience in the pub that evening.

'You should see the computers he's brought,' she said. 'Dozens of 'em. One for this and one for that, and something he calls "video links" so he can talk to people on the other side of the world, and there they are on the screen, large as life. It's like magic.'

The others grinned. Kate had never quite come to terms with the dot-com revolution, and most modern communications struck her as magic. She had little idea that behind its sweet, traditional image Herringdean was a more modern place than it looked.

Darius was also making the discovery, and was delighted with it. For a while he would be able to run his main business and his many subsidiary businesses, controlling everything from the centre of the web. It would be enough until he was ready to turn this place to his financial advantage.

Checking through the figures, he discovered that it was larger than he'd thought, about a hundred square miles with a population of a hundred and twenty thousand. Sheep and dairy farming flourished, so did fishing, and there were several industries, notably boat building and brewing.

Ellarick was not only a flourishing town, but a port with its own annual regatta.

One source of prosperity was tourism. Now summer was coming, the hotels were filling up as visitors began to flood the island, seeking tranquillity in the country lanes or excitement in the boats.

Ellarick also contained an elderly accountant called James Henly, who had dealt with Rancing's business. An early visit from him pleased Darius with the news that the rent paid to him by the other inhabitants was considerable, but also displeased him with the discovery that he was the victim of yet another piece of sharp practice.

'Mr Rancing persuaded several of his larger tenants, like the breweries, to pay him several months' rent in advance,' Henly explained in his dry voice. 'Apparently, he convinced them that there would be tax advantages. I need hardly say that I knew nothing about this. I was away and he took advantage of my absence to act on his own account. When I returned and found out, it was too late. He'd pocketed the money, and within a few days he'd vanished.'

'Meaning that it will be some time before I can collect rent from these establishments again,' Darius said in a mild manner that revealed nothing.

'I'm afraid so. Of course, what he's done is legally open to question since he made over everything to you, so technically it was your money he took. You could always try to get it back.'

His tone made it clear that he didn't attach much hope to that idea. Darius, who attached none at all, controlled his temper. It wasn't his way to display emotion to employees.

'How much are we talking about?' he said with a shrug.

He felt less like shrugging when he saw the figures.

Rancing had staged a spectacular theft and there was nothing he could do about it. But at all costs Henly mustn't be allowed to suspect his dismay.

'No problem,' Darius said as indifferently as he could manage. 'The tourism season is just starting. I shan't let a detail get me down.'

Henly's eyes widened at the idea of such a financial blow being a mere detail. He began to think the stories of Mr Falcon's impending ruin were untrue after all.

Darius, who'd intended him to think exactly that, asked casually, 'Did he leave owing you any money?'

'I'm afraid he did—'

'All right, just send me a detailed bill. That's all for now.'

For several days he remained in the house, rising early to link up with business contacts on one side of the world, eating whatever Kate brought him and barely taking his eyes from the computer screen. As the hours wore on, he turned to the other side of the world where he had business contacts whose day was just beginning. Day and night ceased to exist; all he knew was what he needed to do to survive.

On a whim, he searched the local phone directory until he found Harriet Connor, living in Bayton Street in Ellarick. A map showed him that it was in the centre of the town.

Then he put away the papers quickly. What did he care where she lived?

Thinking back to his work, at last he felt he'd put things on a firmer footing and could dare to hope. Perhaps it was time to venture outside. He'd hired a car but so far not used it. Now he drove into Ellarick, parked in a side street and got out to walk.

No doubt it was pure chance that made him walk down Bayton Street. He reckoned that must have been the reason because he'd forgotten her address. Now he found himself in a place of expensive shops and hotels that looked even more expensive. The tourist trade must be good. No doubt she did well out of the hotels.

There was her shop, on the corner, and through the open door he could just see her with a female customer. There was a child there too, and Harriet was talking to the little boy, giving him all her attention, as though nobody else mattered. He was clutching a large model boat, and Darius saw him turn to the woman and say, 'Please, Mum. *Please.*'

He could just make out her reply, 'No, darling, it's too expensive.'

For a moment the child looked rebellious, but then he sniffed and handed the boat to Harriet. She took it thoughtfully, then suddenly said, 'I could always make a discount.'

The mother gasped, and gasped again when she saw the piece of paper on which Harriet had written the price. 'Are you sure?'

'Quite sure. It ought to go to someone who'll really appreciate it.'

Darius moved quickly back into a doorway as the woman paid up and hurried away with the child. The last thing he wanted was for Harriet to realise that he'd witnessed this scene. Instinct told him that she wouldn't be pleased at knowing he'd seen her kindly side any more than he would be at knowing she'd seen his. Not that he admitted to having a kindly side.

He waited until she put up the shutters before hurrying back to the car.

The following night he was out walking again, much later this time. Darkness had fallen as he headed for the harbour. At last he came to a public house and went inside, only to find the place too crowded for his mood.

'It's nice outside,' the barman suggested. 'Plenty of space there.'

He led Darius to the garden, where a few tables were laid out. From one of them came laughter.

'We're near the lifeboat station,' the barman explained, 'so the crew members tend to come in here to relax after a call out. That's them, just there.'

He pointed to where two women and four men were sitting around a table, laughing and talking. They were well lit, but then the lights faded into darkness, tempting Darius to slip in among the trees, hoping to remain unseen. From here he could catch a distant glimpse of the sea, that mysteriously always had the power to make him feel better.

A cheer rose from the table, making him back away, but not before he'd seen who was sitting there, surrounded by laughing admirers.

It was her. The Bad Fairy. Or was she now the Good Fairy? He wished she'd let him make up his mind.

The man beside her put a friendly hand on her shoulder, roaring, 'Harry, you're a fraud.'

'Of course I'm a fraud, Walter,' she teased back. 'That's the only fun thing to be.'

Harriet, he remembered. Harry.

Was there no escape from the pesky woman? Why here and now, spoiling his quiet contemplation? And why was she wearing a polo shirt that proclaimed her a member of the lifeboat crew?

Phantom was at her feet, and Darius had a chance to study him. Before, he'd sensed only a very large dog of no particular breed. Now he could see that Phantom's ancestry included a German Shepherd, a St Bernard, and possibly a bloodhound. He was a handsome animal with a benign air that at any other time Darius would have appreciated. Now he only remembered the heavy creature pinning him to the ground and making a fool of him.

The crowd around the table were still chattering cheerfully.

'So what are we going to do about this guy who thinks he owns the place?' Walter asked.

'Actually, he really does own the place,' Harriet sighed. 'And there's nothing we can do. We're stuck with him, I'm sorry to say.'

A groan went up, and someone added, 'Apparently, he's spending money like there's no tomorrow, yet according to the newspapers he's a poor man now. Go figure.'

'Hah!' Harriet said cynically. 'What we call poor and what Darius Falcon calls poor would be a million miles apart.'

Now Darius was even more glad of the trees hiding him, so that they couldn't see his reaction to the contemptuous way she spoke his name.

'It's a big act,' she went on. 'He has to splash it around to prove he can afford to, but actually he's a fraud.'

'Gee, you really took against him!' said the other woman sitting at the same table. 'Just because he got mad at Phantom for ruining his suit. I adore Phantom, but let's face it, he's got form for that kind of thing.'

Amid the general laughter, Harriet made a face.

'It wasn't just that,' she said. 'It's also the way I first saw him, with his head thrown back, drinking in the sun.'

'Perhaps he just likes nature,' Walter suggested.

'That's what I thought. I even liked him for it, but then I didn't know who he was. Now I see. He was standing there like a king come into his birthright. He owns the land and he owns us, that's how he sees it.'

'He told you that?'

'He didn't need to. It was all there in his attitude.' She assumed a declamatory pose. 'I'm the boss here and you'd better watch out.'

'Now that I'd like to see,' said Walter. 'The last man who tried to boss you about was me, and you made me regret it.'

More cheers and laughter. Someone cracked a joke about Darius, someone else cracked another, while their victim stood in the shadows, fuming. This was another new experience and one Darius could have done without. Awe, respect, even fear, these he was used to. But derision? That was an insult.

Walter leaned towards her confidentially. 'Hey, Harry, make a note never to rescue him. If you find him in the water, do the world a favour and look the other way.'

Roars of laughter. She raised her glass, chuckling, 'I'll remember.'

That was it. Time for her to be taught a lesson.

Emerging from the trees, he approached the table and stood, watching her sardonically, until the others noticed him and became curious. At last Harriet's attention was caught and she turned. He heard her draw a sharp breath, and registered her look of dismay with grim satisfaction.

'You'd better remind yourself of my face,' he said, 'so that you'll know who to abandon.'

She couldn't speak. Only her expression betrayed her horror and embarrassment.

He should then have turned on his heel and departed without giving her a chance to reply. But Phantom had to spoil it. Recognising his new friend, he rose from where he was nestled beneath Harriet's seat and reared up, barking with delight.

'Phantom, no!' she cried.

'Leave him,' Darius told her, rubbing Phantom's head.

'You daft mutt! Is this how you get your fun? Luckily, I'm in casuals tonight. Now, get down, there's a good fellow.'

After Harriet's dire warnings, his relaxed tone took everyone by surprise and he noticed that puzzled frowns were directed at her. Fine. If she wanted battle, she could have it. He nodded to them all and departed.

When he reached the road he heard footsteps hurrying behind him and turned, half fearing another canine embrace. But it was her.

'That thing about leaving you in the sea—it was just a silly joke. Of course we'd never leave *anyone* to drown.'

'Not anyone,' he echoed. 'Meaning not even a monster like me.'

'Look—'

'Don't give it another thought. The chance of my ever needing to rely on you is non-existent—as you'll discover.'

'Oh, really!' she said, cross again. 'Let's hope you're right. You never know what life has in store next, do you? Let's make sure.'

Grabbing him, she yanked him under a street lamp and studied his face, frowning.

'You look different from last time,' she said. 'It must be the darkness. OK, I've got you fixed. Hey, what are you doing?'

'The same to you as you did to me,' he said, holding her with one hand while the other lifted her chin to give him the best view of her face.

Harriet resisted the temptation to fight him off, suspecting that he would enjoy that too much. Plus she guessed he wouldn't be easy to fight. There was an unyielding strength in his grasp that could reduce her to nothing. So she stayed completely still, outwardly calm but inwardly smouldering.

If only he would stop smiling like that, as though something about her both amused and pleased him. There was a gleam in his eyes that almost made her want to respond. Almost. If she was that foolish. She drew a long breath, trying not to tremble.

At last he nodded, saying in a thoughtful voice, 'Hmm. Yes, I think I'll remember you—if I try really hard.'

'Cheek!' she exploded.

He released her. 'All right, you can go now.'

Darius walked away without looking back. He didn't need to. He knew she was looking daggers at him.

At home in Giant's Beacon, he sat in darkness at the window of his room with a drink, trying to understand what had so disturbed him that night. It wasn't the hostility, something he was used to. Nor was it really the laughter, which had annoyed him, but only briefly. It was something about Harriet—something…

He exhaled a long breath as the answer came to him. She'd spoken of seeing him on the beach, 'standing there like a king come into his birthright.'

That hadn't been her first reaction. She'd even said she'd liked him, but only briefly, until she'd discovered who he was. Then she'd seen only arrogance and harshness, a conqueror taking possession.

But wasn't that partly his own choice? For years he'd assumed various masks—cool, unperturbed, cunning, superior or charming when the occasion warranted it. Some had been passed on to him by a father whose skill in manipulation was second to none. Others he'd created for himself.

Only one person had seen a different side of him—loving, passionate. For twelve years he'd enjoyed what he'd thought of as a happy marriage, until his wife had left him for another man. Since then he'd tried to keep the vulnerable face well hidden, but evidently he should try harder.

He snatched up the phone and dialled his ex-wife's number in London.

'Mary?'

'Do you have to ring me at this hour? I was just going to bed.'

'I suppose *he's* with you?'

'That's no longer any concern of yours, since we're divorced.'

'Are Mark and Frankie there?'

'Yes, but they're asleep and I'm not waking them. Why don't you call during the day, *if you can make time?* I never liked having to wait until you'd finished everything else, and they don't like it either.'

'Tell them I'll call tomorrow.'

'Not during the day. It's a family outing.'

'When you say "family" I take it you mean—'

'Ken, too. You shouldn't be surprised. We'll be married soon, and he'll be their father.'

'The hell he will! I'll call tomorrow evening. Tell them to expect me.' He slammed down the phone.

Darius had a fight on his hands there, he knew it. Mary had been a good wife and mother, but she'd never really understood the heavy demands of his work. And now, if he wasn't careful, she would cut his children off from him.

How his enemies would rejoice at his troubles. Enemies. In the good times they had been called opponents, rivals, competitors. But the bad times had changed all that, bringing out much bile and bitterness that had previously been hidden for tactical reasons.

As so often, Harriet was hovering on the edge of his mind, an enemy who was at least open about her hostility. Tonight he'd had the satisfaction of confronting her head-on, a rare pleasure in his world. He could see her now, cheeky and challenging, but not beautiful, except for her eyes, and with skin that was as soft as rose petals; something that he'd discovered when he'd held her face prisoner between his fingers.

This was how he'd always fought the battles, gaining information denied to others. But now it was different. Instead of triumph, he felt only confusion.

After watching the darkness for a long time he went to bed.

CHAPTER THREE

HARRIET prided herself on her common sense. She needed to. There had been times in her recent past when it had been all that saved her from despair. Even now, the dark depths sometimes beckoned and she clung fiercely to her 'boring side' as she called it, because nothing else helped. And even that didn't make the sadness go away. It simply made it possible to cling on until her courage returned.

She knew that people had always envied her. Married at eighteen to an astonishingly handsome young man, living in apparently perfect harmony until his death eight years later. As far as the world knew, the only thing that blighted their happiness was the need for him to be away so often. His work in the tourist industry had necessitated many absences from home, but when he returned their reunions were legendary.

'A perfect couple,' people said. But they didn't know.

Brad had been a philanderer who had spent his trips away sleeping around, and expected her not to mind. It only happened while he was out of sight, so what was she complaining about? It was the unkindness of his attitude that hurt her as much as his infidelity.

She'd clung on, deluding herself with the hope that in time he would change, presenting a bright face to the world so that her island neighbours never suspected. Finally Brad had left her, dying in a car crash in America before the divorce could come through, and the last of her hope was destroyed.

To the outside world the myth of her perfect marriage persisted. Nobody knew the truth, and nobody ever would, she was determined on that.

All she had left was Phantom, who had been Brad's dog and who'd comforted her night after night when he was away. Phantom alone knew the truth; that behind the cheerful, sturdy exterior was a woman who had lost faith in men and life. His warmth brought joy to what would otherwise have been a desert.

It was the thought of her beloved dog that made her set out one morning in the direction of Giant's Beacon. There was still a chance to improve relations with Darius Falcon, and for Phantom's sake she must take it.

'I suppose I'm getting paranoid about this,' she told herself. 'I don't think he'd really do anything against Phantom, but he's the most powerful man on the island and I can't take chances.'

She recalled that at their last meeting he'd actually spoken to him in a kindly tone, calling him 'You daft mutt' and 'a good fellow', thus proving he wasn't really a monster. He probably had a nicer side if she could only find it. She would apologise, engage him in a friendly chat and all would be well.

The road to Giant's Beacon led around the side of the house, and over the garden hedge she could see that the French windows were open. From inside came the sound of a man's voice.

'All right. Call me again when you know. Goodbye.'

Excellent, she would slip inside quickly while he was free. But as she approached the open door she heard him again,'There you are. I know you've been avoiding my calls—did you really think I'd let you go that easily?—I know what you've been doing and I'm telling you it's got to stop.'

Harriet stood deadly still, stunned by his cold, bullying tone. She must leave at once. Slowly, she flattened herself back against the wall and began to edge away.

'It's too late for that,' Darius continued. 'I've set things in motion and it's too late to change it, even if I wanted to. The deal's done, and you can tell your friend with the suspicious credentials that if he crosses me again he'll be sorry—what? Yes, that's exactly what I mean. There'll be no mercy.'

No mercy, she thought, moving slowly along the wall. That just about said it all. And she'd kidded herself that he had a nicer side.

No mercy.

Quietly, she vanished.

'There'll be no mercy.'

Darius repeated the line once more. He knew that these days he said it too often, too obsessively. So many foes had shown him no mercy that now it was the mantra he clung to in self-defence.

At last he slammed down the phone and threw himself back in his chair, hoping he'd said enough to have the desired impact. Possibly. Or then again, maybe not. Once he wouldn't have doubted it, but since his fortunes had begun to collapse he had a permanent fear that the person on the other end immediately turned to a companion and jeered, 'He fell for it.'

As he himself had often done in what now felt like another life.

That was one of the hardest things to cope with—the suspicion of being laughed at behind his back; the knowledge that people who'd once scuttled to please him now shrugged.

The other thing, even harder, was the end of his family life, the distance that seemed to stretch between himself and his children. It was easy to say that he'd given too much of himself to business and not enough to being a father, but at the time he'd felt he was working for them.

Mary, his wife, had been scathing at the idea.

'That's just your excuse for putting them second. You say making money is all for them, but they don't want a great fortune, they want *you* there, taking an interest.'

He'd sacrificed so much for financial success, and now that too was fading. Lying awake at night, he often tried to look ahead to decide which path to take, but in truth there was no choice. Only one path stretched forward, leading either to greater failure or success at too great a cost. They seemed much the same.

He rubbed his eyes, trying to shake off the mood, and turned on the radio to hear the local news. One item made him suddenly alert.

> 'Much concern is being expressed at the suggestion of problems with the Herringdean Wind Farm. Work has only recently started, yet—'

'Kate,' he said, coming downstairs, 'what do you know about a wind farm?'

'Not much,' she said, speaking as she would have done about an alien planet. 'It's been on and off for ages and we thought it was all forgotten but they finally started work. It'll be some way out in the channel where we don't have to look at the horrid great thing.'

'Show me,' he said, pulling out a map of the island.

The site was located about eight miles out at sea, within

England's territorial waters. As these were owned by the Crown, he would gain nothing. He could even lose, since the island might be less appealing to potential buyers.

'They've actually started putting up the turbines?' he said.

'A few, I believe, but it'll be some time before it's finished.'

He groaned. If he'd bought this place in the normal way, there would have been inspections, he would have discovered the disadvantages and negotiated a lower price. Instead, it had been dumped on him, and he was beginning to realise that he'd walked into a trap.

Fool! *Fool!*

At all costs that must remain his secret. Kate was too naïve for him to worry about, and nobody else would be allowed near.

'Shall I start supper?' Kate asked.

'No, thank you. There's something I've got to see.'

Darius had just enough time to get out there before the light faded. When he'd inspected the turbines he could decide if they were a problem.

For this he would need the motorboat that was also now his property, and that was lodged in a boating shed at the end of a small creek that ran in from the shore. He found it without trouble, opened the door of the shed and started up the engine.

He was expecting problems. The engine might not work, or would at least be complicated to operate. But it sprang to life at once, everything was easy to operate, and since the fuel gauge registered 'full' he reckoned that luck was on his side, just for once.

Briefly he glanced around for a life jacket but, not seeing one, shrugged and forgot about it. A breeze was getting up as he emerged from the creek and set out across the channel. Glancing back, he could see the beach where he'd had his first ill-fated meeting with Harriet. Then he turned determinedly away and headed for the horizon.

At last he saw it—a dozen turbines rearing out of the water, seventy metres high, and, nearby, the cargo ships bearing the loads that would become more turbines. He got as close as he could, trying to think only of the benefit to the island of this source of electricity. But the new self, who'd come to life on the beach, whispered that they spoiled the beauty of the sea.

Functional and efficient, that was what mattered. Concentrate on that.

Now the light was fading fast and the wind was mounting, making the water rough, and it was time to go. He turned the boat, realising that he'd been unwise to come out here. He wasn't an experienced sailor, but the need to know had been compelling. Now he had just enough time to get to shore before matters became unpleasant.

Almost at once he discovered his mistake. The waves mounted fast, tossing his little boat from side to side. Rain began to fall more heavily every moment, lashing the angry water, lashing himself, soaking through his clothes, which weren't waterproof. The sooner he drove on the better.

But without warning the engine died. Nothing he could do would start it again. Frantically, he peered at the fuel gauge and saw, with horror, that it still showed 'Full'.

But that was impossible after the distance he'd already travelled. The reading was wrong, and must have been wrong from the start. He'd set out without enough fuel, and now he was trapped out here in the storm.

He groaned. It went against the grain to admit that he needed help, but there was no alternative. He would have to call Kate and ask her to notify the rescue service. Then it would be all over the island. He could almost hear the laughter. Especially *hers*. But it couldn't be helped.

Taking out his cellphone, he began to dial, trying to steady himself with his feet as he needed both hands for the phone. That was when the biggest wave came, rearing up at the side of the boat, forcing him to cling on with both hands. With despair, he saw the phone go flying into the water. He made a dive for it but another swell hoisted the boat high, twisting it so that he went overboard into the sea.

Floundering madly, he tried to reach the boat, but the waves had already carried it away. Farther and farther away it went, beyond his strength to pursue, until it was out of sight.

Now his own body seemed to be turning against him. The shock of being plunged into cold water had caused his heart to race dangerously, making him gasp and inhale water. His limbs froze, and he could barely move them. He wondered whether he would die of cold before he drowned.

Time passed, tormenting him, then vanishing into eternity until time itself no longer existed. Perhaps it had never existed. There was only darkness on earth and the moon and stars high above.

His wretchedness was increased by the thought of his children, waiting in vain for his call tonight. They would think he'd forgotten them, and only the news of his death would tell them otherwise. Then it would no longer matter.

Darius wanted to cry aloud to them, saying he loved them and they must believe that, for he would never be able to tell them again. But the distance stretched into infinity, and then another infinity that he feared because so much was left undone in his life—so many wrongs not righted, so many chances not taken, so many words not spoken… and now…never…never…

Why was he even bothering to tread water? Why not just let go and accept the inevitable?

But giving in had never been his way. He must fight to the end, no matter how much harder it was.

In his dizzy state he seemed to lose consciousness. Or was he going mad? That might make it easier. But doing things the easy way wasn't his style either.

Yet the madness was already creeping over him, giving him the illusion of lights in the distance. It was impossible but he saw them, streaming out over the water, turning this way and that as though searching. Then the beam fell on him, blinding him, and a cry split the darkness.

'There he is!'

The universe seemed to whirl. Vaguely, he sensed the boat approaching, ploughing through the waves. Another few seconds—

But it seemed that a malign fate was intent on destroying him even now. A wave, bigger than the others, reared up, sweeping him with it, up—then down back into the abyss—up—down—then away from the boat to a place where he would never be found. A yell of fear and rage broke from him at being defeated at the last moment.

Then he felt a hand clasp his, the fingers tightening with fierce determination, drawing him closer. The waves fought back but the hand refused to yield to them. Suddenly he realised that two men were in the water with him, and were loading him onto a stretcher. Gradually the stretcher began to rise, taking him clear of the sea, lifting him to safety.

From somewhere a man's voice said, 'OK, I've got him. You can let go, Harry.'

And a woman replied, "No way. This one's mine.'

Harry! That voice—

Shocked, he opened his eyes and saw Harriet's face.

'You,' he whispered hoarsely.

Harriet was there, leaning close to ask, 'Was there anyone else with you—anyone we still need to look for?'

'No,' he gasped. 'I was alone.'

'Good. Then we can go back. There'll be an ambulance to take you to hospital.'

'No, I must go home—my children—I've got to call them. Wait—' he grasped her '—my cellphone went into the water. Let me use yours.'

'I don't have it here.'

'Then I must call them from home.'

'But the hospital will have—'

'Not the hospital,' he said stubbornly.

'Gee, you're an infuriating man!' she exclaimed.

'Yes, well, you should have left me in the water, shouldn't you?' he choked. 'You had the right idea the first time.'

A coughing fit overtook him. Between them, Harriet and Walter got him under cover, and she stayed with him for the rest of the journey. He slumped in the seat, his eyes closed, on the verge of collapse. Watching him, Harriet was glad she hadn't needed to answer his last remark. She wouldn't have known how.

At the lifeboat station she helped him ashore, and there was another argument.

'No hospital,' he insisted. 'I'm going home.'

'Then I'll take you,' she said. 'Walter—'

'Don't worry, I'll do the report. You keep him safe.'

Darius was about to say that he would drive himself when he remembered that his car was a mile away. Besides, there was no arguing with this bossy woman.

Somehow, he stumbled into her car and sat with his eyes closed for the journey.

'How did you manage to find me?' he murmured. 'I thought I was a goner.'

'Kate raised the alarm. She said you left suddenly after you talked about the wind farm. Later, she went out and bumped into an old man she knows who works on the shore. He said he'd seen you leaving in your motorboat. When you didn't return she tried to call you on your cellphone, but it was dead so she alerted the lifeboat station.'

Kate was waiting at the door when they arrived. Darius managed to stand up long enough to hug her.

'Thank you,' he said hoarsely. 'I owe you my life.'

'As long as you're safe,' Kate insisted. 'Just come in and get warm.'

In the hall, he made straight for the phone.

'Get changed,' Harriet said urgently. 'You're soaking.'

'No, I've got to call them first. They'll be waiting.' He'd been dialling as he spoke and now he said, 'Mary? Yes, I know it's late. I'm sorry, I got held up.'

From where she was standing, Harriet could hear a woman's sharp voice on the other end, faint but clear.

'You always get held up. The children went to bed crying because you didn't keep your word, and that's it. Enough is enough.'

'Mary, listen—'

'I'm not going to let you hurt them by putting them last again—'

'It's not like that—*don't hang up*—'

Harriet couldn't stand it any more. She snatched the phone from his hand and spoke loudly. 'Mrs Falcon, please listen to me.'

'Oh, you're the girlfriend, I suppose?'

'No, I'm not Mr Falcon's girlfriend. I'm a member of the lifeboat crew that's just taken him from the sea, barely in time to save his life.'

'Oh, please, do you expect me to believe that?'

Harriet exploded with rage. 'Yes, I do expect you to believe it because it's true. If we'd got there just a few minutes later it would have been too late. You're lucky he's here and not at the bottom of the ocean.' She handed the phone to Darius, who was staring as though he'd just seen an apparition. 'Tell her,' she commanded.

Dazed, he took the receiver and spoke into it. 'Mary? Are you still there?—yes, it's true what she said.'

A sense of propriety made Harriet back away in the direction of the kitchen but an overwhelming curiosity made her leave the door open just enough to eavesdrop.

'Please fetch them,' she heard him say. 'Oh, they've come downstairs? Let me talk to them. Frankie—is that you? I'm sorry about the delay—I fell in the water but they pulled me out—I'm fine now. Put Mark on, let me try and talk to both of you at once.'

His tone had changed, becoming warm and caressing in a way Harriet wouldn't have believed possible. Now she backed into the kitchen and shut the door, gratefully accepting a cup of tea from Kate.

'He'll go down with pneumonia if he doesn't get changed soon,' Kate observed worriedly.

'Then we'll have to be very firm with him,' Harriet said.

'Like you were just now.' Kate's tone was admiring. 'He didn't know what had hit him.'

'I suppose he'll be cross with me, but it can't be helped.'

'As long as we keep him safe,' Kate agreed.

Harriet look at her curiously. 'You sound as though you really care. But he can't be very easy to work for.'

'I'll take him rather than the last fellow any day. Rancing

just vanished, leaving me here for weeks. He never got in touch, never paid me—'

'Didn't pay you?' Harriet echoed, aghast. 'The lousy so-and-so. How did you live?'

'I had a little saved, but I had to spend it all. I couldn't contact him. Nothing. Then Mr Falcon walked in and said the place was his. I was still living here because I've got nowhere else to go. I thought he'd throw me out and bring in an army of posh servants, but he said he wanted me to stay and he paid me for all the weeks after Rancing left.'

'He—paid you? But—'

'I know. He didn't have to. He didn't owe me and I couldn't believe it when he handed me the cash.'

Harriet stared, feeling as though the world had suddenly turned upside down. This couldn't be true. Darius was a villain. That had been a settled fact in her mind. Until tonight—

'Why didn't you tell anyone?' she asked.

'Because he said not to. He'd be good and mad if he knew I'd told you now, so you'll keep quiet, won't you?'

'Of course. I'm not even quite convinced.'

'No, he said you wouldn't be.'

'He said what?'

'Not at the time, but last night when I was making his supper, I mentioned it, asked if I could tell people, and he said that you especially must never know because you enjoyed seeing him as the devil and he didn't want to spoil your fun.'

'Oh, *did* he?'

There were no words for the unfamiliar sensation that shook her. Darius had looked into her mind and read it with a precision that was alarming. Or exciting. She wasn't sure. One thing was certain. Everything she'd thought she knew about him was now in question. And the truth about his real nature was an even bigger question. The world had gone mad, taking her with it.

And what a journey that might be!

She recovered enough to say, 'But if people knew he could be as generous as this they'd see him differently.'

'Perhaps he doesn't want them to,' Kate said wisely.

That silenced Harriet. This was too much to take in all in one go. She needed space and solitude.

It was time to see how he was managing. Opening the door, they looked out into the hall and saw Darius sitting so still that they thought the call was ended, but then he said, 'All right,' in a hard voice.

After a pause he added, 'You'd better go back to bed now—yes, all right. Goodbye.'

He set the phone down and leaned back against the wood, eyes closed, face exhausted. Something told Harriet the call hadn't gone well.

'Time for bed,' Kate told him. 'Shall we help you up the stairs?'

'Thank you, but there's no need,' he growled.

He hauled himself slowly to his feet and began the weary trek, stair by stair, but waving the two women away if they seemed to get too close. They contented themselves with keeping a respectful distance, following him up and into his room, where he sat heavily on the bed.

'It's all right,' he said. 'I can manage.'

'No, you can't,' Harriet firmly. 'If we leave now you'll just stretch out and go to sleep in your freezing wet clothes. Next stop, pneumonia.'

'Now, look—'

'No, you look. I didn't give up my evening to come out to sea and fetch you to have you throw your life away through carelessness. You're going to take off those wet clothes and put on dry ones.'

Darius looked warily from one to the other, and seemed to decide against argument. His eyes closed and Harriet thought for a moment he would lose consciousness. But when he opened them again an incredible change seemed to come over him.

Astonished, Harriet saw a faint grin that might almost have been good-natured, or at least resigned. Then he shrugged.

'I'm in your hands, ladies.'

He unbuttoned his own shirt and shrugged it off, then unzipped his trousers and stood while they removed them. Kate fetched towels and a bathrobe that Harriet helped him put on. He tried to draw the edges together before removing his underpants, but his grip was weak and they fell open at the crucial moment.

Harriet quickly averted her eyes, but not before she'd seen his nakedness. Just a brief glimpse, but it told her what she didn't want to know, that his personal magnificence measured up to his reputation in business.

Hastily, she began opening drawers, asking, 'Where are your pyjamas?'

'I don't have any. Sleeping in the nude is more comfortable.' He raised an eyebrow at her. 'Don't you find that?'

'I really wouldn't know,' she said primly. It was incredible to her that he'd chosen this moment to tease her. He was half dead, for pity's sake! Did nothing crush him?

'I'm making you a hot tea,' she declared, 'and when I come back I expect to find you in bed.'

'Yes, ma'am,' he said meekly.

Now Harriet was sure she could see a gleam of humour far back in his eyes, but she couldn't be sure.

'I'll leave you in Kate's capable hands.' Some defensive instinct made her add, 'Don't stand any nonsense from him, Kate.'

'Don't you worry,' Kate said significantly.

'Harriet!' She turned at the door in response to Darius's voice. 'Thank you,' he said quietly.

'Don't mention it.'

She departed hurriedly. Downstairs, she made the tea but only took it halfway up the stairs before calling Kate and handing it to her. Suddenly it was important to escape him, above all to escape his knowing look that said he would tease her if he wanted to, and what was she going to do about it?

There was nothing to be done, except get back home—a place of safety, where she knew what was what.

When she got there safety greeted her in the form of Phantom. As they snuggled down under the covers she discussed the matter with him, as she discussed everything.

'What a night! Him of all people. And it seems he's not like… Well, I don't know what he's like any more. He was nice to Kate, I'll admit that. Maybe we were wrong about him. No, not we. Just me. You always liked him, didn't you?

'If you could have seen him getting undressed tonight. It was an honest accident—at least, I think it was. But what I saw was impressive and maybe he meant me to see and maybe he didn't.

'He ticks the boxes—great thighs, narrow hips and the rest—well, never mind. But Brad also ticked the boxes, and he *knew* he ticked them. A man like that wasn't going to confine himself to me, was he? And he didn't. So if His Majesty Falcon is expecting me to be impressed he can just think again.

'You agree with me, don't you? Well, you do if you want that new stuff I bought for your breakfast tomorrow. Yes—yes—that's a lovely lick. Can I have another? Thank you. Now, let's go to sleep. And move over. Give me some room.'

CHAPTER FOUR

HARRIET spent the next morning at her shop, which was doing well. She'd recently taken on a new assistant who was good at the job, something she was glad of when Kate rang, sounding frantic. 'Darius is driving me crazy wanting to do all sorts of daft things.'

'Hah! Surprise me.'

'He's got a nasty cold, but he insists on getting up. He says he's got to go out and buy another cellphone. He's ordered a fancy one online but it'll take a few days to arrive so he's determined to get something basic to fill in. And then he wants to come and see you.'

'All right, I'm on my way. Don't let him out. Tie him to the bed if you have to.'

Distantly, she heard Kate say, 'She says I'm to tie you to the bed,' followed by a sound that might have been a snort of laughter, followed by coughing.

'You hear that?' Kate demanded into the phone. 'If you—'

Her voice vanished, replaced by a loud burr. Harriet hung up, very thoughtful.

Before leaving, she took out an object that until then she'd kept hidden away and looked at it for a long time. At last she sighed and replaced it. But then, heading for the door, she stopped, returned and retrieved it from its hiding place. Again, she gazed at it for several moments, a yearning expression haunting her eyes. Her hand tightened on it and for a moment she seemed resolute. But then she returned it firmly to its hiding place, ran out of the room and downstairs, where she got into her car and began the journey to Giant's Beacon.

Halfway there she stopped, turned the car and swiftly headed back to streak up the stairs, snatch the precious object, ram it into her pocket and flee.

She'd done it now, the thing she'd vowed never to do, and that was that. She told herself it was time to be sensible, but she made the journey with her face set as though resisting pain

Kate was waiting for her on the doorstep, calling, 'Thank goodness you're here!'

'Kate, is that her?' cried a hoarse voice from the back of the house.

'I'm coming,' she called, hurrying into the room he'd turned into an office.

At first she was bewildered by the array of machinery, all of it obviously state-of-the-art. Kate had spoken of wonderful things, but still the variety and magnificence came as a surprise. And one man could control all this?

Darius, in his dressing gown, was sitting at a large screen, his fingers hovering over a keyboard.

'Don't come near me,' he croaked. 'I'm full of germs.'

'You shouldn't be up at all,' she scolded him, sitting down at a distance. 'And Kate says you want to go out. That's madness. It's far too cold.'

'I thought summer was supposed to be coming. Is it always like this in May?'

'The weather can be a bit temperamental. It's been colder than usual the last few days. It'll warm up soon, and then we'll be flooded with tourists. In the meantime, take care.'

'I just need a new cellphone to replace the one I lost last night. I have a thousand calls to make, and the house phone keeps going dead.'

'Yes, the line's faulty and they don't seem able to repair it. You were lucky it held out last night when you were calling your children. All right, you need one to tide you over. Try this.'

Reaching into her pocket, she handed over the object that had given her such anguish earlier.

'You're lending me yours?' he asked.

'No, it's not mine, it…belonged to my husband.'

He took it from her left hand, realising for the first time that she wore a wedding ring.

'Husband?' he echoed.

'He died a year ago. He hadn't used this for some time because he'd replaced it with a better one. But it might get you through the next few days.'

He seemed uncertain what to say.

'That's very kind of you,' he murmured at last. 'But—are you sure?'

'Quite sure. You'll find it blank. I've wiped off every trace of him.'

Something in her voice made him glance at her quickly, but she was looking out of the window.

'I appreciate this,' he said. 'Now I can call my children again. I'll be in touch as soon as I'm a bit more normal. I still have to thank you properly for saving me. Perhaps we could have dinner.'

'You don't need to thank me. I was just doing what I do and I wasn't alone. What about all the others on the lifeboat?'

'I'll show my gratitude by making a donation. But I

think you can tell me a lot about Herringdean that I need to know, so I'd appreciate it if you'd agree to dinner.'

'All right, I'll look forward to it.'

'By the way,' he added as she reached the door, 'how's my ghostly friend?'

'Who?'

'His name is Phantom, isn't it?'

She gave an uncertain laugh. 'You call him your friend?'

'You assured me he was only being friendly. Tell him I look forward to our next meeting. What kind of bones does he like?'

'Any kind.'

'I'll remember.'

As she left the house Harriet was saying to herself, 'I don't believe it. I imagined that conversation. I must have done.'

That evening she poured out her thoughts again to the one friend she knew she could always trust.

'I don't know what to think any more. He's different—well, all right, he nearly died and that changes people—but they change back. In a few days he'll be talking about showing no mercy again. Hey, don't do that! Phantom, *put that down!*—oh, all right, just this once.'

Three days later she looked up from serving in the shop to find Darius standing there.

'It's a nice day so I managed to escape,' he said with a smile. 'I wanted to bring you this.' He held out the phone. 'I've got my new one now, but this was invaluable. Thank you. There seems no end to what I owe you.'

'Did you manage to call your sons?'

'My son and daughter, yes.'

'Oh, I thought—Mark and Frank.'

'Frankie. Her name's Francesca, but we call her Frankie. It's a bit like calling you Harry.'

She laughed. 'Yes, I suppose it is.'

'And there's also this,' he said, reaching into a bag and drawing out a huge bone. 'This is for Phantom, by the way, not you.'

Her lips twitched. 'I'm glad you explained that.'

'About our dinner. Kate's set her heart on cooking it for us.'

'Good idea. She's a great cook, and it would be better for you.'

'If you say I need to stay indoors for a few more days I shall do something desperate,' he warned. 'You two mother hens are driving me crazy.'

'No, I was only going to say that anywhere else you'll get stared at. I'll come to Giant's Beacon.'

'You and Phantom.'

'He's included?'

'It wouldn't be the same without him. Friday evening.'

'I look forward to it. *We'll* look forward to it.'

He thanked her and departed. Outside the shop, he hesitated a moment, then headed for the harbour and the lifeboat station, but after a moment his attention was claimed by a man watching him from across the road with an air of nervousness. Enlightenment dawned, and he crossed over.

'I know you, don't I? You were part of the team that saved me from drowning.'

'I'm glad you remember that,' Walter said, 'and not the other thing.'

'You mean when you advised Harriet to let me drown?' Darius said, grinning.

'Ah, yes—'

'It's in the past,' Darius assured him. 'Look, do you have a moment? There's a pub over there.'

When they were settled with glasses of ale, Darius said, 'I want to show my gratitude in a practical way, with a donation to the lifeboat.' He took out his chequebook. 'Who do I make it out to?'

Walter told him, then looked, wide-eyed, at the amount. 'That's very generous.'

'It's not too much for my life. Will you make sure this reaches the right part of your organisation?'

'It'll be a pleasure. It's good to see you on your feet again. Harry said you were in a bad way.'

'All that time in the cold water. I reckon I was bound to go down with something. But Harriet got me home and took wonderful care of me.'

'She's a great girl, isn't she? Sometimes I wonder how she survived after what she's been through.'

'Been through?'

'Losing her husband. Oh, I know she's not the only widow in the world, but they had a fantastic marriage. Everyone who gets married hopes they're going to have what those two had. We all envied them. When he died we thought she might die too, she was so crushed. But she came back fighting. I don't reckon she'll ever really get over him, though.'

'But she's a young woman, with plenty of time to find someone else.'

'Yes, if she really wants to. But you only get something as good as that once in your life. It wouldn't surprise me if she stayed single now.' He drained his glass. 'Got to be going. Nice to meet you.'

They parted on good terms.

* * *

On Friday Darius came in the late afternoon to collect both his guests. Phantom leapt into the back seat of the car as though being chauffeured was no more than his right.

'Don't worry, I've washed him,' Harriet said.

Darius grinned over his shoulder at his four-pawed guest, who nuzzled his ear.

'Wait,' Harriet said suddenly, bouncing out of the car. 'I'll be back.'

He watched as she ran into her home, then out again a moment later, clutching a small black box.

'My pager,' she said, settling into the front seat. 'It has to go with me everywhere in case the lifeboat gets called out.'

'You're on call tonight?'

'Lifeboat volunteers are always on call. The only time that's not true is if we're ill, or have to leave the island for some reason. Then we give them notice of the dates and report back as soon as we return. But normally we take the pager everywhere and have to be ready to drop everything.'

'Everything? You mean…even if…suppose you were…?'

'At work or in the bath,' she supplied innocently. 'Yes, even then.'

That wasn't quite what he'd meant, and her mischievous look showed that she understood perfectly. For a moment another memory danced between them, when the edges of his robe had fallen open just long enough to be tantalising. By mutual consent they decided to leave it there.

'What made you want to be a lifeboat volunteer?' he asked as he started the car.

'My father. My mother died when I was very young and Dad raised me alone. When he went out on a call I used to love watching the boat go down the slipway into the water. All that spray coming up seemed so thrilling. He was a fisherman and I often went out with him. He taught me to be a sailor and bought me my first boat. My happiest times were spent on the water with him, and it was natural to follow him onto the lifeboats.'

'A fisherman? You mean herring?'

She laughed, 'Yes. There have always been shoals of herring in the water around here. Other fish too, but that's how the island got its name.'

'You've never wanted to leave it behind and move to the mainland?'

She made a face. 'Never! There's nowhere better in the world.'

'You sound very sure? As simple as that?'

'As simple as that. It's the best place on earth, and it always will be; unless something happens to spoil it.'

Darius didn't need to ask what she meant. He had the power to do the damage she mentioned, and they both knew it. But this wasn't the right moment.

The drive ran along the shoreline, from where they could see the sun beginning to set.

'I'd never seen anything like that before I came here,' he said.

'Never seen a sunset?'

'Not like a Herringdean sunset. I haven't been much by the sea. It's usually something I see looking down on from a plane.'

'Stop the car,' she urged.

He did as she asked and the three of them walked to the edge of the beach and stood watching as the water turned crimson, glittering as tiny waves broke softly. None of them made a sound. There was no need. Harriet glanced at Darius and saw on his face a look akin to the one she'd first seen when they met—absorbed, ecstatic. At last he gave a regretful sigh.

'We'd better go.'

'You can see it from the house,' she reassured him.

'In a way. But somehow it's different when you're out here with it.'

As they walked back to the car he glanced appreciatively at her appearance. Her soft blue dress wasn't expensive nor glamorous, but neither did it send out the warning he'd sensed from her functional bathing gear. Her light brown shoulder length hair flowed freely in soft waves. She looked relaxed and ready to enjoy herself and he found himself relaxing in turn.

The evening stretched ahead of him, warm and inviting. Another new experience. When had he last whiled away the hours with a friend?

Two friends, he realised, feeling Phantom nuzzle his hand.

'Just wait until we get home,' he said. 'Kate's got something really special for you.'

'I'm looking forward to it,' Harriet declared.

Man and dog stared at her, then at each other. Darius gave a shrug of resignation, and Harriet could almost have sworn that Phantom returned the gesture.

'You have to explain things carefully to women,' Darius told him.

Woof!

'You meant that remark about something special for Phantom?' Harriet demanded.

'Who else? Kate's taken a lot of trouble with his supper. I told her he was the guest of honour.'

Harriet chuckled. 'I guess you're learning.'

Kate was waiting at the door, beaming a welcome. For Phantom there was the dog equivalent of a banquet, which he tucked into with due appreciation. Her mind at ease, Harriet left him to it and followed Darius into the large dining room at the back where a table for two had been set up by the French windows. From here the lawn stretched out until it shaded into the stretch of private beach where they had first met.

'Remember?' he asked, filling her wine glass.

'I remember, and I shouldn't think you'll ever forget,' she said. 'You never did send me the bill for that suit.'

'Well, maybe I'm not the monster you think me to be,' he said.

'Thought, not think. I wouldn't dare think badly of someone who treats Phantom so well.'

'Ah, you've noticed that I'm grovelling to him. I'm so glad. I knew I had no chance of getting on your right side unless I got on his first.'

Harriet seemed to give this serious consideration. 'I see. And it's important to get on my right side?'

'Well, I can't let you go on being my enemy. It wouldn't be practical.'

'And at all costs we must be practical,' she agreed. 'But I have to say, Mr Falcon, that I'm disappointed at how badly you've misread the situation. I'd expected more efficiency from "the most fearsome man in London."'

'Please,' he protested. 'None of that. It was enough of an embarrassment when I could make a pretence of living up to it. Now—' He shuddered. 'But how did I misread the situation?'

'I was never your enemy.'

'Really? You expect me to believe that when you got a bodyguard for Phantom? Oh, yes, I heard. And then you despised me so much that you made jokes about leaving me to drown.'

'Well, you got your own back by walking in on me right after, didn't you? And I didn't leave you to drown—' She checked herself, alerted by his teasing look. 'Oh, ha ha! Well, I guess you're entitled to make fun of me.'

'Yes, I think I am as well,' he said, smiling and raising his glass. 'Truce?'

She regarded him with her head on one side. 'Armed?'

He nodded. 'Safer that way for both of us.'

'It's a deal.'

She raised her own glass and they clinked as Kate entered with the first dish.

'Just in time to save me from your terrible vengeance,' Darius said.

'Don't fool yourself,' she told him. 'When I wreak terrible vengeance on you, nothing and nobody will be able to save you.'

'Then I'd better have my supper quickly,' he said, leading her to the table.

Kate gave them a strange look and departed, making Harriet say in a quivering voice, trying not to laugh, 'She thinks we're both potty.'

'She's very observant.'

For a few moments they didn't speak, concentrating on the food, which was Kate's best, plain but delicious. Harriet wondered how it tasted to Darius, who must be used to more sophisticated fare, but he seemed happy to devour every mouthful.

'If I had "enemy" thoughts, so did you,' she observed. 'When you came upon us in the garden of the pub you seemed to hate me.'

She thought he wasn't going to reply, but then he nodded. 'I did. I heard you talking about how I looked on the beach, "standing there like a king come into his birthright" according to you.'

'That'll teach me to jump to conclusions,' she sighed. 'You weren't really feeling anything like that, were you?'

'No, I was feeling what a glorious place it was. It took me completely by surprise and I just stood there, stunned, trying to believe such beauty existed.'

'That was what I sensed when I first saw you,' she admitted. 'It was only later that I thought—oh, dear, I'm sorry. I guess I got it all wrong.'

'We both got a lot of things wrong, but this is the moment when we put it all behind us and become friends.'

'Friends…' She considered the word for a moment before saying, 'I must warn you, friends claim the right to ask each other questions.'

'Fire away.'

'Why did you go out to sea at all? It was madness.'

'I needed to see the wind farm, and learn all I could.'

'But surely you did an in-depth investigation before you bought the island?' Something in his wry expression made her say, 'You did, surely?'

'The first I heard about it was when Kate told me.'

She stared. 'I can't believe a smart operator like you bought this place without checking every detail first.'

He shrugged.

'You didn't?' she breathed. 'But why?'

'Perhaps I'm not quite as smart as I like people to think. Look, if I tell you, you've got to promise not to breathe a word to another soul.'

'I promise.'

'Seriously. Swear it on what you hold most dear.'

'I swear it on Phantom's life,' she said, holding up her hand. 'Now, tell, tell! The curiosity's driving me crazy.'

'I didn't buy Herringdean. Rancing owed me money, couldn't pay it, so he assigned the place to me, sent me the papers and vanished.'

'What?'

'My lawyer says everything's in order, I'm the legal

owner. But I had no chance to study the place, negotiate, refuse the deal, anything. Whatever I learn about the island comes as a surprise. My "investigation" consisted of looking Herringdean up online. What I found wasn't informative—fishing, beautiful countryside, but no mention of a wind farm.'

'Probably because it had only just got under way and they hadn't updated the site,' she mused.

'Exactly. So you see I've approached everything like a dimwit. All right, all right,' he added as she choked with laughter. 'Have your fun.'

'I'm sorry,' she gasped. 'I didn't mean to but—he fooled you—'

'Yes, he fooled me,' Darius said, managing to be faintly amused through his chagrin. 'And I'll tell you something else. Before he left, he got a lot of the bigger tenants to pay him several months' rent in advance, then he pocketed the money and ran. So it'll be a while before they pay me anything.'

He knew he was crazy to have told her such damaging things. If she betrayed his trust she could make him look like an idiot all over the island.

But she wouldn't betray him. Instinctively, he knew that he was safe with her.

Harriet was making confused gestures, trying to get her head around what she'd just heard.

'But the papers always say—you know, the mighty entrepreneur, all that stuff—'

'Been checking up on me, huh?' he said wryly.

'Of course. Be fair. Since you control our lives, I had to find out what I could.'

'Control your lives? Oh, sure, it looks like it. I arrive knowing nothing, nearly die finding out, get snatched from the jaws of death by you and the others. Some control! So I suppose you know all there is to know about me?'

Harriet shook her head. 'Only basics. Your father is Amos Falcon—*the* Amos Falcon. Empire builder, financial mogul—all right, all right.' She backed off hastily, seeing his expression. 'And you have lots of brothers. It must be nice coming from a large family. I'm an only child and it can be lonely.'

'So can being in a large family,' Darius said.

'Really? I can't imagine that. Tell me more.'

But suddenly his mouth closed in a firm line. It was as though something had brought him to the edge of a cliff, Harriet thought, and he'd backed away in alarm. She could almost see him retreating further and further.

'What is it?' she asked.

He rose and walked away to the window. She had a strange feeling that he was trying to put a distance between them, as though she was some kind of threat. After a moment's hesitation she followed him and laid a tentative hand on his arm.

'I'm sorry,' she said. 'Of course it's none of my business. I'm always sticking my nose into other people's affairs. Just ignore me.'

With anyone else he would have seized this offer with relief, but with her things were mysteriously different. In his mind he saw again the defining moment of their relationship, the moment when she had reached out to him, offering rescue, offering life. The moment had passed, yet it lived in him still and, he guessed, would always do so.

The need to accept her friendship, trust it, rely on it, was so strong that it sent warning signals. Nothing would ever be the same again. But there was no turning back now.

'I don't think I'll ignore you,' he said softly, taking her hand. 'You're not a woman that's easy to ignore.'

'I'll just vanish if you like.'

'No,' he said, his hand tightening on hers so suddenly that she gasped. 'Stay. I want you to stay.'

'All right,' she said. 'I'll stay.'

He led her back to the table and poured her a glass of wine.

'People always think big families are charming,' he said after a while. 'But it can be an illusion. Most of us didn't grow up together. My father's family was very poor and he had a hard life, which he was determined to escape at all costs. Some of the things he did don't look very sympathetic, but maybe if you have to live as he did—' He made an expressive gesture with his hands.

'Was he very—?' She paused delicately.

'Yes, very. Still is, for that matter. His family were miners, and he was expected to go down the pit. But his father had died down there and hell would freeze over before he went the same way. He did well at school, got top marks in practical subjects like maths. Not literature, or "the soft stuff" as he calls it. He reckons that's for fools. But with figures there's nothing he can't do.

'So he ran away and managed to start up his own business, just a little market stall, but it grew into a big one, and then bigger, until he got a shop.'

'He made enough profit to rent a shop? Wow!'

'Not rent. Buy. By that time he'd married my mother. She came from a rich family and they met when he made deliveries to their house. Her relatives did everything they could to stop the wedding. They believed all he really wanted was her money.'

'But they gave in at last?'

'No way. He simply ran off with her. "If you want something, go after it by the shortest route." That's his motto.

She gave him every penny she had. I know that because I've heard her father complaining about it.'

'But he probably loved her, and you. Surely everything in his life wasn't about money? It couldn't be, could it? There's always something else.'

'Is there?' he murmured. 'Is there?'

His face had changed. Now it wore a look of pain that made her take his hand in hers in a gesture of comfort.

'Don't say any more,' she said. 'Not if it hurts too much.'

He didn't answer. His gaze was fixed on the hand holding his, as it had once before. Then it had offered survival, now it offered another kind of life, one he couldn't describe. He had no talent for words, only figures. She'd spoken of it hurting him too much to talk, but now he knew that the real pain lay in not talking about things that had been shrouded in silence for too long. Somehow the words must come. But only with her.

CHAPTER FIVE

'I'LL tell you something,' Darius said at last. 'Falcon isn't my father's real name. He chose it for effect.'

'He wanted to be named after a bird?'

'No, he discovered that it has connections with a Roman consul and two princes.'

'You're kidding me.'

'Do you mean you've never heard of Pompeyo Falco?' Darius demanded with mock surprise. 'He was a very powerful Roman. The princes were Spanish, and there's even supposed to be a saint in the background. Not that he's ever made too much of that one. Nobody could keep a straight face.'

'I guess your father isn't much like a saint.'

'That's putting it mildly. He called me Darius because it means "wealthy". It was his way of signalling what he expected of me.'

Harriet dropped her face into her hands. 'I can hardly believe it,' she said at last. 'It's like something out of a mad fantasy.'

'That's just what it is. I grew up knowing what I had to do to please my father—or else! Luckily, I'd inherited his head for figures, so I was able to live up to at least some of his expectations.'

'Only some?'

'He's not pleased with me at the moment, losing so much money and letting things crumble under me.'

'But that's happened to a lot of people.'

'Doesn't matter. It shouldn't have happened to a Falcon. He's currently considering whether I, or one of my brothers, does him the most credit. At the moment I think I'm bottom of the list.'

Harriet frowned. 'I think I read somewhere that your brothers come from different parts of the world,' she said carefully.

'If you mean that my father spread himself thinly, yes, that's right. As the business built up he did a lot of travelling, first in England, then abroad. I don't think he was ever faithful to my mother for five minutes; that's how, in addition to a full brother, I come to have a half-brother from Russia, one from France, and one from America.

'In the end my mother couldn't stand it any more and she left, taking my brother Jackson and me with her. But she died after a few years and my father reclaimed us. By that time he had a new wife and a new son. We entered their house as strangers, and that was how we felt for a long time. Jackson coped better, although even he had a tough time with our stepmother.'

'She was furious that we were there at all because that meant that her boy, Marcel, wasn't the eldest. When she caught my father playing around she left him and went back to France. Marcel turned up a few years ago and, oddly enough, we all get on well. Our father has helped him start up in business in Paris, and I understand he's a real chip off the old block.'

'More than you?' she asked shrewdly.

He hesitated before saying, 'Who can say?'

Greatly daring, she ventured to ask, 'Is that what you want? To be like him?'

'I don't know,' he said. 'It's all become confused. When I was growing up my one thought was to follow in his footsteps and be a power in the land. People were awed by him, they hurried to please him, and that seemed wonderful to me. But I was immature and, as you grow up, things happen to you—'

He grew silent. After a while he repeated softly, 'I simply don't know.'

A noise made him look up quickly, smiling as if everything was normal. Nobody, Harriet thought, could guess that the moment of insight had taken him by surprise. Now she felt he was trying to forget it.

'Ah, here's Kate with the next course,' he said cheerfully. 'And not only Kate.'

Phantom had slipped in and came to curl up near the table.

'Have you had enough?' Harriet asked, caressing his ears. 'Has the guest of honour been properly cared for?'

A soft woof was the reply.

'How did Phantom happen to be with you and the rest of the crew that night?' Darius asked when they were alone again. 'I gather you'd been out on a shout. Don't tell me he comes too?'

She laughed. 'No, I left him with my neighbour—'

'To protect him from me?'

'Please.'

'All right, I won't say it again.'

'She was out walking him when she saw the boat coming home across the water, so she waited, then came and joined us.'

'How old is he?'

'Fourteen, maybe. He belonged to Brad, my husband, before we married, and he'd got him from a home for abandoned dogs, so he wasn't sure of his age. I know he's getting on a bit but he's still full of beans.'

There was a hint of defiance in her voice that warned Darius to go carefully. Fourteen was old for a dog, especially a large one, but not for the world would he have voiced his conviction that she would soon lose her beloved companion.

'Talking of being full of beans, are you really better?' she asked.

'I'm fine now. I've spent some time in bed—why that cynical look?'

'I'm getting to understand you now. All that time in bed, I'll bet you weren't alone.'

'No, I haven't seduced any willing ladies—'

'I meant you had your laptop computer with you.'

'Ah...yes...I see.' He met her teasing eyes and grinned sheepishly. 'I fell right into that one, didn't I? Yes, I did have it with me now and then. But not always. I got a lot of sleep and I have to admit you and Kate were right. It was what I needed. And, as well as rest, I've been taking exercise. I go swimming from my private beach. I keep looking out for you, but you're never there.'

Her eyes widened in theatrical innocence. 'But how can I be? I don't have the permission of the owner. He's a terrible man. When he found me there once before he was very annoyed.'

'No, you just imagined that.' He grinned. 'In future you go there whenever you like. And take Phantom too.'

A soft noise from under the table told him that this was appreciated.

'And I'm not glued to the computer all the time,' he continued.

'No, I'm sure you read the *Financial Times* and *The Wall Street Journal*—'

'I've been reading up about Herringdean and its history. It's fascinating.'

'You'll find that this island is two places,' she said. 'We're not behind the times. There's plenty of dot-com. But it's the wildness that makes Herringdean stand out, and draws people.'

'Have you always lived on the island?'

'Yes, I was born here.'

'And your husband?'

'No, he came over because he worked for a tourist firm, and they were setting up a branch.'

'And you met, fell in love and married quickly?'

'A couple of months.'

'Wow! A decisive lady! How long were you married?'

'Nearly eight years.'

'Any children?'

'No,' she said quietly.

'And he died quite recently?'

'Last year.' Suddenly she became animated. 'You know, this coffee is really delicious. Kate is a wonderful cook.'

He was silent. Walter was there in his mind, talking about Harriet's husband, saying, 'When he died we thought she might die too, she was so crushed...I don't reckon she'll ever really get over him...'

Now the way she'd swerved off the subject seemed to suggest that Walter was right. It was a warning to him to be cautious.

'What about your children?' Harriet asked. 'Have you managed to call them again?'

'Yes, several times. There's a dangerous situation building up. Mary's going to remarry soon, and if I'm not careful I could be elbowed aside.'

'But you won't let that happen.'

'No, I won't. I had time to do a lot of thinking while

I was resting. It's incredible how being half-awake, half-asleep can make things clear to you.'

Harriet nodded, and for a moment there was a faraway look in her eyes that roused his curiosity. But it vanished before he could speak, and now he thought he understood. Beneath her cheeky schoolgirl charm lurked a woman who kept her true feelings, and even her true self, safely hidden away. In fact, she was mysteriously like himself.

'So what conclusions have you come to?' she asked.

'Not to let myself be sidelined. I try to call them every day.'

'I'm sure they're glad of that.'

He made a face. 'They're not. I made a hash of it the night of the accident and things haven't really improved.'

'Well, you weren't at ease on the phone, I could hear that, but surely they understood what a state you were in.'

'Maybe, but I'm seldom much better than I was then. I don't know what to talk about. It was easier when we were living in the same house, but I'm not really part of their lives any more. Perhaps I never really was. Mary accused me of never putting them first.'

She nodded. 'Children really do like to feel that they have all your attention,' she mused.

Suddenly he saw her as she'd been that day in the shop, talking to the little boy as though only he existed in the entire world. And the child had responded with delight. When had he seen such a look on the faces of his own children?

'You've got a fight on your hands,' she said, 'but you've got to go about it the right way. Do you want some advice from a friend?'

'If the friend is you, yes.'

'That night when you called them after the accident I heard her voice on the other end. I couldn't make out every word but I heard enough to show me an unhappy situation. You told her you'd been "held up" and she said, "You always get held up. The children went to bed crying because you didn't keep your word."

'And then she said, "I'm not going to let you hurt them by putting them last again."'

She waited to see if he would say anything, but he only clasped his hands on the table and stared at them.

'Again?' she asked.

'Yes, I can't deny it. I would plan to spend time with them, but a crisis would come up, someone I urgently needed to meet would be passing through London for just a few hours.'

'Oh, you idiot!' she breathed.

'I guess I am, but I didn't see it then. I always thought there was time to put things right.'

'Yes, we always think that,' she murmured. 'There never is.'

'You sound as though you really know.'

'I guess we all know one way or another.'

'Sure, but the way you said it sounded as though—'

'The thing is—' she interrupted him quickly '—that you have to find a new way to put things right. Concentrate on that.'

'All right,' he said, retreating before the warning she was sending out. 'But how? One minute I thought I was in control. The next minute they were all gone, and if I was a hopeless father before I'm even worse now. When we talk on the phone I can sense them trying to get away. I'm becoming an irrelevance to them.'

'Then do something about it,' she said urgently. 'Put a stop to it now. Never forget that cunning is better than aggression. Above all, don't lose heart, don't even think of giving in. Remember, you're a match for anyone.'

'If you're going to start on that "mighty man of business" stuff again I'm out of here.'

'Don't worry,' she said wryly. 'I can't take it seriously any more.'

'Thanks. That about says it all.'

'Friends have to be frank with each other,' she reminded him.

'I know.' He suddenly became more urgent. 'Harriet, I wish I could make you understand how much I need your friendship. From the moment I stepped onto that beach I knew I was in a different world, and now I know that it's your world. All the vital things that have happened to me since I came here are connected with you.'

'You never know what fate has in store.'

'Yes, after we got off to such a bad start, who could have guessed that you'd be the one who'd save me?'

'Be fair. It was Kate who really saved you, not just by raising the alarm, but by explaining that you'd probably gone to the wind farm, so that we knew where to look.'

'I know that, and I've shown her my gratitude.'

Harriet nodded. Kate had told her about the huge bonus he'd given her.

'And I didn't pull you out of the water on my own. There were a few hefty fellers there, doing the heavy work.'

'I know. But yours was the hand that stretched out to me first, the hand that I clasped, and when I think of that moment that's what I see.'

It was also what he felt in the night, feeling a firm, reassuring grip on his hand, knowing it was her in the last moment before he awoke to find himself alone. Only a dream, yet his hand still seemed to tingle.

'I've just become a sort of symbol, that's all,' she told him.

'If you say so.'

'But if you want a friend, you've got one in me.'

'Promise?'

'Promise. Call on me any time.'

As long as you're here, she thought. But how long will that be? Are we a financial asset to you, or a financial disaster? And won't it be the same in the long run?

It would have been sensible to say this outright and remind him of the reality of the situation, yet something held her silent. There was an intensity in his eyes that she'd never seen before in any man—not the passionate intensity of a lover, but the desperate yearning for help of a man who needed friendship. It had been her hand he'd first seized in the water and that had set matters between them for all time.

'You may regret saying that,' he said. 'I'll call on you more often than you think.'

'I'll never regret saying it. I'm here for you.'

'Shake on it?'

She took the hand he offered, and felt her own hand engulfed. She could sense the power, as she'd sensed it that other time when he'd held her against her will to study her face. But now she also felt the gentleness deep within him, knowing instinctively that few people were ever allowed to know about it.

He touched her heart—not as a lover, she assured herself. That part of her life had died a year ago. But his need spoke to her, making it impossible for her to turn her back on him.

'Shake,' she said.

A couple of days later she resumed bathing on his beach. After splashing around with Phantom for half an hour she gasped, 'All right, boy. Time we were going.'

But as she turned towards the shore she was halted by

the sight of Darius, striding onto the beach wearing a dark blue towel bathrobe, which he stripped off, showing his black bathing gear beneath.

Instead of tight-fitting trunks he wore shorts, looser and less revealing, leaving many of her questions still unanswered. Even so, she could see that he was more powerfully built than a mere businessman had any right to be. If there was any justice in the world he would be scrawny, not taut and lean, with long muscular arms and legs.

He saw her and waved. Next moment he was running into the water and powering towards her. She laughed and swam away, swerving this way and that until he caught up, reaching out his hands. She seized them and he immediately began to back-pedal, drawing her with him. As they reached the shore she slipped away, laughing, and he chased her up the beach to where he'd dropped his bathrobe next to her towel.

Phantom galloped after them, delighted at the prospect of a rematch, but this time Darius was ready for him, dropping to one knee, greeting his 'opponent' with outstretched arms and rolling on the sand with him.

'I reckon that's about even,' he said, getting up at last.

'Now you really are a mess,' she said, regarding the sand that covered him.

'Yes, I am, aren't I?' he agreed with something that sounded suspiciously like satisfaction. 'All right, play's over. Time for the serious stuff. See you tomorrow.'

So it went on for several days—pleasant, undemanding friendship with almost the innocence of childhood. It seemed strange to think of this man in such a light, but when she saw him fooling with Phantom it was hard to remember his harsh reputation, and the power he held over them all.

Then he vanished.

'He just took off without a word,' Kate said when they bumped into each other while shopping. 'He was sitting at the computer when I took in his morning coffee. I don't know what he saw there but it made him say a very rude word. Then he made a phone call. I got out fast but I could hear a lot more rude words.'

Walter, who also happened to be there, said, 'Only rude words?'

'I heard him say, "I don't care; it mustn't be allowed to happen," and "Do you realise what this would mean if—?" and "When I get my hands on him I'll—" and then more rude words.'

'Sounds like a disaster,' Walter observed.

'Nah,' Kate said. 'Not him. He's too big for disaster. You mark my words, they can't touch him.'

'That's not what the papers say,' Walter insisted. 'This "credit crunch" thing has hit all the big shots. Next thing you know he'll have to sell this place and we'll have someone new to worry about.'

'Oh, stop panicking!' Harriet said, trying to sound amused and not quite succeeding. 'He's better than Rancing. The furniture shops love him now he's started kitting out Giant's Beacon, and he's given quite a bit to charity.'

'Yes, I heard about that donation to the animal shelter,' Walter said. 'I wondered how he knew about it—unless you told him.'

'I may have mentioned it. He likes to be told about things.'

'Yes, everyone's talking about how you and he swim together in the mornings. You're a clever lass, getting on his right side.' He added significantly, 'You probably know more than anyone.'

'I know he looks fantastic in swimming gear,' she agreed.

'That's not what I meant.'

Yes, she thought, she knew what he meant. This was the moment a less loyal friend would tell how he'd been tricked by Rancing, exposing him to ridicule. For the first time she appreciated how vulnerable Darius had left himself by confiding in her.

'We don't discuss business,' she said. 'I wouldn't understand it if we did. I've no idea where he's gone, why he's gone or when he'll be back.'

Or if he'll ever be back, she thought sadly.

She didn't doubt that another financial calamity had befallen him, and that he'd gone to try to head off trouble. It must be urgent because, despite their friendship, he hadn't left her a word. Still she was sure he would call her.

But he didn't. Days passed without a word. Wryly, she decided that this was a lesson in reality. When his real world called she simply ceased to exist, that was something to remember in the future.

If there was a future.

Harriet tried to follow the financial news and learned of the sudden collapse of a property company with global tentacles, but she could only guess whether he had had an interest there.

Then, just when she'd decided that he'd gone for good, Darius turned her world upside down yet again. As she and Phantom headed for their morning swim he suddenly gave a bark of joy and charged onto the beach to where a figure lay stretched out on the sand. Fending off the dog, who was trying to lick him to death, Darius rose on one elbow and watched her approach.

'Hello, stranger,' she said when she could speak through her emotion.

'I hoped you'd be here,' he said as she dropped beside him. 'I got back at three in the morning and came out here so as not to miss you. I dozed off for a while, but I knew someone would wake me. All right, Phantom, cool it, there's a good fellow.'

'Did things go as you'd hoped?' she asked.

'More or less. I averted disaster—until next time.'

'You mean we're safe—here on the island?'

'You're safe. This is the last place in the world that I'd give up. Now, I need to ask a huge favour from you, an act of friendship. It's very important to me.'

'Then consider it done.'

'I told you Mary left me for another man, and they were planning marriage. Well, the date has been set, and I've been invited.'

'To your ex-wife's wedding?'

'Yes, it took a bit of manoeuvring, but I managed it. I told her we should seem friendly for the sake of the children. They'll be there so we'll get some time together and they'll know their parents are on good terms. You see, I really took your advice.'

'*I* advised this?'

'You said cunning was better than aggression, and it took all my cunning to manipulate myself an invitation. Mary finished by saying she completely agreed with me and she praised me for thinking of it. She even said I must be improving.' He gave a self-deprecating grin. 'And I owe it all to you.'

He spread his hands in a gesture of finality, his expression radiating such cheerful triumph that she chuckled and said, 'You're telling me that *I* instructed *you* in cunning?'

'There's cunning and cunning,' he said. 'Some kinds I'm better at than others. Manipulating share prices is easy, but—'

'But a child's heart is more complicated than a share price,' she supplied.

'You see how right I was to listen to you. The best friend and adviser I have.'

'Stop buttering me up,' she said severely, 'and tell me what you want me to do.'

'Come with me to the wedding, of course. How can I turn up alone when my ex-wife is marrying another guy? I'd look like a prat.'

'And we can't have that,' she said in mock horror. 'If the markets got to hear—'

'All right, make fun of me. I wouldn't put up with it from anyone else, but with you I guess it's the price of friendship. OK, I'll pay it.

'And there's another thing. I told you about my father and how he likes to control everyone's life. His latest mad idea is to marry me off to Freya, my stepsister. Either me or one of my brothers, but at the moment it's my head he's trying to put on the block.

'Luckily, Freya's no more keen than I am. We get on all right, but that's all. If I can convince my father that it's not going to happen then he'll turn his attention to one of the others.'

'Poor Freya.'

'That's what I think. You'll like her.'

'But will she be at the wedding? And your father? Isn't he furious with Mary for leaving you?'

'Yes, he is. He's even more furious because she managed to get a decent divorce settlement out of me, but he'll want to see his grandchildren. They're Falcons, which means that in his mind they're his property. He doesn't have much contact with them because they live in London and he can't leave Monte Carlo very often.'

'For tax reasons?' she hazarded.

'That's right. He's only allowed to be in England for ninety-one days. Any more and he'd be counted as an

English resident and liable for English tax. He's nearly used up his allowance for this year so he has to dash to London for the wedding, and get back very quickly.'

How casually he spoke, she realised. How normal he seemed to consider this. It was a reminder that his life was centred around money, just in case she was in danger of forgetting.

'And your brothers?' she asked. 'Will they be there?'

'As many as can manage it. They all like Mary, rather more than they like me, actually. And the kids are fascinated by them coming from so many different countries. To them it's like a circus. So we're all going to bury our differences, but you won't send me into the lion's den alone, will you?'

Harriet regarded him sardonically. 'You really don't feel you can face it without me?'

'Definitely not. I'm shaking in my shoes at the prospect.'

There it was in his eyes, the teasing humour that linked with her own mind in a contact sweeter than she had ever known.

'In that case, I'll just have to come along and protect you,' she sighed. 'It's a dreadful responsibility, but I guess I'll manage.'

'I knew you wouldn't fail me. The wedding's in London in two weeks' time. It'll be a civil ceremony held at the Gloriana Hotel, and that's where the reception will be too, so I'll book us in there. You'll be my guest, of course, but we'll have separate rooms, so don't worry. Every propriety will be observed.'

Propriety. There was that word again. How often it cropped up in her mind with regard to this man, always implying the opposite.

Don't go, said a warning voice in her mind. *To him this is a matter of friendship, but can you keep it as mere friendship? You don't even know the answer, and oh, how you wish you did! Stay here, keep yourself safe.*

'I'd love to come,' she said.

CHAPTER SIX

OVER the next few days Harriet made her preparations, arranging extra hours for her assistant, notifying the lifeboat station that she would be away so that they could arrange a substitute to be on call. Her neighbour would look after Phantom, and she explained her coming absence to him with many caresses. He accepted these politely but seemed far more interested in the box of bones that had been delivered from Giant's Beacon.

On the last day before their departure Harriet and Darius went for a final swim, frolicking like children, splashing each other, laughing fit to bust.

Harriet knew that at the back of her mind there was an unfamiliar aspect to her happiness. Part of her had been so sure that their friendship was over, but then he'd drawn her back in, seeking her help and her warmth again, and it was like a balm to her spirit. Suddenly all she wanted to do was laugh and dance.

As they raced up the beach she stopped suddenly and looked around.

'My towel's vanished. Where—? *Phantom.*'

In the distance they could see him tearing along the sand, her towel in his jaws, deaf to her cries.

'He'll be back in his own good time,' Darius said.

'But what do I do in the meantime?'

'Let me dry you.' In a moment he'd flung his towel around her, drawing it close in front, and began to rub her down. She shrieked with laughter and tried to wriggle away but he held her a prisoner while his hands moved over her.

'You wretch,' she cried, pummelling him. 'Let me go.'

But it was no use. He had ten times her strength, as she was beginning to understand. And there was something else she understood. She'd been mad to engage in this struggle that drew her near-naked body so close to his. The pleasure that was pervading her now was more than laughter with a dear friend. His flesh against hers, his face close to her own, the meeting of their eyes; she should have avoided these things like the plague. Except that he hadn't given her the chance.

Caution, she'd promised herself, but where was caution now? And did she really care?

'Let me go,' she repeated.

But now his arms had enfolded her completely, allowing no movement.

'Make me,' he challenged.

She made a half-hearted attempt to kick him but only ended up with her leg trapped between his.

'Do you call that making me?' he demanded.

'Will you stop this?'

'Nope.'

It shocked her to realise how disappointed she would have been if his answer had been any different.

'What do you think you're doing?' she cried.

'I just thought it was time you learned who was boss around here.'

'OK, you're boss. Now let me go.'

'Only if you pay the ransom.'

'And what's that?'

'This,' he said, dropping his head.

It wasn't a major kiss, no big deal, she told herself, trying not to respond to the gentle pressure of his lips. But it was precisely that light touch that was her undoing, making her want to lean forward, demanding that he kiss her more deeply, and more deeply still, threatening her with her own desires. And with that threat came fear.

'No,' she whispered. 'No.'

'I wonder if you really mean that.'

She too wondered, but now she gathered all her strength together and said more firmly, *'No!'*

He drew back a little, frowning.

'You promised this wouldn't happen,' she reminded him.

'I didn't exactly—'

'Every propriety observed, you said.'

'Does that mean I can't even kiss you?'

'It means you can't kiss me now, just when we're about to embark on this idea of yours, pretending to be together when we aren't really.'

Slowly he released her and she took the chance to step back.

'Isn't this something we have to work out as we go along?' he asked.

'You're a businessman, Darius. I'm sure you know that when exploring new territory it's wise to have a plan.'

'And is that your plan?' he demanded. 'To turn away from all human desire?'

'*I have to.* Can't you try to understand? I'm not sure that I can ever…I don't know, *I don't know.*'

'But how long? For the rest of your life? Was he really that perfect?'

She took a step back and her face was distraught. 'Leave me alone. Just leave me alone.'

He sighed. 'Yes, all right. I'm sorry, Harriet. I should have known better. You have to pick your own time. I can't pick it for you. I shouldn't have—it's just that I've wanted to do that for some time and...well, I guess you don't want to know that.'

'I'd rather not,' she agreed.

'Just try to forgive me, please.'

'There's nothing to forgive,' she said calmly. 'It didn't happen. Now, I think it's time we went and started to get ready. We have a long day tomorrow.'

Harriet left him without a backward glance, followed by Phantom, dragging her towel.

After a moment Darius walked after them, cursing himself for clumsiness.

The trip to London was like nothing Harriet had ever known before. Darius had chartered a helicopter that collected them from the lawn and swept them up and over the channel. Looking down, she drew in her breath.

'Herringdean looks so different, and the sea—nothing is the way I know it below.'

'Yes, they're different worlds,' he agreed, looking down with her. 'And it can be hard to know which one is the place you belong.'

'I suppose it wouldn't be possible to belong in the world up here,' she said thoughtfully. 'You could never stay up that long.'

'True. Sooner or later you have to come down to earth,' he said in a voice that had a touch of regret.

In London, they landed at an airport where a car was waiting, ready to sweep them into the West End, the place of theatres, expensive shops and even more expensive hotels.

The sight of the Gloriana Hotel rearing up eight floors

startled Harriet. She'd guessed that it would be luxurious, but the reality took her by surprise. Again, she wondered if she'd been wise to come here, but it was too late. The chauffeur was carrying their bags to the door. Darius had drawn her arm through his and for his sake she must steel herself. He'd asked this as an act of friendship—and from now on she had only one function; to do him credit so that he could hold up his head.

It needed all her resolution when she saw the inside of the hotel with its marble floor and columns. As Darius had promised, they had separate accommodation but they were next door to each other. When he'd left her alone she studied her surroundings. The bedroom was the largest she had ever seen, and the bathroom was an elegant dream of white porcelain and silver taps. She knew she should have been in heaven, but such luxury intimidated her even more.

Ah, well, she thought resolutely. Best dress forward!

But unpacking was a dismal experience. Suddenly none of her dresses seemed 'best' as it would be understood in the Gloriana.

Then she recalled seeing a gown shop in the reception area. A moment to check that she'd brought her credit cards and she was out of the door, hurrying to the elevator.

The shop exceeded her wildest expectations. The clothes were glorious. So, too, were the prices but she decided to worry about that later. Anything was better than looking like a little brown mouse in the kind of elegant company that Darius regarded as normal.

Two dresses held her undecided for a while, but at last—

'I'll take this one,' she said.

'And the other one,' said Darius's voice behind her. 'They both suit you.'

She whirled to face him. 'How did you—?'

'When I found your room empty I asked the desk and they told me you were here. You should have brought me with you so we could make the decision together. Mind you, I like your choices.' To the assistant he said, 'We'll take both of these, please.'

'No,' she muttered urgently. 'I can't afford them both.'

'You?' He regarded her with quizzically raised eyebrows. 'What has this got to do with you?'

'Evidently, nothing,' she said.

'I invited you here to do me a favour. I don't expect you to buy your own clothes as well.'

Light dawned.

'When you say clothes you mean props, don't you? I'm playing a part and the director chooses the costumes?'

'Got it in one.'

'Next thing, you'll be telling me I'm tax deductible.'

'Now there's a thought! Come on, let's get to work. What have you chosen for the wedding?'

'I thought that one,' she said, indicating her first choice.

'No, something a little more formal.' He turned away to murmur to the assistant, and another flow of gowns was produced.

'Try that on,' Darius said, pointing to a matching dress and jacket.

Turning this way and that before the mirror, she saw it looked stunning on her. As Darius said, it was only right that he should pay the expenses, and when would she get the chance to dress like this again? She fought temptation for the briefest moment before yielding happily. It would take more stern virtue than she could manage to reject this.

While the dress was being packed up Darius said, 'Now, about jewellery.' As if anticipating her protest, he hurried on, 'I'm afraid this will only be hired. Take a look at these.'

If they hadn't been on hire she knew she couldn't have accepted the gold, silver and diamonds that were displayed before her. As it was, she was able to make her choice with a clear conscience.

Before they returned to their rooms Darius led her to the back of the hotel, where a huge ballroom was being decorated.

'This is where they'll hold the party tonight,' he said. 'And tomorrow night the wedding reception will be here.'

More size. This place had been created to hold a thousand. So why was she on edge? she wondered. She was at ease with the much greater size of the ocean. But that was natural, not created artificially to be impressive and profitable. She could never be at ease in an environment like this.

But she smiled, said the right things and tried to look as if she belonged here.

'I've got to go and make phone calls,' Darius said as they reached her room. 'I'll have something delivered for you to eat, then why don't you put your feet up until your attendants get here?'

'Attendants?'

'Hairstyle, make-up. Just leave it to them. You don't need to worry about a thing.'

In other words, she thought, let them array her in her stage costume and make her up for the performance.

'All right,' she said good-humouredly. 'I promise not to interfere with my own appearance.'

'That's my girl! Bye.'

He dropped the briefest kiss on her cheek and was gone, leaving Harriet alone and thoughtful. A mirror on the wall of the corridor showed her a neat, efficient young woman, pleasant but not dynamic.

Still, I've never had much chance to be dynamic, she thought. *And who knows—?*

Her reflection challenged her, sending the message, *Don't kid yourself.*

But why not? she thought. *If I want to kid myself, that's my business. Hey, I forgot to ask him—*

Approaching his door, she raised her hand to knock, then stopped as she heard Darius's voice.

'Mary? So you've arrived at last. Are the kids with you?—Fine, I'm on my way.'

Harriet heard the phone being replaced, and moved fast. By the time Darius emerged, the corridor was empty.

Lying on the bed, she tried to rest as Darius had advised, but her mind was too full of questions. What was happening now between him and his ex-wife, between him and his children? Would the wedding be dramatically called off at the last minute because of a reconciliation?

And why should she care? She'd had her chance and turned it down.

The chance wouldn't come again. She must force herself to remember that.

But after only half an hour she heard him return, walking quickly along the corridor until he entered his room and slammed the door like a man who was really annoyed.

After that she dozed until there was a knock at her door.

Even though Darius had told her about the attendants, what happened next was a shock. They simply took her over, allowing no room for argument, and proceeded to turn her into someone else. She yielded chiefly out of curiosity. She was fascinated to discover her new self.

If she'd been fanciful—which she prided herself on never

being—she might have thought of Cinderella. The fairy godmother, or godmothers since there were two of them, waved their wands and the skivvy was transformed into a princess.

Or at least a passable imitation of one, she thought. How well she could carry it off was yet to be seen.

When she was alone again she surveyed herself in the mirror, wondering who was this glamorous creature with the elegant swept-up hair, wearing the dark red glittering cocktail dress. She had always regarded herself as a tad too thin, but only a woman with her shape could have dared to wear this tight-fitting gown that left no doubt about her tiny waist and long legs, while revealing her bosom as slightly fuller than she had imagined.

A princess, she thought. Princess Harry? Not sure about that.

Even she, self-critical though she was, could see how the expert make-up emphasised the size of her blue eyes, which seemed to have acquired a new sparkle, and the width of her shapely mouth.

From nowhere came the memory of her husband, whose work in tourism had often taken him away on trips.

'I could get jealous of all those expensively dressed women you meet,' she'd teased him once.

'Forget it,' he'd told her. 'You don't need that fancy stuff. You're better as you are.'

'A country bumpkin?' she'd chuckled.

'*My* country bumpkin,' he'd insisted, silencing her in the traditional way, making her so happy that she'd believed him and wasn't jealous. Only to discover at last that she should have been.

And if he'd ever seen her looking like this? Would anything have been different?

Suddenly she wanted very badly to find Darius, see the

expression in his eyes when he first glimpsed her. Then she would know—

Know what?

If she only knew that, she would know everything. And it was time to find out.

A few moments later, she was knocking on Darius's door. As soon as he opened it he grew still. Then he nodded slowly.

'Yes,' he said. *'Yes.'*

'Will I do?'

'You cheeky little devil; I've already given you the answer to that.'

He drew her into the room and stood back to look at her, then made a twirling movement with his hand. She turned slowly, giving him time to appreciate every detail, then back again, displaying herself to full advantage. After all, she reasoned, he was entitled to know that his money had been well spent.

'As long as I do you credit.'

'I'll be the envy of every man there.'

And that, she thought, was what he chiefly cared about, apart from his children. She was there to be useful, and it would be wise to remember that. But it was hard when the excitement was growing in her.

Darius put his hands on her shoulders, holding her just a few inches away, his eyes fixed on her face.

'Beautiful,' he said. 'Just as I hoped. Just as I imagined. Just as—'

'Am I interrupting anything?' said a voice from the doorway.

Darius beamed at the young man standing there. 'Marcel!' he exclaimed.

Next moment, he was embracing the newcomer, thumping him on the back and being thumped in return.

Marcel, Harriet thought. The half brother from Paris.

'I'm sorry to come in without knocking,' he said, 'but the door was open.'

His eyes fell on Harriet, and the pleasurable shock in them was very satisfying.

'You've been keeping this lady a big secret,' he said, speaking with the barest trace of a French accent. 'And I understand why. If she were mine I would also hide her away from the world. Introduce me. I insist.'

'This is Harriet,' Darius replied, moving beside her.

'Harriet,' Marcel echoed. 'Harriet. It is a beautiful name.'

She couldn't resist saying cheekily, 'Actually, my friends call me Harry.'

'Harry?' He seemed aghast, muttering something in French that might have been a curse. 'That is a monstrosity, to give a man's name to such a beautiful lady. And this fellow allows them to treat you like this? You should be rid of him at once.'

'Cut it out!' Darius said, grinning, which seemed to amuse Marcel even more.

'Just thought I'd get in the mood now the circus has come to town,' he said.

'Circus is right,' Darius agreed. 'I've warned Harriet.'

'Harriet? You mean *you* don't call her Harry? But of course, you're not a friend; you are—' He made a vague but significant gesture.

'Hey,' she said and he turned his merry gaze on her. 'Don't jump to conclusions,' she told him impishly.

'Ah, yes, I see. How wise.'

'Can we drop this?' Darius asked.

'Certainly. So, Harriet, Darius has warned you, and you know we're a load of oddities.'

'I'll bet you're no odder than me,' she riposted.

'I'll take you up on that. Promise me a dance tonight.'

'She declines,' Darius said firmly.

'Oh, do I?'

'Definitely.'

Marcel chuckled and murmured in Harriet's ear, 'We'll meet again later.'

'Are any of the others here?' Darius asked.

'Jackson. Travis isn't coming. He can't leave America—some television series he's working on. Leonid tried to get here but an urgent meeting came up at the last minute. And our honourable father arrived an hour ago, but I expect you already know that.'

'No, he hasn't been in touch. I'm in his black books at the moment. Anyone with him?'

'Janine and Freya.'

Harriet's teasing impulse got the better of her again and made her say, 'Ah, yes, she's the one you're supposed to be marrying, isn't she?'

'You can stop that kind of talk,' Darius said, while Marcel grinned.

'A lady with a sense of humour,' he said. 'That's what I like. Believe me, you're going to need it. I said before that it was a circus, and Papa is the ringmaster. He cracks the whip and we jump through hoops—or at least we pretend to.'

'Yes,' Darius growled.

'I gather you're not playing his game,' Marcel said, his eyes on Harriet again.

'Right, and so I've told him. Let's hope he believes me.'

'You realise that means he'll set his sights on Jackson or me next,' Marcel complained. 'Luckily, Freya finds me irritating.'

Darius grinned. 'I can't think why.'

'Neither can I. Right, I'll be off. I'll see you at the reception.'

He blew Harriet a kiss and hurried away.

'I like your brother,' she said when the door had closed.

'Most women do,' Darius observed wryly.

'No, I mean he looks fun.'

'Most women say that too.'

'Which is why you find him irritating?'

'He's a good fellow. We get on most of the time. It may have crossed my mind that he sometimes has it too easy in certain areas. Mary used to accuse me of being jealous of his charm, and perhaps she was right. Charm isn't one of my virtues.' He gave her a wry look. 'As you've found out.'

As he spoke he reached for her hand, and some impulse made her enfold his in both of hers, squeezing comfortingly.

'Charm isn't always a virtue,' she said. 'A man can have too much of it.'

'Well, nobody's ever accused me of that.'

'Good. Just honesty—'

'I hope so.'

'And upright virtue.'

'Nobody's ever accused me of that either,' he said with an air of alarm that made her chuckle. 'You teasing little shrew. What are you trying to do to me?'

'Cheer you up,' she said. 'You really need it.'

'Yes, I do. And I might have guessed you'd be the one to see it. Come on. Let's face them together.'

On the way down in the elevator he said, 'Mary's here. I saw her this afternoon.'

'And the children?'

'Briefly. None of us knew what to say, but that was because *he* was there.'

'He?'

'Ken, the guy who thinks he's going to replace me as their father. They're all in the same suite, a "family", Mary says.'

'How do they get on with Ken?'

'They seem to like him,' Darius sighed.

'Good.'

For a moment he scowled, but then sighed and said, 'All right, say it.'

'If they get on with their stepfather they'll be happier. And I know you won't spoil that because you love them too much.'

A faint ironic smile touched his lips. 'All right, teacher. I've taken the lesson on board.'

'Just make sure that you pay attention,' she commanded him severely.

His eyes swept over her glamorous appearance. 'I am paying attention,' he assured her. 'But that wasn't what you meant, was it?'

'No, it wasn't. Bad boy. Go to the back of the class.'

'Fine, I'll get an even better view of you from there.'

'Behave!'

'Aren't I allowed to say that you're beautiful and gorgeous and—?'

'No, you are *not* allowed to say it.'

'All right, I'll just think it.'

She'd done what she'd set out to do, put him in a cheerful mood for the evening. And nothing else mattered. She had to remember that!

As they emerged from the elevator downstairs they could see people already streaming towards the great room where the reception was to be held.

As soon as they entered Harriet saw their hosts on a slightly raised dais at the far end. There was Mary, smiling, greeting her guests. Beside her stood Ken, the man she was about to marry, and on the other side were the children, dressed up in formal clothes and looking uncomfortable.

Harriet was alive with curiosity to meet the woman Darius had loved and married, who had borne him two children, then preferred another man. An incredible decision, whispered the voice that she tried vainly to silence.

'Ready?' Darius murmured in her ear.

'Ready for anything.'

'Then forward into battle,'

She was aware of heads turned in curiosity as Mary's ex-husband advanced with another woman on his arm, and now she was glad he'd arrayed her in fine clothes so that she could do him proud.

Mary was a tall, elegant woman, with a beauty Harriet could only envy. But she also had a down-to-earth manner and an air of kindness that Harriet hadn't expected from the woman who'd spoken to her sharply on the phone.

'Mary, this is Harriet,' Darius said. 'Harriet, this is Mary, who was my wife until she decided she couldn't stand me any longer.'

There was real warmth in Mary's embrace, and her declaration, 'It's a pleasure to meet you.' But the way she then stood back and regarded Harriet was disconcerting. It was the look of someone who'd heard a lot and was intensely curious. It might have been Harriet's imagination that Mary then gave a little nod.

Ken, her fiancé, was quiet, conventional, pleasant-looking but unremarkable. He greeted Harriet in friendly fashion, acknowledged Darius and escaped as soon as possible.

'We've spoken on the telephone,' Mary said to Harriet. 'I recognise your voice.'

'Yes, Harriet was part of the lifeboat crew that saved me,' Darius said.

'Then she's my friend.' Suddenly Mary's eyes twinkled. 'And I was right about something else, wasn't I? You denied that you were his girlfriend but I knew.'

'Have a heart, Mary,' Darius growled.

'All right, I'll say no more. I don't want to embarrass either of you.'

But Darius was already uncomfortable, Harriet could tell. At the sight of his children his face lit up with relief and he opened his arms so that they could hug him.

She knew that Frankie was ten years old and Mark nine. Both were lively, attractive children with nice manners.

'Here she is, guys,' Darius said. 'This is the lifeboat lady that I told you about.'

Both of them stared.

'You work on a lifeboat?' Mark asked, awed.

'Not work. I'm on call if they need me.'

'But how often do you have to go out saving people?'

'It varies. Sometimes once a month, sometimes twice a day.'

'It must be ever so exciting,' Frankie breathed.

'Hey, she doesn't do it for fun,' Darius protested. 'I didn't find it exciting to be stuck in the water, wondering if I'd ever get out.'

'But Dad, she *saved* you,' Mark pointed out.

'Yes,' he agreed quietly. 'She saved me.'

He might have said more, but something he saw over their shoulders made him straighten up, tense.

'Hello, Father,' he said.

So that was Amos Falcon, Harriet thought. Research had made her familiar with his face, but the reality was startling. This was a fierce, uncompromising man with dark eyes shadowed by heavy brows. His mouth might once have been merely firm, but now it looked as though a lifetime of setting it in resolute lines had left it incapable of anything gentler. This was a giant, to be feared. And she did fear him, instinctively.

More troubling still was the astonishing resemblance between him and Darius. They were the same height and with broad shoulders, features that were similar, even handsome. They were undoubtedly father and son.

In how many ways? she wondered. Was Darius doomed to grow into a replica of a man everyone called awesome? Or was there still time for him to seek another path?

Darius drew her forward for introductions, and she was surprised to see that Amos studied her intently. Of course, he was naturally concerned to know about his son's companion. But she sensed there was more. His eyes, boring into her, seemed to combine knowledge, curiosity and harsh suspicion in equal measure. It was unnerving

He made a polite speech of gratitude for Darius's life, then introduced his wife, Janine, who smiled and also spoke of gratitude. She struck Harriet as a modest, retiring woman, which probably suited Amos.

'And this is my daughter, Freya,' she said, indicating a tall young woman beside her.

This was the wife the powerful Amos had chosen for Darius. She didn't look like the kind of female who would shrink back and let herself be a pawn. She was tall, fair, well, but not extravagantly dressed, with an air of self-possession. She shook Harriet's hand vigorously and said all the polite things before hailing Darius with an unmistakable air of sisterly derision. Harriet discovered that she liked Freya a lot.

There were more arrivals, people approaching the dais

to be greeted, and the crowd moved on and shifted her with it. When Darius began to lead her around the room, introducing her to people, she couldn't resist looking back and found Amos staring after her.

Glancing about her, Harriet was more than ever glad that she was dressed in style. This was a gathering of the rich and mighty, and at least she looked as though she belonged amongst them, however fake it might be.

It was clear that Darius really did belong in this gathering. Many of them knew him and spoke respectfully. They knew he'd taken a hit, but so had they, and his fortunes could yet recover, so they addressed him as they had always done, crossing their fingers.

Harriet found herself remembering the day she'd overheard him on the phone vowing, 'no mercy!' How long ago that seemed now that she'd discovered his other side. But these people had never discovered it, and wouldn't have believed it if she'd told them.

And nor, she realised, would Darius want them to believe it. Much of his power depended on a ruthless image.

'What's the matter?' he asked suddenly.

'Matter? Nothing?'

'Why are you giving me that curious look?'

'I didn't know I was.'

'What's going on in that mind of yours?'

'Nothing. My mind is a pure blank.'

He grinned. 'You're a very annoying woman, you know that?'

'Have you only just found that out?'

'I guess I'm still learning. Come on, let's have a good time.'

CHAPTER SEVEN

SUDDENLY Darius's face lit up at something he'd seen over Harriet's shoulder. '*Jackson, you young devil.* Where have you been?'

The young man approaching them was sufficiently like Darius to be his brother, yet better looking. His features were more regular, less interesting, she thought. Most women would have called him handsome.

He greeted Darius with a friendly thump on the shoulder and stood back to survey him with pleasure.

'I've been abroad,' he said. 'I just got back yesterday to find that nobody had seen hide nor hair of you for ages. Where did you vanish to?'

'Herringdean. I'm the unexpected owner of an island off the south coast. This lady—' he drew Harriet forward '—lives there and has been kind enough to be my guide and friend.'

Jackson beamed and engulfed her hand in his. 'I don't know how you put up with him,' he said.

'Neither do I,' she said, liking him immensely.

'Did I hear right? Herringdean? *The* Herringdean?'

'I don't know of any other,' she said.

Delight broke over his face. 'You've got fulmars there, haven't you?'

'Yes, plenty of them. They're beautiful.' Light dawned. 'Hey, I've seen you before, haven't I? On television?'

'I've done a programme or two,' he agreed. 'But never one about fulmars. Could you and I have a talk some time soon?'

'Of course we can.'

'Then you can really have a deep discussion about fulmars,' Darius observed. 'I don't know how you can bear the suspense.'

Laughing, the other two turned on him.

'They're birds,' Harriet said. 'Very big and lovely. They look like gulls but they're really petrels.'

'Fascinating!' said Darius, who wouldn't have known a gull from a petrel if they'd attacked him together.

'They nest high up on cliffs,' Harriet continued, 'and they're one of the beauties of Herringdean.'

Darius regarded her with comic irony. 'And I've owned these fabulous creatures all this time and you didn't tell me?'

'Nobody owns fulmars,' Harriet said. 'It's they who own the world, especially that bit of it called Herringdean.'

Jackson looked at her with appreciation. 'I see you're an expert,' he said. 'Don't waste yourself on this fellow. Let's go and have that talk now.'

'Yes, be off while I make some duty calls,' Darius said.

She was briefly afraid that the exchange might have offended him, but he kissed her cheek, saying, 'Take care of her, Jackson.'

Now she remembered Darius saying that his brother was a naturalist. 'Not an academic. He just works a lot with animals and charities. Does TV a bit, goes off on expeditions. You'd find him interesting.'

And she did. Jackson knew his stuff, and as she also

knew hers they plunged into a knowledgeable discussion that pleased them both.

Darius did his duty, going from acquaintance to acquaintance, saying the right things, avoiding the wrong things, smiling mechanically, performing as expected. Nothing in his demeanour revealed that he was intensely conscious of Harriet and Jackson sitting at a side table, their heads close together, each so absorbed that they seemed to have forgotten the rest of the world.

Gradually, he managed to get near enough to eavesdrop but what he heard brought him no comfort. He couldn't discern every word, but Jackson clearly said, 'It depends whether you're talking about northern fulmars or southern fulmars…'

His last words were drowned out, but then Harriet said, 'It's a pity that…any old rubbish…almost makes you want to…'

Jackson asked a question and she replied eagerly, 'That's always the way with *Procellariidae*, don't you think?'

'What?'

Jackson looked up and grinned. 'Here's my brother. Perhaps you'd better return to him before he goes out of his mind.'

He touched Darius on the shoulder and departed. Darius drew Harriet's arm through his, saying, 'I hardly dare ask what you were talking about. What the blue blazes are procellar—whatever?'

'*Procellariidae*. It's just the name of the family that fulmars belong to, just like crows and magpies are *Corvids*—'

'Are they really? You'll be telling me next that wrens are dinosaurs.'

'Oh, no, wrens are *Troglodytidae*.' Her lips twitched.

'There, and you thought of me as a silly little creature who didn't know any long words.'

'Well, if I was foolish enough to think that you've made me sorry. I feel as if I've been walked over by hobnailed boots.'

'Good,' she teased. 'Serve you right.'

She was looking up at him with gleaming eyes, and he couldn't have stopped himself responding, however much he wanted to. But he didn't want to. He wanted to take her hand and follow her into the world where only she could take him—the world of laughter and good fellowship that had been closed to him before but now seemed to open invitingly whenever she was there.

A few yards away Jackson watched them, unnoticed, a curious expression on his face. After a while he smiled as though he'd seen something that satisfied him.

Harriet had tried to prepare herself to cope among Darius's family. She told herself that she was ready for Mary, for Freya, even for Amos. But it was the children who surprised her. After doing their social duty, Frankie and Mark effectively took her prisoner, corralling her into a corner and sitting one each side, lest she have ideas of escape. Like all the best hostage-takers, they provided her with excellent food and drink, but there was no doubt they meant business.

First she had to tell the story of Darius's rescue, suitably edited for their childish ears. Then they wanted to hear about other rescue trips, listening in awed silence, until Mark said breathlessly, 'But aren't you scared?'

She thought for a moment. 'Not really.'

'Not even when it's terribly dangerous?' Frankie persisted.

'There isn't time to be scared. There's always so much to do.'

Frankie looked around before leaning forward and whispering, 'It's more fun when it's dangerous, isn't it?'

Harriet hesitated, aware of a yawning pit at her feet. She must be careful what she said to children. Especially these two. Frankie's gleaming eyes showed that she already had her own opinion of the joys of danger.

'No,' Harriet said, trying to sound firm. 'And that is a very irresponsible point of view. Danger has to be taken seriously.'

'Yes, Mrs Connor,' Frankie said, straight-faced.

'Harry. My friends call me Harry, like yours call you Frankie.'

United by the bond, they shook hands.

She liked them both enormously, but with Frankie she also had the connection of like recognising like. As a child, she too had felt that danger could be fun. Truth to tell, she still often found it so, as long as it was only her own. Other people's peril had to be taken seriously, but there was a 'ping' about fighting for one's own survival that most people wouldn't understand, and certainly not sympathise with.

Her father had lectured her about being sensible. Now she had passed on the lecture to the next generation, just as she would have done with a child of her own, she thought wistfully.

But she had no children and probably never would have. Darius's offspring would have to be her consolation.

'Go on about Herringdean,' Mark begged. 'Why did you join the lifeboats?'

'I followed my father. He taught me to love being on the water. I've got a little yacht that I sail whenever I can. Every year Herringdean has a regatta, and I compete in a lot of the races. I win some too.' She added proudly, 'I've got all sorts of trophies.'

'Tell, tell,' they demanded.

They were as sailing-crazy as she was herself but, living in London, had fewer chances to indulge their passion.

'Mum takes us on holiday to the seaside,' Frankie said, 'and she gets someone to take us out in a boat, but then we have to come home.'

'What about your father?' Harriet asked. 'Does he go out in the boat with you?'

'He's never been there,' Frankie said. 'He was always too busy to come on holiday.'

'That's very sad,' Harriet said, meaning it. 'He misses so much.'

'He nearly came once,' Mark recalled. 'We were going to have a wonderful time together, but at the last minute he got a call and said he had to stay at home. I overheard him on the phone—he was trying to stop some deal from falling apart. He said he'd join us as soon as he could, but he never did. It was soon after that he and Mum split up. Now we don't go at all.'

Frankie took a deep breath. 'Harry, do you think—?'

'Ah, there you are, you two,' came Mary's voice from nearby. 'I've got someone for you to meet.'

They groaned but got up obediently. Harriet felt a pang of dismay, wondering if Mary had deliberately sought to separate her from the children. And had she heard Frankie call her Harry? If so, was she resentful at their instant bond?

But the smile Mary gave her before hurrying away was unreadable.

Socially, she knew she was a success. Janine and Freya spoke to her pleasantly, Marcel and Jackson claimed her company, while Amos looked on. When he did address her, his manner was courteous but distant, as though he was reserving judgement.

None of the other men there reserved judgement. Admiring glances followed her everywhere and when the dancing started she had her pick of partners. Jackson was at the head of the queue, finally yielding to Marcel.

'Whatever is Darius thinking of to leave you alone?' Marcel asked as they hot-footed it around the floor.

'Darius has urgent things to attend to,' she said primly. 'I don't get in his way.'

'*Sacre bleu!* You talk like that?' he demanded, aghast.

'Sometimes I do,' she said mischievously. 'Sometimes I don't.'

'You keep him guessing?'

'Definitely.'

'So you believe in ill-treating him?'

'It has its uses.'

'Well, then, you must do this. In the end he will rebel, the two of you will quarrel, and it will be my turn.'

Harriet couldn't have said what made her choose her next words. She'd never been a flirt or a tease, but a delightfully wicked impulse made her say, 'Oh, you're going to wait your turn?'

'If I have to. Does brother Darius know you tease other men?'

'Darius knows exactly what I want him to know.'

'I see. I must remember that. I wonder what he did to be such a lucky man.'

She seemed to consider. 'I think he's still wondering that too. Some day I'll tell him.'

That made him roar with laughter. She joined in, relishing the experience of flirting on the edge of indiscretion, a pleasure she'd never known before. Suddenly the world was full of new delights, and she felt herself becoming slightly dizzy.

No doubt it was coincidence that made Darius appear

at that moment. Marcel made a resigned face and yielded, kissing her hand before he departed.

'Until the next time,' he said.

'Do I get a little of your company at last?' Darius asked. 'I seem to be the only person you're not spending time with.'

'Just trying to do you credit,' she said. 'You wouldn't want to be known as the man who accompanied a little brown mouse, would you?'

'I don't think there's much fear of that,' he said. 'I'm beginning to think I've never really known you.'

'Is that so surprising?' she asked. 'We met only a few weeks ago. Neither of us really knows anything about the other.'

'No, we don't,' he said slowly. 'You've taken me by surprise so many times… You'd think I'd realise by now…'

'Maybe we never realise,' she whispered.

The evening was drawing to a close. The bride- and groom-to-be embraced each other for the last waltz, and other dancers joined in. Darius took her hand and held it gently for a moment.

'My turn,' he said. 'Unless you object.'

'No,' she murmured. 'I don't object.'

No words could express how much she didn't object to dancing with Darius as he took her into his arms. Suddenly the most vibrant sensation she'd ever known was the light touch of his hand on her back, drawing her close but not as close as she would have liked. His hand holding hers seemed to whisper of that other time when he'd clung to her in a gesture that had transformed the world.

And then it had been transformed again, and yet again, with how many more to come? Once she would have wished she knew the answer to that, but now she was content to let the path lead where it might, as long as it ultimately led to him. In the enchanted atmosphere of tonight that didn't seem as crazily impossible as it normally would.

There was warm affection in his smile, but was it real or only part of tonight's performance? Or could she make it real? Was Cinderella's power great enough for that?

The music was coming to an end. The ball was over.

But there would be another ball tomorrow, and Prince Charming might yet fit the glass slipper on her foot.

Darius? she thought. Prince Charming?

Well, it took all sorts.

'Is everything all right?' he asked, searching her face.

'Yes,' she said contentedly. 'Everything's all right.'

As they went upstairs he said, 'You were wonderful. Everything I hoped.'

'I floundered a bit.'

'No, you didn't. My kids love you, even Mary thinks you're terrific. You're a star.'

'So I really have helped you?' she asked hopefully.

'More than you'll ever know. And tomorrow's going to be even better.'

'Would you like to come in and talk about it?' Harriet ventured to suggest. 'You can give me my instructions for tomorrow.'

For a moment she thought he would agree, but then a wry look came over his face.

'I'd love to but…things to do. You know how it is.'

'Yes,' she said a touch sadly, 'I know how it is.'

'And besides, you don't need any instructions from me. You've got it all sussed. Now, go and have a good sleep.'

She smiled up at him. 'Goodnight.'

He didn't reply at first, just stood looking down at her with an expression more gentle than she had ever seen before and the faintest smile on his lips. But then the smile faded, became tight and constrained.

'Goodnight,' he said, and moved away.

For a moment Harriet was too dazed to know where she was or what was happening to her. Hearing her door close, she realised that she had entered her room without even being aware of it. As if from a great distance, she heard his own door being closed.

He'd been about to kiss her. She knew it beyond a shadow of doubt. It had been there in his face, until he changed his mind, probably remembering that other time on the beach when she'd told him to back off. How could she have known then that by now she would feel so differently?

So much had changed tonight. She'd been practically the belle of the ball, surrounded by admirers, seeing herself through their eyes but trapped inside her ivory tower. But it was she who, only yesterday, had slammed shut the door of that tower, and she could blame nobody but herself.

Not so much Cinderella as the Sleeping Beauty.

'Except that nobody could consider me a beauty,' she mused wryly.

But Darius had thought so, perhaps only for a brief moment but a little feminine strategy might have transformed that moment into long-lasting joy. Had retreating into the tower, protecting her safety at the expense of life's joy, really been the right thing to do?

'Curses!' she muttered. 'Why did this have to happen now?'

Brooding thus, she snuggled down in the huge bed, wishing it was smaller. Its size seemed to demand two people and she was attacked by a feeling of loneliness.

It was still dark when she awoke. The illuminated clock showed that three hours had passed since they had parted and she had the feeling that something strange was happening. After a moment she realised that a phone was ringing.

It seemed to come from the other side of the wall, so surely Darius would answer it soon. But it went on and on. Nobody was going to answer it.

Perhaps the sound came from somewhere else? She slipped out of bed, threw on her wrap and went out into the dark corridor. Now there was no doubt. It was Darius's phone and there was nobody to answer it.

He wasn't there. He was spending the night with someone else. And she was a fool not to have realised that it was bound to happen. In London there would be a hundred women he could turn to. Returning to her own room, she had to stop herself slamming the door. She had no right to feel insulted or neglected, but that didn't help.

So, who? Freya? Perhaps he really needed his father's money that much. Or one of the numerous females who'd made eyes at him that evening?

She threw herself back down onto the bed but sleep was impossible, and now she wondered how she could get through tomorrow. How could she look at him without an accusation in her eyes, however illogical?

Restlessly, she jumped up and began to pace the room. From the street outside came the sound of a car and she drew aside the curtain to look down.

Then she grew still as she saw the passenger get out. It was Darius, and he was weighed down with baggage. Three large suitcases were offloaded onto the pavement and collected by the porter, then they disappeared into the hotel.

Harriet scurried to her door, listening. She heard the elevator arrive, the doors open and the sound of a trolley being wheeled across the floor, stopping outside the room next to hers. Only then did she look out.

Darius was opening his door, indicating for the porter to

take the luggage in. When the man had departed he seemed to notice Harriet.

'Sorry if the racket disturbed you.'

'It didn't. I happened to see you arrive downstairs. You look worn out.'

'I've been to my apartment to collect a few things. At least, it was meant to be a few things, but once I started I couldn't stop.'

'You mean—that's where you've been all this time?' she breathed.

'Yes, I decided I couldn't be in London without going home for a few hours. I've had someone going in to collect any mail that arrived, but there was still plenty of stuff on the mat. I didn't mean to stay so long but things built up. What's the matter? What's funny?'

'Nothing,' she said in a trembling voice.

'Then why are you laughing?'

'I'm not—not really.'

'Yes, you are. What's so funny at this hour?'

'You wouldn't understand. Go to bed quickly. I'll see you in the morning.'

She escaped before she could give herself away any more. It was vital to be alone to throw herself on her bed, to laugh and cry, and marvel at where the path was leading her.

Now for the big one.

That was her thought as she sat before the mirror next morning, watching as her make-up was again applied by an expert.

Today her clothes were less ostentatiously glamorous, although no less costly, a matching dress and jacket in light grey heavy silk. Around her neck she wore the diamond pendant.

Now the attendants had gone and there was just time for one last important job. Quickly, she dialled her neighbour's number.

'Hi, Jenny, is everything all right?—Lovely—he's not off his food, is he?— Oh, good, they're his favourite bones but I was afraid he might pine—oh, please fetch him.'

Marcel and Jackson, knocking on their brother's door, found it opened promptly.

'I'm honoured,' he said ironically.

'Not you, her,' Jackson informed him. 'Do you think we're going to miss the chance to be seen with the most gorgeous girl since—? Is this her door? Good.'

All three of them raised their hands, but before they could knock they heard Harriet's voice inside.

'Oh, darling, do you miss me? I miss you so much. I'll be home soon. I love you more than anyone in the world.'

Jackson and Marcel stared at their brother.

'A *ménage à trois*?' Marcel demanded, aghast. 'You?'

'Not in a million years,' Darius declared. 'I leave those kind of shenanigans to you.'

'But she was talking to the one she loves *more than anyone in the world.*'

'She was talking to her dog,' Darius said, grinning. 'She does that a lot. She left him with a friend and she called him as soon as we arrived.'

Jackson nodded. 'She's probably had him since she was a child.'

'No, he belonged to her husband who died a year ago.'

'Ah!' Enlightenment settled over Marcel. 'Then perhaps it is the dead husband whom she loves more than—'

'Shall we be going?' Darius interrupted him, knocking. 'Harriet, are you ready in there?'

'Coming!' She opened the door and stood basking in their looks of admiration.

Instantly, Marcel and Jackson extended their hands to her, but Darius stayed firm.

'Back off, you two,' he said, drawing her hand into the crook of his elbow. 'She's mine.'

And Harriet thought she detected a note of pride in his voice, if only she could allow herself to believe it.

Heads held high, they went downstairs to where the ceremony would take place. It would be a civil ceremony, but the venue had been done up to emulate the grandeur of a church. There were flowers everywhere and chairs laid out in rows, while at the far end a choir was assembling.

It was almost time to begin. Ken took his place and stood waiting, his eyes fixed on the door through which his bride would come.

At last Mary appeared and began to walk slowly towards him. She was magnificently dressed in a long gown of saffron coloured satin, a diamond tiara on her head. Behind her walked Frankie and Mark.

What would Darius be feeling now, she wondered, as his one-time beloved married another man and his children became part of another family? He was between her and the procession, so that his face was turned away, and she could only wonder about his expression. But she guessed it would reveal nothing.

As the children passed she saw that Frankie wore a frilly bridesmaid dress and Mark had a page's costume, also frilly. How he would hate that, she thought.

As if to confirm it, he glanced up at her and made a face of helpless resignation. She made a face back, conveying sympathy. By chance, Darius happened to turn his head in time to see them both.

'Poor Mark,' she murmured.

The procession was slowing down, bringing Mark to a brief halt. Just a couple of seconds but it was enough for

Darius to put his hand on his son's shoulder and grunt, 'Don't give up, lad.'

Then they were on their way again, with only the memory of Mark's look of amazed gratitude at his father.

Slowly, the ceremony advanced until the moment when the bride took her groom's hand, looking up into his face and saying fervently, 'You are mine, and I am yours. We will be together for always, and no other man will ever live in my heart.'

Conventional words for a wedding, but how did they sound to the man who had once been her husband? Carefully, Harriet turned her head, hoping to catch a sideways glimpse of his face, only to find it turned towards her. He wasn't looking at the couple swearing their love. His gaze was fixed on her, and something in it made her turn quickly away.

A few feet away, Amos and his family were seated, their chairs at an angle that enabled Amos to see Darius and Harriet clearly. His eyes narrowed, an expression that Jackson recognised with a sigh and that made him exchange a glance with Marcel.

They knew that look on their father's face, and it didn't bode well.

CHAPTER EIGHT

AS THEY walked out afterwards Amos fell into step beside Jackson, speaking in a low voice. 'What do you know about her?'

'Only that she's delightful, and a very good influence on Darius.'

'And just what does that mean?'

'I've been watching them together.' Jackson fell silent.

'And?' Amos demanded. *'And?'*

'He was laughing.'

'What are you talking about?'

'It's true. Darius was laughing.'

'I've seen that too,' Marcel put in. 'And you know what makes him laugh? She makes fun of him.'

'She makes fun of him? And he likes it? Rubbish.'

'They share jokes,' Jackson agreed. 'I've seen them and heard some of the things they say. Daft remarks tossed back and forth, things that wouldn't make any sense to other people, but they understand each other, and they laugh together. I've never seen that in Darius before. She's transformed him.'

Amos didn't answer this, but he strode on ahead and waited for Darius to appear. He nodded briefly at Harriet and jerked his head for his son to follow him.

'What is it, Father?' Darius asked.

'We need to talk.'

'Right now? They're just starting the reception.'

'It won't take long.'

He walked away without stopping until they'd both entered a little side room and closed the door. Then Amos turned on him.

'I gather things are getting worse.'

Darius hesitated a moment before saying, 'Financially, they're not going well but in other ways—'

Amos brushed this disclaimer aside. 'I was speaking financially.'

'Of course,' Darius murmured.

'You can't raise the loans you need, and when you put property up for sale it won't raise the asking price.'

'May I ask how you know these details?' Darius said grimly.

'You don't imagine there are any secrets, do you?'

'Not from you.'

'You ought to be here in London, working things out. Instead, you waste time on that island that can hardly be worth—well, what *is* it worth?'

'You mean in money terms?' Darius asked in a strange voice.

'Don't play games with me. Of course I mean money. How much could you raise from it?'

'I have no idea.'

'But you've been living there for weeks; you must have investigated.'

'In a sort of way,' he said carefully. 'But it's too soon to form conclusions. I don't want to rush things.'

'I suppose that's the influence of the young woman you brought with you. I hope you're not taking her too seriously.'

'As seriously as a man takes a woman who saved his life.'

'Don't make too much of that. It means nothing to her. It's just her job.'

'But it's not,' Darius said fiercely. 'She isn't employed by the Lifeboat Institution, she's a volunteer. She has an ordinary job, but night and day she's ready to drop everything for the people who need her, even if their cries for help come at awkward moments. She doesn't think of herself, she thinks of them.'

'All right, all right, spare me the speech,' Amos said in a bored voice. 'I get the point. Naturally, I expressed my gratitude and of course you've shown your own gratitude by bringing her here. I hope she enjoys herself. But let it end there. She's no real use to you. She doesn't have a penny and she won't understand your way of life.'

'And how do you know what she has and hasn't?' Darius demanded harshly. 'Have you been having her watched, because if you've dared—'

'No need to be melodramatic. I've merely made a few enquiries. She seems a decent sort, lives a quiet life.'

'As you'd expect from a widow grieving for the husband she loved, and who loved her.'

Amos's smile was coldly self-satisfied. 'Ah, so you don't know. I wondered.'

'Know about what? What the hell are you talking about?'

'Did she ever take you to see her husband's grave?'

'Of course not. Naturally, she prefers to keep it private.'

'Have you known her visit that grave at all?'

'How could I know?'

'How could you indeed since she takes such care to hide the truth? But you'll find the answer here.' He thrust a sheet of paper in Darius's hand. 'Read it and find out just how cunningly she's been keeping her secrets. Then see how much of a heroine she looks.'

Darius took the paper and read its contents. Then he grew very still, trying to control his mounting outrage.

His eyes were hard as he looked up at his father, then down again at the paper in his hand. 'Los Angeles,' he murmured.

'Brad Connor died in a car crash in Los Angeles, and he's buried out there,' Amos said.

'And you read something into that? He was in the tourist industry, so he probably travelled a lot.'

'He wasn't there to work; he was living with the woman he planned to marry as soon as his divorce came through.'

'You can't know that,' Darius declared. But he knew as he spoke that Amos could find out anything he liked. It had always been one of the things that inspired admiration for his business abilities, but now Darius could feel only a horror that he'd never known before.

'Of course I know,' Amos snapped. 'I know everything that's been happening to you on that island.'

'You've dared to plant spies?'

'I've taken steps to assess the situation. That's always been my way and you know it. You should be grateful. Do you think I'd stand back and see you run into danger without doing anything?'

'I'm not in any danger.'

'You're in danger of becoming sentimental, and that's one thing you can't afford. I'd hoped by now you'd be seeing things more sensibly but, since you're not, let me spell it out. This young woman has deceived you, presenting a picture of her life that's far from the truth.'

'She has not deceived me,' Darius snapped. 'She's kept

things to herself, but why shouldn't she? Her personal tragedy is none of my business. If she can't bear to talk about it, that's up to her.'

His eyes were full of fury and for the first time it dawned on Amos that he'd miscalculated. His son was every bit as enraged as he'd wanted him to be, but his anger was directed not against Harriet, but against the man who sought to damage her. Amos decided that it was time to change tack. Reasoning might work better.

'I understand that,' he said, 'but it doesn't change the fact that she's holding things back while pretending to be open. You don't know her as well as you thought you did. What other secrets is she concealing?'

'Whatever they are, she'll confide in me in her own good time, *if she wants to*.'

'Just stop and think what's going on in her head. One husband let her down, so next time she's going to make certain that she scores. She's out to marry you with her eyes on the divorce settlement she'll eventually claim.'

Darius gave a harsh laugh. 'Out to marry me? You know nothing. She's here as my companion, no more. I had to promise to stick to her rules or she wouldn't have come.'

Amos groaned and abandoned reasoning as useless. 'How can any son of mine be so naïve? That's the oldest trick in the book.'

'She doesn't go in for tricks,' Darius said. 'She's as honest as the day is long. You have no idea.'

'You've really got it bad, haven't you?' Amos said in a voice that verged on contempt.

'If you mean that I'm in love with her, you're wrong. Harriet and I are friends. With her I've found a kind of friendship I didn't know existed. I can talk to her without wondering if she'll make use of the information. She gives far more than she takes, and that's something I never thought to find in anyone. Try to understand. She's a revelation. I didn't know women like her existed, and I'm not going to do anything to spoil it.'

Amos regarded him with pity. 'A revelation—unlike any other woman,' he echoed. 'Well, I'll say this for her. She's more skilled and astute than I gave her credit for. All right, maybe she's not out to marry you. Perhaps she's just stringing you along for the sake of her island friends. After all, you're the power there. It would pay her to get on your right side.'

'Stop it!' Darius raged. 'If you know what's good for you, stop it *now*!'

'Or what? Is my son threatening me? I really did underestimate her, didn't I? All right, we'll say no more. I tried to warn you but there's no helping a fool.'

'Maybe I am a fool,' Darius said. 'And maybe I'm happy to settle for that.'

'That makes you an even bigger fool.'

'If you dare make yourself unpleasant to Harriet—'

'I've no intention of doing so. Now, it's time we were getting back to the party.'

He strode out. As he walked through the door Darius saw him position a smile on his face, so that he appeared to the assembled company wearing the proper mask.

Suddenly Darius felt sick.

It was an effort to get his own mask in place and he knew he was less successful than his father, managing only an air of calm that covered the turmoil within. Harriet was sitting with her arm across the empty seat beside her, looking around worriedly. Someone spoke to her and she answered briefly before returning to her troubled search. It was as though the world had stopped in its tracks until she found what she was looking for.

Then she saw Darius and he drew in his breath at the

transformation. Suddenly it was as though she was illuminated from inside, radiant, joyful.

'I'm sorry,' he said, going to sit beside her. 'I got waylaid. Forgive my bad manners.'

'Is everything all right?'

'Everything's fine.' He laid his hand over hers. 'Nothing for you to worry about.'

A waiter poured champagne for them both.

'Now, let's forget everything else and enjoy ourselves,' Darius said, raising his glass to clink hers.

Around the various tables, his family observed them. His brothers grinned. His stepsister smiled with relief. His children rubbed their hands. His father scowled.

It was time for the speeches. The best man spoke, the bride and groom talked eloquently. Various other guests proposed toasts. Darius was barely aware of it. He was conscious only of Harriet beside him, wondering if she was remembering the joy of her own wedding, and the marriage that had ended in tragedy. But he could detect nothing in her manner that gave him a clue. Her barriers were in place.

He'd meant it when he'd told his father that he didn't feel deceived that she had kept her secrets. It was yet more proof of their special friendship that he made no claims on her, demanded no rights.

But he knew a faint sadness that she hadn't felt able to confide in him.

Your fault, he told himself. *If you'd shut up talking about yourself for five minutes she might get a word in edgeways.*

That eased his mind briefly, but he could remember a couple of times when the talk had strayed to her husband and she'd diverted it to something else. The truth was she didn't want to open up to him. That was her right. He'd said so and he believed it. But it hurt.

Nor could he entirely escape the suspicion that if she hadn't warned him off he would have sought more than friendship. She was beautiful, not conventionally, like other women, but with a mysterious enchantment that came from within and that beckoned him on.

He'd made promises about keeping his distance but, with a woman like this, how could a real man keep such insane promises?

Now waiters were clearing away for the dancing. The bridal couple took the floor and were soon joined by the rest of the crowd.

'This time I'm seizing you first,' Darius said firmly. 'Before I get trampled in the rush.'

'Nonsense,' she said tenderly.

'It isn't nonsense. Of course it's nice when the lady on your arm turns out to be the belle of the ball, but it has its troublesome moments too. I don't like sharing.'

'Neither do I, but we both have to do our social duty.'

'Ah, I see. You've gone into teasing mode.'

'Why not? I enjoy new experiences and, after all, you brought me here to help stage a performance. Think of me as a piece of stage scenery. Under this dress I'm just wood and plaster. Hey, what are you doing?'

'Just checking the stage scenery,' he said, letting his hand drift around her waist until it sank immodestly over her hips. 'It doesn't feel like any wood and plaster I've ever known.'

It was shocking and she knew she should tell him to move his hand from where it lay over the smooth grey silk, softly caressing the movements against his fingers. But a little pulse was beating in her throat and she couldn't get the words out. And probably nobody could see it in the crowd, she reassured herself.

She was suffused by a warmth and sweetness so intense that it made her dizzy. She wanted to dance like this for ever, his arms around her, his body close to hers, and never have to think of anything else again.

The music was slowing, couples were pulling apart. Marcel presented himself expectantly.

'Go to blazes,' Darius told him pleasantly.

'Certainly,' Marcel said, and vanished.

Harriet was barely aware of Marcel, or any of their surroundings. Lost in a dream, she let herself drift into a new world, refusing to heed the warnings of danger, although she knew that danger would intrude in the end. But let it, she thought. First she would have her moment, and cherish its memory to see her through the dark times.

With a sigh, she felt his movements slow as this dance too came to an end, and she knew that he would not claim her again. The moment had come and gone until, perhaps, another time.

Harriet wondered if it could possibly have been the same for him, but when she looked into his face she saw that it was troubled.

'What's on your mind?' she asked. 'Something's worrying you. I know it. Tell me.'

For a moment he hesitated on the verge of telling her about his father and what he'd learned, but then he backed off, unable to risk hurting her.

'Can't you tell your friend what's wrong?' she asked gently.

Once, younger and more careless, he'd joked that at all costs a man should avoid a woman who understood him too well. How often had he avoided Mary's piercing mental gaze! Yet with this woman he only felt a renewed sense of comfort, as though her hand had once again stretched out to offer safety.

'No,' he said softly. 'Nothing is wrong.' And at that moment he meant it.

It was just like his brothers to barge in, he thought, finally yielding to Marcel. But there was always later. Patience would bring him everything.

After that they both concentrated on their social duty. Harriet was never short of partners, until finally she glanced up to find Amos approaching, the very picture of geniality.

'I've been hoping to dance with you but there were so many men ahead of me.' He held out his hand. 'Please say I'm not too late.'

'Of course not,' she said, smiling and taking his hand.

Heads turned as he led her onto the floor, the crowd parted for them, and there was a smattering of applause as he drew her into the dance. Darius, passing the time with Freya, turned his head casually, then grew tense.

'What the devil—?' he breathed.

'He seems quite charmed with Harriet,' Freya said. 'Look at the way he's smiling, practically welcoming her into the family.' She gave Darius an amused look. 'I should be grateful to her, really. It helps take the pressure off me, *brother, dear.*'

'Look at them,' he said distractedly. 'Why is he laughing like that?'

'She's laughing too,' Freya pointed out. 'Obviously they're getting on well. He can be so grim, it's nice to see him putting himself out to be nice to her.'

But for Darius, who knew what really lay behind Amos's 'charm', every moment was torment. He was trying to lure Harriet into a trap, hoping she would say something he could use against her. Darius had often seen him wear a pleasant mask as long as it could be useful, and had thought little of it.

But this was different. This was Harriet—great-hearted, innocent, vulnerable—and he was filled with desire to protect her at all costs.

'Dance with me,' he said, taking Freya's hand.

She was too astute to mistake his motive, especially when she realised how determinedly he steered her in the direction of the other couple.

'Is this near enough for you?' she asked.

'Only just. Can you hear what he's saying?'

'Something about a shop on Herringdean—an antique shop—since when was he interested in antiques?'

'Since he found out she owned one,' Darius growled.

'Now he's talking money—how much is the shop worth?'

'Damn him!'

'Don't act surprised. That's always his first thought. Hey, he's watching us. Let's teach him a lesson.'

'How?'

'Look deep into my eyes, then he'll think what a good son you're being. You never know, he might solve all your problems with one cheque.'

'Yes, but he'd post-date it so that I'd have to marry you first.'

'Never fear. I'll avoid that catastrophe with my last breath.'

'So will I,' he assured her cheerfully.

They finished the dance with no hard feelings on either side.

When Amos had bid her farewell and departed, Harriet went to quench her thirst with an orange juice. Standing beside a large potted plant, she was only vaguely aware of movement from the other side until she heard Mary's voice say, 'Wherever did you find that marvellous girl?'

And Darius's eager reply. 'Harriet is marvellous, isn't she? I'm glad you like her.'

'Are you surprised? Did you think I'd be jealous? On the contrary, she's doing me a great favour. If you've got her, I don't have to feel guilty about leaving you. And the children like her, so I can send them to stay with you with an easy mind.'

'Do you really mean that?' Darius demanded urgently.

'I know you thought I was trying to separate you from them, but I wasn't. It's just that you hurt them so often with your stupidity.'

'There was a lot I didn't understand, but now—'

'But now things are beginning to change, and they'll go on changing as long as you stick with her. She's good for you, Darius. You've become almost human.'

'I never thought to hear you say that, Mary.'

'I never thought to be able to say it. That's why Mark and Frankie will be going to my mother while Ken and I are on honeymoon. They'd much rather have come to you in Herringdean, but I honestly didn't think you'd cope on your own. Now it's different.'

'Too late to send them to me?'

'My mother is so looking forward to having them. I can't disappoint her now. But there's plenty of time in the future. Keep up the good work. The kids are really happy about Harriet.'

'I know, and I can't tell you how much that means to me.'

'Well, make sure you keep her for good. You're a clever man and, believe me, that's the clever thing to do.'

They moved away, leaving Harriet deep in thought.

The evening was drawing to a close. Bride and groom

withdrew and reappeared in outdoor clothes. Cars were at the door. Mark and Frankie said their farewells to Darius and Harriet before being scooped up by their grandmother and swept off to her home on the other side of London.

'Are you tired?' Darius asked Harriet, who was yawning.

'Mmm, a bit sleepy. You did say we're going early tomorrow, didn't you?'

'That's right. Time for bed.'

On the way up in the elevator he slipped his arm around her. 'Did you enjoy it?'

'Oh, yes, it was lovely. Everyone was so nice to me, especially your father.'

'Yes, I saw the two of you dancing.'

'I couldn't believe it when he asked me, but he was terribly gallant and charming.'

'You should beware my father's charm,' Darius said wryly.

'Oh, I know he was just being polite but...I don't know... he was nice. He asked me about my antique shop, said he understood antiques were very profitable these days. I had to admit that it's as much of a souvenir shop for tourists as an antique shop. He laughed and said that was life and nothing was really the way it seemed, was it? Hey, careful. Don't squash me.'

'Sorry,' he said, relaxing the arm that he'd tightened sharply about her. Listening to her innocent pleasure when he knew how misguided it was brought a return of the rage that had attacked him earlier. But now it was a million times more intense, nearly blinding him with the desire to lash out against her enemy.

From the start he'd known of her strength, her defiance, her ability to cope, essential in a lifesaver. Suddenly he was discovering her other side, the one that could be slightly naïve, that believed the best of people, the side she hid behind cheerful masks.

But the face she turned up to him now wore no mask. It was defenceless, the mouth soft, the eyes wide and trusting. He knew it would be a sin to betray that trust by kissing her, no matter how much he longed to. So he contented himself with brushing her cheek with his fingertips, and felt her relax against him.

What he might have done next he never knew, for the elevator reached their floor, the doors opened and the world rushed in on them again.

Now she was smiling brightly in a way that set him once more at a distance.

'Sleep tight,' he told her at her door. 'We have to be up with the dawn.'

'I'll be there,' she promised. 'Goodnight.'

He thought she would give him a final look so that the sweet connection they had established might live again. But he was facing a closed door.

Inside her room, Harriet stood in darkness, listening as his footsteps moved away to his own door.

Her heart was heavy. Midnight had struck and Cinders had been forced to leave, not running away and leaving a shoe, but escorted by the Prince who'd been tempted only briefly before his common sense had rescued him.

It's over. All over. Finished. Done with. Get undressed, go to bed, and stop indulging in fantasies. Didn't you learn anything from last time?

Switching on the bedside lamp, she stripped off her beautiful attire with ruthless fingers and replaced it with plain cotton pyjamas. Her packing was done at top speed, and then she was ready for bed. Defiantly, she got under the duvet and switched out the light.

There was a knock at the door.

'Who is it?' she asked without opening.

'It's me.'

CHAPTER NINE

HARRIET opened the door a crack and saw him. He'd removed his jacket and bow tie and his shirt was torn open at the throat.

'Can I talk to you?'

She stood back as he went past her. She would have turned on the bedside lamp but he stayed her hand.

'Better just let me talk. I owe you an apology for my behaviour tonight.'

'Do you? You didn't offend me.'

'That's very sweet of you, but I got a bit possessive in a way that I promised not to. Just friends we said but I didn't really stick to that, did I? I hadn't expected you to look so beautiful—'

'Thanks,' she said wryly.

'No, I didn't mean that,' he said hastily. 'Oh, heavens, I'm making a mess of this. I only wanted to say that you were a hundred times more wonderful than I'd dared to hope and...*Harriet!*'

Then his arms were around her, pulling her tightly against him, and all the sensible restraint drained out of her as she received the kiss she'd been longing for, never completely admitting her own desire. Now there was no chance of denying it to herself or him. She felt herself soften and fall against him, reaching out so that he was enfolded in her arms as she was enfolded in his.

Her hands were exploring him, the fingers weaving into his hair before drifting down to his face. He raised his head from hers, looking down with a question in his eyes, as though wondering if he only imagined her passionate response.

'Harriet,' he whispered, 'why have we…?'

'Shh!' She silenced him with her fingertips over his mouth. 'Don't speak. Words are dangerous. They mean nothing.'

She was right, he realised with a sense of relief. Words were nothing when he had her body against his. He could feel the cheap cotton against his hands and wondered how any woman could feel so lusciously desirable in those almost masculine pyjamas. They taunted him, hiding her beautiful body while suggesting just enough of it to strain his self-control.

Harriet felt as though she had lived this moment before, earlier that evening when he'd allowed his hand to drift indiscreetly behind her dress, but then been forced by propriety to restrain himself. She hadn't wanted restraint either in him or herself, but she'd had no choice.

But she had choice now. She could choose to be warm, intimate, seductive, enticing, passionate. Anything but restrained. Her breathing came fast as he kissed her again and again, little swift kisses covering her face, her forehead, her nose, her eyes, mouth, then sliding lower to her neck.

He was so skilled, she thought in delirious delight. They might have been one person, so sensitively did he know the right way to rouse her—to make her want him—want him more—

'Make sure you keep her for good…'

Without warning, the words screamed at her. Frantically, she fought them off but they danced in her consciousness.

'You're a clever man...'

She'd known that but never thought what it meant—until now—

'Keep her for good...the clever thing to do...the clever thing to do...'

'Kiss me,' he whispered. 'Kiss me as I kiss you... please...'

The clever thing to do. The words went through her like ice, quenching the storm within her.

'Kiss me...'

'Darius, wait...please wait...'

'I don't want to wait any more—Harriet, let me...'

She drew back to meet his eyes, and what he saw in her cooled his ardour as mere words could never have done.

'This wasn't part of the bargain,' she said calmly. 'Friends, remember?'

'The bargain,' he said slowly. 'Ah, yes, the bargain. How could I have forgotten?'

'Exactly. You, of all people, should know about bargains.' As she said it she even managed a faint smile. 'Let's not complicate things by breaking ours.'

She could feel him shaking but he brought himself under control and stepped away.

'You're right, of course. I'll say goodnight...er...sleep well. I'll see you tomorrow.'

The door closed behind him, too quietly to hear, and then there was only darkness.

It was a long night. Darius spent it trying to order his thoughts, dismayed that they were suddenly rebellious, going their own way instead of obeying him as in the past.

Now he was alone he could admit that he was troubled by

what he'd learned that night. How painful Harriet's secrets must be for her to conceal them so determinedly. How sad must be her inner life. And he'd imagined that he knew her.

She had come into his arms, physically and, he'd hoped, emotionally, only for that hope to be dashed when she'd hastily retreated. The message was clear. Briefly she'd weakened, but then her husband's ghost had waked and that was the end. As, perhaps, it would always be.

He opened his window and stood listening to faint noises from next door. Her movements sounded restless, but what was she thinking? And would she ever tell him?

After a while he heard her window close, and then there was nothing to do but go to bed.

Harriet arose next morning with her mind made up. Cool, calm and collected, that was it. But also with a touch of their usual humour, to emphasise that nothing had changed.

In contrast to her glamour of last night, she donned a pair of functional jeans and a plain blouse. Her reflection stared back at her, asking if she really wanted this no-nonsense look when she could have something more enjoyable?

But I can't! It's a trap. No-nonsense suits me fine!

Not any longer. Never mind, it would have to do.

A waiter served breakfast in her room, and as he retreated Darius appeared at the door with a bread roll in one hand and a coffee in the other.

'Glad to see you up,' he said cheerfully. 'I was afraid the evening might have tired you too much.'

'I'm always up with the lark,' she assured him. 'Sit down. I'll be ready in a moment. I've packed up the jewellery ready to go back,' she said, indicating the box. 'Perhaps you'd better check it.'

Looking intent, Darius fingered the contents of the box until he came to the diamond pendant, which he lifted out.

'Not this,' he said. 'It's yours.'

'But it can't be. You hired this stuff.'

'Everything else, yes, but—oh, dear, did I forget to mention that I bought this one?'

'You certainly did.'

'Well, it's done now. Put it away safely.'

His expression was too innocent to be convincing, and she stared at him, open-mouthed with disbelief.

'Who do you think you're kidding?' she demanded.

His face was full of wicked delight. 'Not you, obviously.'

'You deceived me.'

'Yes, and I made a pretty good job of it too,' he said, defiantly unrepentant.

'You know I wouldn't have let you buy me anything as expensive as this.'

'Ah, well, I'm not used to people telling me what they'll let me do. It doesn't suit my autocratic, overbearing nature. I just do what I want and they have to put up with it. So there you are.' He assumed a grim expression. 'Put up with it.'

'You…you…'

He sighed. 'I know it's a great burden, but you'll learn to endure it.'

'It's…it's so beautiful,' she sighed. 'But you shouldn't have done it.'

'Don't tell me what I should and shouldn't do.'

'Yes, but—'

'Stop arguing. That's an order.'

It might be an order but it was delivered with a grin that made her heart turn over.

'Stop bullying me,' she demanded.

His grin broadened. 'I shall bully you if I want to. Now, put it away safely and don't lose it, otherwise I shall have to bully you even more by buying another.'

She ducked her head quickly so that he shouldn't see she was on the verge of tears.

Darius drank his coffee and went downstairs to pay the bill, congratulating himself on having tricked her into accepting his gift without risking the emotion that would have made her reject it.

When he returned she was on the phone to Phantom.

'I'm coming home, darling—see you later today—'

But by now Darius had himself in hand and could cope.

A car took them to the airport, where they boarded the helicopter and were soon soaring to the south and over the ocean, where the brilliant sun made the little waves sparkle.

'I love this time of year,' Harriet said, looking down to where Herringdean was just coming into view. 'The island is at its best.'

'I don't suppose you get called out on the lifeboat so often,' Darius observed.

'It depends. There aren't so many storms, but the fine weather tempts more people out in boats, so things still happen.'

Now they were crossing the coastline, covering the island until they reached the far side, and there below was the beach where they had first met.

'Look who I can see,' Darius said.

'Phantom!' she cried joyfully.

They could just make out the dog racing madly along the beach in pursuit of a ball thrown by a middle-aged woman, bringing it back to her, begging for it to be thrown again, which it always was.

'That's my neighbour, Jenny Bates,' Harriet said. 'She's wonderful with him. Hey, what's he doing now?'

Suddenly Phantom had changed course and raced into the sea. Mrs Bates ran to the water's edge and called him but he took no notice.

'Oh, no!' Harriet wailed.

'He'll be all right,' Darius said. 'He's swum often enough.'

'Yes, when I was with him. But without me he'll do something idiotic like going too far. Oh, look how far out he is! *Come back, you stupid dog!*'

'Land as close to the beach as you can,' Darius told the pilot quickly.

Down they went, finishing in almost the same place as on that first day, a lifetime ago, leaping out and running down onto the beach where Mrs Bates was wailing, 'I can't swim, I'm sorry—he's never done that before—'

'No problem,' Darius said. 'I'll go and—'

He'd been about to say that he would go after Phantom, but Harriet was way ahead of him, powering her way through the waves, calling Phantom urgently. He heard her and looked around, woofed in delight and began to paddle back to her. They met in deep water, greeting each other ecstatically with much crying and barking.

Darius remained where he was, knowing he wasn't needed.

As they emerged from the water Phantom recognised him, yelped joyfully and began to charge up the beach, spraying water everywhere. Quick as a flash, Harriet hurled herself onto the hound, taking him down to the sand.

'Oh, no, you don't,' she said breathlessly. 'Let the poor man have at least one suit that you don't ruin.' She looked up at Darius. 'You'd better run for it. I can't hold him much longer. Hurry up! Go quickly. Thank you for a lovely time, but go before he gets away from me. *Go!*'

There was nothing for it but to do as she said, so he returned to the helicopter. As it took off he looked down and discovered that history was repeating itself in that she was totally absorbed in Phantom, without even a glance to spare for himself.

It was only when he reached home he discovered that he still had her luggage. Briefly, he considered returning it in person, but settled for sending it in a taxi. He knew if he took it himself she would greet him politely while longing for him to be gone so that she could be alone with the one she really cared about.

And he couldn't face that. He could have dealt with her hostility, but her cool politeness would flatten him.

Coward, he thought wryly.

Amos would be ashamed of him.

But Amos could go and jump in the lake.

For a while things seemed peaceful. Harriet slipped back into her old routine, bathing in the mornings, sometimes seeing Darius on the beach for a few minutes, chatting about nothing much, cracking a few jokes before saying a polite goodbye.

One evening, while she was working late in her shop, a knock at the door made her look up and see him through the glass. She unlocked the door.

'Sorry, sir, we're closed for business,' she said cheekily.

'Thanks for the welcome. Hiya, Phantom. Careful not to knock any of these antiques around.'

'He doesn't need you to tell him to behave perfectly,' she said indignantly. 'He's always perfect.'

'Sure, that's why you pinned him to the ground when we landed.'

'Oh, well, that was different. What brings you here at this hour?'

'I'll be honest; I have an ulterior motive. And don't say it.'

'Say what?' she asked innocently.

'That I never do anything without an ulterior motive.'

'I wasn't going to say that.'

'No, but you were thinking it.'

'Very perceptive of you. All right, what's the ulterior motive?'

He held up his mobile phone.

'The kids call me every evening and they always ask to talk to you. I have to invent excuses why you're not there.'

'But surely they don't think we're living together?'

'Well…no, but they're surprised that you're never around.'

'But when they call tonight I will be around?' she hazarded.

'Exactly.'

'Unless I make a run for it.'

'You're too good a friend to do that.'

Before she could answer, the phone rang. Darius answered and his face lit up.

'Frankie, lovely to hear from you, darling. What have you been doing today?'

Harriet studied his face, taking in its warmth and pleasure. Her resolution to keep him at a polite distance was fading with every moment.

'What's that?' Darius asked. 'Harriet? Well…I'm not sure if…' He looked at her with pleading eyes. 'I'll see if she's here,' he said. 'I'm just going looking now.'

Silently, he mouthed, *Please.* Harriet relented and took the phone.

'Hi, Frankie! Boy, am I glad you called and gave me a chance to sit down! Your dad and I are working our socks off. I've just had a delivery at my shop and he's helping me unpack and put things away—he's doing very well.'

From the other end of the phone Darius could hear his little girl chuckling. He grinned.

'Yes, I'm really making him work,' Harriet said. 'He's surprisingly good. Let's face it, he looks like a wimp—oh, dear, I shouldn't have said that. If you could see how he's glaring at me—'

'I'm not,' Darius said indignantly.

'Anyway, he's not as much of a wimp as he looks. He can manage heavy weights—much to my surprise—'

Darius's indignation had faded and he was looking at her with resigned amusement. She laughed back at him, sending a silent message. *That'll teach you!* And receiving his message in return. *Just you wait!*

Harriet rattled away for a while, enjoying the sound of Frankie's delight. Then Mark took over, wanting to know if she'd been sailing. She'd taken her little yacht out only that morning and had plenty to tell him. It was a happy conversation.

At last she handed the phone back to Darius.

'It's a conspiracy,' he told his son. 'She's as bad as you are, or you're as bad as she is. I'm not sure which.'

Sounding relaxed and happy, he bid his children good-night, then turned to her, laughing and exasperated in equal measure.

'Harriet, you little wretch! What are you trying to do to me? Wimp, indeed!'

'Shame!' she soothed him. 'All those hours spent in the gym, for nothing.'

'All right, enjoy your laugh. I suppose I asked for it.

And thank you. You did far more than I hoped for.' He looked around at the large boxes. 'You really have just had a delivery, haven't you?'

'Yes, a big one. Hey, what are you doing?'

'Well, I've got to prove I'm not a wimp, haven't I?' he said, beginning to unpack. 'Call it my gratitude.'

He wouldn't let her refuse, but worked for two hours fetching, carrying, lifting weights, finally breathing out hard and saying, 'I'm ready for a drink. Come on.'

The glass of ale in the pub that followed was in the same spirit of cheerful friendliness, and when they finally said goodnight she was able to feel confident that she'd successfully returned their relationship to safe territory.

She was to discover her mistake.

It was three days before she saw him again, racing towards her on the beach as she and Phantom emerged from the water, seizing her shoulders as soon as he reached her.

'You've got to help me,' he said. 'I know you won't want to but—'

'Why wouldn't I want to?'

'Well, I never stop asking for things, do I? It's always you giving and me taking—'

'Darius, calm down and tell me what it is.'

'Mary called me. The kids can't stay with their gran; she's gone down with a bug. It's not serious but they have to leave, and they want to come here.'

'Of course they want to be with you.'

'Yes, but Mary will only agree if you're part of the deal. I reckon it's really you they want to see rather than me.'

'Nonsense, you're their father.'

'Yes, but I'm still learning. Mary relies on you. If you don't say yes, *she* won't say yes. Please, Harriet.'

It was unfair of him, she thought, to look at her like that. How could she be sensible in the face of that imploring gaze, reminding her of his nicer side—the one that brought her dangerously close to falling in love?

'Of course I'll help you,' she said, 'as long as we agree beforehand what we're going to—'

She stopped as his cellphone had rung.

'Mary?' he said urgently. 'Yes, I've asked her and she's agreeable. It's going to be all right—what's that?—she's right here.' He handed her the phone.

'Harriet?' said Mary's urgent voice. 'Oh, thank heavens. We've got a disaster on our hands but I know you can take care of it.'

'Calm down; I'll be glad to help, and I'm sure they'll love the island.'

'Oh, yes, if you could have heard them talking after you spoke to them the other day. All I need to know is that you'll be there.'

'And I will.'

'They're well-behaved children. You won't have any trouble making them go to bed at the right time, and they're not picky eaters—'

'Mary, hang on, I didn't mean—'

But it was too late. With mounting dismay, Harriet realised that Mary had assumed that she was living with Darius and would be there for the children all the time.

'You don't understand,' she said frantically. 'I'm not actually—'

But she was watching Darius, and what she saw checked her. He'd followed her thoughts and was silently begging her not to destroy his hope.

'Not what?' Mary asked.

'I'm not—' She could tell that he was holding his breath. 'Not…not a very good cook,' she floundered.

'That's all right,' Mary assured her cheerfully. 'He says Kate's a terrific cook. All I'm asking you to do is be nice to them, and I know you will because—'

Harriet barely heard the rest. Dismayed, she realised that she'd committed herself to moving in with him, living close to him day and night, unable to escape the attraction that threatened to overwhelm her.

She'd been caught unawares, but now it was done and it was too late to undo. She could never bring herself to kill the blazing hope she could see in him. Dazed, she bid Mary farewell, handed over the phone and wandered to the water's edge.

What have I done? she whispered to herself. *Whatever have I done?*

Then she heard him calling her name, and turned to see him following her. The next moment he'd flung his arms around her.

'Thank you!' he said. *'Thank you!'*

He didn't try to kiss her, just held her with hands that gripped so tight it was almost painful. But she didn't even think of escape. There was a sweetness in his passionate gratitude that made her heart beat faster.

He drew back and she almost gasped at the sight of his face, lined with emotion, confusion, anguish and a kind of fierce joy that he himself didn't truly believe existed.

'Thank you,' he whispered again. 'Thank you, thank you.'

Now she knew what she'd done, and nothing in the world would ever make her regret it.

'I'm going to collect them in London tomorrow,' he said. 'Will you come with me?'

'If I can. I'll have to call the lifeboat station so that they've got a replacement on call. I'll do it now.'

At the station she was assured that there was no problem. There were plenty of volunteers to fill her place.

'It doesn't give you much time to move in,' Darius said, 'but I'll help you. And don't worry about anything. I know you didn't mean to live there but you can make everything just as you like it. Your word will be law, and you can choose your room. I won't trouble you, my word on it, and if you—'

'Stop, stop!' she said, laughing and touching his lips gently. 'You're babbling.'

He removed her fingers, but not before laying the lightest possible kiss on them, just enough to be felt, not enough for offence.

'I can't help it,' he said humbly. 'It matters so much, I can't risk anything going wrong.'

'Nothing's going to go wrong,' she promised. 'Now, we have a lot of work to do.'

'Yes, let's make a start. And you.' This last was addressed to Phantom, who'd nudged his hand.

'He's included?' Harriet asked eagerly.

'You don't think I'd leave him out, do you? The kids will love him. Now I come to think of it, he's almost more essential than you are.'

She chuckled. 'I think so too. Let's go.'

As they walked home his business side reasserted itself.

'What about your shop? You'll hardly have any time there for the next few weeks.'

'My assistant is reliable, and there's a temporary worker I sometimes use. She's very good.'

'Fine, hire her full-time at my expense. I pay her wages, is that clear? No argument.'

'I wasn't going to give you one,' she said. 'You're not the only one who can do business.'

She danced ahead of him, whistling.

CHAPTER TEN

HARRIET arranged the extra worker as soon as she got home, while Darius called Kate to alert her about Harriet's arrival.

They spent the rest of the day moving her things into Giant's Beacon. Kate ceremoniously showed her round the four available bedrooms, promising to get to work on whichever Harriet chose.

'You'll probably prefer the one at the end of the corridor,' Darius suggested, bland-faced.

It was certainly the most 'proper' room, being furthest from his, and having a lock on the door. It was also extremely ugly.

The nicest room was at the front of the house, just above the front door. There were two bay windows, a thick, newly laid carpet and a large comfortable-looking bed.

It was also directly opposite Darius's room.

'I wouldn't choose this if I were you,' Darius said. 'It's much too close to that fellow, and I've heard he's a bad character. Give him a wide berth.'

'And you'd know him better than anyone else, I suppose,' she riposted.

'Definitely. You shouldn't even have been shown this room, even though it's the most comfortable, and lovely in the mornings when the sun comes in.'

'Yes, I noticed it was facing the dawn.'

'But it doesn't have a lock on the door,' he pointed out.

'Ah, but he's promised not to trouble me. If he keeps his word, why would I need a lock?'

'That's very true.'

'And if he doesn't—I'll set Phantom on him.'

'There's a threat to frighten a man.'

'So I think—' She threw herself onto the soft mattress, and Phantom jumped up beside her. 'Yes, I think we'll have this one.' She turned to her companion. 'Do you agree?'

Woof!

'Then if everyone's satisfied,' Darius said, 'we'll call it a day, and be ready to leave early tomorrow.'

The helicopter was there on the dot, sweeping them off to the airport near London. From there a car took them to the house where the children were staying. Mark and Frankie were watching from the window, and yelled with delight when they saw them.

'Dad! You came!' Frankie cried.

'But of course I came. I said I would.'

They didn't reply, but Harriet wondered how often in the past he hadn't been there when he said he would.

The housekeeper appeared, saying that their hostess wouldn't come downstairs because of her illness, but she sent her thanks and best wishes. Darius returned a message of condolence, and they were ready to go.

As they left the house Harriet happened to notice the children exchanging glances, and was almost certain that she heard Mark whisper, 'I told you she'd come.'

On the journey home they made her talk about Herringdean, yearning for the moment when they could look down at it from high in the air. When that moment finally came they were speechless, gazing open-mouthed at so much beauty. Darius, watching them, understood.

'That's what I thought when I first saw it,' he said. 'The loveliest place in the world.'

They nodded agreement, but Harriet detected a slight bafflement in their manner. Their father had actually said that? Who was he trying to kid?

At last it was time to land and make their way to Giant's Beacon. As she had expected, their first meeting with Phantom was joyful. Since he asked nothing better than to be the centre of attention all the time and they had lots of attention to give, they forged an instant three-way friendship.

After supper she and Kate saw them to bed with the promise of plenty of action next day. They were already yawning and climbed into bed without argument.

Downstairs, Darius poured her a glass of wine and raised his own glass in salute.

'To you,' he said. 'Without you, none of this would be happening.'

'But it is happening. Now it's up to you to make the best of it.'

'Did you see their faces when I told them I felt the same as they when I first saw Herringdean? They didn't really believe I could feel that way.' He added wryly, 'Any more than you did.'

'I wish you'd stop brooding about that. It was a lifetime ago. You're not the same man.'

'Maybe not,' he murmured. 'But who am I now?'

'You'll find that out with them.'

'And you?'

'No. This is you and them. I'm not really a part of it.'

'That's not true and you know it,' he said quietly.

Suddenly she was faced with a dilemma. His words offered her the chance to turn the conversation in a direction that tempted her. Try as she might to stop her heart inclining towards him, it seemed to have a life of its own, beating more intensely when he was near, bringing her alive in his presence in a way that wasn't true at any other time. A little cleverness, a little scheming, and she could secure him. It would be so easy, if only—

If only she could bring herself to settle for second best, for a marriage in which she gave love in return only for gratitude.

'Why did you sigh?' he asked. 'Did I offend you by saying that?'

'No, of course not.'

'I really forced you here against your will, didn't I? I'm sorry.'

'There's nothing to be sorry for. Stop being so gloomy. Now, I'm going to take Phantom out for a walk before I go to bed.'

'I'll come with you.'

'Better not,' she said quickly. 'He wants me to himself for a while. Goodnight.'

She slipped away before he could say any more, escaping from the danger that always hovered in his presence these days, hurrying out of the house, signalling Phantom to follow her. Darius watched them run away in the moonlight, and only when they were out of sight did he climb the stairs to find two little faces looking down at him.

'Dad, *Dad!*'

'What are you two doing up? You should be asleep.'

'Harry's gone,' Frankie wailed. 'She took Phantom with her.'

'Don't panic. They've just gone for a walk. They'll be back.'

'Promise!' she demanded.

'Word of honour. And if she doesn't I'll go and fetch them. Now, back to bed.'

They vanished obediently and he, being naïve, assumed they had obeyed him. It was only later, as he strolled in the garden watching for Harriet's return, that he realised they were looking out of the window over his head.

'Is she coming yet?' Mark called.

Darius was about to admonish them when he had the strangest sensation that Harriet was there, reading his mind, shaking her head in disapproval. Enlightenment dawned.

'Come on down and we'll wait together,' he called back.

They darted away, appearing in the garden a moment later. Kate brought out milkshakes and they sat around a small table, chatting to pass the time. Darius described his first encounter with Phantom. Once, the thought of anyone, even—or especially—his own children—knowing about that undignified incident would have filled him with horror. Now, he found himself describing it in detail, relishing their shrieks of laughter.

Harriet would have been proud of him, he felt.

'Perhaps we should go with her next time,' Frankie suggested.

'You don't have to keep guard over her,' Darius said. 'She's not going to run away.'

'Really? She'll stay with us for ever and ever?'

'That's for her to say,' Darius said quietly.

A mysterious understanding was creeping over him. Like himself, they had seen Harriet in a light that set her apart from everyone else, as though she possessed a special power that acted like a shield against all the evil of the world. Those she defended were safe. Those she loved were fortunate beyond their dreams.

The difference between them was that they had seen at once what he had taken time to understand. And that delay might be his undoing. But for now he must profit by her influence to find the right words for his children's questions. He crossed his fingers, hoping against hope for wisdom.

But before he could speak Harriet again intervened to save him.

'Here she is,' Frankie cried, bounding up and pointing to two figures emerging from the trees.

She and Mark made off at top speed and in the riot of noisy delight nobody noticed Darius closing his eyes and thanking a merciful fate. When he was calm again he strolled towards her, calling, 'Nice to see you back.'

Harriet smiled at him. 'Nice to be back,' she said.

His eyes held hers. 'Really?'

'Yes, really. Right, you kids. Bed.'

When that job was done she leaned against the wall, yawning. 'I'm nodding off right here.'

'Go and get some sleep, because you're going to need it.'

'You too. Goodnight.'

Harriet slept until the early hours, then got up and glanced out of the window. From here she could just see a glow of light that she knew came from Darius's office.

Throwing on her dressing gown, she slipped downstairs. From behind the door she could hear him on the phone.

'I accessed the website half an hour ago and there's no doubt—I know how to fight this—I've already put things in place that'll make them think twice—don't worry, I've got it in hand.'

He sounded almost like the man she'd heard before vowing, 'No mercy', but she sensed something different. The cruelty had gone from his voice and only the determination remained.

As he hung up she opened the door and found him staring at the screen. He looked round and smiled wanly.

'Don't you ever sleep?' she asked.

'I'm trying to catch up at night so that I can be free during the day. There are things I still have to do.'

'You poor soul. Can I do anything to help?'

'I'd be glad of a coffee.'

She disappeared into the kitchen, returning with a full mug a few minutes later, only to find him dozing. She set down the mug and laid a gentle hand on his shoulder, so that he awoke at once, looking up at her with a faint smile. She had never seen him so vulnerable, never been so dangerously close to loving him.

'I'm going to do it,' he said. 'You'll be proud of me, teacher.'

'I was proud of you tonight,' she said. 'When I saw you sitting outside with them, cracking jokes. You must have been telling them a great story to make them laugh like that.'

'Yes, they really enjoyed hearing how their dad looked like a total prat.'

'I don't believe you said anything like that.' When Darius simply grinned she said, 'Well, go on, I can't stand the curiosity. Tell, tell!'

'It was about our first meeting—the way Phantom flattened me on the sand. I thought they'd enjoy it, and they did.'

'You actually managed to tell *that* story?' she breathed in astonishment and admiration. 'How come?'

'You told me to,' he said simply.

'I never—' She stopped. 'When did I?'

'There and then.'

'But I wasn't there.'

'Yes, you were. You were right there with me. You always are. Even when you're not there, you *are* there. Didn't you know?'

'No,' she murmured.

His gaze intensified. 'I guess there are a lot of things you don't know.'

'I guess there are.'

'I'm glad I'm not the only one who's confused.'

Everything was in a whirl. He was telling her something she longed with all her heart to hear, to believe; telling her not with words but with his eyes, with his hesitant tone, with his uncertainty that seemed to say everything was in her hands.

Playing for time, she said lightly, 'The great financier is never confused.'

'That's what *he* used to think,' he agreed. 'So when the confusion came he didn't know how to cope with it.'

A soft buzz came from the screen.

'You've got an email,' she said. 'I'm going back to bed. So should you. Get some sleep.'

She slipped away and ran back to her room, telling herself that she was glad of the interruption that had saved her from saying and doing things that she would regret.

If she tried really hard she might even manage to believe that.

Mark and Frankie were instinctively happy outdoors. Town life bored them, and escaping to the island lifted them to seventh heaven. They revelled in the visit to Harriet's little yacht, and the trip out to sea, gaining particular pleasure from their father's ignorance, even greater than their own, and the way he addressed Harriet as 'Captain'. Several times Harriet caught them exchanging knowing glances.

At home she took charge, banishing Darius to the office to catch up with his work while she and Kate saw to supper.

'Isn't Dad having supper with us?' Mark asked.

'The poor man's got to do a little work,' Harriet said. 'Last night he worked late so that he could spend the day with you. Now, I'll take his supper in to him.'

'Are you and Dad going to get married?' Frankie asked.

'It's much too soon to think of anything like that,' Harriet said quickly. 'We're just friends for now, and we're not rushing it. Don't mention it to him.'

Frankie nodded wisely. Harriet was left staring at Darius's office door. He'd been closing it when Frankie asked her question, and although Harriet tried to believe that he couldn't have heard anything she'd noticed the way the door was suddenly still for a moment, before being shut.

At the end of the evening he emerged to join them for a walk with Phantom, and perhaps only Harriet noticed that he was unusually quiet. Later, when the children had gone to bed and the house was quiet, it wasn't a surprise when he knocked on her bedroom door.

'I just wanted to say I'm sorry that Frankie embarrassed you,' he said, coming in. 'She's too young to understand that…well, things have to happen slowly.'

'You're right,' she said. 'Going slowly can save you from a lot of mistakes.'

'Does that mean anything special?' he asked, almost daring to hope.

'I guess it does.' She fell silent.

'Harriet,' he whispered, 'don't shut me out. Not any more.'

She sighed. 'I rushed into marriage with Brad…I was so young…ah, well…'

'Don't stop there,' he begged. 'Talk to me. You keep everything bolted and barred, and you shouldn't.'

'I know. I don't mean to but I've hidden the truth for so

long that it's hard to change now. My neighbours think we were the perfect couple, and that's what I wanted them to think. I'd have been ashamed for them to know the truth. I loved Brad so much but he…well, he just took my love for granted and did as he liked.'

'Go on,' he said gently. 'Harriet, please tell me everything. You know so much about me, but you hide from me and keep me on the outside.'

She drew away suddenly and went to the window, throwing back her head, breathing harshly. She felt as though she were being torn in two directions. It had taken her so long to reach this point and now her courage was failing her. She saw Darius watching her closely, with an expression so gentle that she reached out to him without even realising.

At once he went to her. 'Tell me,' he said again. 'Don't shut me out. If only I could make you understand how important it is.'

'Why?' she whispered.

He answered by laying his lips tenderly on hers, leaving them for just a moment.

'Can you understand now?' he asked.

She searched his face. 'I'm not sure. I'm so confused.'

'Trust me, Harriet. That's all I ask.'

She rested her head against him. 'Our marriage was a mistake. I rushed into love, and when it went wrong I wouldn't admit to myself that he wasn't the man I'd thought. I don't think he was ever really faithful to me, but nobody else knew because he was away so often.

'In the end he left me for a woman he'd met in America. He went to live with her over there, and they died together in a car crash. I still have the last letter he wrote me, demanding a quick divorce because his lover was pregnant. That really hurt because I'd always wanted children and he was the one who insisted on waiting.

'It's strange, but after what he did to me, the thing I'll really never be able to forgive him for is the way he abandoned Phantom. That poor dog adored him. When Brad was away he'd sit at the window, watching and watching until he returned. Then he'd go mad with happiness.

'I loved Phantom too, but I always knew I was second best to him. And when Brad said he was leaving him behind—I couldn't believe he could be so cruel. It was *her* fault. She didn't want him, so Brad simply tossed him out of his life.'

Darius uttered one word, vulgar and full of feeling.

'That's what I said,' Harriet agreed.

'I'll never forget the day he left. Phantom watched him loading his things into the car. He began to wail, then to howl, and he ran after Brad and tried to get between him and the front door. I'll swear he knew what was happening, and was begging not to be left behind.

'Brad pushed him aside and shouted at him. Then he went out and got into the car. Phantom followed, but suddenly everything seemed to drain out of him, and he just sat there in the road while the car vanished. I hated Brad at that moment. I could forgive him for leaving me, but not for breaking that poor creature's heart.

'After that, Phantom sat at the window every day, waiting for his return. Then one day he didn't go to the window, but just lay there staring into space. He knew it was final.

'I've tried to make it up to him. I tell him how much I love him, and I promise that I'll never, never desert him or let him down in any way.'

'Harriet, you're talking about him as though he was a person.'

'I suppose that's how I think of him, except that he's more loyal and loving than any human being. I think he's happy with me now, but I wonder if he still mourns Brad.'

'Perhaps that depends on you,' Darius said carefully. 'If he can tell that *you* still mourn Brad—'

'But I don't,' she said, a little too quickly, he thought. 'He's a part of my life that's over. I love Phantom for his own sake. How could I not love him when he's so lovable?'

'And when he reminds you of Brad,' Darius said. 'Are you sure you aren't hiding from the truth, just a little? Are you really over him?'

'That was another life, another world. It doesn't even feel like me any more.'

That was a clever reply, he thought wryly, because it sounded like a denial without actually being one.

'What about this world?' he asked, choosing his words carefully.

'This is the one that matters. I know that. It's just so hard to know where I belong in it. Sometimes I feel I never will know.' She searched his face.

'I can help you there,' he said, laying his mouth over hers and murmuring through the kiss. 'This is where you belong, in my arms, in my heart.'

She silenced him with the soft pressure of her own mouth, reaching up to caress his face before sliding one hand behind his head. She'd fought so hard to cling onto caution, but now she banished it without another thought. Whatever pain the future might hold, she would risk it in return for the beauty of this moment.

When she felt him drawing her to the bed she went willingly. Now everything in her wanted what was about to happen. Fear and mistrust were set aside as she felt a new self coming to life within her, and knew that this was the self that was always meant to be, a self that could yield joyfully to passion, but for whom tenderness mattered as much, or even more.

For, dazzling as was the physical pleasure, it was the look in his eyes that made her sigh with happiness as he brought her to the moment they both longed for. And afterwards it was the strength of his arms around her that carried her safely back to earth.

Now, at last, she knew where she belonged.

CHAPTER ELEVEN

HARRIET need not have been worried about the visit. It was blessed from the start by the fact that both children were instinctively at home in the country. Sailing, bathing on the beach, running through fields and trees with Phantom, trips around the island to small villages and communities—all this was their idea of heaven.

In only one respect was the holiday less than perfect. It lacked what they most longed for, and that was to see Harriet called out on a lifeboat rescue.

She'd obtained permission for them to visit the station where her friends greeted them jovially, and showed them around, including a moored lifeboat. But no emergency turned up, and the excitement they longed for failed to materialise.

It was time for the Ellarick Regatta. For the last week the hotels had been filling up, the island was full of visitors and the port was brilliant with flags. Mark and Frankie each had a copy of the programme, which never left them.

'How many races are you in?' Mark had demanded, studying the lists although he knew them by heart.

'It depends,' Harriet said. 'If I get eliminated in an early heat I won't go on to the next, but if I finish in the first three I'll go on to the next heat, and the next and maybe even the final.'

'And then you'll win the small boat trophy,' Frankie said triumphantly. 'Like before.'

'How did you know?'

'It's listed here,' Mark said, showing her. 'You've won once, and come second three times. Did you get a big prize?'

'I got a trophy. I keep it in the shop.'

'Then it's time we all saw it,' Darius announced.

They had a jolly expedition to the shop that, as Harriet had said, sold as many gifts as antiques, and at this time of year was full of souvenirs of the regatta. Darius kitted them out with T-shirts, plus anything else that took their fancy, and they ended the day in an ice cream bar.

That night Harriet went to bed early as she had to be up in the early hours. The children bid her a formal goodnight and blew her kisses before retreating. Darius saw her to her door.

'Aren't you coming in to tuck me up?' she asked innocently.

'You need to be at your best tomorrow. Go to bed, get some sleep,' he commanded.

'If you say so. Just one goodnight kiss—'

She took possession of his mouth before he could protest, kissing him softly, then with more vigour, then fiercely.

'Harriet, you're not being fair,' he murmured desperately.

'So who's fair?' she whispered back.

'I'm trying to protect you from distractions—'

'When I need your protection I'll ask for it. Now, come inside and stop arguing.'

This was another new person, one who could shamelessly demand a man's attentions while equally shamelessly offering her own. No, not offer her own, insist on her own, for he was trying to be virtuous and resist her, and she wasn't going to have that.

It was a week since they had found each other, and she had spent every moment of that week wanting to enjoy him again, that might have embarrassed her if she hadn't known he felt exactly the same. They'd been careful. The need to put the children first had meant there were fewer chances than they might have hoped. But tonight was a chance she was determined to seize—whatever nonsense he might talk.

When at last they lay dozing together, he murmured, 'Now you must go out and win.'

'But I did win,' she whispered. 'Just now. Didn't you notice?'

'I kind of thought I was the winner.'

'We'll call it a tie.' Her lips twitched. 'But I'm not sharing the trophy.'

'That's all right. We'll compete for another one in the next round.' He kissed her. 'And now I'm leaving—'

'Are you?' she said, moving her hand.

'Yes, you little wretch—Harriet, don't do that, it isn't fair—'

'I'm not trying to be fair—'

'I know what you're trying to do—*Harriet!*'

After that there was silence for a long time. Then he gathered his energy enough to say, 'Now I really am going so that you can go to sleep. You have to be at your best tomorrow. You've got to triumph in that race and go into the next round and win there, and we're all going to be there when you get the trophy. I'll be cheering and the kids will be cheering—'

'Ah, yes, the children,' she sighed. 'It's all for them. Don't let's forget that.'

Rejoicing in the pleasure of this wonderful time, she

often forgot the conversation she'd overheard, suggesting that Darius had another motive for securing her. Not only the passion they shared, but also the sense of being close in heart and mind, rescued her from fear. All would be well, she was increasingly sure of it.

From the door he blew her a kiss and was gone.

In the early hours of next morning she was up with the lark, finding the taxi waiting at the door. By mutual agreement, Darius was remaining at home with the children rather than driving her.

Then the port came in sight, and she forgot everything but the excitement of the regatta. She got to work on her yacht, making sure everything was ready, then settled in, feeling herself become one with it.

Forty yachts were entered for the race, but only ten could compete at any one time, so it began with heats. Some of the crowd watched from the shore, but the view was better from the large ferries that had positioned themselves out at sea, and Harriet knew that the three of them would be on one of these, eagerly watching for her.

They were off. She managed to keep ahead of most of the other boats, without actually getting into the lead. Halfway through the race she saw Darius and the children leaning over the railing of a ferry, cheering her. Inspired, she redoubled her efforts and managed to arrive second.

'That's it,' Darius said as they welcomed her ashore. 'You're in the next heat.'

'And next time you'll be first,' Mark said loyally.

'You'll show 'em,' Frankie cried.

And she did. Whether it was the sense of a loyal family rooting for her, or whether it was simply her time, she won the next heat, came second in the next, and won the final race. When she came ashore the band was playing as she went up to the dais to receive the trophy. There were photographs to be taken, herself holding up her prize, with Frankie and Mark one each side, then Frankie and Mark holding the prize. Darius was in some of the pictures too, but usually in the background, rather to her disappointment.

The day ended in a restaurant, being ecstatically toasted not only by the family but by her many friends. Then home to be toasted again.

Darius ended the evening, as he always did, at the computer, catching up with the work he'd been unable to do during the day. He looked worn out, she realised. With every day he seemed to get less and less sleep. She crept away and left him.

He came to her two hours later. 'I was afraid you might have gone to sleep by now,' he said, closing the door behind him.

'I'm just about to.' She yawned theatrically. 'I simply can't keep awake.'

Laughing, he took her into his arms. 'Let's see if I can help you find sweet dreams.'

She slipped her arms about his neck. 'Hmm, let me think about that.'

'Don't think too hard,' he murmured, dropping his head so that his lips were against her neck.

'You're a wicked man, you know that?'

'Would you like me to go away?'

'I'm not sure. Do that again and I'll decide.'

Their first love-making had been full of tender emotion, and because of that it had been perfect. Over the next few days, a new pleasure had revealed itself, love and laughter at the same time, and she discovered that its joy could be as great as any other. She hadn't known before that she could be a tease, but she was learning it now and revelling in the lesson.

He caressed her, watching her expression intently.

'Are you any closer to making your mind up?' he wanted to know.

'I'm not sure. Some things take longer to decide than others.' She stretched out luxuriously. 'But we have plenty of time.'

'Yes, all the time in the world,' he said with relish.

As he spoke he was drawing his fingers down her, touching lightly so she took a long breath as her desire rose.

'I've thought about nothing but this since last time,' he murmured. 'And the time before.'

'Neither have I. You're here now, and I'm going to enjoy every moment.'

'I intend to make sure you do—*what the blazes is that?*'

A shrill noise had rent the air, then again, and again and again.

'Oh, no,' Harriet groaned. 'That's my pager. I'm needed on the lifeboat. I've got to dash.'

'You're going to run away *now*?'

'I don't have any choice,' she cried, shoving him aside and making a grab for her clothes.

For a moment he was too stunned to speak, but lay on the bed, his heart pounding as he fought to bring himself under control. This couldn't be happening. It mustn't happen. To have the prize snatched from him as the climax mounted—to be defeated at the last moment and told to put up with it. His head was spinning.

'Bye,' she cried and headed for the door.

'Wait!' he cried, getting command of himself at the last minute, 'I'll drive you there.'

'I can't wait for you. I'm on my way.'

She was gone. A moment later, he heard her car start up.

Dazed, he wrenched on his clothes and went out into the corridor, to find his children already there.

'Dad, what's happened?' Mark demanded. 'There was a funny noise and Harry dashed off. She hasn't been called, has she?'

'That's right, she's on her way to the lifeboat station now.'

'Oh, wow!' Both children began to leap about. 'Let's go too, please, Dad.'

'They won't let us in. They're doing a serious job and we'd be in the way.'

'But we can watch from the shore and see the boat go out. Please, Dad, please, please, *please*.'

They were bouncing up and down, looking up at him beseechingly.

'All right,' he said, relenting. 'Get dressed fast.'

In ten minutes they were sweeping out of the drive. On the journey he switched on the car radio, tuned to the local station, that was carrying news about a small party out on a jaunt who'd sent a frantic radio message that their boat had sprung a leak.

By the time they arrived they were several minutes behind Harriet, who had completely vanished, but the station was buzzing with life. A crowd had gathered just outside, and they quickly joined it. A cheer rose as the lifeboat went down the slipway, hitting the water so that spray rose up high.

'Was it like this for you, Dad?' Mark breathed.

'I don't exactly know,' he said wryly. 'I wasn't here. I was a few miles out, going down for the third time.'

That was roughly how he felt right now. His mind told him that she'd had no choice but to leave and save others as she had saved him. He had no reasonable complaint.

But that was only his mind. The rest of him was complaining bitterly at losing the prize at the crucial moment.

She had laid in his arms, tender and sweet, giving him the look he loved, the one that said he could bring her a pleasure and happiness she'd never dreamed of before. That look had the power to open his heart, inviting her to reach out to him, as he reached out to her more with every day that passed.

Until now he'd shown his growing feelings through touch, waiting until he was sure of the right words. Since the night she'd confided in him he'd felt his defences collapse. The barrier of her husband's memory, once looming so high between them, no longer existed. She'd trusted and confided in a way he hadn't expected, filling him with happiness but also with a slight sense of guilt that he hadn't matched her openness with his own.

Honesty demanded that he admit he already knew the secret she was finally revealing, but he hadn't been able to bring himself to do it. It would involve telling her about his father's spies, and in her anger and dismay she might have laid some of the blame on himself. Not for the world would he risk damaging the bond between them. At least, not yet.

Soon he would be able to tell her of his feelings. It might even have been that night. But then—

He groaned. There were two Harriets—the passionate loving one, and the brave efficient one who put duty before everything. Tonight, the second one had taken over, leaving him stranded. Life with her would be more complex than he'd ever dreamed. Also more intriguing . That suggested an interesting future.

But tonight he was aching with frustration and thwarted feelings.

Hours passed. Occasionally someone would come out of

the station to brief the watchers on how things were going. So they knew that the lifeboat had reached its destination, rescued everyone safely, and was on its way back.

At last it appeared on the horizon, just visible in the faint gleam of the dawn. The children watched, thrilled, as it came closer and was hauled back up the slipway. When Harriet appeared they ran to greet her and be introduced to the rest of the crew. They were in seventh heaven.

'Gosh,' Mark exclaimed. 'Wasn't that the most wonderful thing that ever happened?'

'Oh, yes,' Darius said wryly. 'Wonderful.'

But his personal feelings vanished when he saw Harriet on the edge of total exhaustion.

'Let's get you home fast,' he said. 'Leave your car here; you're too tired to drive. I'll fetch it later. Let her have the back seat, kids, so that she can stretch out.'

She did manage to stretch out, falling asleep almost at once, and waking to find her head resting in Frankie's arms.

'We're home now,' the little girl said kindly. 'I'll help you to bed.'

With Kate's assistance, she did, finally emerging to where Mark and her father were waiting in the corridor.

'All right for me to go in?' Darius asked.

'Just for a moment,' she told him sternly. 'She needs to sleep.'

Darius gave her a comic salute. 'Yes, ma'am. Anything you say, ma'am.'

He vanished into Harriet's room too quickly to see his children stare at each other with an unmistakable message; Dad said *that?*

Going quietly to the bed, Darius whispered, 'Hello.'

Silence.

Leaning closer, he heard her faint breathing and realised that she was asleep.

'I guess Frankie was right to protect you,' he murmured. 'You need it sometimes. It's a pity about tonight because I was going to say…all sorts of things. Now they'll have to wait until the time is right.' He touched her face with gentle fingers. 'Let's hope that day comes soon.'

He kissed her softly, and left the room without her knowing that he'd been there.

The last few days of the holiday built on the success of the first week. Darius's relationship with his children was becoming everything he had hoped, and his manner towards Harriet was full of affection and gratitude.

'Without you, this would never work,' he told her. 'However much I want to, I can't spend all my time with them. I have to keep an eye on what's happening out there.'

'I know. You were up almost until dawn last night,' she said. 'I don't know how you manage to stay awake.'

'I don't always,' he said ruefully. 'Thank goodness for you distracting them. I swear if I nod off they barely notice.'

The end of the holiday was near. The four of them would fly to London, where the children would be reunited with Mary. After that, she hoped she and Darius would have a little time together before returning to Herringdean.

But the day before they were due to leave the financial world began to call to Darius more urgently. Hardly a minute passed without a text, an email or a call on his cellphone.

'Is it bad news?' she asked him urgently.

'Not bad, just interesting. It could go either way, depending on how I handle it. I think we need to change our plans.

It's best if you don't come to London after all. I'll have to stay there a few days, sort some things out. So I'll take the kids back to Mary and stay out of your hair for a while.' He grinned. 'You'll be glad to have a rest from me.'

'Of course I will,' she said in a dead voice. 'Who could think otherwise?'

The children complained bitterly about her not coming with them.

'I've got work to do,' she said cheerfully. 'It's time I took over the shop and I have to go to training sessions for the lifeboat.'

'But we will see you again?' Frankie urged.

'I'm sure you will. Who knows what's around the corner?'

She spoke brightly, but she couldn't help being glad Darius wasn't there to hear. She couldn't have helped watching for his reaction, and now something in her was warning her to expect the worst.

On the day she saw them off and stood looking up into the sky as the helicopter rose higher and higher, then swung away until it disappeared completely and the sky was empty but for a few seagulls.

How lonely it was now. After the pleasures of the last week, the quiet and emptiness were almost unbearable. Worse still was the fear that what had gone was gone for ever. He had said the news could be good, depending on how he handled it, and she guessed he would handle it with skill, perhaps ruthlessness. The 'no mercy' side of him would rise and take over again.

He would leave Herringdean, having no further use for it, or for her. He'd learned how to reach out to his children and he could carry those lessons forward without her help. He'd settle back in London, find a wife who suited him better, sell Herringdean and forget she existed.

And I should have known it would happen, she thought. *All this time the truth has been staring me in the face, but I wouldn't let myself see it.*

It was time to be sensible. She was good at that, she reminded herself. She had a shop to see to, and Phantom to look after. He was showing signs of depression now his two adoring young friends had gone.

'People always go off and leave you, don't they?' she said, caressing him. 'Well, not me. I'll always be here for you. That's a promise.'

Moving back into her home, she filled up the time by cleaning it. More time was occupied at the lifeboat station, but mostly in training sessions. For some reason, very few boats got into trouble.

Now she began to understand Mark and Frankie's frustration at the lack of action. Why couldn't people obligingly get into danger so that she could have the satisfaction of saving them? Not that she wanted anyone to suffer. She just wanted to feel needed, and that was becoming hard.

For the first few days Darius called her regularly, but the calls were always brief. Then they were replaced by texts, friendly, cheerful but unrevealing. Exactly the kind of message a man might send if he was easing his way out of a relationship.

One evening she and Phantom went out for a long walk. As she strolled back home a car passed her going in the other direction, and slowed down. It was Walter.

'I just drove past your place,' he called, 'and there's a fellow standing there.'

'Did you see who it was?' she asked eagerly.

'No, I wasn't that close, but he looked as if he was waiting for you.'

'Thanks, Walter.'

Her heart soaring, she sped away, racing Phantom until

her shop came in sight and she dashed around the corner, to where a man was walking impatiently up and down.

It was Amos Falcon.

CHAPTER TWELVE

'GOOD evening, Mrs Connor.'

Harriet wondered if she'd only imagined that he stressed 'Mrs' very slightly.

'Good evening, Mr Falcon. What a surprise. You didn't tell me you were coming.'

'It was a sudden decision. Aren't you going to invite me in?'

'Of course.'

She led him up to her apartment over the shop, keeping her hand on Phantom's collar, dreading that he might give one of his displays of friendliness. But she need not have feared. When they were inside, Phantom moved as far away from Amos as possible and sat huddled in a corner, eyeing him distrustfully.

When the door had shut, Harriet said, 'If you were hoping to see Darius—'

'I wasn't. I know he's in London. I've seen him several times in the last few days.' He was watching her face carefully, easily seeing that this disconcerted her. 'Did he not tell you that? Strange.'

On first finding him there she had remembered how pleasantly he'd spoken to her when they danced at the wedding. But now she saw that his smile was cold, and she remembered how Darius had described his father—ruthless, scheming, implacable; a man who was determined to make others do his will. She recalled too that Amos had chosen a wife for his son, and wondered uneasily what had brought him such a distance to see her.

'So you don't know what's been happening to him?' Amos said in a genial voice that struck a false note to her ears.

'I don't ask Darius about his business,' Harriet said. 'I doubt if I'd understand it, anyway.'

'Possibly, but when a man is taking hold of his problems and dealing with them successfully it's not hard to understand. Anyway, never mind that. You and I have things to discuss.'

'Coffee?' she asked politely.

'Thank you, I will. You know, I really took to you when we met before. You're an admirable young woman, not just because you helped save my son's life, but also because of the way you've built up this shop. It's worth a lot more than you'd think by just looking at the outside.'

'How do you know what it's worth?' she asked.

He shrugged. 'That kind of information isn't hard to come by. It belonged to your husband but he had very little time for it so the running of it fell to you. It was you who arranged the loans and made sure they were paid on time.'

'So you've been looking at my bank records?' she asked in outrage.

She knew that a man like this, who stood at the summit of the financial universe, would have no difficulty in accessing any figures that he wanted, yet the discovery that he'd had her investigated was a nasty shock that made her seethe.

'And I've been very impressed by what I found. You've turned this place into twice what it was before. I'm prepared to pay a high price for it.'

'It's not for sale.'

He gave a harsh chuckle. 'Of course it isn't. That's exactly what I expected you to say.'

'And I meant it.'

'Naturally. But you and I don't need to waste any time. We both know what the score is. You've gained a real influence over my son, but now that he's returning to his old life I don't want him harking back to you. The fight isn't over yet and he's going to need all his faculties to come out on top.'

Then Harriet did something that she did very rarely. She lost her temper, turning on him with such a look that he nearly backed away.

'Understand me,' she said. 'I will not discuss Darius with you. If he wants to consign me to the past then he can tell me himself, and I'll open my hands and let him go. I will not try to keep a stranglehold on him, and you don't have to buy me off. Is that clear?'

Amos Falcon's response was a genial smile that made her want to murder him.

'Perfectly clear and I respect your strength of mind, but you should allow me to show that respect by purchasing your shop at twice its value. You won't get such an offer again.'

'You're crazy,' she breathed. 'You think everyone's for sale.'

'No, I simply think you should be considering the long-term implications. After the appalling way your husband treated you, you should be protecting yourself.'

His words were like a douche of ice.

'The appalling way—? Darius told you about that?'

'Not at all. I told him.'

Suddenly the world had turned into a nightmare through which she could only stumble.

'You told—? When?'

'At the wedding. I discovered I knew rather more about you than he did, so I brought him up to date.'

Now she couldn't speak at all, only look at him from wide, horrified eyes.

'He was very chivalrous,' Amos went on. 'He said it was entirely a matter for you if you wanted to keep your secrets, which, of course, is right. But I think he was a little disturbed to discover that you'd been holding him off while pretending to be close to him.'

Harriet's head swam. There in her mind was the sweet moment when she'd confided in Darius what she'd told nobody else, meaning in this way to prove her trust in him.

But he'd known all the time, and never told her.

'Get out,' she breathed. 'Get out now, if you know what's good for you.'

'He doesn't,' said a voice from the door. 'He's never known what was good for him.'

Shocked, they both turned to see Darius standing there, a look of dark fury on his face.

'You heard her,' he told his father. 'Get out. Get off this island and don't ever come back.'

'What are you doing here?' Amos shouted.

'When I found out where you'd gone I came after you as fast as I could. I knew you'd try something like this. Luckily, I arrived in time to spike your guns.'

'I was only trying to do my best for you,' Amos growled. 'You've done so well these past few days.'

'Yes, I've put a lot of things right, not everything but enough to survive. And now I'm coming back here to stay. For good. I'm moving my centre of operations here permanently. From now on I'll operate out of Giant's Beacon, with the help of my wife.'

'Your wife!' Amos snapped. 'You mean you've asked her? Of all the damn fool—'

'No, I haven't asked her,' Darius said with a glance at Harriet. 'And after what you've told her I wouldn't give much for my chances. But I'm a man who doesn't give up. When I want something I keep on and on until I get it. *You* taught me that, and I was never more glad of a lesson in my life.

'It won't be easy. Why should any woman in her right mind want to marry into this family? But I'll keep going until she forgives me for keeping that little matter of her husband to myself, and understands that I can't live without her. Then, perhaps she'll take pity on me.'

Harriet tried to speak but she couldn't. Her eyes were blinded with tears and something was almost choking her.

'Now go,' Darius said quietly.

Amos knew when he was beaten. With a scowl at them both, he stormed out of the door and they heard his footsteps thundering on the stairs.

'I meant every word of it,' Darius said, coming to stand before her. 'I love you. I want to have you with me always. That's why I went to London, to set up the arrangements that would make it possible for me to move here permanently. I suppose I ought to have told you first—*asked* you first—but that's not my way. I fix things to suit myself, and then other people just have to fit in. Once I knew I wanted to marry you, you never had a choice.

'Harriet, Harriet, don't cry. I don't mean it. I'll do anything to marry you. You'll just have to be a little patient with me. Don't cry, my darling, please.'

But she couldn't stop crying. Tears of joy, of hope, of released tension, they all came flooding out, making it impossible for her to speak. Mysteriously, he also found that words had deserted him, so he abandoned them altogether, carried her into the bedroom and revealed his love in other ways. She responded with heartfelt tenderness, and they found that their mutual understanding was once more perfect.

'I can't believe the way you stood up to my father,' he murmured as they lay together afterwards. 'The world is littered with strong men he crushed beneath his feet, but he didn't stand a chance against you.'

'He tried to turn me against you,' she said. 'How dare he!'

'I heard him tell you that he and I had had several meetings while I was in London, but he didn't tell you what those meetings were about. He tried again to get me to marry Freya, offered me money, all useless. Freya was cheering me on, and actually drove me to the airport. The last thing she said to me was, "Go for it. Don't let her escape!"'

'Mary said much the same thing. There'll be a huge cheer when I tell them that we're engaged.' Suddenly, he sounded uncertain. 'Harriet, we are engaged, aren't we?'

'I thought you weren't going to take no for an answer.'

'I'm not.'

'And neither am I.' She drew him close.

'That old man thought he was being clever when he found out about your husband,' Darius said, 'but it just made me angry with him. It only affected me in that I longed for you to confide in me willingly, and when you did—I wanted to tell you that I already knew, but I was afraid to spoil what was happening between us. Say you forgive me.'

'There's nothing to forgive,' she whispered.

'And we'll marry as soon as possible?'

'I want to, of course I do. I love you. I thought I'd never love another man, but you're different from them all. But can you really give up your old life to come and live here? Aren't we being unrealistic?'

'I shan't have to give it up completely. I'm going to have to downsize, but that suits me. My London home is up for sale and I'll be selling quite a few other properties. I'll pay off some debts, reschedule others, and what's left can be controlled just as easily from here as from London.'

'But can you do it all alone?'

'I won't have to. I have staff who are willing to move here permanently. I couldn't ask them before because I didn't know where I'd be myself, but now it can all be arranged. I've got plans to create a little village for them.'

'And they won't mind leaving London for such a quiet place?'

'Mind? They were falling over themselves to volunteer. This will be a whole new life for a lot of people. It isn't going to be the "great financial empire" I once had. It'll be about a third of the size, but that's fine with me. Then I'll have more time to spend with my wife and our children.'

'Our children?'

'If that's what you'd like.' He was silenced suddenly as she took him into a fierce embrace.

'That's what I'd like,' she whispered at last. 'Oh, yes, that's what I'd like, as soon as possible.'

'Then we'll have a dozen children, and I'll spend my time pottering about the house, and sometimes helping you in the shop.'

'Now you're getting carried away,' she warned.

'So what's wrong with being carried away?'

'Nothing,' she sighed blissfully. 'Nothing at all.'

'And I'm going to do my best to make Herringdean glad I'm here. There must be things I can do for the community. I expect they'll come and suggest them to you soon, and you can tell me. I'm going to have a good look at that wind farm. There may be some arrangement I can make to get a good electricity price for the island.'

'Do you really think you can?'

'I don't know.' His voice rose to a note of exhilaration. 'I simply don't know.'

'Darling, you're sounding a bit mad. Anyone would think not knowing was the best thing in the world.'

'Maybe it is. Maybe it's better to have things that you know you don't know, that you've got to learn about, because that's all part of having a new life. There's so much I don't know, and I'm going to have a great time finding out.'

'*We'll* have a great time finding out,' she suggested.

'Maybe. The trouble is that you already know so much more than me. I'm going to have to learn from you—teacher.'

She regarded him tenderly. She wasn't crazy enough to take all of this too seriously. Darius was caught in the exhilaration of their love and their new life, and he was celebrating with wild dreams. But he hadn't completely changed character, no matter how he sounded. Part of him would always be the fierce, dynamic man who'd first arrived on Herringdean weeks ago.

But she knew also that part of him would be this new man coming to life in her arms. And just how the mixture settled would be up to her in the years ahead. He'd put himself in her hands and she was eager for the challenge.

'You make it sound so wonderful,' she said. 'Oh, yes, everything is going to be perfect. No, no, it's perfect now.'

'Not quite,' he said. 'There's still one thing I want, although I don't suppose I'll ever have it.'

'Whatever can that be?'

'You've done so much for me. Saving my life was just the start of it. There are so many other ways in which you've saved me, I couldn't begin to count them. If only there was something I could do for you that would mean as much.'

'But it's enough that you love me.'

'Not for me. I want to give you something so precious that it's like a jewel, but I don't know that I can. I can't make it happen—it just has to happen, and maybe it never will.'

'Stop fretting,' she told him. 'We'll just have to be patient. It may take a long time to happen.'

But it happened before anyone could have expected, and in a way that nobody could have foreseen in a million years.

Preparations for the wedding started at once, with Harriet moving out of her tiny apartment and into Giant's Beacon, where she could take immediate charge of the renovations.

'Is Phantom pleased with his accommodation?' Darius enquired after the first day.

'Yes, he's asked me to express his approval of your efforts on his behalf. Putting him in the room next door to ours was pure genius.'

'Next thing, he'll have to meet the family. We'll start this afternoon.'

'What?'

'It's simple. We go into the computer room, switch on the video link—' he was doing so as he spoke '—and the family will appear.'

It was her first encounter with video link and it took her breath away. Jackson connected from his computer in London, and Marcel appeared from Paris. Then there was Mary and Ken, raising their glasses to her, and Frankie and Mark, bouncing with happiness.

Like Darius, she was discovering the joys of new experiences and they were exhilarating.

'It's all working out,' she told Phantom, stroking him as he settled for the night. 'We're going to have such a wonderful life, my darling—Phantom—are you all right? *Darius.*'

In a moment he was there, dropping to his knees beside the dog, who was heaving violently.

'Call the vet quickly,' he said.

The vet lived nearby. He was soon there, listened to Phantom's heart and shook his head.

'He's very old, and his heart's worn out,' he said. 'This was bound to happen soon. I think you should prepare yourself for the worst. Would you like me to put him to sleep now?'

'No,' Harriet said fiercely. 'I want him until the last possible moment.' She scooped Phantom up in her arms. 'There, darling, we'll stay together and you'll feel my arms around you all the time.'

Darius watched her wretchedly, torn apart by her grief.

'We'll stay with him together,' he said, touching her face gently.

But then the worst thing possible happened. A sound split the air, making them both start up in horror.

'My pager,' she gasped. 'No—no—I can't. I can't leave him to die alone.'

'Harriet, you've got to go,' Darius said urgently. 'Not for their sake but for your own. You swore to do your duty and put it above all personal considerations. If you fail now, you'll never forgive yourself as long as you live.'

Her wild eyes showed that she knew he was right, and tears streamed down her face as she fought between her duty and her feelings for her beloved dog.

'How can I leave him alone?' she whispered.

'He won't be alone. I'll stay with him until the last minute. He'll be in my arms, just as he would have been in yours. He'll know that he's loved, I promise you. Trust me, Harriet. *Trust me!*'

'Yes—' she gasped. 'Yes—' She caressed Phantom's head. 'Goodbye, my darling—goodbye—'

Darius never forgot the look on her face as she backed out of the room. Or the look on Phantom's face as he took the dog into his arms.

'She'd have stayed if she could,' he told him. 'We both know that, because she loves you more than anyone in the world. And I'm not even jealous.'

Incredibly, he felt the great furry body in his arms relax. Phantom's eyes closed, but he was still alive for a moment later they opened again.

'It's time we had a good long talk,' Darius murmured. 'We both love her so much, we had to get together sooner or later.'

He talked on, only faintly aware of the passage of time. He wondered where Harriet was now. Had she reached the station yet? He knew she was suffering, thinking of Phantom dying without her. But he had made her a promise, and he would keep it at all costs.

The hours passed. Daylight faded. He knew he was repeating himself, but that didn't matter. What counted was the love in his voice, reaching out to the dog as Harriet herself would have reached out to him.

At first he listened for her step on the stairs, but gradually he ceased to be aware of anything but the living animal dying softly in his arms. It might be madness but he had no doubt that Phantom could understand every word, just as he would have done from Harriet.

And then the truth came to him as a revelation. This was

the sign he'd longed for, the proof that he and Harriet were one. Phantom's eyes on him were full of trust.

Harriet, slipping into the house downstairs, listened to the silence, knowing what it meant. Phantom had died when she wasn't there to care for him. And however much she tried to believe that Darius had helped him, he would know that she herself had abandoned him when he needed her most. Tears streamed down her face as she climbed the stairs.

And then, halfway up, she stopped, holding herself tense against the incredible sound that reached her. Surely that was Darius's voice? He was talking to someone, that meant—?

Hardly daring to believe it, she sped up the rest of the way, pausing outside the door, then moving quietly into the room. There she stood just outside of Darius's vision, listening, entranced, to his words.

'I'm not sure she really understands even now how much I love her,' he was saying. 'I've tried to show it but I'm clumsy. I never knew anyone like her existed and I'm afraid that she'll leave me. That's why I'm hurrying her into our marriage before she has a chance to think. But she's turning me into someone else. This other guy, he doesn't do any of the things I'm used to, so I'm having to get to know him from scratch.

'I wish I could be more like you. You were never lost for what to do next, were you? Toss them to the ground and jump up and down on them, that's your way.

'I used to be jealous of you. How about that? I thought she loved you because she still loved Brad, but it's got nothing to do with him. I know that now. You're lovable and precious, and you've got to be here for us a while yet.

'Hey, you're restless. That's good. Hold on there, boy.

Don't give up now. She'll be home soon—just a little longer. *Harriet!*'

She dropped down beside him, her hands caressing Phantom, but her eyes turned up to him in a passion of love and gratitude.

'You did it,' she whispered. 'You kept him alive for me. Thank you, thank you—oh, if only you knew—'

'I think perhaps I do,' he murmured, his eyes meeting hers in a moment of total understanding that was normal with them now.

'I reckon he's got a little longer yet,' Darius said.

As if to prove it, Phantom shifted in his arms and leaned forward to lick Harriet's face.

'You've got to live a bit longer, you hear that?' she said. 'I want you there at our wedding. Promise me.'

Woof!

They were married three weeks later, on the beach. Of Darius's family, only Amos and his wife were missing; but his brothers and Freya all said they wouldn't miss it for the world. Mary and Ken said the same thing, watching with satisfaction as Darius laid claim to the most valuable property of his life.

Frankie walked behind the bride, pretty in frills and flowers. And beside her walked Mark, his hand on Phantom's collar, guiding him to a place at the front where he could curl up and watch the ceremony.

The vet had expressed astonishment at his survival, but Harriet wasn't surprised. Darius had done what he longed to do—given her something so precious that it was like a jewel. If she had doubted his love before, she could doubt it no longer. She knew now that the jewel would shine for ever.

* * * * *

WHO WANTS TO MARRY A MILLIONAIRE?

BY
NICOLA MARSH

Nicola Marsh has always had a passion for writing and reading. As a youngster she devoured books when she should have been sleeping and later kept a diary whose content could be an epic in itself! These days, when she's not enjoying life with her husband and son in her home city of Melbourne, she's at her computer, creating the romances she loves in her dream job.

Visit Nicola's website at www.nicolamarsh.com for the latest news of her books.

This one's for my writing buddies,
Fiona Lowe and Joan Kilby.
Thanks for the camping tips.
If you convinced my hero to give it a go,
there's hope for me yet!

CHAPTER ONE

'WE HAVE a problem.'

Four words Rory Devlin did *not* want to hear—especially at his first Devlin Corp Shareholders' Ball.

He glanced around the Palladium ballroom, ensuring everyone was engaged in drinking, dining or dancing, with no visible crisis in sight, before acknowledging the waiter hovering at his elbow.

'What kind of problem?'

The kid, barely out of school, took a backward step and he belatedly remembered to temper his tone. It wasn't the waiter's fault he'd been dealing with non-stop hold-ups on the Portsea project all day.

Attending this shindig was the last thing he wanted to do but it had been six months since he'd stepped into the CEO role, six months since he'd tried to rebuild what had once been Australia's premier property developer, six months of repairing the damage his dad had inflicted.

The waiter glanced over his shoulder and tugged nervously at his bow tie. 'You better see for yourself.'

Annoyed at the intrusion, he signalled to his deputy, who saluted at his 'stepping out' sign, and followed the waiter to a small annexe off the main foyer, where the official launch of the Portsea project would take place in fifteen minutes.

'She's in there.'

She?

He took one look inside the annexe and balked.

'I'll take it from here,' he said, and the waiter scuttled away before he'd finished speaking.

Squaring his shoulders, he tugged at the ends of his dinner jacket and strode into the room, eyeballing *the problem*.

Who eyeballed him back with a defiant tilt of her head, sending loose shoulder-length blond waves tumbling around her heart-shaped face.

She wore a smug smile along with a flimsy blue cocktail dress that matched her eyes.

He hoped the links around her wrists and ankles were the latest eccentric fashion accessory and not what he thought they were: chains anchoring her to the display he had to unveil shortly.

'Can I help you?'

'I'm counting on it.'

Her pink-glossed lips compressed as she sized him up, starting at his Italian handmade shoes and sweeping upwards in an all-encompassing stare that made him edgy.

'Shall we go somewhere and discuss—?'

'Not possible.'

She rattled the chains at her wrist and the display gave an ominous wobble.

'As you can see, I'm a bit tied up at the moment.'

He winced at her pitiful pun and she laughed.

'Not my best, but a girl has to do what a girl has to do to get results.'

He pointed at the steel links binding her to his prized display.

'And you think chaining yourself to my company's latest project is going to achieve your objective?'

'You're here, aren't you?'

What *was* this? Some kind of revenge?

He frowned, searching his memory banks. Was she someone he'd dated? A business associate? Someone he'd slighted in some way?

If she'd gone this far to get his attention, she wanted something. Something he'd never give, considering the way she'd gone about this.

He didn't take kindly to threats or blackmail—or whatever *this* was.

Having some bold blonde wearing a dress that accentuated rather than hid her assets, her long legs bare and her toenails painted the same silver as her chains, bail him up like this…no way in hell would he cave to her demands.

She wanted to sell him prime land? Put in a tender for a job? Supply and interior decorate the luxury mansions on the Portsea project?

Stiff. She'd have to make an appointment like everyone else. This kind of stunt didn't impress him. Not one bit.

She chose that moment to shift her weight from one leg to the other, rattling the chains binding her slim ankles, drawing his attention to those long bare legs again…

His perfectly male response annoyed him as much as the time he was wasting standing here.

'You wanted to see *me* specifically?'

'If you're Rory Devlin, CEO of the company about to ruin the marine environment out near Portsea, then, yep, you're the man.'

His heart sank. Since he'd taken over the reins at Devlin Corp six months ago he'd borne the brunt of every hippy lobbyist and environmentalist in town. None that looked quite as ravishing as the woman before him, but all of them demonstrating the same headstrong fanaticism.

Eco-nuts like her had almost derailed the company. Thankfully, he had a stronger backbone than his father, who'd dilly-dallied rather than making firm decisions on the Port Douglas project last year.

Devlin Corp had ensured the rainforest in far North Queensland would be protected, but that hadn't stopped zealot protestors stalling construction, costing millions and almost bankrupting the company in the process.

If he hadn't stepped in and played hardball he shuddered to think what would have happened to his family legacy.

'You've been misinformed. My company takes great pains to ensure its developments blend with the environment, not ruin it.'

'Please.' She rolled her eyes before focussing them on him with a piercing clarity that would have intimidated a lesser man. 'I've researched the land you develop—those flashy houses you dump in the middle of nowhere and sell for a small fortune.'

She strained against her chains as if she'd like to jab him in the chest, and his gaze momentarily strayed to hers before her exasperated snort drew his attention upwards.

'Your developments slash trees and defile land and don't give a rat's about energy conservation—'

'Stop right there.'

He crossed the room to stand a foot in front of her, feeling vindicated when she had to tilt her head back to look up at him, and annoyed when a tantalising fragrance of sunshine and fresh grass and spring mornings wrapped around him.

'You're misinformed as well as trespassing. Unlock yourself. Now.'

Tiny sapphire flecks sparked in her eyes before her lips curved upwards in an infuriatingly smug smile.

'Can't do that.'

'Why?'

'Because you haven't agreed to my terms yet.'

He shook his head, pressing the pads of his fingers against his eyes. Unfortunately, when he opened them, she was still there.

'We do this the easy way or the hard way. Easy way: you unlock yourself. Hard way: I call Security and they use bolt cutters to humiliate you further.'

Her eyes narrowed, not dimming in brilliance one iota.

'Go ahead. Call them.'

Damn, she knew he was bluffing. No way would he draw attention to her and risk the shareholders getting curious.

'Give me the key.'

He took a step closer, deriving some satisfaction from the way she inhaled sharply and wriggled backwards before he realised his mistake.

He'd wanted to intimidate her; he'd ended up being an inch away from her.

'Make me.'

Her tongue darted out to moisten her bottom lip and he stared at it, shaken to the core by the insane urge to taste those lips for himself.

Hell.

He never backed down—ever. He'd taken on every challenge thrust upon him: changing schools in his mid-teens so he could be groomed to take over Devlin Corp one day, ousting his layabout father from the CEO role, stepping up when it counted and dragging an ailing company out of the red and into the black.

She wanted him to capitulate to her demands?

As if.

'I'm not playing this game with you.'

He used his frostiest, most commanding tone. The one he reserved for recalcitrant contractors who never failed to delay projects. Predictably, it did little for the pest threatening to derail his evening.

She merely smiled wider.

'Why? Games can be fun.'

Exasperated beyond belief, his fingers tingled with the urge to throttle her.

Dragging in deep, calming breaths, he stared at the model of Portsea Point, the largest project he'd undertaken since assuming CEO duties.

He needed this project to fly. Needed it to be his biggest, boldest success to push the company back to its rightful place: at the top of Australia's luxury property developers.

If he could nail this business would flood in, and Devlin Corp would shrug off the taint his father had besmirched the company with in his short stint as CEO.

Failure was not an option.

He glanced at his watch and grimaced. The unveiling would take place in less than ten minutes and he needed to get rid of this woman pronto.

Thrusting his hands into his pockets and out of strangling distance, he squared his shoulders and edged back to tower over her.

'What do you want?'

'Thought you'd never ask.'

His gaze strayed to her glossed lips again and he mentally kicked himself.

'I want a little one-on-one time with you.'

'There are easier ways to get a date.'

Confusion creased her brow for a second, before her eyes widened in horror.

'I don't want a *date* with you.'

She made it sound as if he'd offered her some one-on-one time with a nest of vipers.

'Sure? I come highly recommended.'

'I bet,' she muttered, glancing away, but not before he'd seen the flare of interest in her eyes.

'In fact, I can give you the numbers of half the Melbourne female population who could verify exactly how great a date I am and—'

'Half of Melbourne?' She snorted. 'Don't flatter yourself.'

Leaning into her personal space, he savoured her momentary flare of panic as she eased away.

'You're the one who wanted one-on-one time with me.'

'For an interview, you dolt.'

Ah…so that was what this stunt was about. An out-of-work environmentalist after a job.

He had two words for her: *hell, no.* But against his better judgement he admired her sass. Most jobseekers would apply through an agency or harass his PA for an appointment. Not many would go through this much trouble.

He crooked his finger and she warily eased forward. 'Here's a tip. You want an interview? Don't go calling your prospective boss nasty names.'

'Dolt isn't nasty. If I wanted nasty I would've gone with bast—'

'Unbelievable.'

His jaw ached with the effort not to laugh. If his employees had half the chutzpah this woman did Devlin Corp would be number one again in next to no time.

'What do you say? Give me fifteen minutes of your time and I'll ensure you won't regret it.'

She punctuated her plea with a toss of her shoulder-length blond hair and once again the tempting fragrance of spring outdoors washed over him.

He opened his mouth to refuse, to tell her exactly what he thought of her underhand tricks.

'I don't want to disrupt your Portsea project. I want to help you.'

She eyeballed him, her determination and boldness as attractive as the rest of her.

'In the marine environmental field, I'm the best there is.'

Worn down by her admirable persistence, he found himself nodding.

'Fifteen minutes.'

'Deal.'

Her triumphant grin turned sly. 'Now, if you don't mind fishing the key out of its hiding spot, I'll get out of your way.'

'Hiding spot?'

Her gaze dropped to her cleavage.

Jeez, could this evening get any crazier?

'Uh...okay.'

He'd reached a tentative hand towards her chest when she let out a howl of laughter that had him leaping backwards.

'Don't worry, I've got it.'

With a few deft flicks of her wrists she'd slipped out of her chains and kicked the ones around her ankles free.

'You set me up.'

He should have been angry, should have cancelled her interview on the spot. Instead he found himself watching her as she deftly wound the chains and stuffed them into a sparkly hold-all she'd hidden under the table, wondering what she'd come up with next to surprise him.

'I didn't set you up so much as have a little fun at your expense.'

She patted his chest. 'I snuck a peek at you earlier in

the ballroom and it looked like you could do with a little lightening up.'

Speechless, he wondered why he was putting up with her pushiness. He didn't take that from anyone—ever.

She pressed a business card into his hand and the simple touch of her palm against his fired a jolt of awareness he hadn't expected or wanted.

'My details are all there. I'll call to set up that interview.'

She slung her bag over her shoulder, the rattle of chains a reminder of the outlandishness of this evening.

'Nice to meet you, Rory Devlin.'

With a crisp salute she sauntered out through the door, leaving him gobsmacked.

CHAPTER TWO

GEMMA SHULTZ strode from the ballroom, head held high, success making her want to do a little shimmy.

With Rory Devlin boring holes in her back with his potent stare, she waited until she'd rounded a corner before doing a triumphant jig.

She'd done it. Scored an interview with the high-and-mighty CEO of the company threatening to tear her family's land apart.

An interview she had every intention of nailing.

The project to build luxury mansions out at Portsea would go ahead, she had no illusions about that, but the moment she'd heard about it she'd headed back to Melbourne with the sole intention of ensuring Devlin Corp didn't botch the beachside land she'd always loved.

Crazy, when she had no room for sentiment in her life these days, but that land had been special, the only place she'd ever felt truly comfortable in her topsy-turvy teenage world.

It was her dad's lasting legacy. A legacy her mum had upped and sold without consulting her.

Her neck muscles spasmed when she thought of her immaculately coiffed mother, who valued grooming and designer clothes and social standing, a mother who had barely acknowledged her after her dad died.

Though she'd never doubted Coral's love for her dad, she'd often wondered why the society princess had married a cabinet-maker. While her folks had seemed devoted enough, Gemma hadn't been able to see the attraction. Her dad had spent his days holed up in his workshop while Mum attended charity events or garden parties.

No surprise how Coral had viewed her passion for mudpies, slugs and rats as pets. Though she had to give her mum credit: she'd never stopped her from being a tomboy, from trailing after her dad like an apprentice. They hadn't had a lot in common but they'd been a close family; it hadn't been till later, when she'd turned fourteen and her dad had died, that a yawning chasm had developed, a distance they hadn't breached since.

People started filtering from the ballroom into the annexe and she bit back a grin. She'd bet Mr Conservative was hovering over his precious display, ensuring she hadn't scratched it with her chains.

Laughter bubbled up from within and she slapped a hand across her mouth to prevent a giggle escaping. The look on Rory Devlin's face when he'd caught sight of her chained to his display…priceless didn't come close.

She'd hazard a guess no one ever stood up to the guy. He had an air of command; when he snapped his fingers people would hop to it.

She'd been counting on the element of surprise, had wanted to railroad her way into an interview to show him exactly who he was dealing with.

Her toes cramped and she slipped out of the three-inch heels she hadn't worn in two years: the last time she'd been home and her mother had insisted she attend a charity ball for sick kids.

She couldn't fault the cause, but having to swap her denim for chiffon and work boots for stilettos had been unbearable. Though she'd been thankful she'd kept the outfit, for no way would she have gained access to the Devlin Corp shindig unless she'd looked the part.

She'd timed her entrance to perfection, waiting until a large group bearing invitations had gathered at the door before inveigling her way in by tagging along.

No one had questioned her. Why would they, when her mum would have forked out a small fortune for her blue designer dress and matching shoes?

The rest had been easy, and with her objective achieved she almost skipped down to the car park where she'd left the battered car she'd picked up from the airport earlier today.

She had no idea how long she'd be in town for, no idea how long it would take to ensure her dad's land wasn't pillaged by the corporate giant.

For now, the ancient VW would have to do. As for lodgings, she had one destination in mind.

Come first thing in the morning she'd confront Coral, demanding answers—like what had possessed her mum to sell the one place in the world she valued most?

Gemma awoke to the pale pink fingers of a Melbourne dawn caressing her face and a scuttling in the vicinity of her feet.

She yawned, stretched, and unkinked her neck stiff from sleeping on her balled-up jacket, squinting around her dad's workshop for the culprit tap-dancing near her toes.

Noise was good. Noise meant scrabbling mice or a curious possum. It was the silent scuttlers—like spiders—she wasn't too keen on. She might be a tomboy but arachnids she could do without.

A flash of white darted under the workbench and she

smiled. How many times had her pet mice got loose in here? Too many times to count, considering she'd left the door open to let them have a little freedom.

Her dad had never complained. He'd spent eons searching for them, affectionately chastising her while promising to buy new ones if Larry, Curly and Mo couldn't be found.

Her dad had been the best, and she missed him every second of every day. He'd died too young, his heart giving out before she'd graduated high school, before she'd obtained her environmental science degree, before she'd scored her first job with a huge fishing corporation in Western Australia.

Her dad had been her champion, had encouraged her tomboy ways, had shown her how to fish and catch bugs and varnish a handmade table.

He'd fostered her love of the ocean, had taught her about currents and erosion and natural coastal processes. He'd taken her snorkelling and swimming every weekend during summer, introducing her to seals and dolphins and a plethora of underwater wildlife she hadn't known existed.

They'd gone to the footy and the cricket together, had cycled around Victoria and, her favourite, camped out under the stars on his beachside land at Portsea.

The land her mum had sold to Rory Devlin and Co.

Tears of anger burned the backs of her eyes but she blinked them away. Crying wouldn't achieve a thing. Tears were futile when the only place she'd ever felt safe, content and truly at home had been ripped away. The only place where she could be herself, no questions asked, away from scrutinising stares and being found lacking because she wasn't like other girls her age.

She'd dealt with her grief at losing her dad, and now

she'd have to mourn the loss of their special place too. Not fair.

As she glanced around the workshop, at her dad's dust-covered tools, the unfinished garden bench he'd been working on when he died, his tool-belt folded and stored in its usual spot by the disused garden pots, her resolve hardened.

Now the land was gone, memories were all she had left. They'd been a team. He'd loved her for who she was. She owed him.

Unzipping her sleeping bag, she wriggled out of it and glanced at her watch. 6:00 a.m. Good. Time for her mum to get a wake-up call in more ways than one.

To her surprise, Coral answered the door on the first ring.

'Gemma? What a lovely surprise.'

Coral opened the door wider and ushered her in, but not before her sweeping glance took in Gemma's crushed leisure suit that had doubled as pyjamas, her steel-capped boots and her mussed hair dragged into a ponytail.

As for last night's make-up, which she'd caked on as part of her ruse, she could only imagine the panda eyes she'd be sporting.

A little rattled her mum hadn't commented on her appearance, or the early hour, she clomped inside and headed for the kitchen, about the only place in their immaculate South Yarra home she felt comfortable in.

'You're up early.'

Coral stiffened, before busying herself with firing up the espresso machine. 'I don't sleep much these days.'

'Insomnia?'

'Something like that.'

A flicker of guilt shot through her. She remembered her mum pacing in the middle of the night after her dad had died, but she'd been too wrapped up in her own grief to worry.

That was when the first chink in their relationship had appeared.

Coral had always been self-sufficient and capable and in control, and she had handled Karl's death with her usual aplomb. While she'd cried herself to sleep each night for the first few months, her mum would stride around the house at all hours, dusting and tidying and ensuring her home was a showpiece.

It had been a coping mechanism, and when the pacing had eventually stopped she'd thought Coral had finally adjusted to sleeping alone, but considering the early hour and the fact her mum was fully dressed, maybe her sleep patterns had been permanently shot?

'Coffee?'

Gemma nodded. 'Please.'

'Have you come straight from a work site?'

There it was: the first foray into critical territory, a territory Gemma knew too well. How many times had she borne her mum's barbs after her dad died?

Have you washed your hair?

Can't you wear a dress for once?

No boy's going to ask a tomboy to the graduation ball.

She'd learned to tune out, and with every dig she'd hardened her heart, pretending she didn't care while wishing inside she could be the kind of daughter Coral wanted.

'I actually got in last night.'

Coral's hand stilled midway between the sugar bowl and the mug. 'Why didn't you stay here?'

'I did. I bunked down in Dad's workshop.'

Horror warred with distaste before Coral blinked and assumed her usual stoical mask. 'You always did feel more comfortable out there.'

'True.'

Gemma could have sworn her mum's shoulders slumped before she resumed bustling around the kitchen.

Why did you do it? It buzzed around her head, the question demanding to be asked, but she knew better than to bail Coral up before her first caffeine hit of the day. She'd clam up or storm off in a huff, and that wouldn't cut it—not today. Today she needed answers.

'How long are you here for?'

As long as it takes to whip Rory Devlin's butt into shape.

Devlin's butt...bad analogy.

An image of dark blue eyes the colour of a Kimberley sky at night flashed into her mind, closely followed by the way he'd filled out his fancy-schmancy suit, his slick haircut, his cut-glass cheekbones.

At six-four he had the height to command attention, but the rest of the package sold it. The guy might be a cold-hearted, infuriating, corporate shark who cared for nothing bar the bottom dollar but, wow, he packed some serious heat.

She hated the fact she'd noticed.

'I'm here for a job.'

She sighed with pleasure as the first tantalising waft of roasted coffee beans hit her.

Watching her mum carefully for a reaction, she added, 'Out at Portsea.'

Coral's head snapped up, her eyes wide with fear. 'You know?'

'That you sold out? That you got rid of the one thing that meant everything to Dad?'

To me?

She slid off the bar stool and slammed her palms on the island bench. 'Of course I know.'

'I—I was going to tell you—'

'When? When I returned to Melbourne to build my dream home on that land? The home Dad helped me plan years ago? The home where I'd planned on raising my kids?'

Okay, so the latter might be stretching the truth a tad. She had no intention of getting married, let alone having kids, but the inner devastation she kept hidden enjoyed stabbing the knife of guilt and twisting hard.

Coral's lips compressed into the thin, unimpressed line she'd seen many times growing up. 'Sorry you feel that way, but you can't bowl in here every few years, stay for a day, and expect to know every detail of my life.'

Shock filtered through Gemma's astonishment. She had *every* right to know what happened to her dad's land, but she'd never heard Coral raise her voice above a cultured *tsk-tsk* if they didn't agree.

'I'm not asking for every detail, just the important ones—like why you had to sell something that meant the world to me.'

Fear flickered across Coral's expertly made-up face before she turned away on the pretext of pouring coffee.

'I—I needed the money.'

She spoke so softly Gemma strained to hear it.

Coral—who wore the best clothes, used the most expensive cosmetics and lunched out daily—needed money?

'You've got to be kidding me,' she muttered, sorrow and regret clogging her lungs, making simple inhalation impossible.

She wanted to explain why this meant so much to her, wanted her mum to understand how she'd travelled the world for years, never feeling as sheltered as she did at Portsea.

She wanted her mum to truly comprehend the vulnerabilities behind her tough-girl exterior, the deep-seated need for approval she'd deliberately hidden beneath layers of practised indifference.

She wanted her mum to realise her anger was about the loss of another childhood security rather than not being consulted.

She opened her mouth to speak but the words wouldn't come. Not after all this time. Not after the consistent lack of understanding her mum had shown when she'd been growing up. Why should now be any different?

When Coral turned around to face her she'd donned her usual frosty mask.

'I don't question your financials; I'd expect the same courtesy from you.' Coral handed her some coffee with a shaky hand, making a mockery of her poise. 'You're welcome to stay here as long as you like, no questions asked, because this is your home. But I won't tolerate being interrogated like a criminal.'

Instinctively Gemma bristled—until she realised something. She valued her independence, lived her own life and answered to no one. Including the mother she rarely visited. How would *she* feel if Coral landed on her doorstep demanding answers to sticky questions? She'd be royally peed off.

Some of the fight drained out of her and she gave a brisk nod, hiding behind her coffee mug. Besides, the damage was done. The land was sold and nothing could change that. She'd be better off focussing on things she could control, like ensuring Devlin Corp respected the beach while they built their mansion monstrosities.

'There's a spare key behind the fruit bowl.' Coral patted her sleek blond bob, an out-of-place, self-conscious gesture at odds with her air of understated elegance. 'I know we haven't always seen eye to eye, Gemma, but I'm glad you're here.'

By the time she'd recovered from her shock and whispered, 'Thanks…' Coral had sailed out of the room.

CHAPTER THREE

RORY flipped the rough-textured business card between his fingers. Recycled paper, no doubt, but there was nothing second-hand about the information staring him in the face.

He'd had the company's PI run a background check on Gemma Shultz last night, after she'd thrust her business card in his hand and exited his display like a queen.

He had to admit the results of the investigation surprised him as much as the woman had last night. She wasn't some crackpot lobbyist, hell-bent on delaying his project or, worse, ruining it.

Gemma Shultz was the real deal.

He ran his finger down the list: qualified as an environmental scientist at Melbourne University, spent a year at a major fishing company in Western Australia, specialising in marine conservation, two years working for a beachside developer in Spain, and the last few years freelancing for seaside construction companies keen on energy-saving and protecting the planet.

Impressive.

Not a hint of scandal among the lot: no throwing herself in front of bulldozers, no chaining herself to trees, no arrests for spray-painting corporate headquarters or flinging paint at fur-wearers.

Thank goodness. Bad enough she'd blackmailed him into giving her an interview. The last thing he needed was for the media to get a whiff of anything untoward.

His dad had done enough while he'd been in charge, gracing the covers of magazines and the front pages of newspapers with a constant parade of high-profile women while living the high life.

It was a pity Cuthbert Devlin—Bert, to his friends, and there had been many hangers-on—had been more focussed on squandering money than on running the company entrusted to him.

Rory shuddered to think what would have happened if Bert hadn't abdicated in favour of chasing some model to Europe, though he had a fair idea.

Devlin Corp would have been driven into the ground and his grandfather's monumental efforts in building the company from scratch would have been for nought. And what *he'd* been trained to do from his teens would have meant nothing.

He still couldn't understand why Bishop Devlin had handed the reins to his recalcitrant son—not when he'd been groomed for the job for so long. Until his grandfather had explained he needed to give Bert a chance to prove himself, to see if his son was made of sterner stuff.

Rory loved his dad, faults and all, but he couldn't understand why anyone would pass up the opportunity of a lifetime to run a major company.

A small part of him had been glad his dad had botched the top job, because he'd known it was only a matter of time till he got his chance. Now he had that chance no way would he let anything derail him—including a smart-mouthed, intelligent environmental scientist with seawater in her blood.

His intercom beeped and he hit the answer button. 'Yes, Denise?'

'Gemma Shultz to see you.'

'Send her in.'

He threw her business card into the dossier and snapped it shut. Armed with more information than last night, he was prepared for a confrontation: on *his* terms. When the sassy blonde sauntered through his door he'd be ready.

Until the moment his door opened, she stepped into his office and his preparation of the last few minutes evaporated.

His gut inexplicably tightened at the sight of her in a staid black trouser suit and a basic white business shirt. Nothing basic about the way she wore it, though. The top two buttons were undone to reveal a hint of cleavage, and her fitted trousers accentuated her legs. Legs that ended with her feet stuck into work boots.

And what were those God-awful dangly things hanging from her ears? Dolphins? Whales? Burnished copper fashioned into cheap earrings that did nothing for her plain outfit.

His mouth twisted in amusement. Gemma Shultz was nothing if not original. She wore an off-the-rack outfit, no make-up, ugly shoes and horrid earrings. Yet she intrigued him.

He couldn't fathom it.

She'd blackmailed her way into this interview and that had had his back up from the start. He didn't like having his authority questioned, didn't like some upstart environmentalist bulldozing her way in with unethical tactics, but what made it infinitely worse was he couldn't for the life of him fathom why he'd agreed to this meeting.

What was it about this woman that had him so tetchy?

'We meet again.'

Rather than offering her hand for him to shake, she surprised him again by shrugging out of her jacket and draping it over the back of a chair, making herself completely at home. And making his hands clench with the effort not to yank it off the chair and insist she put it back on again, so he wouldn't have to notice the faint outline of a lace bra beneath the semi-transparent white cotton of her blouse.

Weren't environmentalists supposed to wear hessian sacks and hemp bracelets and dreadlocks?

Annoyed at his reaction, he mentally slashed her interview allotment by five minutes. The sooner he got rid of her, the sooner he could get back to what he did best. Building the best luxury homes Melbourne had ever seen.

'Considering your tactics last night, you left me no choice.'

A smug smile curved her lips, and in that moment he knew that whatever came of this meeting Gemma Shultz could become the bane of his existence if he let her.

'I half expected you not to follow through on your promise of an interview.'

'I always keep my promises.'

He crossed his arms, recognised his defensiveness, and immediately uncrossed them. Only to find his hands itching to reach across the desk and see if her hair felt as silky-soft as it looked.

Damn, what was *wrong* with him?

She was nothing like the perfectly polished women he dated, with their trendy fashions and manicures and cleverly highlighted hair. Women who wouldn't be caught dead in a cheap suit and work boots. Women who wore diamonds for earrings, not copper marine life. Why the irrational buzz of attraction?

'Your fifteen minutes has been cut to ten. Start talking.'

Unfazed by his curtness, she pointed to his computer. 'By now I'm sure you've researched me and found a virtual plethora of information. So how about we skip the formalities and cut to the chase?'

Intrigued by her forwardness, he nodded. 'Which is?'

'I want you to hire me for the Portsea project.'

'And I want to buy the island next to Richard Branson's—but, hey, we don't always get what we want.'

Her eyes narrowed at his levity.

'I'm the best in the business. Give me a month on the project and I'll ensure every home you build is energy-efficient while maintaining viability in the surrounding environment and ensuring the beach is protected.'

'I've already had consultants look over the project—'

'Hacks.'

She leaned forward and planted her palms on his desk, her chest temptingly at eye level.

'You're a smart man. You know in the construction business it's the bottom dollar that counts. That beach? Last on the priority list. Which is why you need me. I incorporate scientific knowledge with environmental *nous.*' She straightened, shrugged. 'I'm a specialist in the marine field. You'd be a fool not to hire me.'

After the public debacle his father had made of the Port Douglas project, the company and himself, if there was one thing guaranteed to push his buttons it was being seen as stupid.

He stood so fast his chair slammed into the filing cabinet behind him, and he leaned across his desk—within strangling reach.

'I can assure you, Miss Shultz, I'm no fool. You've had your say. Please leave.'

She didn't recoil or flinch or bat an eyelid and his admiration notched further.

'Not till you've interviewed me.'

She sat, crossed her legs and rested her clasped hands on one knee.

'You promised me an interview so start asking questions.'

Stunned by her audacity, he shook his head. 'I can call Security.'

'You won't.'

Her blue eyes grew stony as she met his stonewalling gaze head-on. 'I've done my research too. You're new to this job. You want the best for Devlin Corp. Let's cut the small talk and use my remaining minutes here wisely.'

He fell into his seat and rubbed his forehead, where the beginnings of a headache were stirring.

Fine, he'd play this her way. He'd go through her little game for the next five minutes, then he'd personally escort her out and slam the door on headstrong, pushy women once and for all.

'Why don't you go ahead and tell me why a successful, headhunted, environmental scientist who has worked around the world wants to work on a Devlin Corp project?'

For the first time since she'd strutted in he glimpsed uncertainty as she tugged on an earring, before she quickly masked it with a toss of her hair.

'I like to diversify. The size of a project isn't important to me. It's the probable impact on the surrounding environment. And the Portsea project captured my attention for that reason.'

Her eyes glittered with unexpected fervour as she sat forward, her hands waving around to punctuate her words. 'Portsea's a gorgeous spot. Beaches along the Mornington Peninsula are special. You can't just dump a fancy-schmancy housing development in the middle of it and hope for the best.'

Increasingly frustrated that she saw him as some dollar-grabbing corporate raider, he had to cut this short.

'Contrary to your belief, Devlin Corp doesn't *dump* anything. When we take on a project of this magnitude we do extensive environmental studies—'

'Done by consultants. So you've said.'

She waved away his explanation, leaving him gob-smacked for the second time in twenty-four hours.

'I'm not besmirching your company's reputation. All I'm asking for is forty-eight hours to head out to the site, collate my findings and present them to you.'

'That's all?'

She ignored his sarcasm, beaming as if he'd agreed to share CEO duties with her.

'I promise you won't regret it.'

'I already do,' he muttered, thinking he must be mad to contemplate giving in to her demands.

But something she'd said rang true: he'd hired consultants previously used by his dad, and while he couldn't fault their findings he had to admit environmental outcomes weren't his area of expertise.

The consultants presented their findings, he went ahead with the project regardless, and while no red flags had jumped out at him, how well had the consultants studied how the land lay, so to speak?

He had an expert in the field sitting in front of him, offering her services for two days. Businesswise, he'd be a fool to pass up expertise of that magnitude. Personally, he wanted to boot her out before she coerced him into anything else.

'What do you say?' She held up two fingers. 'Two days is all I'm asking for.'

'If I agree to this—' her grin widened and he held up a hand to rein her in '—and it's a big *if* at this stage, how much are you charging?'

She leaned forward as if to impart some great secret. 'For you? Free.'

He reared back. He'd learned from a young age that if something looked too good to be true it usually was.

'What's the catch?'

She shrugged. 'No catch.'

He glimpsed a flicker of uncertainty in her eyes, the pinch around her mouth, the fiddle with her earring.

'Here's the deal. If you tell me the truth about why this is so important to you, I'll give you two days.'

She paled and he almost felt guilty for holding her over a barrel. Almost. For all the grief she'd put him through he should rejoice he'd finally gained the upper hand. No one got the better of him, but in twenty-four hours this woman had come close.

Indecision warred with yearning, before she finally sagged into her chair, the fight drained out of her.

'My family owned that land.'

There she went again, flooring him without trying.

'We bought it from the Karl Trust.'

She gnawed on her bottom lip. Her vulnerability was softening the hard shell he'd erected around his heart. Not from any grand passion gone wrong but for the simple reason he didn't have the time or inclination for a relationship.

He dated extensively, squiring women to corporate events and charity balls and the theatre. But dating and getting involved in a relationship were worlds apart and he liked to keep it that way. He had one love in his life—Devlin Corp—and it suited him fine.

'Karl Shultz was my dad. The land had been in his

family for a few generations, in trust. It meant a lot to us—him.'

Her slip-up told him all he needed to know. This land had personal value to her, which made him wonder why she'd let it be sold in the first place. Financial liability, most likely, but it wasn't his place to question her personal status.

'I get it. This land meant something to you and you want to ensure it's treated right.'

She clasped her hands so tight her knuckles stood out. Her reluctance to discuss anything deeper than superficialities was obvious.

'Something like that.'

She clamped her lips shut to stop herself from saying more but he'd heard enough.

'I'm a stand-up guy, Miss Shultz, and I value honesty. Especially in business.'

He held out his hand for her to shake. 'You've got yourself forty-eight hours to do your worst.'

Her answering smile made something unfamiliar twang in his chest.

'Thanks, you won't regret it.'

She placed her hand in his, her callused fingers skirting along his palm and creating a frisson of electricity that disturbed him as much as the urge to hold on longer.

'And call me Gemma. I have a feeling we'll be seeing a lot more of each other before this project is through.'

He opened his mouth to correct her, to reiterate it was two days only, but as she shook his hand and smiled at him as if he'd announced she'd won the lottery he couldn't help but think seeing more of her might not be such a bad thing after all.

CHAPTER FOUR

As THE elevator doors slid open on the ground floor, and Gemma stepped into the elaborate glass-and-chrome foyer of Devlin Corp, she wrinkled her nose. The place was lit up like a Christmas tree, despite the gorgeous sun outside, and she'd hazard a guess those lights weren't dimmed at night. What a waste of electricity.

Not to mention the fancy flyers lying in discreet piles on strategically placed tables—way to go with conserving trees—and enough water coolers to irrigate an entire African village.

Maybe once she'd finished with the Portsea project good old Rory would let her overhaul his business.

Considering his perpetually bemused expression whenever she was around, she doubted it.

Exiting the glass monstrosity, she skipped down the marble stairs onto bustling Collins Street.

She'd hustled her way into that interview using bold tactics, and she intended on continuing to bombard Mr Conservative from left field.

He'd read up on her, from that folder sitting in front of him that he'd tried to slide under a pile of documents when she'd entered.

She'd expected nothing less from a go-get-'em businessman in his position, but he'd surprised her with his intuition. He'd picked up on why the land was important to her and laid out a little blackmail of his own.

He'd left her no choice but to come clean about her reasons for wanting to be involved, but rather than criticism she'd seen understanding in those perceptive blue eyes.

He'd understood. Surprising. It made her like him a tad. Enough to wonder why a rich, successful, good-looking guy in his early thirties—her research had been thorough too—wasn't engaged or married or in a relationship.

She'd seen only a few internet hits of him in the glossies or newspapers. A guy like him should have had loads printed in the gossip columns, but there'd been surprisingly little bar a few pictures of the requisite arm-candy blondes/brunettes/redheads—stick-thin women in *haute couture* accompanying him to various corporate events.

For the CEO of Australia's biggest luxury property developer, she'd expected more enlightening hits. Interesting.

As she threaded her way through the corporate suits rushing down Collins Street, with everyone in a great hurry to get where they needed to be, she took the time to look around. It had been years since she'd strolled through her home city. Her flying visits usually consisted of work and a quick obligatory visit with her mum.

As much as she loved Melbourne's beautiful gardens and trams and café culture, she'd never really felt at ease here. Attending a private girls' high school had exacerbated her alien feelings. She'd had few friends once the girls had discovered she enjoyed windsurfing and rock-climbing and camping more than sleepovers and manicures and make-up.

Throw in her love of physics and chemistry over art and literature, of participating in soccer games rather than tittering on the sidelines watching the local boys' school, and her classmates' shunning had been ensured.

She'd pretended she didn't care—had blissfully retreated to Portsea on the weekends, where she could truly be herself in a non-judgemental environment that nourished rather than criticized. But after her dad died and her relationship with her mum went pear-shaped, the insecurities her mother fed at home had festered at school, leaving her emotionally segregated from everyone.

She'd learned to shelter her emotions and present a blasé front to the world. A front that thankfully had held up in Rory Devlin's intimidating presence and gained her an opportunity to pitch. She had complete confidence in her abilities and knew once he'd heard her presentation he'd hire her.

Besides, she thought he had a soft spot. She'd seen the shift from cool businessman to reluctantly interested when she'd mentioned her family had owned the Portsea land. Who would've thought the guy had a heart? It humanised him and she didn't like that. Didn't like how it added to his appeal. He was a means to an end, nothing more.

The fact she hadn't been on a date in months had to be the reason she'd noticed how his eyes reminded her of a Santorini sky, how his lips would tempt a nun to fantasise.

When they'd shaken hands her fingers had tingled with the residual zap, making her wonder what he'd do with those strong, masterful hands in the throes of passion.

Not good to be thinking along those lines. Not good at all.

She loved her job, threw herself into it one hundred percent, but moving from place to place had consequences: she didn't have time to form attachments to any guy.

If she were completely honest, she didn't have the inclination either. She socialised—dinner, drinks, the occasional movie—but no one had captured her attention for longer than a few dates. Leading a transient life suited her. Moving on to the next job site gave her the perfect excuse to not get emotionally involved.

Garett, her regular date for functions in London, had accused her of being deliberately detached, of putting up barriers against a deeper relationship. Probably true. She'd switched to a new date for the next business dinner.

She'd mulled over her reluctance to pursue a long-term relationship at length, and while it suited her to blame her work, she knew deep down she wanted what her mum had had: the complete love of a man who adored and one hundred percent accepted you.

Her dad had been patient, kind, generous with his time and affection, and completely non-judgemental. He had been the one person who truly understood her, and once he'd died her mum's rejection had only served to increase her feelings of being an outcast.

The emotional walls she'd erected had been deliberate, a coping mechanism at the time, but they'd become such an ingrained part of her she didn't know how to lower them. Or didn't want to.

Letting a guy get too close, opening herself up to possible rejection again? Uh-uh. She might be many things, but a masochist wasn't one of them. Better to push them away before they shut her out. She'd learned that the hard way.

She had a brilliant job she adored, a freedom envied by her married colleagues, and the ocean—a place she could immerse and lose herself anywhere in the world. Why risk all that? No guy was worth it, not in her experience.

That buzz she'd experienced when Rory had shaken her hand? Nothing more than static from the posh rug in his office.

She bumped into a businessman, who shot her a filthy glare, and she apologised, sidestepped and picked up the pace, obliterating thoughts of a handsome millionaire—the least likely guy she'd be attracted to.

Rory stood on the crest and surveyed the endless indigo ocean stretching to the horizon.

Gemma's place.

That was how he'd started thinking of this stretch of beach, and he shook his head. He didn't have room for sentimentality in his life, and certainly not in his business, but there was something about her never-say-die attitude in regards to this land that plucked at his heartstrings.

She'd gone to extreme lengths to gain his attention, and while he didn't approve of her methods he couldn't fault her enthusiasm. This place meant a lot to her. He'd granted her request to provide him with assessment findings to humour her, but he had to admit he was curious. Curious about her scientific skills, curious about her work ethic, and curious about what she'd do once he vetoed her findings.

The project was ready to go, excavation set to commence in a month, and he had every intention of getting it done on time. Houses were sold, shareholders had invested, sub-contractors had been hired. Amendments were doable at this stage, but anything else she might come up with? Pie-in-the-sky dreams.

A gunshot made him jump and he whirled around, squinting at the road where it had come from. When a dented pale blue VW rolled over the hill, and backfired again before pulling up next to his Merc in a cloud of dust, he stifled a grin.

Of course she'd drive a beat-up old banger; though how environmentally safe a car like that was remained debatable.

She tumbled out of the car, all long denim-clad legs and red jumper, a gaudy floral scarf fluttering in the wind and her plait unravelling as she hurried towards him.

'Sorry I'm late.'

He jerked a thumb in the direction of the vehicle. 'Car trouble?'

'How'd you guess?'

'That thing belongs in a museum. Where'd you get it? Rent-a-Bomb?'

She blushed.

'You know the emissions from that can't be good for the environment?'

It was like waving a chainsaw in front of a greenie.

She squared her shoulders, her eyes flashing blue fire. 'Considering some of us aren't flush with funds like other people—' her scathing glare encompassed him and the Merc '—we make do with what we've got.'

He opened his mouth to respond and she held up a finger.

'As it so happens, they had nothing else available. Once I know how long I'm in town for I'll be chasing up something more suitable. Satisfied?'

'Immensely.'

Her eyes narrowed at his tongue-in-cheek response, but before she could flay him again he gestured to the land.

'How long since you've been here?'

'Five years.'

Her wistful sigh cut through his distraction.

'That's a long time to stay away from home.'

She angled her head away from him, but not before he'd glimpsed fleeting pain.

'Work keeps me pretty busy.'

'Same here.'

He knew exactly how many years she'd worked overseas, but hearing her audible regret only exacerbated his curiosity. If she loved her job so much, her regret must be personal. He'd bet some jerk had done a number on her.

'Melbourne doesn't hold good memories for you?'

She reared back as if he'd poked her in the eye. 'What makes you think that?'

'Your time spent away, your defensiveness.'

He expected her to clam up. So of course she did the opposite, surprising him yet again.

'There's nothing much left for me here any more.'

She sank onto a nearby log, resting her elbows on her knees, her chin on her hands. He eyed the log warily and she raised an eyebrow at his pause.

'No bull-ants, no spiders—nothing to bite your butt.'

She blushed again, the faint pink staining her cheeks highlighting the blueness of her eyes, making him forget his five-thousand-dollar suit as he sat just to be close to her.

'Bad break-up?'

She shook her head, the addictive fragrance of spring mornings and sunshine he'd smelt when they'd first met wafting over him.

'Uh-uh. I just don't fit in here.'

'What about family?'

'My mum lives in South Yarra. We catch up occasionally. It's been five years since I've been to the beach here, but I made a flying visit to Melbourne two years ago and saw Mum then.'

She made it sound as if she'd flown in to have a root canal.

'You don't get on?'

'Something like that.' Her hand gestured to the vista before them in an all-encompassing sweep. 'She never understood how special this place was. My dad and I used to camp here. We did a lot of stuff together…'

She trailed off and for one horrifying moment he thought she might cry. He didn't do tears, didn't know how to offer comfort, and he rushed on.

'I take it you didn't know she'd sold the land?'

'No.'

That one syllable held so much regret and rawness and retribution he almost felt guilty for delving.

'This means a lot to you.'

'You think?'

Her sarcasm, tinged with sadness, made him wish he hadn't probed for answers. If he'd kept this on a purely business level he wouldn't be feeling like the grinch that stole Christmas.

When it came to business, he didn't have time for a conscience. He didn't feel anything other than soul-deep satisfaction that he was doing what he'd been groomed to do: preserve his family legacy.

That was when it hit him.

Their situations were reversed. He'd been given an opportunity to continue his family legacy, to make it flourish, to stamp his flair, to make his mark.

How would he feel if his dad had run Devlin Corp into the ground or, worse, sold it off to the highest bidder? He'd be gutted. That was exactly how Gemma would be feeling.

'You came home especially for this, didn't you?'

'Yep.'

'You know I can't retract the sale or stop the project from going ahead?'

The moment the words spilled out of his mouth he wondered where they'd come from. He didn't owe her any explanations, but something in her defeated posture tugged.

'I wouldn't expect you to,' she said, derision curling her upper lip. 'I'm not some charity case.' She swivelled to face him, then fired back, 'You're a hard-headed businessman. I get it. All this? Gone. But if I can preserve one iota of this beauty, maybe the people who live here will appreciate it as much as we did.'

She ended on a little hitch of breath and leaped to her feet, dusting off a butt moulded temptingly by denim.

'Now, let's get to it.'

He stood, and before he'd realised what he was doing he placed a comforting hand on her shoulder.

'I'm willing to hear your ideas and keep an open mind.'

She allowed his hand to linger for a few long, tension-fraught seconds before she shrugged it off.

'Thanks. That's all I ask.'

She switched into business mode, the contrast intriguing him as much as her steely determination underlined with a thread of vulnerability.

He'd never met anyone like her.

The businesswomen he worked with were only intent on climbing the corporate ladder, while the women he dated were poised, polished and excessively cool.

They never fought for a cause or were passionate about what they believed in. They didn't care about the environment unless a passing shower ruined their blow-dried perfection. They rarely wore skinny jeans or paisley scarves.

They were nothing like Gemma.

'The marine ecosystems in Port Phillip Bay need to

be preserved.' Her eyes narrowed as they swept the horizon. 'Human-induced environmental changes, such as the mansions you're proposing to build along here, can contribute to the breakdown of sustainability.'

Although impressed by the passion shining in her eyes, he kept his tone light. 'You're trying to dazzle me with scientific speak.'

Her glare made him wish he'd kept his mouth shut.

'See these dunes below us? Destroying the vegetation in sand dunes lets the wind blow them away, increasing the coast's vulnerability to erosion.' She pointed to the scrubby bush a few feet in front of them. 'If you're building mansions behind us, you'll probably construct a sea wall along here.' She shook her head. 'Bad move. Seriously bad move. A sea wall built along a beach only protects the landward property, but ruins the beach by isolating sand behind the wall from the active beach system. This eventually leads to serious erosion problems, and eventually no beach exists in front of the wall…'

Her voice faded but her eyes had lost none of their spark as they pinned him with ferocious accusation.

'If this beach were left to erode naturally, without a sea wall, it would always be here.'

And her dad's legacy would last for ever. She didn't have to say it. It was evident in every line of her rigid body: in her defensive stance, her crossed arms, her upthrust chin daring him to disagree.

Her fervour, her passion for her cause was staggering.

'No sea wall. Got it.'

One eyebrow arched in imperious disbelief. 'You're mocking me?'

Considering he'd noticed her clenched fists, he wouldn't dare. 'Honestly? Your dedication is impressive but plans are in place, houses are sold, this project is going ahead.'

With or without your approval. It was a comment he wisely confined to his head.

'Houses? Don't you mean luxury mansions worth millions? Millions designed to make your precious company mega-wealthy.'

'You of all people know what land prices are worth along here. I'm just doing what any developer would do.'

'Yeah, plunder the land,' she muttered, her sagging shoulders the first sign of defeat.

'Construction is going ahead.' Feeling sorry for her, he softened his tone. 'What would you suggest to facilitate environmental conscientiousness?'

He listened carefully as she outlined her plans for solar panels and double glazing and toilets flushed by tank water, trying not to be distracted as the wind toyed with the strands escaping her ponytail and flushed her cheeks.

When she'd finished, she stared at him with an eyebrow raised in question.

'What do you think?'

'Collate your ideas, back them up with documented research and be ready to present to my project managers day after tomorrow.'

Her eyes widened in disbelief. 'You mean it?'

'I'm not in the habit of saying things I don't mean—'

She cut him off by flinging herself at him and wrapping her arms around his neck, that infernal scarf smacking him in the face.

He floundered, propriety dictating he unwind her arms and set her back, so as not to blur their business relationship. But by the time his brain processed what he should do it was too late.

His arms slid around her of their own volition, savouring her soft curves and the way she fitted into him.

He knew it was wrong, knew he shouldn't do it, but he

rested his cheek on the top of her head, buried his nose in her hair and inhaled, committing the fresh outdoor scent he'd associate with her for ever to memory.

For ever?

It was the reality check he needed, and he quickly eased away, grateful when she laughed off their embrace as if it meant nothing.

'Guess you can't fault me for exuberance.'

His terse nod belittled the special moment they'd shared and he glanced at his car, desperate to extract himself from an already precarious situation. One more moment in her 'exuberant' company and goodness knew what he'd do.

'Thanks for meeting me out here. I'll have that presentation ready for you.'

'Ring Denise and she'll schedule a time.'

'Great.'

He made a grand show of glancing at his watch, when in fact time meant nothing and he'd much rather spend the afternoon here than listen to a bunch of builders drone on about material costs.

'You go.' Her face softened. 'I want to spend a few more minutes here.'

On her own.

He couldn't give her the land back but he could give her the privacy she craved.

'Sure, see you in a few days.'

'Count on it.'

She smiled, and this time something beyond scary twisted in the vicinity of his heart.

He did the only thing possible.

He bolted.

CHAPTER FIVE

GEMMA waited until the purr of Rory's Mercedes faded before she found the nearest ti-tree and banged her forehead against it. Repeatedly. It didn't help.

She'd hoped it might knock some sense into her—or, better, eradicate the memory of flinging herself at Rory.

What had she been *thinking?*

That was the problem; she hadn't been thinking. She'd been so blown away by his offer to present her recommendations to the project managers logic had fled and she'd been running on pure emotion.

When it came to this place it had always been about emotion, and that was what hurt the most: the fact her mum hadn't realised its importance in her life—the haven it had provided to an isolated teenager. Or if she had she'd upped and sold it without consulting her regardless.

She rubbed her forehead, her rueful wince tempered by the incredible view. How many times had she camped here with her dad? Pitching tents, cooking sausages over an open fire, roasting marshmallows. Everything had been an adventure because her dad had made it so. He hadn't berated her for not brushing her hair or not wearing a dress or not playing with dolls. Her dad had understood her, and standing here in their spot she missed him more than ever.

She inhaled the briny air, its familiar tang infusing her lungs, releasing some of her residual tension. She'd always been more relaxed here, more at home. From the distinctive ti-trees to the grassy fringes, from the pristine sand to the untamed ocean, she'd never felt anything other than comfortable here. It was a feeling she could never replicate anywhere else—a feeling of righteousness, of oneness, that had been ripped away by a mother who had never understood.

Another major head-slapping moment. She'd divulged some of her family history to Rory. She should have known the familiarity and contentment of being here would loosen her lips. Her inhibitions too, going by that cringeworthy hug.

Though it hadn't been all bad. While she'd been regretting her impulsiveness, and searching for a dignified way to extricate herself and laugh it off, he'd hugged her back. That had been a bigger surprise than his offer to let her present to the team.

Having his strong arms wrapped around her, being wedged against his firm body, her nose pressed into the side of the neck, where she'd breathed in his woodsy aftershave…after the first few seconds, when the shock had worn off, she'd reluctantly, irrationally, enjoyed it.

His common sense had kicked in first and she'd braced herself for awkwardness, been pleasantly surprised when they'd moved past the moment.

The guy kept astounding her, and if she wasn't careful he'd pull a bigger surprise and actually get her to lower her defences.

Not on her agenda—and certainly not with a corporate hotshot like him—but for a second, with the recent memory of his arms around her, it was nice to dream.

When Rory spied the daily newspaper in his stack of periodicals his heart sank.

His PA left a selection of current financial newspapers and magazines on his desk, refreshing them as needed, but she steered clear of newspapers featuring gossip columns.

Unless Devlin Corp had rated a mention he'd rather avoid.

Snatching it out of the stack, he laid it flat on his desk and flipped to the middle pages, his suspicions confirmed as he spied a half-page article, complete with picture, about his dad and his latest conquest—a statuesque redhead half his age.

The article, and the number of times he spied the words *Devlin Corp* at a glance, riled him.

Rubbing his forehead, he read the article: the usual drivel about his dad flying the redhead up to the Gold Coast for a whirlwind weekend of wining and dining, speculation whether she'd be the fifth Mrs Cuthbert Devlin, and questions raised over Bert's uncanny ability to fritter away the family fortune.

Rory's fingers convulsed, bunching the newspaper, as the journalists reiterated the fall of Devlin Corp under Bert's reign, rehashing the frequent overseas jaunts on the company jet, all-nighters at the casino and a birthday bash featuring international singing sensations and chefs and French champagne, while people who'd bought homes in a Devlin Corp project were left homeless when the company stalled.

The news vultures had even brought up the Port Douglas debacle, citing some protestor's quote about the rainforest and how big developers pillaged the land.

He hated having the mistakes of his father flung in his face.

With an angry growl he balled the newspaper and lobbed it into the bin, where it belonged.

It had been six months since he'd taken over—six months during which Devlin Corp had fulfilled its obligations and clawed its way back to the top of the property game.

Reading rubbish like that in the newspaper eradicated all his hard work and that of his dedicated employees. It sucked. Why couldn't they concentrate on all Devlin Corp had achieved in the last half year? The new communities built, the new homes, the new projects on the horizon.

The company needed positive publicity, not the same old, same old, from a bunch of journalistic hacks.

His gaze fell on the scrunched newspaper in the bin as the wheels slowly turned in his head.

Positive publicity...

The hacks kept on churning out the environmental angle as often as they reported Bert's latest arm candy. What if he gave the media a more upbeat focus for their Devlin Corp mentions, affirming the company's role in protecting the environment?

No more belittling or second-guessing or implying that Devlin Corp didn't care about anything but the almighty corporate dollar. No more dubious, inconclusive, unsubstantiated implications.

What he had in mind would ensure Devlin Corp came out looking like the company most likely to sponsor Greenpeace.

Maybe it had been fortuitous Gemma Shultz had bulldozed her way into his life? He had a bona fide environmental scientist muscling in on the Portsea Point project. Why not use that to his advantage?

Having her onboard for this project would raise the profile of his business while ensuring he wouldn't face the same problems his dad had had with the eco-warriors at Port Douglas.

Win-win all round.

A definite solution to the publicity problem.

Give the newshounds something constructive rather than destructive.

Clenching his fist in a victory salute, he glanced at the digital clock on his PC screen.

Time to see how Gemma performed for the project managers and if she had what it took to be the public face for his latest campaign.

Rory joined in the light applause as Gemma's pitch concluded.

For the last half-hour he'd watched her enchant his project managers, each and every one of the hardened building professionals falling under her enthusiastic and passionate spell.

The guys were putty in her hands, and as they vied for her attention on the pretext of asking questions he sat back, folded his arms, and studied her.

She'd pulled her hair back into a low ponytail today, every strand slicked into place, and the severity of the style accentuated her heart-shaped face and large blue eyes.

She wore no make-up bar a slick of lipgloss he'd hazard to guess had more to do with keeping her lips moist than any reverence to fashion. Her simple tan shift top skimmed to mid-thigh over matching trousers. An unremarkable outfit on a remarkable body. Not that he could see much of it in the drab get-up, but he'd felt it. The way her curves had pressed against him was burned into his memory.

He didn't like his gut twisting with unexpected need, so he focussed on another pair of ridiculous earrings—

orange starfish surrounded by a silver circle—taking the marine theme to extremes.

As she elaborated on costing for solar panels as an electricity source for all housing on the Portsea project, he pondered if she'd be right for the job he had in mind.

He wanted positive PR for Devlin Corp. But depending on Gemma to put a positive spin on his latest project…? Her commitment was undoubted, but no amount of prep work could ensure success.

Rory had aced everything he touched—from high school exams to his master's degree in economics. Not from any luck the universe had bestowed on him, but through sheer hard work and determination.

Nothing beat him. Ever. His grandfather said it was because his mum was an artist with her head in the clouds and his dad couldn't concentrate on anything for longer than five seconds, so he strove to be nothing like them.

Not a bad assumption. How his flaky parents had managed to connect longer than a minute to conceive him was unfathomable.

They'd split when he was young—his mum flitting to some hippy arty commune in California, his dad bedding every female within a hundred-mile radius.

Bert had the attention span of a hyperactive-gnat in both his personal and professional lives, but his generosity and conviviality and his zest for life made him lovable.

He tolerated his dad for those qualities, loved him in his own way, but the fact that Bert had nearly driven Devlin Corp into the ground only cemented what he already knew: rely on no one, trust no one. If he wanted a job done, best to roll up his sleeves and get it done.

Relying on someone else left him feeling strangely uncertain—a foreign feeling that didn't sit well with him.

'What do you think, Rory?'

He blinked like an owl awakening, embarrassed at being figuratively caught napping. Every occupant at the boardroom table stared at him, expecting an answer, while Gemma's disappointment slapped him across the face.

She thought he hadn't been listening. Way to go with getting her onside.

'I think the idea to have a marine conservation area as part of the community is an interesting one, but I'll have to ponder further. Time we adjourned.'

He stood and strode to the front of the room, placing a hand in the small of her back, noticing her slight stiffening.

'I'd like to thank Miss Shultz for her presentation today. It was enlightening.'

She straightened her shoulders at his praise and he lowered his voice. 'Wait in my office. I'll chat with the guys and you'll have a decision shortly.'

'You're considering this?'

If her eyebrows shot any higher they'd reach her hairline.

Touched by this rare show of vulnerability, he nodded. 'Great presentation. One of the best I've seen. The energy efficiency stuff sounds feasible, the marine proposal more complicated—but, yeah, I'm considering it.'

Her eyes sparkled with enthusiasm, and before he risked having her fling her arms around him in front of the team he gave her a gentle nudge in the direction of the door.

'I'm not making promises, because the team has to vote—'

'Cut the spiel. You're the boss. You get the deciding vote and we both know it.'

Amazed at her boldness, he nudged her again. 'Go wait for me.'

With a brisk nod, she picked up her portfolio and waved to the team. Before she took a step, she murmured under her breath, 'Just for the record, I wait for no man.'

'You'll wait for *me*.'

A spark in her eyes flared at his cockiness. He didn't care. He had to get the last word in, had to establish control after her über-professional presentation had left him nonplussed.

She strode for the door; he watched—along with ten pairs of wistful eyes. The married guys were wishing they weren't, the single guys were wishing they had a shot.

Like him.

Startled by the unwelcome thought, he moved to the front of the conference room. The faster he wrapped things up, the faster he could instigate the first stage of his PR plan.

Gemma paced the office, her toes cramping in the stupid high-heeled pumps she'd worn for the occasion. How women wore these torture devices she'd never know. Give her a pair of hiking boots any day.

She was playing a part today and the shoes were an essential item in her ensemble: the professional marine environmental scientist businesswoman, who knew her stuff, who could deliver on promises.

The project guys had eaten it up, but the one man she'd had to convince had appeared unmoved during the presentation.

Rory Devlin was one cool customer and she hated not being able to read him.

She'd tried, surreptitiously watching him while she extrapolated her data to the project managers. But his face had remained an impassive mask and to her horror he'd zoned out during question time.

Not good.

Whichever way the vote went, the moment he stepped into this office she'd have to give the pitch of her life to ensure her dad's legacy was well looked after.

This was it. Last ditch stand.

If she failed she'd have to pack up and ship out. Something she'd done many times over the years. It never fazed her, yet somehow this time the thought of leaving so soon after she'd arrived left her surprisingly morose.

Living out of a suitcase, moving from job site to job site, didn't bother her—but being back in Melbourne had triggered an emotional reaction she hadn't banked on.

It had to be the loss of the land. No matter how far and wide she travelled, she'd always had Portsea to come home to, secure in the knowledge it would always be there. The one place she could be herself, cosseted by fond memories and a feeling of belonging she never had elsewhere.

Losing that felt like losing a piece of her soul, and this unusual sentimentality had her more rattled than she cared to admit.

That was the moment Mr Conservative chose to stride into his office, impressive in his black pinstripe suit, white shirt and aubergine tie. She'd never gone for suits, but the way *he* filled one out she was sorely tempted to re-evaluate her preferences.

'You disappoint me.'

Her heart plummeted. 'How?'

'I expected you to be handcuffed to my desk at the very least.'

She managed a tight smile in relief. The fact he'd made a joke had to be a good sign.

'What's the verdict?'

He paused, his poker face driving her crazy as she shuffled her weight from foot to foot, impatience taking precedence over the annoying pinching of the infernal shoes.

When he finally looked her in the eye, she had her answer before he spoke.

'You're in.'

She let out an exalted whoop, her spontaneous happy dance, complete with hip swivel and shoulder shimmy, earning an amused lip quirk.

At least it was an improvement on flinging herself into his arms: she'd given herself a stern talking-to on that front. The memory of her *faux pas* had lingered way too long, popping into her head at inopportune moments, like last thing at night, first thing in the morning and at regular intervals throughout the day. Beyond annoying.

'On one condition.'

'Anything,' she said, buoyed by the fact he'd hired her to ensure her dad's beach was preserved in the construction phase, as well as ensuring the mansions he built were energy efficient and environmentally sound.

'Anything?'

He stepped into her personal space and her pulse took off like a rocket.

'You sure about that?'

Never one to back down from a challenge, she tilted her head to look him in the eye.

'Whatever it takes to get the job done.'

The sudden, unexpected flare of heat in his eyes caught her off guard and she eased back, only to have his hands shoot out and grip her arms.

The answering zing of electricity pinging through her body short-circuited her self-preservation mechanism—the one that warned standing this close to him, having him hold her, was tantamount to sticking her finger in a power point.

'You want to work on this project? Sell your ideas to the investors. They're the money men.'

His confident grin snatched her breath.

'Without their approval, my backing means nothing.'

Another pitch? Not a problem. She'd wowed the project managers, had convinced him. She could do this.

So why the clammy palms, fidgety fingers and tumbling tummy? Had to be his proximity. Hyper-awareness zapped between them, their bodies radiating enough heat to fuel the entire project.

She noticed small, inconsequential things—like a tiny mole beneath his left ear, a shaving nick along his jaw, an old scar near his right temple. Seeing his imperfections made him more accessible, leaving her seriously unnerved.

'I'll do it.'

She eased away and he released her, his expression inscrutable.

'Great. We leave tonight.'

'Pardon?'

'The investors are holding a golf tournament at the Sebel Heritage in the Yarra Valley. They're playing all day tomorrow, so if you want to make a pitch it'll have to be later tonight. They'll convene and give a decision tomorrow.'

'We're staying overnight?'

He nodded. 'Problem with that?'

His confident stance grated: legs apart, hands in pockets, shoulders squared. He held all the power—knew she'd have to do whatever he said if she wanted to nail this and have a say in how her dad's land was treated.

She didn't like over-confident men: their cockiness, their self-assurance that the world revolved around them. While Rory didn't come across as arrogant, he had total control over this situation and it irked, big time. Or was that because his aura of assurance made him slightly irresistible?

'No problem. E-mail me the details.' Gritting her teeth at being left no option, she forced a smile. 'What time do you want me there?'

'I'll pick you up.'

She opened her mouth to protest and he held up a hand.

'Doesn't make sense to drive down in separate cars. Surely car-pooling is more environmentally friendly?'

His mouth curved into a sardonic smile and her heart gave a strange *ka-thump.*

'Besides, you can prepare for your presentation on the way.'

Damn him for his perfectly logical, perfectly thoughtful reasons.

She didn't want to spend a few hours holed up with him in a car, didn't want to rely on him for anything. But she had to wow the investors, and honing her pitch made more sense than battling evening traffic in the decrepit rental.

His probing stare focussed on her ear, and she belatedly realised she'd been tugging on her earring. She hated showing a sign of nerves.

With a brisk nod, she hitched her portfolio under her arm.

'Okay, sounds like a plan.'

She didn't understand the triumphant glint in his eyes, and nor did she like it.

CHAPTER SIX

GEMMA didn't care that the VW backfired as she pulled into her street. She had more important things to worry about, like nailing a presentation twice in the same day.

She'd kicked some serious butt with the project managers, and had been riding high on Rory's decision until he'd added the stipulation about wowing the investors. Made sense. The money-men had to approve her proposed changes. But it didn't make it any easier.

A golf trip, he'd said, and she'd inwardly groaned. She could imagine a boys-only club where she'd be scrutinised for what she wore, how much make-up she slathered on and how her hair fell.

Nightmarish, but she'd do it, play whatever game she had to, in order to protect the Portsea land that should have been hers.

As she neared home, she saw cars worth more than her annual salary lined the driveways and kerbs around the house, which could only mean one thing: Coral was entertaining.

With a scowl, she parked halfway up the street and trudged back, her ire building with every step. Yep, the stupid shoes were still pinching, but her sour mood had more to do with the well-modulated, well-cultivated voices floating on the breeze and the clink of martini glasses than any shoes.

How many times had she hidden away during one of her mum's sojourns, or snuck out of a window to avoid the stares? There'd been plenty of those on the odd occasion when she'd been sprung, from women with their noses ten feet in the air, looking down on the scruffy tomboy, their confusion unable to crinkle their Botoxed brows as they wondered how coiffed Coral could produce an offspring like her.

They'd never said anything, not to her face, but what had rankled more than their visible derision had been the pinching around her mum's mouth—as if she'd sucked on a lemon. Not once had Coral wrapped an arm around her and included her in the conversation, proud of her daughter no matter what clothes she wore.

No, Coral had flashed a brittle smile, sagging in relief when she left, and that had hurt more than all those snooty cows put together.

The voices grew louder as she neared the back garden and she stopped, hating how the insecurities of the past had the power to affect her now. She was a professional, head-hunted by beach authorities the world over, years away from the teenage tearaway she'd been. No way would she slink around as she'd used to. She'd walk through their snobby soiree, head held high.

Decision made, she stepped around the side of the house and walked into a wall of expensive perfumes, each as overpowering as the next, trying to outdo each other as much as their owners.

They sat around a glass-topped wrought-iron table—hat-wearing socialites in dresses worth more than her rent-a-bomb car. The buzz of gossip hung in the air, and the G&Ts were flowing as freely as the name-dropping. She took a deep breath, bracing herself for the inevitable air-kisses.

Hitching her portfolio higher under her arm, she pasted a bright smile on her face and strode forward.

The buzz faded into silence as eight pairs of eyes looked her up and down, expressions ranging from puzzled to suspicious.

'Hi, ladies,' she said, enjoying their bemusement as Coral entered the back yard holding a tray of canapés. Her expression was the best of the lot: a mixture of surprise and wariness and ill-disguised discomfort.

In that moment some of her exhilaration at this morning's success evaporated on a cloud of regret. Regret that she could never be the daughter her mum wanted, regret that they were so different, regret that the one person she wanted to share her successes with was so inaccessible.

'Would you care to join us?' Coral's brusque tone made her bristle.

'No, thanks. Wouldn't want to disrupt your private party.'

Her mum hovered, uncertain, and Gemma waved her forward. 'Go ahead. I'm going to grab a bite to eat then work on the Portsea project.'

Coral's lips compressed at the P word. 'The Portsea project?'

'I mentioned it.'

But she hadn't elaborated, considering she hadn't spoken to her mum beyond pleasantries since she'd arrived. The two of them had been doing an avoidance dance bordering on the ludicrous.

While she liked not having to make polite small talk like a stranger, a small part of her—the part that wished Santa existed—wished her mum would just welcome her with open arms.

'I've been hired as the marine environmental consultant on the luxury mansions Devlin Corp is building on Dad's land, pending final approval from the investors.'

'That's wonderful!'

Coral's exuberance stunned her. But not half as much as her mum putting down the tray of canapés to give her a swift hug.

'I'm so proud of you,' she said, before releasing her.

Gemma would have reeled back in shock without the wall behind her.

'Thanks.'

Her jaw ached from the effort not to gape at her mum's rare display of affection as she watched Coral play the perfect hostess, offering canapés and topping up drinks.

Had she imagined the last few minutes, or had her mum actually said she was proud of her? Better—embraced her in front of the blue-rinse brigade?

This was why she loved the ocean. Tides and ecosystems and shifting sands were real—much easier to understand than humans.

A low tittering filled the air as Coral waved in her direction with a smile and Gemma took that as her cue to bolt. They were talking about her, and she had no intention of being a bystander.

After an hour spent honing her presentation until she could recite it in her sleep, Gemma had no option but to consider the next part of impressing the investors: her limited wardrobe.

Cold, hard facts she could handle. A mascara wand and stilettos? No way.

She'd taken a step towards her bedroom when Coral entered the kitchen.

'Guests gone?'

Coral nodded, her shoulders drooping in weariness, and Gemma noticed the wrinkles fanning from the corners of her mum's mouth. They shocked her as much as her mum's hug and declaration had earlier, for Coral had used to spend a fortune on cosmetics to maintain her youth.

A sliver of guilt lodged in her conscience. She'd been so wrapped up in her life the last few years she'd barely paid attention to her mum on her brief visits home. Whenever they'd caught up it had been out of obligation, but while they'd never be bosom buddies something had shifted when she'd walked into that garden party and been welcomed.

'Want a drink?'

Considering the number of used empty glasses on the tray, she raised an eyebrow. Coral shrugged and topped up two glasses from the pitcher she'd brought in.

'After sitting through another of those shindigs, I need it.'

Shock number two—hearing her mum voice anything other than cultivated glee at gossiping with her cronies.

Maybe she needed that drink after all. 'Sure.'

Coral handed her a glass and raised hers. 'To my clever daughter.'

Shock number three, and Gemma couldn't resist saying something. Aiming for levity, she pointed at Coral's glass. 'How many of those have you had?'

'Not enough,' she muttered, downing half her G&T in one gulp.

Oo-kay, something was definitely wrong—but Gemma wasn't skilled at this kind of thing. She didn't know whether Coral got stuck into the gin regularly and this was the alcohol talking, or a sign of some deeper malaise.

Whatever the cause, awkward and out of her depth

didn't begin to describe how she felt having this kind of conversation.

'Is something wrong?'

Coral focussed cloudy eyes on her for a long moment before shaking her head. 'Just tired.'

There was more to it, but Gemma didn't want to delve—not when she'd be ill-equipped to handle the answers.

Desperate to change the subject, she blurted, 'I'm going away tonight.'

Coral instantly perked up. 'With who?'

'Rory Devlin.'

Coral definitely didn't do Botox, for her eyebrows shot so high her forehead resembled a Sharpei.

'He gave the go-ahead on my pitch this morning, but the investors need to have the final say and they're golfing in the Yarra Valley, so we're heading down there this evening.'

Coral clearly hadn't unglued her tongue from the roof of her mouth, for she nodded and downed the rest of her drink, but there was a glint in her eyes that made Gemma want to clarify the purpose of this trip.

'It's business.'

The glint turned into a matchmaking gleam. 'Sounds lovely.'

She hadn't seen her mum so animated in years, and she wondered if it was the gin or genuine interest in her life.

'I'm good friends with his father's second wife.'

Gemma hated gossip, but she couldn't pass up an opportunity to learn more about the guy she'd be working with.

'Second wife?'

Coral grimaced. 'Cuthbert's been married four times.'

'No way!'

Coral nodded. 'I know—unbelievable. He's had about the same number of facelifts and has been between wives for a year now, so his exploits are frequently fodder for the gossip columns.'

Poor Rory. Coral might be set in her ways but at least her life wasn't plastered in the tabloids, embarrassing her kids.

'Rory seems a pretty staid guy.'

'Ethel says he's nothing like his father. In fact, he's taken over the reins of the family company after Cuthbert almost ran it into the ground.'

Ah… So that was why he was so business-focussed. She couldn't blame him there. If Devlin Corp was his family legacy he'd be fighting tooth and nail to save it—as she would have fought if she'd known her father's land was being sold off.

As much as she'd have liked to interrogate her mum again as to why she needed the money, she craved information on Rory more.

'Is Ethel Rory's mum?'

'Lord, no.'

Coral's laugh, devoid of humour, spoke volumes. 'I can't see Ethel being a mother to anyone. She married Cuthbert after Rory's mum took off when he was a youngster. The marriage lasted two years before Cuthbert moved on.'

Once again she sympathised with Rory. It had killed her to lose her dad. What must it have been like for him, losing his mother, then having to accept a stepmother only to have her move on shortly after? Not the best upbringing to build emotional attachments.

While she might not have been as close to her mum as she would have liked following her dad's death, they'd been a family when he'd been alive, and she'd been lavished with the attention and affection every kid needed to thrive.

'Funny thing is they're still the best of friends.'

'Who? Ethel and Cuthbert?'

Coral nodded. 'They frequently hit the town together. Ethel loves the high life; Cuthbert lives it.'

A shrewd gleam entered her mum's eye. A gleam she didn't like one bit.

'I could have a dinner party…invite them and—'

'Stop right there.'

Gemma held up her hands and slid off the bar stool. 'I don't need you interfering.'

The last thing she needed was her mum poking her nose into her business relationship with Rory and turning it into something it wasn't.

'I'm only trying to help.'

She'd never heard her mum's voice wobble, let alone seen her with a wounded expression, but she couldn't afford to waver on this. Before she knew it Coral would have them marching up the aisle.

'Thanks, but I can handle it.'

Coral topped up her glass and Gemma gritted her teeth to stop herself telling her to take it easy. She had no right and if she didn't want her mum interfering in her life, she had no place doing the same.

'Do you date much?'

Hell, this was what happened when she tried to bond with her mum. She faced an interrogation she'd rather avoid.

'Enough.'

'Anyone serious?'

She could bluff and throw in a few fake names, but she was proud of her choices, proud she'd built a solid, commendable career at the expense of a meaningful relationship.

And those doubts that crept into her head late at night, whispering that she'd end up alone if she kept pushing guys away for fear of letting anyone too close? Not worth worrying about—not when she felt more comfortable with marine life than living the high life on the dating merry-go-round.

'Not really.' This time *she* reached for the pitcher. 'Work keeps me busy and I move around a lot.'

Coral stared at her over the rim of her glass, her eyes huge and filled with worry. 'What about starting a family of your own one day—'

That was her cue to leave. She downed the G&T in two gulps and grabbed her laptop, wishing she'd never mentioned raising kids as an argument to flay Coral with for selling her dad's land.

'I appreciate your concern, Mum, but I'm fine. I'm going away with Rory on *business.* So don't over-analyse anything or feel sorry for me, because I like my life just the way it is.'

'Okay.'

Coral's easy capitulation raised her suspicions, but she couldn't see anything beyond an aggravating pity in her eyes before she lowered them to concentrate on her drink.

'I need to get ready.'

'Would you like some help?'

If the impromptu chat she'd had with her mother hadn't bamboozled her enough, Coral's invitation to help her get ready sent her into a tailspin.

She'd rarely dated as a teenager—guys had tended to be intimidated by her ability to kick the football further, score more points in basketball and swim the fastest and furthest in any race—so they'd never done the mother/daughter tizzy stuff. Surely it was too late to start now?

Then she made the fatal mistake of glancing at her mum. Her hopeful expression combined with her trembling hand as she twirled the glass undermined her instant refusal.

'I could do your hair? Lend you this incredible new mineral make-up that looks like you're not wearing any?'

She'd never seen Coral anything other than poised and elegant and confident, even after her dad's death, and the fact her mum was practically begging to help went some way to breaching the yawning emotional gap between them.

Besides, in the dress-to-impress department she needed all the help she could get.

'Okay.'

Coral's tremulous smile made her feel something she hadn't in a long time when it came to her mum: hope. Maybe it wasn't too late to bridge the distance between them after all this time?

'You go up. I'll finish stacking the dishwasher and be up to give you a hand shortly.'

Feeling more light-hearted than she had in years, Gemma took the stairs two at a time, the fizz in her veins lending an extra spring to her step.

Had to be the gin, and nothing at all to do with the tentative overtures of her mum or the prospect of spending the night in the company of one seriously hot guy—albeit for business.

That was her excuse and she was sticking to it.

'What on earth is all that?'

Gemma took one look at the paraphernalia in her

mum's arms and stepped back, instantly regretting her acceptance of Coral's offer to help her get ready.

Moving faster than Gemma had seen in years, Coral dumped her booty onto the bed and rubbed her hands together.

'Hair straightener. Curling tongs. Epilator. Eyelash curler. Make-up brush set. Light mirror.'

Gemma shook her head, not encouraged by her mum's determined smile.

'I was going to wear my hair in a ponytail, so I don't need all that hair stuff.' She batted her eyelashes. 'That curler? Redundant. Nothing could curl these straight pokers.' Puffing out her cheeks, noting their pallor, she exhaled. 'The make-up? Couldn't hurt.'

Coral picked up a small square device with a bristly steel head. 'What about the epilator?'

'That depends. What does it do?'

'Hair removal.'

Coral's glance dipped to her legs as realisation hit: her mum thought she might need to de-fuzz. Which meant her mum also thought there was a fair chance her legs would be bared tonight.

Dying from embarrassment, she held up her hands. Yeah—as if *that* would ward off an incoming beauty expert hell-bent on making her over.

'Let's stick to the make-up.'

Coral swapped the epilator for one of the hair thingies. 'And the hair. Nothing like sleek hair to glam up.'

'I don't do glam,' she muttered, but her protest fell on deaf ears as her mum urged her to sit on the stool in front of the mirror while she bustled around, plugging in the straightener, unfolding her satchel of brushes, laying out make-up on the dresser.

As she glanced at her bare face in the mirror, at the

frizzy blond strands spiking out of her loose plait, she couldn't help but be thankful she'd accepted her mum's offer.

She might be confident in her abilities, but she'd be lying if she didn't admit to being the teensiest bit intimidated at the thought of standing up in a room full of suited-up guys who'd probably pick her proposal apart.

She'd be judged on appearances too, and presenting a confident front would work wonders. She'd nail this pitch if it killed her.

She loved a challenge—always had. Land the biggest fish of the day? She wouldn't move off the pier until she'd caught it. Swim in the freezing ocean on a winter's day? She'd be first off the boat and ride the boom-net the longest. See the first Bottlenose dolphin of the season? She'd don wetsuit and fins every day, waiting for a glimpse of her beloved creatures.

Have a super-confident, commanding millionaire in control, thinking she'd quiver in her work boots in front of a roomful of his high-flying cronies?

Bring it on.

'Ready?'

Coral hovered over her and Gemma nodded, trying not to stiffen when her mum tugged the elastic off the end of her plait and unravelled it with her fingers.

How old had she been when she'd last submitted to having her hair done? Eight? Nine? It was one of the few girly things she remembered truly enjoying as a kid, having her mum brush her hair every morning and night with strong, smooth strokes that lulled.

'You've always had such lovely healthy hair,' Coral said, picking up a brush and running it from her scalp to the ends in the same reassuring way she'd done as a child.

'Thanks,' Gemma said, the word squeezing past the

unexpected lump in her throat, and when their gazes met in the mirror she knew Coral understood her gratitude was for more than brushing her hair.

In a way, she hadn't only lost her dad when he'd died. She'd lost her mum too. She'd put it down to mourning at the time, both of them withdrawing into their private worlds to cope. But later, when the initial horror had faded, replaced by an insidious sadness invading on a daily basis, she'd needed her mum. Had needed comforting and hugs and reassurance.

She hadn't got it. They'd been so consumed by their initial grief that once it eased they were different people, virtual strangers, and neither knew how to reach out to the other.

The lump in her throat grew as Coral gently ran thick strands of her hair through the heated straightener, a small satisfied smile curving her lips as she bit down on the tip of her tongue in concentration.

How could something so simple bring so much satisfaction to her mum?

'There. All done.'

As Coral ran her palms over her shiny hair, hanging like a sleek curtain past her shoulders, their gazes caught in the mirror again and Gemma had her answer.

Her mum's eyes were filled with hope and yearning, and the sheen of tears accentuated what she'd already suspected. Offering to help her prep for her presentation meant more than the grooming and appearances Coral valued.

This had been an olive branch.

When she tried a tentative, grateful smile, and watched her mum's expression transform into one of joy, she knew she'd done the right thing.

Interrogating her about the land could wait.

CHAPTER SEVEN

RORY had always been upstanding, always played by the rules, always played fair.

Hiring Gemma for her profile more than her expertise niggled, but after seeing Devlin Corp besmirched yet again in the papers, courtesy of dear old dad, he had to do something.

Not that his plan was all *that* nefarious. Gemma's presentation had genuinely impressed him, and he could see the viability of her proposal. But he'd orchestrated the meeting with his investors with one goal in mind.

To have her front and centre as the environmental face of the Portsea Point construction.

The investors had already received a memo from him this afternoon, outlining why hiring her was a viable proposition.

They'd been amenable to seeing her presentation, and from early feedback he'd received via e-mail she'd have to botch it for them not to go for it.

Not that he'd told her any of this. He wanted to see her pull out all stops, wanted her to prove herself—if for no other reason than to cement this decision as a purely business one, and eradicate the constant nagging feeling that he wasn't averse to having her stick around for a while.

He'd been distracted at work all afternoon, thinking

about her unusual qualities and why she piqued his interest when she was nothing like the women in his sphere. No smoothness, no polish, no artifice; she intrigued and terrified him.

He didn't like surprises as a rule. He'd had a gutful of them growing up, whenever Bert had brought home his latest conquest and introduced her as yet another stepmum-to-be. Those vacuous, self-absorbed usurpers who'd seen his dad as an easy meal-ticket and had sucked up to him because they'd thought it would curry favour with the old man.

He'd hated every moment of it and had grown immune to them, relying on practised indifference to get him through.

Surprises sucked. Yet Gemma Shultz had been one big surprise wrapped up in a very attractive package since he'd met her.

Who knew? Maybe some surprises weren't so bad after all?

As he strode up the manicured path towards her front door she slipped out, hoisting a small, scruffy backpack that had seen its fair share of travel, and quickly shut the door.

He raised his hand in greeting, immediately regretting the dorkish gesture. The whisky he'd consumed at work with his deputy burned in his belly, spreading its heat outwards, making him sweat, and he surreptitiously slid a finger between his tie and collar.

He couldn't breathe. The air was sucked out of his lungs as she strolled towards him. He was confounded by his reaction to this extraordinary woman.

'I knew you'd bring your fancy car.' She jerked her thumb towards the Merc.

'Better than squeezing into that.' He pointed at the

rusty rental and she nodded, toying with an earring—a black seal in spun gold this time.

'It's not so bad.'

He'd rarely seen her anything other than bold and sassy, so her flash of uncertainty as she glanced at the run-down car made him want to haul her in for a comforting hug.

'You look great, by the way.'

'Really?'

Her fingers tugged at the end of her flowing peasant top, smoothed the sides of her denim skirt, and her nervousness struck him again.

'Yeah, really.'

His gaze skimmed her glossy hair, shimmering like the sun. Her eyes were accentuated by subtle cosmetics, making them appear glistening and seductive.

His gut wrenched. He liked it better when she stuck to ugly suits, ponytails and no make-up.

Her eyes widened, as if she'd read his thoughts. 'I've got my suit in here.' She tapped the backpack. 'Benefits of non-crushable fabric and travelling light.'

'Your room should be ready, so you'll have plenty of time to change once we check in.'

Considering the way his mind had taken a detour from the business at hand, he felt the need to state the obvious—separate rooms—if only for his benefit.

'Good to know.'

Her mouth quirked into a playful smile, socking him like a jab to the jaw.

'Just in case I had the wrong idea.'

Her soft laughter taunted and, unable to rein in the insane impulse to touch her, he reached out and slid his palm over her hair, shiny and sleek, framing her expertly made-up face like a stunning backdrop.

It trailed through his fingertips like silk, tantalisingly

soft, and he bit back a groan when his bemused gaze clashed with hers.

He had no idea if her eyes held promise or if his imagination was working overtime, but whatever the hell was going on here he had as much control over it as he did over his father: absolutely none.

Her tongue flicked out to moisten her bottom lip and his fingers convulsed.

Screw propriety. Screw appearances.

He'd spent a lifetime doing the right thing, trying to be the opposite of his dad, but in that second he'd never wanted to kiss a woman more.

So he did.

He leaned forward and placed a kiss just shy of her glossed mouth, lingering longer than he should, but not giving a damn. The way he was feeling—reckless and floundering—she was lucky he didn't go for the lips.

He stiffened when she smiled against his mouth and eased away.

'If you're trying to distract me in the hope I'll botch the presentation and you'll be rid of me, think again.'

Her teasing smile slugged him in the chest. Time to back-pedal. Fast.

'We're going to be late.'

He picked up her backpack, wishing he'd never offered to pick her up, wishing he'd never kissed her. He hated his abrupt tone, hated the laughter in her eyes chastising him for being a stuffy fool, but if he didn't get behind the wheel right now and concentrate on the road who knew what he'd end up doing?

'Wouldn't want that.'

He ignored her smirk, mentally chastising himself for being a fool and unnecessarily complicating matters.

It wasn't until they'd hit the freeway that Rory realised

he hadn't given the Portsea project a second thought once Gemma had strutted out through her front door.

The moment Rory drove through the Sebel Heritage front gate and along its long, winding, tree-lined drive Gemma was catapulted back to her teens.

Arriving at a party to find the girls decked out in make-up and dresses while she wore jeans and her best T-shirt.

Walking into class to find her classmates discussing manicures while she wanted to chat about the weekend footy scores.

Coming downstairs every day to find her mother immaculately made-up, no matter what the hour, while she slouched around in whatever shorts were clean.

She'd never fitted in.

Since her teens she'd been the odd one out, and while she'd grown to value her individuality as she got older entering *this* exclusive enclave resurrected her old doubts like nothing else.

As if she wasn't nervous enough already. She'd agreed to pitch tonight. She hadn't agreed on kissing Rory Devlin.

'We're here.'

'Great.' She managed a tight smile as he meandered along the never-ending driveway, looking but not seeing the designer townhouses lining the fairways, the Heritage Retreat and Mii Spa, the sprawling clubhouse.

If driving into this place hadn't rattled her enough, his kiss had done it. The way he'd touched her hair, along with his genuine compliment, had made her feel special and desirable and feminine. As she'd mulled over his motivation for the entire two-hour drive, while pretending to hone her presentation, she'd come to the startling conclusion that she could end up feeling more for this guy than was good for her.

He pulled up under an elaborate portico, increasing her foreboding.

She didn't belong in a place like this.

It might be for only one night, and on business, but staying in an exclusive resort raised her hackles. She'd rather be roughing it in a tent than holed up in some posh hotel room, trying not to climb the walls.

She might have been raised in an upper-class suburb and attended a private school but she'd been an outcast, and being surrounded by obvious wealth disconcerted her, reminding her of every instance when she hadn't belonged growing up.

It was why Portsea meant so much—why losing the land had ripped a hole in her carefully constructed confidence. Having a safe place to go to, *her* place, where she could be herself, had meant the world to a tough girl determined on hiding her vulnerabilities. Take that away and she risked stripping down the rest of her defences too. Scary.

Clamping down on the urge to balk and stay in the car, she entered the cosy foyer alongside Rory, trying not to stare at her dishevelled backpack next to his designer overnight bag.

The faded denim backpack had frayed straps, a broken zip on the front pocket, and a tiny hole in the bottom left corner. Next to his bag, with the designer's shiny logo embossing it, it looked tacky, reinforcing the yawning gap between them.

She was natural, earthy, without pretence.

He was smooth, slick, without a clue as to what made someone like her tick.

So why the hell couldn't she forget that kiss?

'Here's your keycard.'

He handed her a small folder and she tried not to

snatch it so she could bolt for the sanctuary of her room. 'Thanks.'

'We're next to each other.'

Goody.

'The presentation's at eight?'

He nodded, his probing stare making her uncomfortable. Not that she blamed him for trying to fathom why she'd switched from enthusiastic to withdrawn.

'There's a conference room next to the Lodge Bar.' He snapped his keycard against his palm repeatedly, on edge. 'I can make a dinner reservation at the Bella if you like—'

'Thanks, but I couldn't possibly eat anything before the presentation. I'll grab some room service later.'

'No worries.'

But there were plenty of worries, judging by the awkward, stilted conversation. She'd gone from having the upper hand, savouring her power to unsettle this uptight businessman, to perpetually remembering how he'd loosened up long enough to kiss her.

'We better head up to our room…s,' he said, his slip lightening the tension, making her chuckle while he ducked his head to grab the bags.

'Let's do that,' she said, back to her confident best as she shot him a coy smile.

His lips thinned as he shouldered the bags and strode ahead, as fast as his long legs could carry him.

After a sleepless night, Rory rolled out of bed at 6:00 a.m., punching his pillow in frustration along the way.

How on earth had Gemma messed with his head in twenty-four hours? If she'd impressed him during her pitch to the project managers yesterday morning, her presentation to the investors last night had blown him away.

He knew the investors had been sold, even though they'd made a grand show of deliberating and making them wait for a final decision until after their early-morning golf game today.

He should be rapt. His plan to use her as the face of Portsea Point would come to fruition.

If he didn't go insane in the process.

He'd sat through a full hour of her presentation, using the sixty minutes to mentally list every reason he shouldn't be attracted to her.

Nothing in common; complete opposites; eco-obsessed versus city-savvy; batty scientist versus levelheaded businessman.

When he'd still found himself staring at her legs and working his way up he'd started nit-picking, adding average fashion sense and atrocious taste in jewellery and awful shoes to his list.

Only to find himself counteracting each and every one of his petty arguments by noticing the way her nose crinkled when she was really concentrating, how she smiled with her eyes as well as her mouth, how she lit up a room by being in it.

He didn't want to be attracted to her—didn't want to complicate their business arrangement. But no way would he let Devlin Corp suffer if he made bad decisions from lack of sleep.

He confronted issues head-on.

He'd do the same with Gemma.

Starting today.

'You don't strike me as the picnic type.'

Gemma stifled a grin as Rory tightened his grip on the picnic basket. She shouldn't bait him, she really shouldn't, but who went on a picnic wearing a suit?

'We need to wait for the investors to make their final decision—better to wait outside than in.'

A logical explanation—she'd expect nothing less from him—but she couldn't shake the feeling there was more behind his impromptu invitation.

'True.'

While breakfast at the Bella Restaurant had been superb, she'd been too fidgety to enjoy the amazing Bircher muesli and delicious crêpes.

She'd been hyped-up after her presentation last night, hadn't slept, and the adrenalin hadn't subsided this morning. That was her excuse for placing her palm flat against the wall next to her bed, wistfully imagining Rory doing the same on the other side.

Unbelievable. For a woman without a romantic bone in her body she'd done a good job of romanticising that brief greeting kiss. All night.

At least she'd been smart enough not to tempt fate and had bolted after the presentation finished. The last thing she'd needed was to sit around with Rory in a cosy bar downing drinks.

If he'd seemed distracted during her morning pitch, he'd been one hundred percent focussed last night—to the point she'd almost squirmed under his intense scrutiny.

At one stage his stare had been so potent, so mesmerising, she would have sworn he could see right down to her soul.

She'd soldiered on, pretending she was talking to a roomful of blobby jellyfish—her technique for being at ease during public speaking—not risking another glance his way.

It had worked, and she'd been suitably confident she'd nailed her presentation. She wished she could be as confident of handling Rory and his strange mood this morning.

'How's this spot?'

They'd strolled along the walking trail on the periphery of the hotel for ten minutes before he'd stopped on the banks of the Yarra River.

'Perfect.'

He produced a purple picnic blanket from the basket, spreading it like an amethyst cape on a field of emerald.

She slipped off her sandals and stared pointedly at his shoes. He looked at her feet, his, and frowned.

'Come on—you're not seriously having a riverside picnic wearing shoes?'

'I guess not,' he muttered, slipping off his shoes and stuffing his socks into them.

He had sexy feet, she thought, belatedly realising she was staring when he wriggled his toes.

She sighed as her feet hit dirt, savouring the warm grittiness on her soles. She loved the gravel texture under her feet almost as much as she loved the grating of sand.

No matter how many beaches she visited around the world, when she first dug her toes into the sand it always felt like coming home.

Her dad had sworn the only reason she'd got good grades at school was because she'd lived for their weekends at the beach. He'd been right. She'd always finished her work in class, because homework meant time away from the outdoors after school and homework on the weekends meant no Portsea.

She'd loved those weekends. Loved the ocean spray in her face and the sand between her toes and the icy brace of the sea. Loved swimming and building sandcastles and playing beach cricket.

Mum would set up the umbrella and lay out lemonade

and peanut butter sandwiches on the towels before settling back to read, while she cavorted with her dad. They'd been happy—a close family unit. She'd missed that familial bond after her dad died as much as she'd missed him.

Thinking of her dad and how her relationship with her mum had been fractured always made her melancholy, and she wished she hadn't headed down memory lane.

No beach came close to what Portsea meant to her and never would. The thought that some rich folk who probably wouldn't appreciate it would be living on her land in their fancy mansions… Best not go there. No use spoiling this picnic before it had begun.

'Great spot.'

He nodded and sat next to her, knees bent, forearms resting on top of them, as he stared out over the sludgy Yarra.

She mirrored him, content to stare at the water and feel the warmth of his deliciously close body radiating towards her.

She never felt completely comfortable around guys like Rory: rich, powerful, able to command attention with a wave of their pinkie. She'd worked with enough of them to know.

Yet sitting here with Rory seemed different. *He* was different, with a heart of gold underlying his steely exterior.

Despite her unusual tactics, he hadn't had to grant her an interview. And he certainly hadn't had to give her an opportunity to pitch her ideas to his project team or the investors while footing the bill.

People usually did things for a reason, were motivated by all sorts of causes from money to recognition and everything in between. She'd like to think Rory wasn't like that, but how well did she really know him?

A corporate go-getter like him wouldn't cave easily to demands, yet he'd given her a chance when she'd expected she'd need to browbeat him. More than that, he understood her rationale and seemingly supported her environmental quest. The sad thing was, she wondered why.

This picnic only served to heighten her suspicions. She never let people close for a reason: if even her mother rejected the real her, why was a busy businessman taking time out? And why was he being so darn nice to her?

She didn't like her defences crumbling and that was what was happening. With every smile, with every nicety, he was slowly chipping away at the emotional armour she'd been developing since the first time she'd realised her uniqueness wasn't always appreciated. So she went in for the kill.

'Why did you kiss me yesterday?'

He didn't answer, his forehead creased in thought. When he finally looked at her, the confusion in his eyes mirrored hers.

'I have no idea.'

She snorted. 'That's a cop-out.'

He rubbed the back of his neck, out of his comfort zone. 'You're not like any woman I've met before.'

'Good to know.'

He winced, as if her sense of humour pained him as much as his momentary slip in kissing her.

'I don't want you to get the wrong idea.' His nose crinkled, as if the river had washed up rank reeds. 'I don't do complications and drama and the inevitable fallout of getting involved.'

She should have been pleased he was a fellow relationship cynic, but his answer disappointed her somehow.

'Then why do it?'

He plucked at blades of grass, tossing them in the air,

watching them fall, buying time before reluctantly meeting her curious gaze.

'Because you intrigue me. You bowled me over the way you barged your way into an interview with gumption and sass. But most of all because I really want to do this.'

He captured her face in his hands and lowered his lips to hers, brushing them once, twice, before giving in to the irresistible pull between them and kissing her. A deep, hot, luscious kiss that lasted for ever and left her leaning all over him—because she didn't have a hope of sitting up straight with her boneless spine.

'Wow.'

She touched her lips and his gaze darkened.

'Wow is the effect you have on me.'

Their stunned gazes held for five long, loaded seconds before she glanced away, her heart pounding in exhilaration, her head throbbing with confusion.

Having Rory kiss her might set her on fire physically, but logically it didn't make any sense.

She didn't want to like him.

He was the enemy—a money-oriented, autocratic property developer who defiled the environment she loved.

On the flipside, he'd demonstrated an unexpected spontaneity by organising this picnic, and an admirable honesty in professing confusion over his rationale for kissing her.

She confused him? The feeling was entirely mutual.

'You hungry?'

'Ravenous.'

He wasn't looking at the hamper.

Before she straddled him and cut loose, she flipped open the basket on the pretext of looking at the food.

The hotel had done well, and her stomach rumbled

as she helped set out salmon and asparagus rolls, figs wrapped in prosciutto, crusty baguettes slathered in duck and walnut pâté, cheese scones with caramelised onion jam, brie quiche and tropical fruit skewers.

When she pulled out a bottle of Shiraz, she studied the label in surprise. 'Great drop. My dad had this vintage in his cellar.'

She handed it to him for the uncorking honours.

'You know this is on a par with Grange Hermitage, right?'

'In that case I'm surprised Mum didn't sell that too,' she muttered, wishing Coral had flogged the wine before the land.

'Her selling the land must've really divided you.'

She didn't want to discuss this, not with him, but it was the lesser of two evils.

Talk about her mother or dwell on that kiss? Considering her heart rate hadn't slowed and her lips still tingled, no contest.

'We were already divided.' She picked at the edges of the wine label until it frayed. 'After Dad died we drifted apart and nothing I did seemed good enough.'

He raised an eyebrow. 'You must've had decent grades to get into science at uni?'

'Academically I wasn't a problem.'

She laid the bottle down, half its label stripped. 'I was a tomboy and our interests never matched. We co-existed in the same house but were worlds apart. It felt like…'

Heck, why had she opened up? He didn't want to join a pity-party any more than she did.

'Like what?'

Balling her hands, she willed the sting of tears away.

'Like she couldn't accept me for who I was so she rejected me instead.'

She focussed on a far tree-line, waiting for the blur in her eyes to clear.

'I'm sorry.'

He touched her shoulder and she struggled not to flinch.

'Don't be. I learned a long time ago to depend on no one.'

'Me too.' He squeezed her shoulder and released it. 'Not sure what's worse. Having a mum emotionally shut down or not having a mum at all.'

She knew via the Coral gossip grapevine his mum had left, but she couldn't let on—not without giving away the fact she'd been discussing him.

'What happened with yours?'

He shrugged, his expression impassive. She'd bet he'd spent a lifetime honing it, as she had.

'She was an artist, pretty flighty. Couldn't tolerate Dad's infidelities—not that I blame her—so she left when I was five.'

'That's so young.'

'Yeah, I missed her at the start.'

'Did your dad step up?'

He snorted. 'My dad stepped *out.* Continually. But at least he hung around and didn't ship me off somewhere, so it's all good.'

'Do you hear from your mum?'

The tightness around his mouth softened as he nodded. 'All the time. We e-mail, Skype, chat on the phone. She's the same scatterbrain, wrapped up in her pastels and oils, oblivious to reality. But she stays in touch—guess that's the main thing.'

She envied him. He was a guy whose parents seemed flaky at best, but he'd come to terms with it. Shame she couldn't say the same for herself.

Sadness clogged her throat, and she grabbed a glass from Rory's outstretched hand and took several sips of the exquisite wine.

'Easy.' A worry line had appeared between his brows. 'How about we forget our dysfunctional families and enjoy the picnic?'

Annoyed she'd become maudlin—though it had succeeded in distracting her from that kiss—she smiled and gestured at the food.

'Let's eat.'

Gemma glanced at her empty driveway and breathed a sigh of relief. Her mum wasn't home so there was no risk of her interrogating Rory and embarrassing her.

'Would you like to come in?'

She issued the invitation out of politeness, hoping he'd refuse. The last thing she wanted was to spend more time with him after blurting out her innermost fears during that picnic.

Thankfully, apart from that hiccup, it had been a success. They'd eaten—or he'd eaten. She'd toyed with a cheese scone, her appetite lost along with all common sense when she'd divulged her private thoughts—and they'd talked. They'd shared an impulsive hug when the investors had rung through their decision.

She had the job.

They'd headed back to the clubhouse and shared a drink with a few of the guys post-game at the Nicklaus Bar, but their back-slapping camaraderie had reeked of old boys' club exclusivity and she'd been relieved when Rory had indicated it was time to leave.

There'd been no buffer of her work on the ride home, and she'd been forced to chat and smile and pretend as if nothing had happened between them at the Sebel: the kiss, the shared family tales, the inevitable bonding.

It had been the longest drive of her life.

'Do you make a wicked espresso?'

His adorable smile made her heart leap—she couldn't do this, couldn't risk blurring the lines further.

She'd already revealed too much, had allowed him to get closer than any guy ever had. The faster she slammed her defences back in place, the happier she'd be.

'Sorry, instant's all I've got on offer.'

His smile faded at her abruptness. 'Thanks. Maybe another time?'

'Sure.'

She heard the disappointment in his glib reply. She'd bet it wasn't a patch on hers. 'I e-mailed the project manager from the car. We're meeting on-site tomorrow. Will you be there?'

'Not sure. Back-to-back meetings all day.'

'See you next week, then.'

He frowned, staring at her, trying to convey some silent message she had no hope of interpreting.

'Come down with me Saturday,' he blurted, folding and unfolding his shirt cuff. 'I'd planned on heading down for the day, and we can get a lot of work done without tradesmen buzzing around.'

Her heart leapt at his initial invitation before reality slapped it down. Of *course* he'd join her on the Peninsula for work. What did she expect? After one picnic he'd be romancing her?

While he'd been attentive and chivalrous, he couldn't have stated his intentions any plainer: he didn't do involvement. What had he said? Something about no dramas and complications?

Normally she would have agreed with him, but then

he'd kissed her…and what a kiss. A kiss to remember, a kiss to resurrect on lonely evenings, a kiss to build foolish dreams on if she was that way inclined. She wasn't. Thank goodness.

'Getting a jump start on work sounds good.'

His brisk nod was a world away from the passionate way he'd kissed her next to the river, and her resident imp couldn't resist pinching his propriety.

'It'll be fun.'

'Fun?' he parroted, as if he couldn't quite comprehend the meaning of the word.

She laughed. 'Yeah, fun. I love Portsea Beach, so working on my passion—it'll be great.'

She accentuated *passion,* drew the word out, vindicated when his Adam's apple bobbed as he swallowed.

'Yeah, great.'

He flung open the door so fast he almost tumbled out. She opened hers.

'Rory?'

'Yeah?'

He ducked his head, but not far enough, and it clunked against the doorframe. She winced but he didn't react, his gaze fixed on her.

'Thanks.'

For giving her this work opportunity, for being so understanding, for telling her he'd see her on Saturday albeit for work.

'No worries.'

He straightened and she stepped out, snagging her backpack from the foot well.

'Now, go—before—'

'Before what?'

Before I blurt any more deep, dark secrets.

Before I re-evaluate my stance to reassemble my tattered emotional defences against you.

Before I forget every logical reason why I shouldn't like you and fall for you regardless.

A myriad of emotions flitted across his face and she focussed on the desire darkening his eyes to indigo.

'Before I turn into a pumpkin.'

Lame by any standards. His slight grimace made her laugh.

'See you Saturday.'

He headed towards the driver's door, not breaking eye contact until he'd slid into the car.

When he gunned away, and her heart roared in response, she deliberately walked towards the house without a backward glance.

CHAPTER EIGHT

IT HAD BEEN a while since Gemma had pulled an all-nighter, and as she rolled out of bed she blinked at the alarm clock. Her gritty eyes and stuffy head were testament to three hours' broken sleep, and she yawned, did a few yoga poses, and tried to figure out if she'd dreamt yesterday.

Rory's candid admission that she intrigued him, the impromptu picnic, the shared confidences, the kiss.

In the grand scheme of things it meant little, and she wanted it that way, but during those sleepless hours she'd imagined what it would be like to be involved with a guy like him.

Not the usual dating merry-go-round she rode, content not to have demands placed on her, but *really* involved: mentally, physically, emotionally. Equals in every way it counted.

Stupid, because they were poles apart, but a girl could dream, right? That kiss had been the catalyst for her fruitless fantasies.

He should never have done it.

She should never have let him.

It had blurred the edges of their relationship, taking it beyond business, tempting her to be take a risk and show him exactly how intriguing she could be.

His supreme confidence brought out the worst in her, prompting her to tease a reaction out of him. Maybe she'd invited the kiss? In which case, note to self: *stop taunting him, unless you want more.*

She'd analysed it at great length last night when she couldn't sleep. Her practical side said she must be different from every woman he'd ever dated so he'd been tempted to explore why. Her wistful side, the side she hadn't known existed until *the kiss,* basked in the unexpected power she could exert over a commanding guy like him.

Thankfully, practicality won out. He'd gotten too close yesterday, creeping under the barriers she'd erected many years ago out of necessity, tempting her to trust.

She'd never spoken of her mother to anyone, had never articulated her fears of rejection and not being good enough. Deep, personal fears she barely acknowledged let alone divulged to a virtual stranger.

Rory had a way about him, a way of crawling under her guard and getting her to believe in him, and it terrified her.

No doubt about it: she had to forget that kiss, forget her momentary lapse yesterday, forget his empathy, and focus.

Satisfied she'd clarified the situation in her own mind, she pulled on work jeans and a khaki drill shirt, slipped her feet into steel-capped boots and tied her hair into a ponytail. No fuss, no frills—exactly how she liked it.

Flipping open a small wooden box with a dolphin carved on the lid, she chose a pair of earrings—clownfish today—and threaded them through the holes in her ears. They were her one concession to frippery, and she liked having her marine friends dangling from her ears and brushing against her neck.

She'd collected the earrings all around the world, hoarding them in the special box hand-carved by her dad.

Her fingertip traced the outline of the dolphin and she smiled, remembering her adamant demands that he carve a dolphin and his indulgent smile as he'd quietly done just that.

This box had travelled with her from Jamaica to Jaipur, Mexico to Marbella, and everywhere in between. It gave her comfort, a solid link to her dad, one of many memories to treasure. Even more important now his land had been sold.

Pulling a face at the mirror, she adjusted the elastic on her ponytail. While she could do without make-up, she liked the sleek hair. Not that she'd succumb to the ritual of virtually ironing her hair every time she washed it, but having it hang past her shoulders in a shiny tail was kind of nice.

She had ten minutes to grab a piece of toast and hit the road before she ran into peak hour traffic. The project managers were meeting on-site at seven-thirty. She planned on being there first.

The light under the kitchen door surprised her, and she edged it open, stunned to see her mum cradling a steaming mug of coffee and poring over the early-edition morning papers.

'I have a reason to be up at this ungodly hour—what's yours?'

Coral glanced up from the papers, her shy smile as confusing as seeing her in a dressing gown and without make-up.

'I'm up at five every morning these days.'

'Really?'

'Becomes a habit after a while.'

When Coral didn't divulge why, Gemma popped two

slices of bread into the toaster. She didn't have time to delve into the reasons behind her mum's insomnia, and even if she did she wouldn't want to. Yesterday had been nice, a tentative start to bridging the gap between them, but she wasn't in the mood to get all deep and meaningful on a few hours' sleep.

'Have a nice time away?'

'It was business.'

And that was all she'd say on the matter. Until her mum smirked and pushed the newspaper across the table.

'Looks like Rory Devlin was impressed by your business.'

Confused, she glanced at the paper upside down. It was some features snippet between the gossip column and the horoscopes she'd never read in a million years.

Except today. Considering she was front and centre.

Coral chuckled as she snatched the paper and flipped it to read the accompanying article.

Millionaire CEO Rory Devlin is pleased to announce the addition of environmental scientist and marine specialist Gemma Shultz to the project team at Portsea Point, the latest of Devlin Corp's high-end developments.

Since taking over the reins of Devlin Corp six months ago the CEO has been busy boosting profit margins and re-establishing the business as Australia's premier luxury property developer.

Devlin Corp's exclusive enclaves have flourished along the east coast of Australia, with their signature opulent mansions built in Port Douglas, Surfers Paradise, Byron Bay, Coffs Harbour and Manly.

With Devlin Corp commencing work on a new

lavish development in Portsea shortly, Ms Shultz's expertise will be welcomed to maintain the ecology along the coastline.

Rory Devlin couldn't speak highly enough of his new consultant.

'I bet,' she muttered, shoving the paper away with one finger.

'He must be impressed with you to give a glowing recommendation already—'

'News must be on a go-slow if that's the kind of boring stuff they're printing.'

Coral's grin widened. 'Perhaps you're irked they used an old CV photo and not one of you with lovely sleek hair?'

Gemma shot her a death glare. 'I'm a professional, Mum, who spends her days on a beach. Wind. Salty air. Think my hair's important?'

Coral filled a mug with coffee and placed it in front of her, tweaking her ponytail. The simple action was so reminiscent of her childhood that a lump lodged in Gemma's throat.

'It pays to always look your best.'

'No one cares how I look when I'm testing E. coli levels.'

Except you. But she wisely kept that to herself. They were getting along. No use aggravating the situation.

Coral wrinkled her nose at the mention of E. coli, and Gemma took the opportunity to slather butter on her toast while casting surreptitious glances at the article.

Mr Conservative couldn't speak highly enough of her, huh? She'd never let him live this down.

When she looked up, her mum was studying her as if she were a micro-organism under a microscope.

'You like him, don't you?'

'Mum, I'm not in high school,' she mumbled, taking a huge bite out of her toast to stop herself blurting exactly how much.

Coral tapped the article. 'You could do worse than marrying into that family.'

Gemma choked. 'Gotta go,' she mumbled, snatching up the keys in one hand, juggling her bag and toast in the other.

Thankfully, her mum merely waved as she backed out of the door.

She wasn't the marrying kind. She'd have to let a guy get close enough for a relationship first, and that was as likely as her taking up spear-fishing.

Even if she took the risk, getting hitched to a millionaire bachelor who didn't do romantic entanglements would be the last thing she'd do. High-maintenance, rich designer guys weren't her type.

If she kept telling herself long enough, she might start to believe it.

Rory sat through three early-morning meetings, drank four cups of espresso and ate half a bagel, clock-watching the entire time.

Not that heading to the Portsea site for an impromptu visit would lessen his uneasiness. If anything, seeing Gemma would exacerbate it.

He'd been horrified when he'd blurted the invitation to work all day Saturday, second-guessing himself in a way he never did in the business arena.

He shouldn't have kissed her.

Since when did he give in to impulse? Never.

He'd succumbed twice now: first when picking her up, then on that picnic.

Another huge *faux pas,* organising the picnic. He'd seen her nerves the night before, when she'd bolted after her presentation, and thought it might put her at ease to be out in the open rather than pacing her room waiting for the investors' decision. With the added bonus of confronting his baffling attraction for her and getting it out of his system.

His motives had been pure. His execution? Lousy.

He should have known a picnic would throw them together in an intimacy that made him squirm. She'd asked him why he'd kissed her when he'd picked her up. He'd responded by kissing her again, properly this time. Schmuck.

Throw in that awkward, revealing little chat about their parents and he mentally kicked himself—hard.

He could blame his lunacy on any number of factors: his admiration for her work ethic and chutzpah, his attraction to her intelligence and understated beauty, his genuine excitement following her presentation about what she could bring to his project.

In reality, he'd blurted the truth when she'd asked: she intrigued him, like no woman had before.

That was what had prompted his invitation for them to spend Saturday together, work or otherwise. He'd done it out of desperation, cloaked in business terms, because he feared he didn't want to go a whole three days without seeing her.

Not good.

Then he'd spied the newspaper in his periodicals pile and guilt had ripped through him when he'd seen evidence of his plan coming to fruition.

His father and the associated negative press for Devlin Corp had been wiped from the gossip columns, replaced by news of his appointing Gemma, as he'd intended, with the added bonus of their other luxury developments mentioned. The kind of positive publicity money couldn't buy.

Seeing the half-page picture of her taken from her CV, reading the accompanying article, he should have been stoked.

He'd achieved what he'd wanted: establishing her as the face of his new development, showing the country Devlin Corp cared about the environment, and hopefully guaranteeing he wouldn't run into the same problems his dad had up at Port Douglas.

Instead, all he could do was stare at that picture and the way Gemma glowed. Even in a grainy professional shot, eyes wide and bordering on startled, her hair loose and mussed, she captivated him.

Which meant he'd have to do his damnedest to keep things strictly business. Getting involved with Gemma would be messy, and he didn't have time in his life for mess—not when Devlin Corp was finally starting to kick corporate ass.

He'd never mixed business with pleasure, had deliberately avoided dating anyone in his work sphere because of the possible complications and fallout. And there *would* be fallout. That was a given.

The women he dated always said they weren't interested in anything heavy at the start, but once they'd progressed past the first few dates the claws were unsheathed, ready to hook into him and not let go.

While Gemma didn't seem the type, with her transient job and London base, he didn't want to botch this opportunity. He had a top-notch marine expert willing to ensure his Portsea project dotted all the *i*'s and crossed all the *t*'s. The mansions would be environmentally certified as well as lavish, guaranteeing top dollar for those wealthy few lucky enough to afford them.

He'd be a fool to jeopardise all that for the sake of a self-indulgent fling.

As his marketing manager droned on about a new campaign he studied the newspaper article again, via the search engine on his smartphone.

He didn't want to use Gemma, but the phone had rung off the hook this morning—land-owners from Cairns to Launceston, enquiring about Devlin Corp's luxury development packages, asking for quotes. It was the first time in six months they'd had this kind of buzz, thanks to Devlin Corp showing its eco-friendly side.

People were environmentally conscious these days: forgoing plastic shopping bags, composting, recycling, using water tanks, harnessing solar energy. They didn't take kindly to large corporations felling trees and churning land, as his dad had found out on the rainforest fringe in Port Douglas.

Seeing a marine environmental scientist associated with his beachside project would bring kudos to his company and boost profit margins, without drawing unwanted attention from protestors.

Win-win.

Then why the nagging guilt that he'd unwittingly drawn her into this and she'd be furious if she knew?

He shut down the article and hesitated, his thumb poised over the keypad. He needed to keep Devlin Corp front and centre with positive publicity, needed to ensure the public saw Gemma doing what he'd hired her for.

Blowing out a long breath, he brought up his in-box, firing off an e-mail to his PA. Denise knew the drill. She'd leaked his whereabouts to the press at opportune moments over the last six months, claiming to be 'an unnamed source' when the company needed a boost or was desperate to counteract Bert's bad publicity.

Time for his 'source' to let the press know where Gemma would be on Saturday.

Gemma's morning had been manic: inspecting the beach, revising plans, going over new energy sources, scoping out the beach surrounds to ensure the managers knew where the amendments were to take place.

The guys had been nothing but professional, and she'd been buoyed by their acceptance of her. Until the boss man roared up in his Merc mid-afternoon and they scattered, leaving her to face him alone.

Her throat constricted as he stepped from the car in a grey suit offset by a pale blue shirt and navy striped tie, his long strides closing the distance between them at a rapid pace.

For one crazy, irrational second she wanted to run to meet him. The thought alone was enough to eradicate her sudden breathlessness and have her focussing on work.

'How's it going?'

'Fine.'

He raised a brow at her abrupt response and she glanced away, pretending to study the markers already scattering the ground.

'Productive morning?'

'Uh-huh.'

An awkward silence descended and she shuffled documents, flipped through plans, studying them as if they held the answers to eternal youth.

'Still happy to work tomorrow?'

He'd lowered his voice, and its deep timbre strummed her like a caress, her body responding on a visceral level that scared the heck out of her.

'Yeah.'

If he was tiring of her monosyllabic answers he didn't show it.

'Great. I'll pick you up at your place around six.'

And have early riser Coral accidentally-on-purpose orchestrate a meeting? Not likely.

'I can drive.'

He glared at her VW. 'I don't think so.'

'I'll borrow Mum's car—'

'I'll be there at six.'

To her astonishment, he walked away, leaving her wanting to tell him what he could do with his orders.

But as she watched him meet up with a few of the managers and gesture towards the land, his animation obvious even at a distance, some of her animosity at his command waned. It made sense for him to drive. Car-pooling preserved the ozone. It wasn't *his* fault she couldn't stop thinking about him or those distracting kisses.

Judging by his authoritative behaviour, he hadn't given them a second thought.

Good. At least one of them was thinking clearly.

As for the potential problem with matchmaking Coral? Time to shout her mum a treat.

CHAPTER NINE

GEMMA didn't feel the slightest twinge of guilt when she bundled her mum off to a swanky South Yarra day-spa for a Saturday-morning facial.

Coral had been sweetly surprised and very eager to head out. After scribbling a nondescript note saying she'd be out all day and late back, Gemma flung a few essentials into her backpack and waited impatiently for Rory to arrive.

The faster they hit the road, the less likely she'd be to call today off. She'd been tempted—boy, had she been tempted. Seeing him yesterday on the job site after the picnic episode had erected an unseen wall between them; she'd been stilted and nervous, he'd been aloof and distant. Who knew how they'd manage to interact one-on-one today?

When his Merc slid to a smooth stop in front of the house she hitched her backpack higher and bounded down the path, eager to get underway.

She almost stumbled when he got out, walked around the car and opened the passenger door. His impeccable manners were not surprising, but the simple action reminded her of her dad. He'd always used to open doors for Coral and her—a small thing she'd forgotten until now.

Sadness lodged in her throat but she cleared it, pasting on a bright smile as she neared the car.

'Right on time.'

He gave a funny little half-bow. 'Was there ever any doubt?'

'Punctuality is part of the workaholic's handbook, so I guess not.'

The corners of his mouth twitched. 'Hey, I'm heading out of town for the day. Does that sound like a workaholic to you?'

'Considering you're heading out of town for *work,* that'd be a resounding yeah.' She pointed at the car boot. 'Bet you've got a laptop stored in there.'

'Care to sweeten that bet?'

'Sure.'

He hooked his fingers beneath the straps of her back-pack to help her shrug out of it, effectively trapping her, and she tried not to breathe in his addictive masculine scent.

'What did you have in mind?'

She pondered, while her imagination took flight, envisaging him giving a little tug on the straps, bringing their bodies so close she could feel his radiant heat.

There were so many bets that sprang to mind, most of them X-rated, but she couldn't make a flirty joke—not when he hadn't cracked a smile yet. Regardless of that picnic kiss, they had to focus on business.

Tell that to her inner mischief-maker, hell-bent on getting Mr Conservative to lighten up.

'Okay, here's the deal. If there's a laptop in there, we get to play hooky for a while today. If there's no laptop, you work to your heart's content the whole day.'

At last a breakthrough. Interest flared in his eyes.

'Sounds doable. As long as you don't have me diving with sharks if I lose.'

'Would I do that?'

He shot her a dubious glance as he slid the straps off her shoulders and held the backpack in one hand as if it weighed nothing.

'Guess we better pop this boot and see who wins?'

'You're on.'

Gemma crossed her fingers behind her back. While she was all for work, they needed to lose the residual awkwardness from that kiss. If he was anything like her he'd retreated because of it, and the way they'd connected.

She hadn't expected his candour. Most guys would have lied about why they'd kissed her when she'd asked, even though that first kiss when he'd picked her up hadn't been particularly passionate.

But he'd revealed he liked her and his inherent honesty had blown her away. If she'd back-pedalled, too scared to lower her defences, how must *he* be feeling? A guy who confessed he didn't do complications would be petrified.

She'd withdrawn yesterday. He seemed determined to continue their emotional avoidance today. She couldn't blame him for it—not when she agreed—but the thought of spending her Saturday working with this tension between them didn't sound fun.

'Do you want to do the honours or should I?'

He held out the car's remote control. 'Go ahead. I wouldn't dream of depriving you of your fun and games.'

Annoyed by his impassivity, she grabbed the remote and hit the button, inadvertently holding her breath as the boot popped. When he raised it to place her backpack inside, she scanned the huge space: golf clubs, gym bag, no laptop.

Dammit.

He gestured towards the boot, the hint of a grin playing about his mouth. 'Well?'

Not giving up that easily, she pointed to the gym bag. 'Could be in there.'

'Why don't you open it and see?'

'And rifle through your undies? No, thanks.'

The imp in her rejoiced as he blushed and held up his hands.

'You win. My laptop's stored under the passenger seat.'

'Gotcha!'

She did a little victory shimmy, and at last he smiled.

'Fine. We get to play hooky *after* we've put in a solid six hours work.'

'Good. Even workaholics need to play every now and then,' she said, her gaze drawn to his mouth, remembering exactly how fantastic he could be while playing.

She'd never been a weak-kneed, belly-flopping female, but when she tore her gaze from his mouth, only to see the blatant yearning in his eyes, her knees shook and her stomach tumbled.

He'd given a resounding answer to her unspoken question as to whether he still felt the spark.

'You're playing with fire,' he said, his expression reverting to guarded as he closed the boot and guided her to the passenger seat, his hand in the small of her back gently supportive.

For a confirmed independent gal, it felt nice to be supported for once.

As long as she didn't get used to it.

'We're almost there.'

Gemma struggled to consciousness, trapped halfway between a luscious dream of waking up next to Rory and the startling reality of having his voice next to her.

'You've slept the whole way.'

Opening her eyes, she blinked, yawned and stretched, her confusion clearing as she remembered where she was.

'We're in Portsea already?'

'Yeah, easy drive without peak-hour traffic.'

'Did I really sleep the whole way?'

'The moment we hit the freeway about five minutes from your place.'

She grimaced and used her pinkie to wipe the gritty sleep from the corners of her eyes, before making a subtle dab around her mouth, hoping she hadn't drooled.

'Some travel companion I make.'

'The snoring was rather soothing after a while.'

Mortified, she couldn't look at him. 'I don't snore.'

'Keep telling yourself that.'

He chuckled and, glancing over his shoulder, turned left, slowing the car as he pulled into the project's makeshift car park. 'Next time I'm investing in a decent pair of earplugs.'

She whacked him and he laughed, the sound giving her hope that he'd loosen up after all.

In a way, falling asleep had been a bonus, as she'd avoided the small-talk nightmare they'd had on the way back from the Yarra Valley. Yet a small part of her couldn't help but wonder what would have happened if she'd been awake.

Would they have delved deeper into that *moment* they'd had outside the car at her place? Would they have moved beyond discussing their families onto something more meaningful, like their hopes and dreams? Or would he have retreated again? She'd bet the latter.

Stepping from the car, she stretched, marvelling at the view. The lights of the Mornington Peninsula twinkled in the early-morning dimness, curving around the bay like the fine diamonds on Coral's bracelet.

Thinking of her mum and the jewellery she could have sold rather than her dad's land if she needed money soured her mood, and she wrapped her arms around her middle.

'Cold?'

'A little,' she said, but her inner frostiness was from the loss of something emotionally valuable rather than the chilly sea breeze.

'You'll warm up soon enough.' She shot him a glance and he rolled his eyes. 'From work. What do you think? I'm going to jump you?'

She could always live in hope.

He compressed his lips, regretting his comment, but there was no disguising his eyes, darkened with desire, and her body flushed, warmth oozing through her like heated honey.

She knew what she wanted.

For him to slide his hand into hers and tug her towards him. For him to say *Screw work. Let's play.* For him to admit they'd started something neither of them might understand or want but couldn't deny.

She wanted to live in the moment, forget her inherent fears and insecurities and open herself to this guy in every way.

What she wanted was irrelevant, considering he didn't say a word as he spun on his heel and marched towards the site office, unlocking the door and entering without looking back.

So that was how it was going to be.

Well, he could retreat all he liked and bury himself in work—but later today, during their down time, she'd get him to unwind if it killed her.

CHAPTER TEN

RORY liked working weekends. Liked the peace and quiet while people bustled between sporting games and shopping malls and barbecues. Liked the amount of work he caught up on. Liked the ability to focus without interruption.

Sadly, that wasn't happening today.

Not entirely fair, as Gemma wasn't interrupting so much as distracting. His fault, not hers.

He glanced at her strolling along the beach and speaking into a Dictaphone, her head constantly moving as she looked around. She'd been a dervish of activity since they'd arrived at Portsea at seven-thirty, surveying the beach, making amendments to her recommendations, jotting notes.

He liked the fact she kept out of his way. Gave him time to figure out what the hell he'd been thinking, inviting her for the day to work.

Work? Right. What a joke.

Their word games, their sparring, their parry and retreat rammed home what he'd suspected. Today was about being with her rather than any great desire to work.

And keeping his hands off her was slowly but surely killing him.

He'd tried to be the epitome of the polite business acquaintance/friend, had tried to maintain a distance. But she'd undermined him with her silly bets and loaded looks and crazy earrings.

Those earrings really bugged him. Rose quartz sea lions today, their frivolity in stark contrast to the rest of her practicality. A woman who wore khaki cargoes, a brown T-shirt, beige hiking jacket and steel-capped boots shouldn't wear giddy earrings. They got him wondering... Would she be light-hearted and playful in other areas of her life, particularly the bedroom, once stripped of her practical armour?

Damn, he couldn't keep thinking like this.

He never second-guessed any decision he made. When he wanted something in the business arena he made it happen. No room for uncertainty. So why this burning desire to yell *Screw work,* sweep Gemma off her feet and head straight for the privacy of the sand dunes?

As if sensing his stare, she looked up and waved, her ponytail whipping in the gusty wind, her face glowing. Her clothes might be plain but in that moment, silhouetted against the morning sun, which gilded her hair and created a halo around her, she was the most beautiful woman he'd ever seen.

He returned her wave, knowing he should head back to the site office and type up some last minute ideas he'd had to improve driveway access. Instead he found himself heading down the rickety wooden steps to the beach.

She met him halfway and his chest almost caved with the weight of pretending they were nothing more than work colleagues.

His earlier assessment hadn't done her justice. Up close, he saw a faint pink flushed her cheeks, accentuating the incredible blue of her eyes, and her smile was a poleaxing combination of joy and wickedness.

'Was wondering when you'd give up on the boring stuff up there and head down to the beach where it's all happening.'

He couldn't help but return her smile. 'That "boring stuff up there" is what you're being paid to ensure doesn't impact on down here.'

She snapped her fingers. 'I knew I was here for a reason.'

He stared at the ocean, unable to bear her radiant smile a second longer. They needed to get back on solid ground, work ground, and forget the teasing—no matter how lighthearted. It would be his undoing.

He cleared his throat. 'What did you think of the amended plan on the high-end homes?'

Her right eyebrow twitched, the only sign she was surprised by his abrupt switch from playful to business.

'Love it.' Her gaze swung to the land on their left. 'Angling the upper storey will capture the sun perfectly, enhancing utilisation of solar power.'

'That's the idea.'

He followed her line of vision, imagining the finished product: opulent three-storey mansions, rendered pale mocha to blend in with the sandy surrounds, expansive floor-to-ceiling glass windows, contemporary angles adding uniqueness.

He loved the luxury homes Devlin Corp built, had admired them since he was a kid, when his grandfather used to take him from site to site. Back then he'd thought they were palaces fit for kings and queens. His parents' open plan home had been the signature design back then.

Pity the queen hadn't stuck around and the king had kept trying to fill her shoes with ugly stepsisters.

He was mixing his metaphors. Better than mixing business with pleasure.

'And dropping the water tanks underground is a stroke of genius.'

He couldn't help but be buzzed by her praise. 'They're a bit of an eyesore. Better not to detract from all this.'

He gestured towards the beach around them, and this time her eyebrow arched all the way.

'Careful, you're almost sounding human.'

'Just because I'm a businessman it doesn't mean I've lost sight of the bigger picture.'

He held up a finger when she opened her mouth to respond.

'But the sea wall on the highest point of the beach stays.'

She paled. 'But that will exclude the sand behind the wall from the normal onshore and offshore movement characteristic of normal beach behaviour.'

Making a wisecrack about beach behaviour at this point wouldn't be a smart move—not when her playfulness had vanished, replaced by five feet six inches of fervent, riled environmentalist.

'It could make the beach unusable for long periods after heavy wave action, and considering the people who'll live here that's sad.'

'There's plenty more beach access around here. It's only a small section.'

She sighed, her exasperation audible. 'You're already developing a park on the upper part of the beach. That's cutting off a vital reserve of sand for the beach during erosion phases, when the sand is moved off the beach by waves. Any sea wall, no matter how small, can lead to severe depletion of dune sand and ultimately no beach.'

While she'd kept her tone surprisingly calm, her chest heaved with the effort of her conviction. He wanted to bundle her into his arms and squeeze her tight.

He was proud of her—proud of her convictions, her knowledge, her dedication to preserving nature.

'Let me look over the proposed plans again and I'll see what I can do.'

Her answering grin had enough power to slug him where he feared it most: his heart.

'You get it, don't you?'

He held up a finger in warning. 'I said I'd take another look at the plans. If it's economically feasible, I'm willing to implement changes. You've already twisted my arm to include your marine conservation centre. Don't push your luck.'

She screwed up her nose. 'Yuck, you're going all corporate bottom-dollar on me.'

'I have investors to consider, shareholders too—'

'I know what'll convince you.'

She did a funny little dance that kicked up sand and he couldn't help but laugh.

'What are you up to?'

'Leave everything to me. This afternoon when we're playing hooky I'm taking you to meet some friends, and if they can't convince you to help preserve this beautiful marine environment, nothing will.'

'These friends aren't going to ply me with suspect cookies and homebrew before pushing me off a pier?'

'Wait and see.'

He didn't trust her exaggerated wink any more than his resolution to keep things between them casual.

Gemma slipped her mask and snorkel on, trying not to ogle Rory in his wetsuit. How the man managed to make rubber look good was beyond her.

He seemed unfazed by the whole adventure, and she wondered if anything ever rattled him.

When she'd procured bathing suits and they'd boarded the boat at Sorrento, he'd merely raised an eyebrow and settled in for the ride.

How many times had her dad brought her out here? Twenty? Thirty? She never tired of snorkelling at Popes Eye Marine National Park, a small semi-circle of rocks between Queenscliff and Sorrento. The shallow protected waters teemed with colourful fish and marine life, and today she'd get to share that with Rory.

Before the main event.

'Ready?'

He nodded and gave a thumbs-up. 'As I'll ever be.'

'You've done this before, right?'

He dangled his snorkel and mask on the end of his finger, swinging along with the gentle swell buffeting the boat. 'Snorkelling? Yeah. Here in the icy waters of Port Phillip Bay? Not on your life.'

'Trust me, it's worth it.'

Especially the way he was looking at her at that moment, with admiration and something deeper darkening his eyes.

They joined the group entering the water, and for the next half-hour stayed close as they snorkelled around the national park.

As a kid, she'd loved the fact this place had been constructed as an incomplete island fort during the late 1800s, and had imagined herself as a pirate, a sea captain and a mermaid—in that order.

When they finally broke the surface of the water Gemma pointed upwards, delighting in Rory's open-mouthed awe.

'There's a unique rookery of Australasian gannets around here. Watch this.'

A large gannet with an impressive two-metre wingspan

swooped fast, plunging into the bay at high speed. Rory held his breath, and she revelled in his surprise when the bird reappeared with a fish in its beak.

'They're excellent plunge divers.'

'I can see that.'

They bobbed in the water for a few moments, but this time he wasn't looking at the local wildlife. He had the strangest expression as he stared at her, as if he was seeing her for the first time.

The group leader gave a shout to round them up, and when she climbed back aboard she put the shivery feeling shimmying through her body down to the frigid water rather than the intensity of his stare.

'What's next?'

'You'll see.'

He didn't push her for info, content to sit next to her, close enough that their rubber-clad thighs brushed. Those shivers were tiptoeing down her spine with increasing frequency, making her want to snuggle into him.

A short time later he shifted and sat upright. 'Are those seals?'

'Uh-huh. Welcome to Chinaman's Hat seal platform.'

His genuine grin gladdened her heart. 'Are these your friends?'

'No, you'll meet them shortly. But you'll like these guys too—you have something in common.'

'We do?'

'Yeah. They're a bachelor community of Australian Fur Seals and they can get grumpy if approached.'

He laughed out loud. 'By "something in common", I'm hoping you mean we're bachelors?'

'And the rest,' she said, her sickly sweet smile garnering her a hip-to-shoulder bump.

'I'm not grumpy.'

She wondered how far she should take this, before deciding to give him another nudge. 'Maybe not grumpy. A tad withdrawn?'

His eyes clouded and she immediately regretted bringing it up out here and spoiling their outing.

'End of a long working week. I'm usually mellow.'

Mellow? Was that what he called a well-executed retreat?

'Uh-huh,' she mumbled in vague agreement.

She was a fool. What had she expected? For him to admit he was back-pedalling because he didn't want this to get complicated between them? For him to confess he was as scared as her of any emotional involvement but was sorely tempted regardless?

An awkward silence stretched between them and she plucked at the rubber stretched taut on her thigh. Then he said, 'Gemma, I don't want—'

'Dolphins!'

Once the cry went up everyone crowded to the side of the boat and the moment vanished.

As they re-entered the water, she wondered if he'd been about to say *I don't want complications, I don't want a relationship* or, the worst possibility, *I don't want you.*

Before she slipped on her mask and snorkel she waved at the small pod of Bottlenose dolphins nearby.

'Meet my friends. If they don't convince you to look after the local beaches, nothing will.'

Wisely, he remained silent, but the understanding flash in his eyes before he slid his mask on gave her hope.

They slipped into the water in small groups, and while they held on to mermaid lines and allowed the curious dolphins to come to them Gemma watched Rory.

She saw the first moment a dolphin swam within touching distance and his eyes crinkled at the corners in delight, saw the awe on his face when a group of five dolphins leapt out of the water, saw the workaholic executive melt away beneath the onslaught of these beautiful creatures.

When they'd finally made it back on the boat and stripped out of their gear it took him a full ten minutes before he spoke.

'I get it,' he said, his voice low, his tone reverent, and she refrained from flinging her arms around his neck and hugging the life out of him—just.

She settled for touching his hand. 'I'm glad.'

He turned his hand over, sliding his fingers between hers, holding on tight, and that was how they remained for the return journey to Sorrento.

Holding hands, her head resting on his shoulder, watching the sun set in a dazzling display of mauve and gold and pink, streaking the sky with beauty.

Gemma didn't believe in romance or fairytales or happily-ever-afters. But this? It came pretty darn close to topping her list of life's perfect moments.

CHAPTER ELEVEN

RORY had swum in the crystal clear ocean around the Maldives, had snorkelled in Fiji and dived in the Caribbean with Bert on a rare child-friendly trip in his early teens. But nothing beat the swim he'd had today.

Initially unimpressed by the icy waters of Port Phillip Bay, he'd quickly warmed up—courtesy of Gemma's wide-eyed enthusiasm and her 'friends'.

The laughs had been on him when he'd realised his vision of dreadlocked hippies was in reality a pod of dolphins.

Devlin Corp donated to various conservation causes, but he'd be lying if he didn't admit that had more to do with tax breaks than any real love of marine wildlife.

Gemma had opened his eyes today, and while he wouldn't be diving into that shiver-inducing water on a regular basis, he knew he'd take a more personal role in his company's causes.

What he'd seen on that dolphin dive—her enthusiasm, her animation, her verve—had reaffirmed that marine science wasn't just a job to her. She truly believed in the cause and her ethics blew him away.

He couldn't fathom how he could have been attracted to women who were torn between the Caesar salad and the wonton soup, women who valued their six-hundred-dollar pairs of designer shoes more than the ozone, women who prided themselves on etiquette and appearances but were shallower than the rock pools where the boat had docked.

Being with Gemma, her refreshing honesty and exuberance and lack of pretence, made him feel like a new man—a man capable of handling a spontaneous, vivacious woman, a man capable of change.

He couldn't remember the last time he'd played hooky. He was rarely sick and never lolled around. The closest he came to relaxing was the occasional sauna at the gym, and even that had him edgy after fifteen minutes.

Spending the afternoon swimming with dolphins should have had him going stir-crazy. Instead he'd loved it. Gemma had intrigued him from the start, and now, after discovering another side to this incredibly multi-faceted woman, he knew he was in serious trouble.

He'd bounded up the wooden steps of the Baths Café in Sorrento, where they were stopping for a snack before heading home, when his phone buzzed.

He'd left it in the car all afternoon: another first. He never went anywhere without his phone—needed to be connected to his business at all times. Yet he hadn't given Devlin Corp a second thought all day and that sobered him.

He was acting just like his dad. Putting personal needs first, acting on a whim, forgetting the implications for Devlin Corp.

Hell.

He'd sworn never to be like Bert—had made a commitment to Devlin Corp. So what was he doing, losing his head over a woman who would be out of his life sooner rather than later?

Annoyed at his afternoon lapse, he scrolled through

the messages. He tensed when he spied the latest from his PA Denise.

Check out the Melbourne Daily late edition.

With a few taps on his bookmarks he brought up the online paper and flipped through the pages. On page eight, in full Technicolor glory, was a picture of Gemma talking into her Dictaphone on the beach this morning: focussed, wind-blown, magnificent.

He skimmed the article, vindicated by the numerous mentions of Devlin Corp and its continual rise to the top, interspersed with the story of the company's dedication to the environment in hiring Gemma. They extolled her virtues at length, listing her credentials and how her presence at Portsea Point would ensure marine viability alongside Devlin Corp's signature homes.

He'd got what he wanted. Bert and his associated bad publicity for Devlin Corp had been wiped from the media, replaced by Gemma as the face of his new project. Positive spin all the way.

As his gaze focussed on that picture of Gemma in her natural glory, doing what she loved best, he wondered at what cost.

With Devlin Corp at stake he'd done what he had to do. But how would Gemma feel about it? Technically he wasn't using her, merely boosting her profile as the company's latest and greatest consultant, but would his genuine motivation count for anything when he told her the truth?

With her waiting for him inside the café, guilt twanged his conscience—hard. He should tell her. It was the decent thing to do.

Turning off his phone for the first time ever, he stuck it in his pocket, mentally rehearsing what he'd say, how he'd explain his rationale without sounding like a jerk.

By the time he pushed through the glass door and caught sight of her, sitting on the veranda, all his good intentions flew out of the open window.

Her hair fluttered in the breeze like gold silk, and her eyes were wide and sparkling, reflecting the stunning blue of the bay behind her, as she caught sight of him and waved.

His resolve shot, revelations forgotten, he strode across the café, focussed on nothing but being with her.

Gemma never lazed around. She spent every moment of every day at high velocity, packing as much into her life as she could. She liked being busy at work, liked the satisfaction of a job well done. In her down-time she hiked and swam, preferring to keep moving.

The guys she'd dated hadn't been interested in her frenetic pace. They'd preferred women to sloth around, lazing by a pool in a bikini rather than actually swimming. Guys who needed attention, guys so blatantly wrong for her she often wondered if that was the reason she'd dated them.

She'd never had the grand dream of settling down and getting married and raising a family, was too used to hiding behind the job she loved to avoid the pain of emotional involvement. Too used to her independent lifestyle, too used to packing up at a moment's notice and traversing the world for work. She thrived on it and, while many might call her selfish, she liked her life just fine.

Getting to know Rory had changed all that.

It made no sense.

She hadn't known him long.

He was a corporate big-wig; she was an environmental specialist.

He liked designer duds; she liked cheap, functional and funky.

They were light years apart in every way.

Yet seeing him come alive in the bay this afternoon, watching him open his eyes and his heart, see her for who she really was and what mattered, had shattered her illusions for ever.

It was okay to have the happily-ever-after dream with the right person.

Unexpectedly—catastrophically—she'd found him.

The guy she could see herself changing her life for.

A guy special enough that she could stay in Melbourne and build a life with him.

A guy worthy of investing in emotionally for the first time.

It wasn't one specific thing but the whole package: his ability to make her laugh, to say the right thing, to make her feel like a beautiful woman with a glance.

She didn't need compliments to feel good about herself; growing up a tomboy and working in a male-dominated environment, she was used to being one of the boys.

Facials, manicures and hair straighteners were as foreign to her as sequins and clutch bags and stilettos. Yet spending time with Rory made her feel more feminine, more appreciated, than she'd ever been.

The question was, what was she going to do about it?

She had a job to do on the Portsea project; that much was clear. Once the month was up? What then? Rory expected her to pack up and leave, a job well done. Should she tell him she might stick around?

The implications of a revelation that momentous made her shiver.

'You cold?'

Rory sat beside her and draped an arm across her shoulders, rubbing her arm to warm her up. Holding hands on the boat after sharing the dolphin swim had changed something between them, breaking down his barriers, bringing them closer in a way she'd never expected.

He'd been more relaxed than she'd ever seen him, unconsciously touching her in unspoken agreement that he liked her despite not admitting it.

They were a fine pair: dancing around each other, emotionally stunted, terrified to take the first step. After that ride she felt as if they'd taken a leap into a scary abyss.

'Not any more,' she said, snuggling into him as if it was the most natural thing in the world, giving him a clear signal that she'd like to do this on an ongoing basis.

'Fancy another coffee?'

'No, thanks. I'm content to sit awhile if you are?'

'I'm exactly where I want to be,' he said, his expression inscrutable as he stared out at the choppy bay, at small waves created by a blustery wind.

Over two lattes each, and a massive blueberry muffin for her, all-day breakfast for him, they'd watched the ferry from Queenscliff dock and depart again, people strolling along the beach, kids playing in the icy shallows.

Gemma could have sat there all evening, letting the world pass her by, but as Rory's arm remained wrapped around her she knew she had to tell him.

Someone like him didn't come along every day and she'd be a fool to pretend otherwise. They might not have a lot in common, and she knew next to nothing about him, but she'd taken risks her entire life. What was one more?

The fact previous risks had been physical and this risk was emotional? She'd waste time second-guessing that later.

'Rory?'

'Hmm?'

Reluctant to move, but needing to see his reaction when she dropped her bombshell, she eased back and he removed his arm. She missed the contact, and emboldened by her decision, she placed a hand on his thigh.

'I'm thinking of sticking around.'

Confusion creased his brow for a second, before realisation widened his eyes.

'In Melbourne, you mean?'

'Uh-huh.'

His thigh flexed beneath her palm, and she resisted the urge to stroke the firm sinews.

'Once this job is finished, I might look around for something else to work on. What do you think?'

For a horrifying second panic flared in his eyes, before his lips curved into a smile.

'I think that's a great idea.' He covered her hand with his.

She waited for him to say more, waited for him to say it would give them a chance to get to know one another, waited for him to say he was willing to take a chance if she was.

His silence unnerved her, but he hadn't released her hand so she'd have to be happy with that. What had she expected? For a self-professed commitment-phobe to jump for joy?

It had taken *her* long enough to get to this point. She needed to give him time to get used to the idea that they might share more than a spark.

'Good.'

She had the impression he wanted to say something, but a waitress came to clear the table and the moment passed.

'We better make a move.'

A chill settled over her as they stood. It had little to do

with the wind and more to do with the nagging feeling that, despite his words, her declaration had scared him more than he let on.

Coral usually spent Saturday evenings having dinner with friends. Gemma was counting on it as Rory dropped her off, but one glance at the driveway had her giving him a hurried kiss.

Coral's Honda sat in front of her VW, meaning at any moment her mum would come waltzing out on the pretext of checking that a possum wasn't devouring her roses, or some such guff, when in reality she'd want to scope out Rory. Gemma could only imagine how inadequate Coral might make her feel about spending time with someone as smooth and suited as him.

'Today was great. We got heaps of work done, and you were a trooper on the dolphin swim, and the café was lovely, and—'

'Is anything wrong?'

Darting a quick glance over her shoulder, and seeing an upstairs curtain twitch, she grimaced. 'My mum's queen bee on the local gossip grapevine. She thrives on it. So I'm trying to beat a hasty exit and leave you unmolested before she descends.'

He laughed. 'She can't be that bad.'

'Worse.'

Harsh, and not entirely true, but the last thing she needed right now was her mother crossing paths with Rory and the inevitable comparison and judgement that would follow.

'Will I see you Monday?'

The moment the question fell from her lips she inwardly winced. Since when had she sounded like a needy female?

'Actually, I'll be tied up in meetings Monday to Wednesday, then I'm heading interstate towards the end of the week.'

'Right.'

But it wasn't. Things were far from right. Since she'd declared her plans to stick around he'd been acting strange. Nothing overtly obvious, but a subtle withdrawing that left her wondering if she'd misread the afternoon and feeling more than a little hurt.

'I'll call you when I get back.'

'Sure.'

She snagged her backpack from the backseat and leaped from the car before he could say anything else. She'd heard enough for now.

When he didn't try to kiss her again, or touch her or speak, she held her head high, hitched her backpack higher, and strode towards the house.

Not having a clue about relationships sucked. Emotionally clueless, she had a sinking suspicion she'd made a mess of the best day of her life.

Rory tooted as she reached the front door and she waved, glancing over her shoulder in time to see him pull away. Could he leave any faster?

Tension banded her forehead with the promise of an incoming headache, and she patted her pocket for her key—only to have the door swing open.

On the bright side, Rory had left.

On the down side, Coral hovered on the other side of the door like an avenging angel, clad in head-to-toe Chanel and waving her in like a signaller waving in a jet on an aircraft carrier.

'You've got some explaining to do, my girl.'

Gemma rolled her eyes and trudged inside. 'At twenty-nine, I don't need to justify myself to anyone.'

Coral placed a hand on her shoulder. 'I'm teasing.'

Great. Now parting with Rory had her edgy. She heard the uncharacteristic tremor in Coral's voice and, hating taking her mood out on her mum, she dumped her backpack on the floor.

'I'd kill for a peppermint tea.'

Coral's genuine smile made her feel like a cow. 'Coming right up.'

Gemma followed her mum into the kitchen, determined to give her the bare basics, scull her tea, and head for her room where she'd grouch and grumble and mull in peace.

'How was your day?'

'Good.'

'You were with Rory?'

'Uh-huh.'

Maybe if she kept up the brief responses Coral would move on to another topic.

Fat chance.

'Portsea must've been chilly with that southerly today.'

Gemma's head snapped up. 'How did you know I was in Portsea?'

'Honey, everyone knows.'

Her expression benign, Coral pushed the late edition newspaper across the counter and she snatched it, flicking through the pages with flustered fingers.

There she was again: page eight, on the beach early that morning. She looked a mess, ponytail whipping in the wind, Dictaphone shoved to her mouth, her eyes squinting against sand and sun. She'd never looked good in photos and this one proved it.

'Did you read the article?'

She rolled her eyes and did just that. Most of the article centred on her expertise and what she brought to the project, along with singing Devlin Corp's praises.

The thing reeked of a PR stunt—as if someone at the company had fed some gossip-hungry journo her whereabouts, a few choice lines, and they'd run with it.

'Does it bother you, being in the media?'

Tossing the paper away, Gemma shook her head. 'Not really.'

Coral poured boiling water into teacups and dangled the bags. 'Was it just you and Rory at Portsea today?'

'Mum, drop it.'

Sliding a cup across the bench, Coral perched on a bar stool opposite. 'You're awfully touchy.'

That tended to happen when you finally took the plunge and put yourself out there, and the guy you thought was into you didn't return the enthusiasm.

Knowing she'd have to give her mum something, she shrugged. 'We worked most of the day, then chilled out. Nothing serious.'

Coral raised a knowing eyebrow. 'You never had a boyfriend growing up. You've never mentioned anyone on your brief visits home. Now you seem to be spending a lot of time with this guy—'

'Stop.'

Gemma slid off her stool so quickly she almost upended the scalding tea. The sensible thing to do would be to zip her lips and march out of there, take time to cool off. But the uncertainty and second-guessing of the last few hours coalesced into an anger directed at the person in front of her—a person who had no right to start acting maternal now, after years of making her feel worthless.

How she'd yearned for these questions as a teenager, when she'd never fitted in at school but wanted to, when she'd needed her mum's advice on boys and make-up and clothes but didn't know how to ask, when she'd craved her mum's approval and support.

The lack of support had hurt. It was a hurt she'd locked away and kept hidden beneath an outer layer of bravado and boldness. A hurt that had festered. And having Rory pull away from her, just as her mum had pulled away all those years ago, brought back her insecurities in a rush: maybe she wasn't girly enough, wasn't beautiful enough, plain wasn't enough?

Shaky and out of her depth, she jabbed a finger in Coral's direction. 'Tell me this. Why the interest now? You never gave a damn when I needed you most.'

She spat each word out, punctuated with the underlying hurt she'd buried deep now bubbling to the surface.

'You pushed me away, Mum. Rejected me. And I had no idea why.'

Coral staggered as if wounded, adding to Gemma's guilt, but the pain of neglect and wishing things had been different flooded out in a torrent she couldn't control.

'It's a bit late to pull the caring act now. Where were you when Dad died, when I really needed you? And all those years after, when I needed some kind of acknowledgement you loved me? Where was the concern then, huh?'

Coral plopped down onto the bar stool, her face a deathly white.

'I—I—don't know what to say…'

'That's just it. When I needed you most, you never did.'

Clutching her churning belly to stop herself being sick, Gemma turned and ran.

CHAPTER TWELVE

RORY had botched Saturday.

Big-time.

He hadn't told Gemma the truth about those newspaper photos. And he sure as hell hadn't told her the truth about how he was feeling.

Therein lay the problem, because damned if he knew.

As much as he liked her, as much as he wanted to explore what they'd started with their spasmodic flirting, he'd freaked out when she'd said she was sticking around.

Not that she'd spelled out exactly why, but he knew. By the softness around her mouth when she told him, by the unguarded zeal in her eyes, by the hope on her face, he knew she was doing it for him.

He couldn't handle that much responsibility.

Shove him into the CEO's chair at an ailing company? Yep, he could cope with his eyes closed. But being responsible for someone's feelings? Hell, no.

He'd grown up independent, taking care of himself from an early age, learning not to depend on anyone. It suited him.

Deep down, he knew this freak-out was probably based on some long-buried rebellion against his parents—a mother more wrapped up in her art than him for the first five years of his life before she bolted, and a father who paid more attention to his constant parade of unsuitable girlfriends.

He'd accepted his dysfunctional family as a kid with resignation, but he'd be kidding himself if he thought his upbringing hadn't left a lasting legacy.

He wanted to be nothing like his parents.

Didn't want to let a woman close for fear of letting her down like Bert did. Didn't want to get emotionally involved for fear of finding it too claustrophobic and bolting like his mum.

The only problem was his deep-seated fear of emotional attachment might cost him a woman he could seriously fall for given half a chance.

He'd been so blown away by her declaration he'd backpedalled, desperate to buy time, deliberately staying away an entire week.

Sadly, time away hadn't changed the situation. He needed to acknowledge the truth. They'd connected on some innate level that defied logic or explanation, and he needed to recognise it or lose her.

Considering he'd mucked up appointments, turned up late to an interstate flight and made a general cock-up of things over the last week, he couldn't lose her.

He'd missed her that much.

If losing her wasn't an option, he had to face facts. Was he ready for a real relationship? What were his expectations? What were hers?

If she stuck around, for how long? Would she flit off at the first opportunity if a great job offer came her way? If so, how would that affect them?

Too many questions, not enough answers; none beyond his wild speculations.

They had to talk.

After he finished grovelling.

* * *

This had better be good.

Gemma pushed through the glass door and entered the vegetarian café, wondering what surprised her more: the fact Rory had called or his choice of meeting place.

Until she realised he probably assumed because she was an environmentalist she was vegetarian too. Considering she'd barely managed to nibble on a cheese scone at their picnic, followed by a blueberry muffin at the Baths Café while he devoured fried eggs and bacon, she could understand how he'd make the leap. She'd save her carnivore side for another time; *if* there was another time.

True to his word, he'd been busy all week. Too busy to call or e-mail or text. No one was *that* busy.

She'd pretended not to care. She'd worked harder and longer than everyone else, stoked by her plans for energy efficiency and marine conservation and reducing carbon footprints at Portsea coming together.

During the day and well into the evening she didn't have time to dwell on Rory's rationale. But at night, when she lay on her back and stared at the ceiling, she'd rehashed every second of Saturday afternoon, wondering how she could have misread the situation.

The tiny bell over the door tinkled and the skin on her nape prickled. She knew who'd entered behind her without having to turn around. Crazy how in tune they could be after knowing each other a fortnight.

'Thanks for coming,' he said, placing a hand in the small of her back. The barest pressure sent an instant zap of awareness through her.

Her brain might know there was no future for them; try telling that to her body.

'No worries,' she answered, aiming for blithe, sounding ridiculously perky instead.

He guided her through the small tables, choosing the

corner booth furthest from the door, ensuring privacy. That figured. He'd start off with, *It's not you, it's me.*

He picked up the grease-stained menu, gave it scant attention before sticking it back between the salt and pepper shakers.

'You hungry?'

'Not really.'

'Me either.'

He clasped his hands together, rested them on the table. Combined with his sombre expression, he looked like a judge about to give an unfavourable ruling.

Considering the surprising ache in her chest, she was probably not far off the mark.

'I had this spiel worked out—'

'Let me save you the hassle. It's okay. I get you're not into me, that you're not interested in complications. Don't worry—'

'I'm into you.'

She only just caught his muttered *'Way too much to be good for me.'*

For the first time all week her mouth curved upwards. 'You could sound a little more enthusiastic.'

He frowned. 'Sorry, I'm making a hash of this again.'

She could make it easier for him, but after the week he'd put her through? Not likely.

He leaned back in his chair and hooked his clasped hands behind his head—a powerful businessman out of place in this tiny café in a Melbourne side street. What really commanded her attention was the play of emotions across his face: uncertainty, regret, hope. She focussed on the hope.

He took a deep breath, blew it out through pursed lips. She waited.

'You threw me.'

He wasn't the only one. She'd done a fair job of shocking herself the last fortnight.

'You come across as this independent, fearless, in-control woman who travels the world and muscles her way into jobs and doesn't like permanency. And that suited me just fine.'

He ruffled the top of his hair, spiking it. 'I liked you, but after the way we'd been flirting, then how we connected on the boat, hearing you say you were sticking around…' He shrugged. 'I kinda freaked out.'

'I noticed.'

Some of the tension drained from his rigid shoulders when she didn't snap, and he lowered his hands, stretching his neck from side to side like a boxer about to enter the ring.

'I guess what concerns me is you're giving up some of your freedom.'

He didn't add *for me* but he knew. Knew how much her independence meant—knew what she'd be sacrificing if she stuck around. For him.

'I don't play games. That's why I gave it to you straight. I like you. I want to spend some time exploring the spark we share. I'm not *giving up my freedom* for anyone. This is for *me.*' She clapped a hand to her chest. 'It's what *I* want to do.'

Admiration glittered in his eyes but she wasn't finished.

'I can't give you any promises about how long I'll stick around, and I'm certainly not angling for a commitment, but for the next few months I want to stay in Melbourne.' She pointed at him. 'To hang out with you.'

He snagged her hand and brought it to his lips, pressing a kiss in her palm and curling her fingers over it. She needed little encouragement to hold on to a kiss like that.

'There's something else—'

'Do I really need to hear it? Because right now we're in a good place.' She waved her free hand between them. 'If you're going to disturb that, leave it.'

He hesitated, the frown between his brows only finally easing when she pulled a face, imitating him.

'Don't look so serious. We're dating, not getting married.'

She couldn't blame him for chuckling in relief.

'Am I allowed to say *anything?*'

'Only if it's good news.'

His smile faded. 'The building commencement date has been moved forward. They start Monday.'

While she'd known this day was coming—heck, she'd been working towards it with a team—it didn't make the reality any easier. Her dad's land was being carved up. And there wasn't one damn thing she could do about it.

'In a fairytale world I'd give you back the land if I could. But there are too many people's livelihoods invested in this project—people's jobs, millions of dollars—'

'You don't have to justify this. You bought the land fair and square, and I gave up believing in fairytales a long time ago.'

She tried to sound matter-of-fact, but her voice quivered and he clasped her hands across the table.

'You mentioned you used to camp out there with your dad. How about we do that this weekend?'

As a distraction technique from her misery, it worked.

'Seriously?'

He nodded. 'Give you a chance to say goodbye.'

A chance of closure, to farewell her favourite spot in the world, to move on in her mind. She'd never forget how safe Portsea made her feel, its familiarity warming her as much as her memories, but her haven would soon be gone and she needed to come to terms with that. It made sense. But did she really want to share a guaranteed poignant, sad and potentially blubbery weekend with Rory?

Sensing her reticence, he squeezed her hands. 'Or, if you'd prefer, you camp out there alone. Though it's mighty lonely along that stretch of beach and I'd probably worry—'

'Fine. You can come.'

She rolled her eyes—an effective move against the sting of tears.

'Though I have to warn you there's this wombat that used to attack us, and he had a few feral wallaby mates. Then there's the snakes and redback spiders and—'

To her amazement, he paled.

'You've been camping before, right?'

Being a typical male, he squared his shoulders and uttered famous last words. 'How hard can it be?'

CHAPTER THIRTEEN

'NEED some help?"

Rory straightened and clutched at his middle back. 'No, thanks, I'm almost done.'

'Right.'

Gemma sent a pointed glance at the storm clouds gathering, before staring at his lame attempt at pegging the tent.

He frowned and turned his back on her, hefting the mallet high over his head and bringing it down with a resounding thud. It skidded off the peg and landed on his boot.

He cursed, and she turned away in case he looked up and caught her smiling. It wasn't her fault the guy had to go all macho on her—especially when he'd never been camping before.

In a way it was very sweet, him giving her the opportunity to camp here one last time. It had touched her in a way she hadn't expected—especially coming from a business-oriented guy who wouldn't have a sappy bone in his body. But he really should have let her take care of everything instead of divvying up tasks.

She understood he needed to feel in control. Typical guy. But judging by the time it had taken him to struggle to this point in erecting the tent, perhaps he should've assigned that particular task to her. Goodness only knew what he'd packed in the way of food.

'Isn't there something you should be doing?'

'Nope.'

She dusted off her hands, earning a filthy look. 'I've scooped out a fire pit, set up the kindling and a metal grille over it, and strung up some rope for tarps in case we need it.'

He frowned and glanced up into the trees. 'Why would we need tarps? That's what the tent's for.'

Not wanting to dent his manly pride, already suffering under the hatchet job he was making of the tent, she shrugged.

'The weather forecast sounded grim, so thought it'd pay to be doubly prepared.'

He grunted in response and resumed his mallet-swinging.

Funnily enough, she hadn't been camping in ages, and sharing this experience with him meant a lot—despite her constant teasing.

She knew he'd offered because he felt bad about the building date being brought forward, but it had been inevitable anyway. Whether the bulldozers arrived on Monday or next month made little difference. Her sanctuary would be irreversibly changed for ever.

Her light-heartedness in teasing Rory faded. Thinking of her refuge being demolished brought Coral to the forefront of her mind—a place she didn't want her to be. She'd avoided her the last week—had stayed out late working at the office and waited until she'd heard her mum head for her morning walk to shower and slip out.

Childish, but their last confrontation had been ugly, and freshly fragile after having Rory MIA for a week, with no contact, she hadn't been up to it. She regretted her harsh words, wished she hadn't verbalised the pain lodged in her heart all these years.

What would change in discovering why her mum had rejected her all those years ago? It wouldn't bring back those lost years, when she would have given anything for a hug or a genuine smile or maternal support.

She liked the fact they'd been getting along better this trip, that her mum had been making an effort. It reminded her of the good times when her dad had been alive, when Coral would roll her eyes at their woodworking and experiments yet ply them with lemonade and cookies while she made frequent trips to the shed to chat or offer inane advice they'd all laugh at.

Or the times her mum would sit in the stands at the local pool while her dad coached her in butterfly and freestyle and backstroke, encouraging her to be faster than the boys' swim team.

Or the times they'd indulged her passion for hiking, when her mum would wait patiently in the car for hours while she raced her dad up the highest peak.

While shopping and gossiping at cafés held little interest for her, Gemma would have done it if her mum had invited her along.

Sadly, verbalising her rejection hadn't helped and she regretted blurting the truth and the devastation on her mum's face when she'd stormed out.

She wanted to make amends but didn't know how. If they hadn't been able to breach the gap after her dad died, how would they recover from this?

But the small part of her that still craved her mum's attention, the part she'd deliberately shut down years ago, couldn't be ignored and demanded she make peace.

If she planned on staying in Melbourne she'd have to make an effort to repair the damage, to get their relationship back on civil terms. But she had to get out of the house—couldn't risk another potential blow-out tearing them apart completely.

She'd investigated a few short-term rentals yesterday, and expected to hear back on Monday. Until then her date was erecting the Taj Mahal of tents.

Glancing over her shoulder, she checked his progress and stifled a laugh. The tent resembled a lean-to rather than a monument.

She could offer to help, but considering his prickliness earlier he'd take it as a slight on his manly pride and refuse.

Her time would be better spent doing really important stuff. Like putting the finishing touches on her surprise. She reached for her mobile to do just that.

Rory prided himself on his construction skills. He might spend his days behind a desk, but he had a set of tools bestowed upon him by his grandfather that the old guy had taught him to use. He knew his way around hammer and wrench and screwdriver, had replaced worn washers and fixed busted water pipes, and he'd constructed a rudimentary workbench at home.

But this tent business? Major pain in the ass.

He'd read the instructions online after purchasing it. Looked simple enough. But he'd soon learned getting the damn walls to stay upright while he hammered in pegs was tougher than it looked. What he'd anticipated as being a fifteen-minute job max had taken him an hour, and the thing still looked lopsided.

As long as it kept them sheltered it would do its job. He'd wasted enough time when he could have been with Gemma.

He flicked a glance in her direction and his chest contracted. She sat in the passenger seat of his car, her feet curled beneath her to one side, engrossed in her phone, one thumb tapping a text message, the other hand absent-mindedly twirling the end of her ponytail round and round a finger.

No make-up, clad in jeans and a loose sweatshirt and hiking books, she looked like the sexiest woman he'd ever seen.

He'd been a fool to almost lose her because he couldn't handle feeling like this.

He could use all the excuses in the world—his parents' disaster of a marriage, his grandfather throwing out titbits of affection sparingly, his never having been involved in a long-term relationship—but they were just that: excuses.

He had the power to control his destiny, so why this inability to let Gemma into his heart? No one to blame but himself. He knew why too.

Plain, old-fashioned fear. Fear of losing control, fear of not being in command, fear she'd get to know the real him and run a mile.

That was the clincher: he might have an ounce of Bert in him and drive her away, as Bert had driven away his mother all those years ago.

Not that he was a philanderer, like his dad, but he'd seen beneath Bert's suave veneer over the years and the fact was Bert couldn't commit. To anyone or anything. He had power and prestige and looks, could command a room with a tilt of his head, but there was an inner coolness women found irresistible and yet it prevented him from growing close.

Rory felt the same way. Apart from Devlin Corp, he'd never felt truly passionate about anything.

Until now.

That was what really scared him—that once he'd allowed himself to truly feel for the first time, and if the relationship went pear-shaped and Gemma left, he'd be sapped of some of his strength and the power that made him invincible in the business arena.

Stupid? Maybe. But for now he'd shelve his fears and make the best of it. In it for a good time, not a long time, and all that jazz.

As if she sensed him watching her she glanced up and smiled. That slow, sexy curving of her lips called him to action.

He flung down the mallet and strode across the distance between them, squatting next to the open door and snagging her hand. 'What're you doing?'

'You'll see.'

He entwined his fingers with hers, noting her short nails, ragged cuticles, the lack of polish, finding them more appealing than the many manicured talons he'd artfully dodged over the years. 'A surprise, huh?'

'Something like that.'

Her eyes twinkled with mischief and he'd never wanted to kiss her more. 'When do I get to see this great surprise?'

She glanced at her watch and screwed up her nose, pretending to think. 'In about an hour, when it's dark.'

'Sounds intriguing.'

She squeezed his hand. 'If you finish that tent super-quick, might be in forty-five minutes.'

'Slave driver,' he said, his mock grumpy tone eliciting a laugh.

'And don't you forget it.'

His gaze swung to the pathetically lopsided tent and he cringed. He'd rather be with her, but if they planned on sleeping he'd better fix it.

Then again, perhaps there were other perks to not sleeping tonight?

* * *

'Ready?'

He nodded, his admiration for the amazing woman by his side tinged with unstoppable desire. How the hell he'd keep his hands off her tonight he had no idea.

'Should I be worried?'

She pretended to ponder, her eyes crinkling, her pert nose screwed up, and he'd never wanted to kiss anyone as much as he wanted to kiss her at that moment.

'Depends. If you're scared of the monster from the deep coming up the beach to gobble you at night, then maybe you *should* be afraid.' She wiggled her eyebrows. 'Very afraid.'

Snagging her hand in his, he tugged her down the final steps to the beach. 'I'm willing to risk it if you are.'

'Hey, I'm not the one who'd never ventured into Port Phillip Bay before.' She bumped him with her hip in an intimate gesture he liked. 'Deep-sea monsters are particularly attracted to newbies, and seeing as it was your first time in the bay last week…'

All he could focus on was one word: *attracted.* He was intensely, irrationally, imploringly attracted to her.

His self-proclamation to keep this weekend about her saying a proper goodbye to the land she loved and keeping his libido in check was in serious danger—not helped by the fact she'd brought him to a deserted beach for a moonlit walk.

'They wouldn't dare come near me with you by my side.'

She stopped and placed a hand on a cocked hip. 'Are you saying I'm scary?'

'No.'

'Then what *are* you implying?'

He loved this playfulness and her inherent ability to make any situation fun.

'You're a sea nymph. No monster in his right mind would mess with you.'

Her lips curved into a devastating smile and he knew right then he was in trouble—big trouble.

Not the kind that could be dismissed, but the kind he'd have to confront if he wanted to sleep again some time this century.

'Come on, your surprise is ready.'

Curious as to what she had in store, he fell into step alongside her, slowing down his strides to match hers, content to stroll.

He never strolled. He power-walked or jogged or strode, always moving at a chaotic pace. *You snooze, you lose* had been his motto for so long he'd forgotten what it was like to slow down and take a good, long, hard look around.

Who knew you could snorkel in Port Phillip Bay? Or that seals and dolphins and a plethora of wildlife were out there, waiting to be appreciated?

As for the Portsea land Devlin Corp had snapped up for a bargain price—he never would have fully appreciated it if Gemma hadn't come on board. He was proud of the luxury mansions his company constructed, proud of every single development around the country. But having her insight, her expertise, had opened his eyes to environmental issues he'd previously overlooked despite hiring specialists.

Portsea was only a two-hour drive from Melbourne, and yet the only time he'd ever visited was for the annual summer polo day. As for walking on this beach? Try never.

He liked his life, liked the frenetic pace and cut-throat energy of the corporate world, but this camping weekend with Gemma was teaching him something. It was okay to chill. Not that he'd become hooked on it or anything, but maybe he'd be making more trips to the beach in the future.

They rounded a small headland and he gaped.

'Surprise.'

She bounced on the balls of her feet, the white of her teeth reflected in the campfire on the beach.

'How did you manage this?'

'Called in a favour from one of dad's old fishing buddies.' She tugged him towards the fire, where her contact had left a cooler, and glanced at a rocky crop overhead and waved. 'Chester's a crabby old bachelor but he has a weakness for soap operas, so when I asked him to prep a fire on the beach for me he threw in this as well.'

'This' happened to be a cooler stocked with expensive champagne, strawberries and chocolate.

'A closet romantic?'

'Like you?'

'My fridge has three ingredients. What do you think?'

She laughed. 'Let me guess. Mouldy cheese, long-life milk and a six-pack of boutique beer—the classic bachelor staples.'

'Don't knock it till you've tried it.'

He picked up the bottle and made quick work of the cork, surprisingly piqued by a twinge of loneliness. He rarely cooked, hence his barely stocked fridge. When he ate he had an ordered-in snatched sandwich at his desk or a business dinner where he didn't taste the food while wrangling problems.

Being a bachelor suited him, but Gemma made it sound as appealing as soggy seaweed on toast.

'I've tried it,' she said, holding out the plastic flutes she'd dug up from the cooler. 'I lead a busy life, rarely in one place for long, so I guess your fridge has three more items in it than mine usually does.'

He poured champagne into the flutes and stashed the bottle on ice when he was done, not wanting to get into the deep and meaningful with her but curious about her life.

'Do you ever wish for stability and a picket fence and kids?'

She thrust a flute at him and retreated a step. He guessed he had his answer.

'Why? Because I'm a woman?'

'No, because you've got a lot to give. The way you throw yourself into work. The way you care about the environment and marine life. You'd bring that same passion to a family.'

He'd rendered her speechless.

He blundered on. 'Don't mind me. The stress of constructing that tent is making me ramble.'

She sank to the sand and patted a spot next to her—a spot he was all too willing to take. Better than having her kick sand in his face for raving like a lunatic about private matters no concern of his.

'When things matter to me I give them my all.' She twirled the flute, and tiny shards of flame reflected off the champagne. 'Always thought I'd never have time for a family.'

She downed half her champagne, lowering the flute to pin him with a probing stare.

'Why the questions? Bachelorhood not living up to expectations? Secretly pining for a family?'

'Hell, no.'

'Would you like some time to think about that?'

He managed a rueful chuckle, wondering why he felt so empty inside. Devlin Corp was his life. Anything else would be a complication he didn't need.

He'd seen first-hand what having a distracted father

meant to a family: a neglected wife who eventually left, and a kid who learned far too young to fend for himself.

He'd never make the same mistakes his dad had. So why did his instant vehement refusal leave him hollow?

'I'm not a family man,' he said, and the champagne left sourness in his mouth as he wondered what madness had possessed him to head down this track.

'You're nothing like your dad,' she said softly, her touch on his hand scaring him as much as her insight.

'I sometimes wonder.'

Her fingertips flittered across the back of his knuckles, and he shuddered with the effort not to ease her back onto the sand and cover her body with his.

'Wonder what?'

Unaware where his urge to unburden his soul was coming from, he clamped his lips.

She didn't pressure him for answers. Her fingertips continued their leisurely exploration, unhurried.

One of her many qualities he liked was the absence of the usual female necessity to badger, to know everything. She wouldn't have asked unless she genuinely cared for his answer, and that more than anything loosened his lips.

'I wonder if I'm like Bert after all.'

Her fingers stilled, rested over his, the warmth from her palm reassuring.

'Not professionally, because I know we're nothing alike there, but in our personal lives.'

'You haven't been married four times.'

'No, but at least Bert connected with those women long enough to want to marry them.'

'Couldn't have been much of connection—' She stumbled and he raised an eyebrow. 'Except with your mum, I mean. He must've loved her. They had you.'

He smiled at her blunder. 'It's okay. I'm just musing

out loud. Forget it.' He turned his hand over and threaded his fingers through hers. 'Now, how about we dunk those strawberries?'

'Later.'

She scooted closer until she pressed into his side and they sat in silence, staring into the fire.

Her closeness, both physically and emotionally, should have scared him, but he found himself relaxing, drunk on her warmth and openness rather than any alcohol buzz.

'Guess we all have our self-doubts,' she said, drawing spirals in the sand. 'You don't want to be like your dad, and I wish I was more like my mum—but that's impossible.'

He laid his hand over hers. 'You mentioned at the picnic you thought she rejected you because you weren't worthy?'

Her lips thinned and a tiny crease appeared between her brows. 'All in the past.'

He picked up her hand, turned it over and traced the lines in her palm, wanting to distract her, wanting to eradicate the sorrow in her voice.

'You shouldn't do that.'

'What?'

'Doubt yourself—ever. You're amazing, Gemma. I admire everything about you, from your work ethic to your spontaneity—' he gestured at the fire '—and everything in between. You're more than worthy. You're incredible. Don't let anyone make you think otherwise, okay?'

She mumbled an agreement, the quaver in her tone ensuring he gave her time to gather her emotions. When the silence stretched to uncomfortable, it was time for a topic change, and he squeezed her hand.

'Thanks for taking me on that dolphin swim last week. I can't stop thinking about it. It was a real eye-opener.'

She cleared her throat. 'You're welcome.' She tilted her face up to him, her skin glowing in the firelight. 'Your adaptability surprised me.'

'You didn't think I'd like it?'

'Let's just say I have a newfound respect for a guy who can swap a designer suit for a wetsuit and still manage to look exceptionally cool.'

'You think I'm cool?'

'Hot, more like it.'

She held his gaze, her eyes sparking with daring. Daring him to cross the line, daring him to kiss her, daring him to go for it.

The fire crackled. Waves crashed. He resisted.

This was it. The definitive moment where he crossed a line in the sand—literally.

If he kissed her now he wouldn't stop. Not this time.

'I warned you once about playing with fire,' he said, his free hand reaching up of its own volition to cup her cheek.

Defiant to the end, she half turned her head, nipping the pad of his thumb and sending heat streaking to his groin.

'I can handle it if you can.'

With one gigantic jump, he leapt over his metaphorical line and didn't look back.

Gemma lived in the moment.

She'd always been a daredevil, but losing her dad had cemented her reckless streak. Life was too short to waste. It was a mantra she lived by daily. A mantra that had her knees wobbling ever so slightly as she strolled across the sand hand in hand with Rory.

She had a million thoughts whirring through her head,

ranging from *I hope that tent holds* to *With this kind of tension this promises to be the best sex ever.*

Despite being opposites, they'd connected on so many levels, and tonight, by the fire on the beach, he'd revealed more than she could have hoped for.

Rory Devlin really understood her. He'd honed in on her feelings of rejection in the past and said exactly the right thing. She *was* worthy. Worthy of a guy like him. And the fact he liked her for who she was, without artifice, without pretence, had ultimately lowered her emotional defences.

She wanted to be close to him. In every possible way.

After their revealing chat he'd tortured her, holding her hand, cupping her cheek, staring into her eyes…and not kissing her.

She'd willed him to close the distance between them, to ravage her lips as he'd done previously on that memorable picnic. Instead he'd leaned so close their breaths had mingled, increasing anticipation, before moving his mouth towards her ear. Where he'd proceeded to tell her in great detail what they'd be doing tonight.

All night long.

They'd doused the fire so fast she hadn't had time to grab a torch and, laughing, they'd grabbed the cooler and made a run for their camping area.

Her body buzzed, her knees shook, her senses were on high alert. To his credit, he didn't break stride as they all but ran across the sand, and when she stumbled he caught her.

'Nice save.'

His fingertips grazed the sliver of skin exposed between her jeans and T-shirt where it had ridden up.

'Can't have you breaking a leg now. Not with what I've got planned for tonight.'

The bold declaration hung in the air between them, brash, provocative. Barely restrained tension was zapping between them, creating more energy than any solar panel.

Her skin prickled with it—a sensuous tingling that made her want to strip off and bare her body to the faint moonlight.

'Show me.'

Without saying another word Rory slid an arm around her waist and backed her through the unzipped tent flap towards the airbed, his slow, leisurely perusal like an intimate caress.

As moonlight spilled into the tent and the breeze cooled her skin Rory peeled her clothes off, worshipped her body and made love to her until she almost passed out from the pleasure.

Living in the moment had a lot to be said for it.

CHAPTER FOURTEEN

GEMMA had been a conscientious camper in the past. She'd ensure the tent had been erected properly, she'd check the food had been sealed properly, and she'd anticipate possible problems before they happened.

But she'd never camped with a sexy distraction before—and therein lay her downfall.

After making love twice they'd gleefully tumbled into their sleeping bags, spending a blissful few hours in each other's arms, only to be awoken at dawn soaked to the skin.

'You did fasten the fly?'

Rory sent a quick glance in the direction of his groin and she rolled her eyes.

'The fly for the tent. The sheet that goes over the tent to stop condensation on the inside and to keep it rainproof. In case of bad weather.'

His shamefaced expression said it all. 'Told you I'd never camped before.'

'Yeah, but…'

No use blaming him. She should have checked it. And would have if he hadn't started kissing her and the rest…

Wriggling out of a squelching sleeping bag and the wet tent, she tried to think quickly.

'I could erect the tarp, but we're already soaked.

Hopefully it was a passing shower and we can dry off before—'

'Freaking hell!'

Her jaw dropped as Rory started hopping around as if a bee had bitten his butt.

'What's wrong?'

He pointed towards his feet and downgraded his hopping to hobbling.

'Something's attacked the soles of my feet.'

She winced in sympathy. 'You fell asleep with your bare feet outside the tent?'

He nodded and muttered another curse. 'The tent's too small for me, so when you dozed off I stuck my feet out the end of the tent.'

'You've probably been bitten by bull-ants.' She gestured towards a wet log. 'Take a seat. Let me see.'

Glaring at her as if this was all her fault, he sat and presented his soles for inspection. And promptly lost his balance and fell backwards into a hole. A grumbling hole.

'What the—?'

He struggled to get upright—only to come face to face with a growling wombat the size of a baby elephant.

Okay, so she was exaggerating, but the way Rory had paled she should amend her analogy to stegosaurus size.

'What do I do?' he breathed, scrambling backwards on his hands and sore soles, doing a fair crab imitation.

'Don't worry. Willemena won't hurt you.'

'Won't hurt me? She's growling at me like I'm supper.'

'You disturbed her snoozy hidey-hole. She has every right to be upset.'

Rory tried to keep on eye on the wombat while giving her a death glare. 'You're siding with this creature?'

'"This creature" has lived here for years. The workers have probably been feeding her or leaving food scraps.

That's why she's hanging around here. She's made a shallow burrow near our campsite because she's expecting food.'

His eyebrows rose further the longer her explanation lasted, and she stifled a laugh.

'You fell on her while she was snoozing. I'd be growling too if I got woken like that.'

He eyeballed the wombat, which took a waddling step towards him.

'She can't hurt me, right?'

'Those claws have been known to rip a man apart, but you should be all right.'

With another mumbled curse he managed to gain purchase on his sore soles and surge to his feet—only to start hopping around again.

Willemena—or more likely her offspring, though Gemma had left out that part—lost interest when no food was forthcoming and trundled off in the direction of the bush.

Smiling, Gemma swung her gaze back to Rory, and in that instant, with his wet jeans clinging to his legs and his hair mussed, his mouth compressed in an unimpressed line, her heart flipped over without a hope of righting itself.

She loved him.

Loved this man for all his intriguing facets: the powerful businessman, the commanding lover, the flexible guy who had accepted her chained to his precious display, camped on her dad's land for the first time, the guy who truly understood her and liked her for it.

Their gazes met and his mouth relaxed, curving into a rueful smile that confirmed it.

How could she *not* love a guy who tolerated getting drenched, getting bitten and getting an up-close-and-personal encounter with a wombat, and still managed to smile about it?

She flew across the space between them and flung herself into his arms, wrapping her arms around his waist and burying her face in his chest.

'If this is a sympathy hug, maybe I should get tortured by the local fauna more often.'

She didn't answer, hugged him tighter, and her heart sighed with the rightness of it when he held her close as if he'd never let go.

She could always wish.

When Gemma steered his Merc into the underground car park of his penthouse and killed the engine he sent a silent prayer of thanks heavenward.

Aborting their camping trip should have made him guilty, but with his feet still stinging, despite a liberal dosing of calamine lotion, and his ego still smarting from making a fool of himself, all he felt was relief.

A nice hot soak in his Jacuzzi followed by a night tucked up in one-thousand-thread-count sheets with Gemma by his side sounded a lot more appealing than roughing it.

'Home sweet home,' she said, handing him the keys. 'How are the feet?'

He wiggled his toes. 'I'll live.'

She grinned. 'Remind me never to take you to the Amazon. The pythons, the killer tarantulas—'

'I get the picture.' He snapped his fingers. 'If we're heading in that direction, how about we skip the Amazon and head for Rio instead? *Carnivale?* Great beaches? Top hotels?'

'You're such a wuss,' she said, shaking her head, her soft smile making something twist in his chest.

But I'm all yours, he wanted to say, needing to tell her how much she meant to him but unsure of the words.

He was kidding himself if he thought they weren't in this for more than a fling. Which meant before they went any further he had to tell her the truth. He took a deep breath.

'I need to tell you something.'

'Let me guess. You're planning on standing on a scorpion nest next, or crawling up a tree to wake a rabid koala?'

There was no easy way to say this. He searched for the right words, came up empty, and settled for the blunt truth.

'I orchestrated that publicity about you in the newspaper.'

Her smile faded. The joy in her eyes was replaced with wariness and disappointment and disgust.

'Why?'

'For the company.'

'The company?' she parroted, her tone eerily flat.

It terrified him.

'My dad's constantly in the paper, flaunting some totally inappropriate woman, making a laughing stock of himself and the company—'

'And you decided to use me to oust him and take centre stage?'

He nodded, ashamed he hadn't told her sooner. 'Devlin Corp was headed for disaster when I took over from dad six months ago. We had problems with protestors on that other job and the media constantly dredges it up. I needed to raise our environmental profile and you came along at the right time.'

Her eyes narrowed, sparking blue fire. 'I get it. Hire

the eco-warrior, tout her association with the company constantly, get your money's worth. So *did* you?'

Her face had crumpled, and she made a god-awful strangled sound that slugged him.

'Gemma, listen—'

'What I want to know is was I an *inappropriate* woman too?'

She spoke over him, as if she hadn't heard a word he'd said, and by the impenetrable mask settling over her face he knew he was in trouble. Nothing he could say or do would get through to her.

'Is that what our relationship's based on? You start something with me so once the papers get tired of my professional qualifications they can plaster us over the stupid society pages?'

Her voice wobbled and he reached for her but she slapped his hands away, her shoulders rigid.

'Tell me this. Was this weekend just some dumb publicity stunt too? Get me onside as part of your ruse? Should I expect to see pictures of our beach campfire or worse spread across the papers tomorrow?'

'Course not.'

'I don't believe you,' she murmured, and turned away to stare out of the window, but not before he'd seen the shimmer of tears.

Those tears slugged him as much as her lack of faith in him. His grandfather hadn't believed in him—not really. Preferring to hand the company over to his flaky dad rather than the kid he'd groomed.

His dad hadn't believed in him either. He'd given him a year before Devlin Corp was bankrupt, but slapped him on the back regardless, with a jolly 'Don't worry, son. Business isn't everything.'

His dad was wrong. The family business *was* everything to him. It had been all he'd had. Until Gemma. Now she didn't believe in him either, and that hurt most of all.

His grandfather's lack of faith? Almost expected. His dad's? Foregone conclusion. Bert didn't have faith in much beyond Jack Daniels and the next warm bed.

But Gemma? He'd grown to value her opinion, grown to treasure those moments when she looked at him as if he was a giant among men.

He'd grown to love her.

The revelation slammed into him like a kick to the gut, leaving him just as winded.

Blindsided, he stared at the woman he loved, wanting to tell her all of it, desperate for her to understand his motivations, but unsure how to make her believe.

He needed her to believe in him.

'Gemma?'

She half turned towards him, a blond strand curling over her cheek, her top teeth worrying her bottom lip as she deliberately averted her eyes.

'I love you,' he blurted, cringing at his delivery but frantic to get the words out there, for her to hear him out.

Before he could say anything more she muttered, 'I don't believe that either,' flinging open the door and making a run for it.

CHAPTER FIFTEEN

FOR a girl who never cried, hooking up with Rory-bloody-Devlin had made a true mockery of her.

Gemma sobbed all the way home in the car, thankful she'd left her VW at his place.

Everything they'd shared had been a sham. He'd hired her for positive publicity and to deflect environmental lobbyists; he would have had to keep her sweet and what better way than to charm her and woo her?

Every tender moment they'd shared flashed before her eyes: his sweet, tentative greeting kiss when he'd picked her up for the Yarra Valley jaunt, the passionate picnic kiss, holding hands on the boat, making love in the tent.

Had it all been a lie? A calculated ploy to keep her on-side so his all-important damn company could complete the Portsea project on time?

Her anger rose exponentially as her sorrow petered out. By the time she'd battled Chapel Street traffic and pulled into her driveway she was ready to thump something.

Stomping into the house, she headed straight for the coffee machine. Not that she needed to be any more wired, but she was desperate to do something familiar to soothe her rampant fury.

And she *was* furious: furious at Rory for lying to her,

furious at him for using her, but most of all furious at herself for falling in love.

There were reasons she didn't take risks with her emotions, and this all-pervading, cloying, utterly soul-shattering devastation was one of them.

She enjoyed her life too much to feel this crappy, and from what she'd seen with colleagues over the years the moment you let love into your life was the moment you said goodbye to clarity and perspective and independence.

She should be thanking Rory for snapping her out of this so called love before she really invested her heart.

More than she already had.

She slammed the cupboard shut and plonked a cup on the counter, glaring at the coffee machine in the futile hope it would produce coffee sooner.

When it didn't, she whirled around to head for the fridge. And her gaze clashed with Coral's.

Great—that was all she needed. Another draining confrontation.

Unable to speak past the lump in her throat, she waited for her mum to speak. Instead, Coral stepped into the kitchen and opened her arms.

Gemma froze.

When was the last time her mum had embraced her? At the funeral? At the wake?

Too much had happened for her to want comfort from a mother who hadn't been available when she'd needed her most, but in that moment, looking into her mum's understanding eyes, she needed a hug more than she would have thought possible.

She took a few hesitant steps, stiff-legged and awkward like a colt, before Coral met her halfway, bundling her into her arms.

The sobs in the car were nothing to the tears tumbling down her cheeks now.

She had no idea how long her mum smoothed her back and murmured 'Shh…' in her ear, but eventually her tears ran out and she was left feeling awkward and embarrassed.

Coral didn't give her time to dwell. 'Sit. I'll make coffee.'

For once Gemma did as she was told, waiting for a barrage of questions that didn't come.

Finally, when she couldn't stand the silence any longer, she blurted, 'I've fallen in love with Rory Devlin.'

Coral didn't spill a drop of milk as she topped up the stainless steel jug.

'I figured as much.'

'How?'

Coral shrugged. 'The only time I've seen you cry is over your father, so I assumed this had to be over another man.'

Gemma didn't know if that made her sound like a weak female but she left it alone. Her mum was being nice, they'd glossed over their last confrontation, and she was dying for that coffee.

'What's the problem?' Coral placed a steaming cappuccino in front of her and took a seat opposite.

'He used me.'

Coral's eyes narrowed and her lips thinned. This evidence of her mum's protectiveness meant a lot.

'How?'

'He only hired me for my credentials, not my skills. Then he tipped off journos about me for good publicity in the paper for his precious bloody company, and got close to me to keep me onside.'

Coral nodded. 'Smart lad—trying to go one up on

Cuthbert's antics spread over the tabloids for all and sundry to see.'

Gemma gaped. 'You're *agreeing* with what he did?'

Coral's exasperated sigh blew the froth off her cappuccino. 'From a business perspective only.' She wiped the froth with her fingertip. 'From a personal viewpoint, I don't believe he used you for a minute. He cares about you. Any fool can see that.'

'How would you know?'

Shock number one had come when her mum had offered her a comforting hug. Shock number two blew her away now, as Coral slid open the third drawer of the dresser—the one that had used to house rubber bands and paperclips and recycled plastic bags—and pulled out a bulky scrapbook with her name on the cover.

'Here. See for yourself.'

Coral flipped towards the back of the scrapbook and pointed at a carefully clipped picture of her and Rory at the campsite yesterday, of him squatting next to the open car door, gazing up at her and holding her hand.

He'd lied.

She'd asked him if their camping weekend would be media fodder too. He'd said no.

She should have known better than to believe a word from his devious mouth. A guy who'd used her from the beginning would say anything to squirm his way out of trouble—all in the name of protecting his precious company.

'If that's not the expression of a smitten man, I don't know what is.'

Speechless, Gemma ignored the picture of Rory and flicked back through the scrapbook, her mind reeling as she scanned pages filled with her earliest drawings, the first Mother's Day card she'd made, a short story she'd written in second grade, yearly school photos, sporting achievements, the invitation to her graduation…

She'd known about the kiddie stuff, but all these clippings of her achievements after her dad had died? News to her.

When she came to the last page, the one with the newspaper clippings about her and the latest addition with her and Rory, she finally risked glancing at her mother. The woman who'd cared a lot more than she'd ever admitted.

'Why did you keep all this stuff?'

Coral tried to appear as poised and cool as ever, but Gemma noted her hands trembling as she picked up her coffee cup.

'No bull, Mum. The truth.'

Taking several long sips that grated on Gemma's nerves, Coral finally replaced the coffee cup on the table.

'Because I was proud of you, and it helped me feel close to you after your father died.'

The sip of coffee Gemma had taken soured in her mouth. Had her mum wanted to get close but hadn't known how?

'What do you mean, you couldn't get close to me?'

Coral paled and the corners of her mouth drooped. 'Maybe this isn't the best time to have this conversation—'

'There'll never be a good time.' Dragging in a breath, Gemma blew it out slowly, calming. 'You want me to start? Fine. After Dad died an invisible wall sprang up between us and I never knew why. Then I see this—' she waved at the scrapbook '—and it makes a mockery of every self-doubt I've ever had. So 'fess up. What's this all about?'

Anguish clouded Coral's eyes before her head sagged in defeat. 'Your father.'

Of all the answers Gemma had expected that hadn't been one of them. 'What does Dad have to do with this?'

Coral clasped her hands tightly and laid them in her lap, squaring her shoulders as if readying for battle. Her rigid posture was the epitome of prim and proper, without a hint of the defeat of a few moments ago.

'You were always your father's daughter from the time you could walk, and I could never compete with that.'

Shocked at the admission, Gemma shook her head. 'We were a close family. We did stuff together all the time. There was never a competition between you.'

'That's because I fitted in with whatever you wanted to do with your dad.' Coral's hands twisted, the knuckles stark white against her crimson suit. 'As a toddler you were already building block towers and pushing dump-trucks and demolishing trains. You weren't interested in dolls or fairies or sparkles. Then as you grew you trailed after your father constantly, spending hours locked away in that workshop of his. Shutting me out,' she added, speaking so softly Gemma almost didn't hear.

A pang of guilt shot through her misery. *Had* they shut her out? Gemma remembered rushing through her homework so she could spend a few hours after school watching her dad build something. And weekends had been heaven, when they'd lock themselves away in the workshop or trawl markets for parts.

Gemma had always thought her mum didn't mind because she'd watch them and ply them with snacks—when she wasn't busy hosting a garden party or having coffee with her friends on Chapel Street.

But maybe Coral had done those things to occupy her time? To fill the void left by a husband and only child so wrapped up in each other's hobbies they'd ignored her?

'We never meant to exclude you,' she said, the guilt

pressing more heavily against her chest when Coral blinked back tears.

'I know. And it didn't matter so much when we were a family. But after your father died…' Coral wrung her hands, twisting them over and over, until Gemma reached out and stopped her. 'I was afraid.'

'Of what?'

'Of having nothing in common with you, of not being able to relate to you in the same way you'd always related to your father, of having you reject me.'

Coral sniffed and dabbed her nose with a tissue while Gemma absorbed the enormity of the truth and regretted they hadn't had this conversation years ago.

'By the time I'd dealt with my grief and pulled myself together the gap between us had grown and I didn't know how to breach it.'

What could Gemma say? She knew exactly what her mum meant because she'd felt the same way. Wanting to be closer to her mother but not knowing how to approach her, especially when they had nothing in common. But if her mum could confess her innermost fears, so would she.

'I was only a teenager, Mum. I felt like I'd let you down in some way.'

Coral shook her head fiercely. '*Never.* I hate that you think you weren't good enough in some way. I never meant to reject you, darling. I was always proud of you.' She nodded at the scrapbook. 'That's proof of it…' Her mum trailed off, unable to meet her eyes.

'There's more, isn't there?'

Coral's teary gaze snapped to hers, her nod reluctant. 'I'm ashamed to admit I was jealous.'

'Of me?'

'No, of your relationship with your father. When you

hit your teens I expected you to grow apart from him, like my friends' kids, but you didn't. You two seemed to get closer, and that really irked.' Her gaze dropped to focus on her wringing hands. 'I—I thought it was me, that I was at fault somehow.'

'Mum—'

'No, let me finish.' Coral dabbed at her eyes, not a telltale blob of mascara to be seen. 'Losing your father ripped me apart, but in my own twisted way I thought it'd bring us closer. I didn't expect you to share my love of fashion or manicures or glossy magazines, but I wanted us to be close. When the opposite happened I didn't know how to deal with it.' Coral dragged her tear-filled gaze to meet hers. 'I let you down and I'm sorry.'

Gemma didn't know what to say. Not that she could say anything with that giant lump of regret stuck in her throat.

'You needed me after Karl died and I wasn't there for you. By the time I wanted to be it was too late…'

'It's never too late.' Gemma reached across the table and covered one of her mum's hands with hers. 'We can't change the past but we can make more of an effort in the future. We can both be there for each other.'

But, considering her relationship with Rory was over, would she still stick around?

'I've planned on staying longer in Melbourne once the Portsea project wraps up…'

Panic flared in Coral's eyes at the mention of Portsea, igniting Gemma's latent anger.

'I have to tell you, Mum, I'll never understand how you could've sold Dad's land for your own needs.'

Coral gnawed on her bottom lip, removing the carefully applied lipstick and leaving an ugly smudge.

Puzzled by her conflicted expression, Gemma removed

her hand, but Coral's hand snaked out and snagged hers, her eyes suddenly bright and clear.

'It wasn't for me.'

'What do you mean?'

'I sold the land to pay off your father's debts.'

Shock ripped through long-held belief. 'What about your lifestyle? This house?'

Coral squeezed her hand and released it. 'Your father's family bestowed this house, the Portsea land and some shares on us when we married. We lived off those investments. But your father insisted on sending you to private school, and he spent a lot on those experiments of his...'

She trailed off and the reality of the situation hit. Her mum hadn't sold Karl's land on a whim; she'd done it out of necessity.

'Are you in financial trouble now?'

Coral shook her head. 'The sale of the land cleared your school fees debt and paid off the rest of what we owed.'

Now stricken with guilt, Gemma said, 'Why didn't you tell me? After what I said to you, what I accused you of—'

'Because I didn't want to taint the image you had of your father. You idolised him, were devastated when he died. Better you should think I sold the land out of selfishness than blame him.'

Her mum was *that* selfless? It only made what she'd thought that much meaner.

Anger mingled with regret. Anger at her dad for putting them in this predicament, anger that the perfect father she'd adored hadn't been so perfect, anger that her memories of him would now be tainted by disillusionment.

Anger at herself for blaming her mum for something that wasn't her fault.

'I'm sorry, Mum. For everything.'

Tears glistened in Coral's eyes again. 'I'm sorry too. For wasting all those years when I should've made more of an effort to reconnect with my only child.'

Gemma had never been a hugger, but embracing her mum now seemed the most natural thing in the world.

When they'd resumed their seats, Coral tapped the scrapbook.

'If you're in such a forgiving mood, maybe you should extend some towards that young man of yours?'

Gemma's reluctant gaze fell on the photo of Rory. He *did* have a starry-eyed expression, as if she was the best Christmas present he'd ever received. Probably an act, but damn, it was a good act—one she'd fallen for.

'I'm not only upset because he used me.' She knuckled her eyes, annoyed at the persistent burn of tears since she'd discovered the truth behind their relationship. 'It's more than that. I told him about *us*—how I felt worthless and not good enough when you rejected me.'

'Oh, honey, I'm so sorry—'

'It's okay, Mum, we've discussed it. We're moving on. But I opened up to Rory, the first guy I've ever trusted, and he's done the same thing. I thought he saw beneath my bravado, saw the real me and liked me for it regardless. But it was all a lie.'

A sob bubbled up and she swallowed it, determined not to cry over him any more.

'He doesn't respect me for who I really am. All he sees is what I can do for him professionally. He doesn't know me at all.'

That was what cleaved her heart: the fact he'd said she shouldn't doubt her self-worth, she was amazing, incredible, blah, blah, blah. And all the while he'd been buttering her up, getting cosy to suit his own ends.

He'd done exactly what she'd divulged had hurt her most: rejected her for no other reason than being herself.

She could throttle him.

'How did you find out?'

'The louse told me.' She breathed deeply, in and out, calming. 'We had this amazing weekend, connected on so many levels, then he blurted the truth.' Her hands fisted. 'I could kill him.'

'I'd help you if I thought he'd done what you're accusing him of.'

Gemma frowned at her mum's defence. 'He did it. He told me.'

'Why would he have told you the truth unless you mean something to him? He could've continued the lie but he didn't.'

Probably couldn't sleep at night with a guilty conscience. How she wished that wombat had gnawed on his bits.

'I'm not wasting time figuring out his motivations.'

Coral pursed her lips, deep in thought. 'Maybe you should? We've wasted a lot of years doubting ourselves, second-guessing, unable to reach out for fear of rejection.' Coral touched her cheek in brief reassurance.

'Shouldn't you challenge him and hear his rationale, so you'll have no regrets whatever happens?'

Gemma sulked. Great time for her mum to pull out the maternal advice—especially when it made perfect sense.

'Take it from someone who knows. Don't waste a minute of your life wishing you could change a situation without giving it a damn good shake-up first.'

Was it that simple? Should she confront Rory? Give him a chance to explain?

She'd been so consumed by hurt when he'd told her the

truth she hadn't wanted to hear any more, let alone some misplaced declaration of love.

But what if he *did* love her? Could they make this work?

Only one way to find out.

Raising her coffee cup in Coral's direction, she smiled for the first time in an hour.

'Here's to more wise motherly advice.'

Coral's lower lip wobbled in response, a fat tear plopping into her coffee before she returned a watery smile.

Gemma couldn't cry any more. She'd used up her yearly quota. Tears were wasted.

Having her mum's reassurance meant the world to her: she *was* special and unique and loved—not some freakish outcast as she'd misguidedly thought all these years.

The knowledge gave her confidence. Confidence to confront her future head-on.

CHAPTER SIXTEEN

CONSIDERING he'd had his feet ravaged by killer insects, his ass almost chewed by a crazed wombat and his declaration of love flung back in his face over the weekend, Rory knew the week had to get better.

It didn't.

He spent Monday troubleshooting in Brisbane, Tuesday schmoozing in Sydney, and Wednesday delegating in Adelaide. Three full-on days of check-ins and airline food and Devlin Corp business.

The airport stuff he could do without, but the business side of things? Usually he thrived on it. Not this week. This week sucked.

Big-time.

He'd handled problems non-stop—from insubordinate contractors to fluctuating market values, bank errors to threatened strikes.

He'd had a gutful.

His only consolation? Business problems kept his mind off problems of another kind: namely Gemma.

In that annoying time before drifting off to sleep, when his mind blanked, the memory of their last encounter would surface, ramming home the fact that the woman he loved didn't believe in him.

Sure, he'd stuffed up with not telling her sooner about

why he'd initially hired her and the newspaper publicity, but what sort of a cold, heartless woman flung a sincere declaration back in his face?

Okay, so she wasn't cold or heartless—far from it. But he couldn't believe she wouldn't give him a chance to explain.

He'd compulsively checked his phone for messages or e-mails the last few days, hopeful she'd relent and contact him. Nothing.

He'd deluded himself into believing it was probably better this way: clean break, no emotional fallout.

Yeah, right.

He was kidding himself.

Aside from the fact he had to see her in the business arena for the next few weeks, until her tender ran out, he couldn't pretend what they'd shared meant nothing.

He might have chosen to shut emotions out of his life for years, but now he'd let them in there was no turning back.

He'd never be like his dad, going through women like socks, but he could see the appeal of never staying with one woman long enough to get involved. Lack of emotional ties meant pain-free disentanglements. Something he had a feeling would definitely *not* apply to him and Gemma.

A dull ache resided between his brows and had done for the last few days. Pinching the bridge of his nose to stop it from escalating, he strode through the deserted hallways of Devlin Corp.

He wasn't in the mood for an all-nighter, but he needed something to take his mind off Gemma now he'd mentally conjured her again.

Annoyed he'd had another lapse, he flung open the door to his office. Stopped dead.

Gemma had managed to surprise him yet again.

She raised an eyebrow, looked him up and down. 'About time you showed up.'

Speechless, he stared at the woman he loved, chained to his desk, wearing grungy camouflage pants, a black T-shirt, ugly fuchsia jellyfish earrings and a smile that could tempt a saint.

Considering he'd seen what she had beneath those awful clothes, he sure as hell was no saint.

Several long seconds later, when he'd managed to quell the urge to run across the office and scoop her into his arms, he shut the door and covered the distance between them to stand less than a foot away.

Close enough to smell her light spring sunshine fragrance. Close enough to see the flicker of uncertainty behind the sass in her eyes. Close enough to touch her.

He wanted to touch her—boy, did he want to. But he couldn't afford to get distracted. Not when they had a few issues to sort out. Namely, did they have a future?

'How long have you been tied to that thing?'

She shrugged and the chains around her wrists rattled. 'About thirty minutes.'

'How did you—?'

'Denise let me in. She knew your estimated time of arrival. I said I had important business that couldn't wait.' A tiny line creased her brow. 'Considering she's probably seen that picture of us in the tabloids, like the rest of Melbourne, I'm guessing she didn't buy my business excuse.'

She'd given him the perfect opening line to dive into an explanation about that latest publicity shot, but he didn't take it. He wanted to know why she was here before putting himself on the line again.

'Why the chains?'

She'd captured his attention the first time she'd pulled that trick and it hadn't waned since.

'Because I thought you needed to be reminded of my whacky, insane personality, and factor that into the way I behaved the last time we were together.'

'Oh.'

So much for being the articulate consummate professional.

'If you promise to listen, I'll untie them.'

He liked having her tied up at his mercy, but voicing that particular opinion wouldn't get them anywhere except naked and hot—two things he'd like, but would do little to solve their problems.

'Go ahead.'

It was bad enough reining in his rampant impulse to devour her while she was hog-tied, but when she bent forward to slip the chains off her ankles and he glimpsed a flash of black lace at her cleavage he clenched his fists to stop from reaching for her.

Instead he headed for the discreet bar tucked away in a cabinet, poured himself a double shot of whisky and downed it straight. When he heard blissful silence, meaning she'd finished slipping out of those damn chains, he risked a glance over his shoulder.

'Want a drink?'

'No, thanks.'

She was fiddling with an earring, twisting it till the thing should have snapped.

'Can we talk?'

'Sure,' he managed to croak out, before clearing his throat and gesturing towards the modular suite forming an L in the far corner.

He waited for her to sit before choosing the sofa opposite. The double shot might have cleared his head momentarily, but he had a feeling sitting too close to Gemma would befuddle it faster than he could blink.

She sat with her hands clasped in her lap, shoulders squared, spine straight, as if someone had stuck a rod down the back of her T-shirt. It was so far at odds with the laid-back woman comfortable in her own skin he knew she had to be as nervous as he was.

'I want to apologise for freaking out on you when you told me about the publicity and why you hired me,' she said, staring at some point over his left shoulder. 'It came from left field and really shook me up.'

She took a deep breath, straining against the fabric on her T-shirt, and he maintained eye contact with great effort.

'I don't do relationships as a rule, and you're the first guy I've dated in a while, so I felt betrayed and confused and— Ah, hell, this is becoming long-winded.'

She tugged on both earrings, managing to twist off a tentacle or two.

'What I'm trying to say is I shouldn't have run like that. I wanted to call, but thought this apology warranted a face-to-face meeting.'

She finally looked at him, expecting an answer, but his mind blanked.

What could he say? That he'd had an awful week because he missed her so much it felt like a permanent ache lodged in his chest? That he'd given up on them? That even if they tried this again how would he know she wouldn't do a runner again at some point in the future?

He settled for the simplest response.

'I'm glad you're here.'

One eyebrow rose in a sceptical arch. 'Really? Because you don't look it.'

'I'm thrown, that's all.'

That wasn't all, and they both knew it.

'You're peed off at me.'

He could lie, try to smooth things over, but what would be the point? If they stood any chance it had to be truth all the way from now on. 'Guess it's not every day I tell a woman I love her and she flings it back in my face.'

She winced. 'That was tactless. Not one of my proudest moments.' Her fiddling fingers stilled and she raised a hesitant glance. 'Did you mean it?'

'I'm not in the habit of saying things I don't mean.'

Jeez, could he sound any more uptight and pompous if he tried? Yeah, he was angry with her, but he had to let it go. Or walk away. Something he couldn't imagine doing at this point.

'I—I thought you said it to get me to forgive you.'

The thought had struck him while mulling it over these last few days. *Had* he thrown it out there in desperation? For fear of losing her? He didn't think so. Then again, did he really have a clue what love was?

'Honestly? I haven't had good role models in the love stakes. My grandfather was a tyrant who showed affection with gruffness. And you know my mum upped and left when I was a kid. Dad equates love with the latest model he can sweet-talk into his bed. I date. I don't do love.'

Her shoulders sagged at his bluntness, but the defiance never left her eyes. 'I keep hoping you'll clarify that with *until now.*'

'Do you want me to?'

'I just want the truth,' she said, her weary tone echoing the tiredness seeping through him. 'It's something I haven't had too much of lately.'

'What—?'

'Just some stuff I've learned from my mum.' She took a deep breath and eyeballed him. 'Let me get this straight.

I've apologized. You've semi-forgiven me. You say you love me but you don't do love.' She held her hands out palm-up and shrugged. 'Where do we go from here?'

'Damned if I know,' he muttered, hating the confusion clouding his head.

He wanted to clear up this mess and move on, but he was tired and grumpy—and wary. Wary of taking a chance, wary of having it blow up in his face again, but most of all wary of the power she held over him.

He didn't like having someone else responsible for his happiness, didn't like depending on anyone. Yet in a short period of time he'd done just that, and while Gemma had come here to apologise she hadn't given him any clue as to *her* feelings.

He wanted to give her a definitive answer, but right now he was running on empty.

'My work here is done.' She stood so abruptly she banged her knee on the table. He instinctively reached out to touch it but she swiftly sidestepped. 'I came here to see where we stand. Guess I have my answer.'

He should have stopped her, should have blurted out his innermost thoughts and deepest fears. But that would involve taking a monumental risk—even bigger than the one he'd taken when assuming the CEO role at Devlin Corp.

Could he do it?

One look at her downturned mouth and shimmering eyes and slumped shoulders was all the incentive he needed.

'Gemma, wait—'

She didn't, and he watched her walk out through the door, taking a piece of him with her again.

Gemma made it to the lift before the tears burning the backs of her eyes fell. Of all the stubborn, emotionally repressed, uptight jerks she had to go and fall in love with *him.*

She'd known it had been a mistake from the start, had lowered her defences regardless. *Idiot.*

Slow-burning anger replaced her indignation. Anger at herself for reneging on her staunchly independent stance and getting emotionally involved.

Mistake. *Big* mistake.

Her tears evaporated as anger took hold, refusing to be ignored.

Who the hell did he think he was? Telling her he loved her, then retreating behind his austere front despite her taking a risk and coming here?

He wasn't the only emotionally repressed person around here. She saw one in the mirror every morning, but *she'd* managed to reach out. Why couldn't he?

Fuming, she dashed a hand across her eyes and punched at the button, willing the numbers to accelerate quickly so she could get the hell out of here.

'Gemma, wait!'

Damn. She jabbed at the button repeatedly, her heart sinking as the lift stuck on the tenth floor. Swearing, she eyed the fire escape and wondered if she could jog down eighteen flights of stairs even as a hand clamped on her shoulder, effectively ending her escape plans.

'Please, come back to the office—'

'Why? So you can sit there and pretend you don't care? No, thanks.'

He blanched. 'You need to hear the truth.'

She shrugged off his hand, but he didn't let her go so easily, grabbing both her upper arms, blocking her, giving her no option but to look up at him.

'The truth? After the charade you've been perpetuating? Like you'd know what *that* is.'

She scored a direct hit and shame shadowed his gutted gaze. ‘Please, Gemma, just five minutes.’

She owed him nothing. Apart from a swift kick where those bull-ants really should have bitten.

‘Give me one good reason why I should go back into that office with you.’

He had exactly one second to make his answer count.

‘When I said I love you, it wasn’t an excuse to justify what I did. I do. Love you. And I want a chance to show you how much.’

The lift pinged and the doors slid open.

She had two options. Walk away now and preserve what was left of her shredded heart. Or give this one last shot.

‘I won’t let you down again, I promise.’

Her chest constricted, making it difficult to breathe. Her dad had used to make promises all the time.

We’ll build that go-kart on the weekend, Gem. Promise. We’ll check out my new secret fishing spot on the bay next week. Promise. We’ll go hiking at the Grampians next summer. Promise.

Her dad had kept every promise he’d ever made to her. Would Rory? She’d done so much with her dad—at the expense of her mum, so she’d learned.

Ironically, thinking of Coral cemented her decision.

Don’t waste a minute of your life wishing you could change a situation without giving it a damn good shake-up first.

Her mum was right. She didn’t want to spend the next few months, maybe a lifetime, regretting that she hadn’t given this a shake-up.

Not wanting to give in too easily, she tilted her head up, silenced him with a haughty glare before he could plead again.

'Just so you know, if a guy breaks a promise to me I use these chains to lash him to a concrete block and drop him off the end of Station Pier.'

She rattled her bag for emphasis and the corners of his mouth curved.

'I'll keep that in mind,' he said, slipping a hand under her elbow and guiding her back to his office.

When she hesitated at the door his grip tightened, as if he expected her to bolt.

'We owe this to ourselves,' he said, his breath fanning her hair, tickling her scalp.

She nodded in agreement, but was nervous nonetheless. What could he possibly say to convince her to take a chance?

They entered the office and he spun to face her, but before he could speak she held up a hand. 'Start at the beginning and tell me everything. The truth this time.'

He frowned, his hand unsteady as he jammed it through his hair, ruffling his usually immaculate short back and sides.

'Devlin Corp had problems with protestors on our last big project. It almost ruined us. Dad was in charge up at Port Douglas. There was a huge fuss and negative media input, saying we were ravaging the rainforest and worse.'

'Were you?'

He tensed, started pacing. 'My father isn't a businessman. He didn't have a clue. Hired the wrong consultants, took shortcuts, didn't read the fine print. Whatever he touched, it was a mess.' He drew in a long breath, blew it out. 'I stepped in to clean it up.'

'Then I came along and you thought you'd use me to fend off similar potential problems?'

He had the grace to nod imperceptibly. 'You were so gung-ho at the start I wanted to get rid of you. Then I saw your pitch and it blew me away. I knew you'd be an asset to the project. Around the same time I saw another mention of my father in the papers…' He winced. 'It was all about timing. You were hell-bent on scoring the job to protect your father's land. I was hell-bent on protecting my project from my father.'

She couldn't fault his logic, but it didn't detract from the fact he'd unashamedly used her.

'You saw it as a win-win.' She wanted to jab a finger in his direction but was too afraid it would shake. 'The consummate businessman, thinking about the bottom dollar, screw emotions.'

Stricken, he locked his gaze on hers. 'I didn't expect to fall for you.'

'That must've mucked up your perfectly constructed plan. Tell me—that picture of us together at Portsea. What was that about?'

He shook his head. 'A mistake. The publicity highlighting your strengths was all I wanted in the papers. Some over-enthusiastic journo must've wanted a scoop and continued to tail you.'

'Nice.'

He held his hands out to her, palms up. 'I'm sorry. I should've told you the truth from the beginning.'

'Yeah, you should've.' She twisted an earring, deriving little comfort from her marine friend. 'I opened up to you, told you how Mum had made me feel, like I was never good enough. Then you go and do the same.'

Horror widened his eyes, but she held up her hand to stave off a response.

'You told me not to doubt myself, that I was amazing, then you belittled me by doing this. Do you know what it felt like? A double betrayal. I thought you really understood me, the first guy to ever do that, then I discovered it was a ruse to protect your precious bloody company.'

'My love for you was never a ruse,' he said, the anguish contorting his mouth not detracting from its sensuous curve. 'I would never fake anything like that.'

Resisting the urge to rub away the agonising ache over her heart, she headed for the door. 'Good to know, but it doesn't change a thing—'

'Marry me.'

She stopped dead and stared at him in disbelief.

'I know what you're thinking. Who wants to marry a boorish workaholic who spends his life worrying about his business, using the people he loves for it, and can't see the best thing that ever happened to him even when she chains herself to whatever's handy to grab his attention?'

He waved his hand around the office.

'See this? It was my life till I met you. I'd have done anything for the business, including risk losing you. Using you for publicity and good PR and to deter protestors. Stupid. Monumentally stupid. Not any more.'

He took her hand and dropped to one knee. She was too stunned to do anything but gape.

'I've stuffed up again, blurting that proposal like I blurted how much I love you.' He raised her hand to his lips and kissed the back. 'This time I'm doing it right. I love you, Gemma. Love your quirkiness and exuberance and your conviction in standing up for what you believe in. Love you for who you are, inside and out. Love how you've opened my eyes in so many ways. Love how you make me feel a better man when I'm with you.'

He turned her hand over and kissed her palm, sending dizzying warmth spiralling through her.

'I'm hoping you can forgive me for stuffing up and not

telling you the truth earlier. I'm hoping you can believe in me. Enough to be my wife.'

Gemma stared at the man she loved kneeling in front of her, genuine love radiating from his eyes.

To see this strong, powerful, commanding man vulnerable to her made her realise she wasn't the only one with insecurities. When it came to love, it made nervous ninnies of them all.

'An answer some time this century would be nice, before I chain myself to a concrete block.'

She tugged on his hand, waiting till he stood before flinging herself into his arms, savouring the security of being held by the man she'd thought she'd lost.

He hugged her tight, mirroring her desire to never let go. She'd hold him to that.

When he released her, an eternity later, she stared into his incredible blue eyes, needing no further assurances.

People like them, who didn't trust their feelings, didn't open up easily. She believed him when he said he'd wanted to tell her the truth earlier, probably at that tiny café when she'd asked him not to spoil the moment.

But he'd opened up to her in every other way that counted, and to have the unswerving love of a guy like him…? She'd be a fool to walk away from what they could have.

While his declaration had been amazing, and she'd needed to hear him articulate his feelings, she should have trusted the depth of his love all along—for no one could fake the emotion shining from his eyes.

'So?'

She cupped his face. 'So I'm thinking October would be perfect for a spring wedding.'

He let out a jubilant whoop, picked her up and swung her around until they were breathless.

Rory pulled an all-nighter.

Gemma didn't mind. She was right there by his side, and work was the furthest thing from their minds.

EPILOGUE

'I NOW pronounce Portsea Point officially open.'

As the mayor cut the ribbon across the main road leading into the precinct, Rory squeezed Gemma's hand.

She glanced up at her husband and smiled through her tears.

Today had been bittersweet in so many ways: walking through the houses which would soon be filled with laughter and cooking aromas and squabbling siblings, touring her dad's land where the newly built marine preservation park would soon be enjoyed by families and tourists and anyone with a passion for this beautiful beach.

Rory and Devlin Corp had come through for her, constructing the conservation area exactly the way she'd envisaged, and she hoped the people who lived here would love this place as much as her dad had.

'Let's get out of here.'

Rory tugged on her hand and she didn't need encouragement to follow his lead. He'd done his duty, making an inspiring speech before the mayor. Besides, she knew where he was leading her.

Their spot.

They slipped through the crowd and turned left, walking in silence till they reached the end of the road where it opened into a car park. A huge wooden sign hung over the entrance.

KARL SHULTZ MEMORIAL PARK. The words had been carved into the wood by a local craftsman, and her throat constricted as it always did when she saw the evidence of how much her husband loved her.

They didn't speak. Rory allowed her time to absorb the significance of this as he always did, respecting her need for private memories as she silently connected with her dad.

They walked through the sand-gravel mix to the entrance of the park—a sprawling acre edged by a natural ti-tree border. There was no sea wall that would have long-term disastrous consequences for the beach beyond.

There was no newfangled plastic play equipment or electric barbecue here. Just rudimentary wooden climbing frames and benches, and that spectacular view over the ocean—a view she'd treasured from the first time she'd camped here at seven years of age.

They stood on the edge of the park, hand in hand, and her heart swelled with love for this man who understood her and accepted her and loved her unconditionally.

He'd put up with her buying an old house in Kew and renovating it to six-star energy efficiency, he'd tolerated her chickens taking up the sole corner of their back yard that hadn't been converted into a veggie patch, and he hadn't blinked when she'd taken up the next greatest environmental cause and spent two months in the Gulf of Carpentaria.

He let her be herself while demonstrating his love in so many ways. When she woke before him each morning and watched him sleep, his mouth relaxed, his eyelashes shadowing his cheeks, she wondered what she'd done to deserve him.

'How can I ever thank you for doing this? For merging our dreams for the land together and creating harmony? For understanding how much preserving the marine area here meant to me? For everything?'

He touched her earring—a platinum killer whale with a twinkling diamond eye—and smiled.

'The day you agreed to marry me was thanks enough.'

'That's incredibly corny.'

Adorably bashful, he shrugged. 'What can I say? I'm a novice in this love business.'

'Lucky for us, we can learn as we go along.'

Sliding her hands around his neck, she lowered his head and kissed him.

Perfect.

When her husband kissed like a dream she could quite happily look forward to a lifetime of hands-on practice in the love stakes.

* * * * *

THE BILLIONAIRE'S FAIR LADY

BY

BARBARA WALLACE

Barbara Wallace is a life-long romantic and daydreamer, so it's not surprising that at the age of eight she decided to become a writer. However, it wasn't until a co-worker handed her a romance novel that she knew where her stories belonged. For years she limited her dreams to nights, weekends and commuter train trips, while working as a communications specialist, PR freelancer and full-time mum. At the urging of her family she finally chucked the day job and pursued writing full time—she couldn't be happier.

Barbara lives in Massachusetts, with her husband, their teenage son and two very spoiled, self-centred cats (as if there could be any other kind). Readers can visit her at www.barbarawallace.com and find her on Facebook. She'd love to hear from you.

To the fabulous Donna Alward, who talked me off ledges and pushed me to get this story on paper. You're the best!

To Flo, the best editor a woman could ask for. To the real Fran and Alice for providing the legal background information. Thanks for the help.

And, as always, to my boys Pete and Andrew, who put up with an awful lot so I can live my dream of writing stories for a living.

CHAPTER ONE

HE DIDN'T believe her.

Color her not surprised. *You've got to go uptown to fight uptown.* Minute the thought entered her brain, she should have shoved it aside. After all, bad ideas were a Roxy O'Brien specialty. But no, she opened the phone directory and picked the first uptown law firm whose ad mentioned wills. Which was why she now sat in her best imitation business outfit—really her waitress uniform with a new plaid blazer—waiting for Michael Templeton, attorney at law, to deliver his verdict.

"Where did you say you found these letters?" he asked. His gold-rimmed reading glasses couldn't mask the skeptical glint in his brown eyes. "Your mother's closet?"

"Yes," she replied. "In a shoe box." Tucked under a collection of seasonal sweaters.

"And you didn't know they existed before then?"

"I didn't know anything until last month."

That was putting it mildly. Her head was still reeling.

The attorney didn't reply. Again, not surprising. He'd done very little talking the entire meeting. In fact, Roxy got the distinct impression he found the whole appointment something of a trial. Something to get through so he could move on to more important, more believable business.

To his credit, disbelief or not, he didn't rush her out the

door. He let her lay out her story without interruption, and was now carefully reading the letter in his hand. The first of what was a collection of thirty, all lovingly preserved in chronological order. Her mother's secret.

You have his eyes.

The memory rolled through her. Four words. Fourteen letters. With the power to change her life. One minute she was Roxanne O'Brien, daughter of Fiona and Connor O'Brien, the next she was… Who? The daughter of some man she'd never met. A lover her mother never—ever—mentioned. That's why she came to Mike Templeton. To find answers.

Well, maybe a little bit more than answers. After all, if her mother told the truth, then she, Roxy O'Brien whoever, could be entitled to a far different life. A far better life.

You have his eyes.

Speaking of eyes, Mike Templeton had set down the letter and sat studying her. Roxy'd been stared at before. Customers figured ogling the waitress came with the bar tab. And they were the polite ones. So she'd grown immune to looks long ago. Or so she'd thought. For some reason, Mike Templeton's stare made her want to squirm. Maybe because he'd removed his glasses, giving her an unobstructed view of what were really very intense brown eyes. It felt like he wasn't so much looking at her as trying to see inside. Read her mind, or gauge her intentions. A self-conscious flutter found its way to her stomach. She recrossed her legs, wishing her skirt wasn't so damn short, and forced herself to maintain eye contact. A visual Mexican standoff.

To her relief, he broke first, sitting back in his leather chair. Roxy found her eyes drawn to the black lacquered pen he twirled between his long, elegant fingers.

Everything about him was elegant, she thought to herself. His fingers, his "bearing" as her high school drama teacher would say. He fit the surroundings, that's for sure, right down to the tailored suit and crisp white shirt. Roxy wasn't sure, but she thought she'd seen a similar look on the pages of a men's fashion magazine. Simply sitting across from him made her feel every inch the downtown girl.

Except, if what her mother said was true, she wasn't so downtown after all, was she?"

"Are all the letters this…intimate?" he asked.

Cheeks warming, Roxy nodded. "I think so. I skimmed most of them." Like the man said, the letters were intimate. Reading them closely felt too much like reading a stranger's diary.

A stranger who was her father. Come to think of it, the woman described on those pages didn't sound very much like her mother, either.

"You'll notice the dates, though," she told him. "The last letter is postmarked. Nine months before I was born."

"As well as a couple of weeks before his accident."

The car accident that killed him. Roxy had read a brief account when doing her internet research.

The attorney frowned. Somehow he managed to make even that expression look sophisticated. "You're positive your mother never said anything before last month?"

He was kidding, right? Roxy shot him a long look. What was with all these repetitive questions anyway? She'd already laid out her whole story. If he planned on dismissing her, then dismiss her. Why waste time? "I think I would have remembered if she did."

"And she didn't explain why?"

"Unfortunately she was too busy dying."

The words were out before Roxy could pull them back, causing the lawyer's eyebrows to arch. Clearly not the best way to impress the man.

Seriously though, how did he expect her to answer? That while on her deathbed, her mother laid out a detailed and concise explanation of her affair with Wentworth Sinclair? "She was pretty out of things," Roxy said, doing her best to choke back the sarcasm. "At first I thought it was the painkillers talking." Until her mother's eyes had cleared for that one, brief instant. *You have his eyes....*

"Now you think otherwise."

"Based on what I read in those letters, yes."

"Hmmm."

That was it. Just hmmm. He'd begun twirling the pen again. Roxy didn't like the silence. Reminded her too much of the expectant pause that followed an audition speech while the casting director made notes. Here the expectation felt even thicker. Probably because the stakes were so much higher.

"So let me see if I have this straight," he said finally, drawing out his words. "Your mother just happens to tell you on her deathbed that you're the daughter of Wentworth Sinclair, the dead son of one of New York's wealthiest families. Then, when cleaning out her belongings, you just happen to find a stack of love letters that not only corroborates your claim, but lays out a timeline that ends right before his death." He gave the pen another couple of twirls. "Ties up pretty conveniently, wouldn't you say? The fact both parties are dead and unable to dispute your story?"

"Why would they dispute anything? I'm telling the truth." Roxy didn't like where this conversation was heading one little bit. "If you're suggesting I'm making the story up—" She *knew* he didn't believe her.

"I'm not suggesting anything. I'm simply pointing out the facts, which are convenient." He leaned forward, fingers folded in front of him. "Do you know how many people claim to be long-lost heirs?"

"No." Nor did she care about any claim but hers, which happened to be true.

"More than you'd realize. Just last week, for example, a man came in saying he'd traced his family tree back to Henry Hudson. He wanted to know if he was eligible for reparation from the city of New York for his share of the Hudson River."

"And your point?" Anger ticking upward, she gritted her teeth.

"My point," he replied, leaning closer, "is that he had more paperwork than you."

Son of a— The man all but called her a fraud. No, worse. He was implying she made up the story like it was some kind of scam. As if she hadn't spent the past month questioning everything she'd known about her life. How dare he? "You think I'm lying about being Wentworth Sinclair's daughter?"

"People have done more for less."

"I— You—" It took every ounce of restraint not to grab the nameplate off his desk and smash it over his head. "This isn't about money," she spat at him.

"Really?" He sat back. "So you have no interest at all in gaining a share of the Sinclair millions?"

Roxy opened her mouth, then shut it. She'd like nothing better than to say absolutely not and make him feel like a condescending heel, but they both knew she'd be lying. If it were only her, or if she lived in a perfect world, she could afford to be virtuous, but it wasn't only about her. And Lord knows her world was far from perfect. That was the point. Being Wentworth Sinclair's daughter could be her only shot at not screwing up the one worthwhile thing in her miserable life.

Try explaining that to someone like Mike Templeton, however. What would he know about mistakes and imperfect worlds? He'd probably spent his whole life watching everything he'd touched turn to gold.

Right now, he was smirking at her reaction. "That's what I thought. Sorry, but if you're looking for a payout, you'll have to do better than a stack of thirty-year-old love letters."

"Twenty-nine," Roxy corrected, although really, why bother? He'd already made up his mind she was some lying money-grabber.

"Twenty-nine then. Either way, next time I suggest you try bringing a document that's more useful, like a birth certificate perhaps."

"You mean the one naming Wentworth Sinclair as my father?" The battle against sarcasm failed, badly, and she mockingly slapped her forehead. "Silly me, I left it at home." When he gave her a pointed look, she returned it with an equally pointed expression of her own. He wasn't the only one who could do judgmental. "Don't you think if I had something like that, I would have brought it with me?"

"One would think, but then one would think your mother would have named the correct father thirty years ago, too." He was folding the letter and placing it back in its envelope. Roxy wanted to grab his long fingers and squeeze them until he yelped. One would think. Maybe her mother had been afraid no one would believe her either.

"You know what," she said, reaching for the stack of letters, "forget this."

What made her think uptown would want to help her? Uptown didn't care about people like her, period, and she'd be damned if she was going to sit here and let some stuffed-shirt lawyer look down his nose at her. "The only reason I came here was that your directory ad said you handled wills and estates, and I *thought* you could help me. Apparently I was wrong."

She snatched her leather coat off the back of her chair. If Mike Templeton didn't think her problems were worth his time, then he wasn't worth hers. "I'm sure another law firm will be willing to listen."

"Miss O'Brien, I think you misunderstood. Please sit down."

No, Roxy didn't feel like sitting down. Or listening to any kind of explanation. Why? Rejection was rejection regardless of how many pretty words you attached to it. She should know. She'd heard enough "thanks but no thanks" in her lifetime. And they felt like kicks to the stomach.

She jammed her arm into her coat sleeve. Emotion clogged her throat, and she absolutely refused to let him see her eyes water.

"By the way," she said, adjusting her collar. "Your ad said you welcomed all types of cases. If you don't mean it, then don't say so in the headline."

An unnecessary jab, but she was tired of playing polite and classy. Besides, being called a gold-digging fraud should entitle her to at least one parting shot.

"Miss O'Brien—"

She strode from the office without turning around, proud that she got as far as street level before her vision grew blurry.

Dammit. She'd have thought she'd be cried out by now. When would she stop feeling so raw and exposed?

You have his eyes...

"Why didn't you say anything, Mom?" she railed silently. "Why did you wait till it was too late to tell me?"

Was she that ashamed of her daughter?

Not cool, Templeton, Not cool at all.

Mike had to admit, though, as indignant exits went,

Roxy O'Brien's was among the best. Ten years of estate law had shown him his share of scam artists and gold diggers, but she was the first who'd truly teared up upon storming out. She probably didn't think he noticed, but he had. There was no mistaking the overly bright sheen in those green eyes of hers, in spite of her attempts to blink them dry.

Pen twirling between his fingers, he rocked back and forth in his chair. Couldn't blame her for being upset. Like a lot of people, she must have thought she'd stumbled across the legal equivalent of a winning lottery ticket. If she'd stuck around instead of stomping off like a redheaded windstorm he'd have explained that making a claim against the Sinclairs wasn't that simple, even if her story was true. There were legal precedents and statutes of limitations to consider.

Of course, he thought, stilling his pen, she didn't have to completely prove paternity for her claim to work. Simply put forth a believable argument.

He couldn't believe he was contemplating the thought. Had he fallen so low he'd take on an audacious case simply for the potential settlement money?

One look at the meager pile of case files on his desk answered his question. At this point, he'd take Henry Hudson's nephew's case.

This was what failure felt like. The constant hollow feeling in his stomach. The weight on his shoulders. The tick, tick, tick in the back of his head reminding him another day was passing without clients knocking on his door.

It wasn't supposed to be like this. Templetons, as had been drilled in his head, didn't fail. They blazed trails. They excelled. They were leaders in their field. Doubly so if you were named Michael Templeton III and had two generations of namesakes to live up to.

You're letting us down, Michael. We raised you to be better than this. A dozen years after he first heard them, his father's words rose up to repeat themselves, reminding him he had no choice. Succeed or else. He took on the challenge of starting his own practice. He had to make it work, by hook or by crook.

Or audacious case, as it were. Unfortunately his best opportunity stormed out the door in a huff. So how did he get the little hothead to come back?

A patch of gray caught the corner of his eye. Realizing what he was looking at, Mike smiled. Perhaps his luck hadn't run out after all. He picked up the grey envelope Roxanne O'Brien had left behind.

God bless indignant exits.

Thursday nights were always busy at the Elderion Lounge. The customers, businessmen mostly, their out-of-town visits winding down, tended to cut loose. Bar tabs got bigger, rounds more frequent, tables more boisterous. Normally Roxy didn't mind the extra action since it meant more money in her pocket. Tonight, though, she wasn't in the mood for salesmen knocking back vodka tonics.

"Six vodka tonics, one house pinot and two pom martinis," she ordered. Despite being cold outside, the air was stifling and hot. She grabbed a cocktail napkin and blotted her neckline. This afternoon's business jacket disappeared long ago and she was back to a black camisole and skirt.

The bartender, a beefy guy named Dion, looked her up and down. "You look frazzled. Table six isn't giving you trouble, are they?"

"Nothing I can't handle. Bad day is all."

Who did Mike Templeton think he was anyway? Arrogant, condescending… Just because he was lucky enough to be born on the right side of town, what made him think he had the right to judge her or her mother or anyone else for that matter?

Wadding the napkin into a ball, she tossed it neatly into the basket behind the bar. "You'd think by this point I'd be immune to rejection."

"I thought you gave up acting," Dion said.

"I did. This was something else." And the rejection stung worse. "You don't know a good lawyer, do you?"

The bartender immediately frowned. "You in trouble?"

"Nothing like that. I need a business lawyer."

"Oh." He shook his head. "Sorry."

"'S'all right." Who's to say the next guy wouldn't be as condescending as Mike Templeton?

"Oh, my God!" Jackie, one of the other waitresses rushed up, earrings and bangle bracelets jangling. "Please let this guy sit at my table."

Busy stacking her tray, Roxy didn't bother looking up. At least once a week, the man of Jackie's dreams walked in. "What's the deal this time? He look like someone famous?"

"Try rich."

Here? Hardly. Unless the guy was lost and needed directions. Rich men hung at far better clubs. "I suppose he's gorgeous, too."

"Put it this way. If he was poor, I'd still make a move. He's that sexy."

Roxy had to see this male specimen for herself. Craning her neck, she surveyed the crowd. "I seriously doubt anyone with that much to offer—"

Mike Templeton stood by table eight, peeling the gloves off his hands one finger at a time. His eyes scanned the room with a heavy-lidded scrutiny. Roxy's stomach dropped. Jackie was right, he was the best-looking man in the room. Stood out like a pro in a field of amateurs. What on earth was he doing here?

"Told you he was breathtaking," she heard Jackie say. Before she could reply, he turned and their eyes locked. She stood rooted to the spot as he shrugged off his camel hair coat and draped it over the back of his chair. His actions were slow, deliberate, all the while holding her gaze. Goose bumps danced up her bare arms. It felt like she was the one removing layers.

"I don't suppose I can convince you to switch tables, can I? You're not interested in dating anyway. I'll give you both my twelve and fifteen."

Eyes still glued to the lawyer, Roxy shook her head. "Sorry, Jackie, no can do. Not this time."

Grabbing her tray, she purposely served her other tables before making her way toward him. With her back to that stare, his pull diminished a little, though she could still feel him watching her with every move she made. Reminding her of his existence. As if she could forget.

Finally she had no choice—or customers—left and sauntered her way to his table.

"You're a difficult person to pin down, Miss O'Brien," he greeted. "I went by your apartment first and some guy told me you were 'at the bar.' I took a chance and assumed he meant here." He smiled, as though being there was the most natural thing in the world, which it was decidedly not. "We never finished our conversation from earlier."

The guy had to be joking. "What was there to finish? I pretty much heard everything I needed to hear when you insulted me and my mother."

"You misunderstood. I wasn't trying to insult you. Had you stuck around, you would have realized I was merely pointing out your story has some very questionable holes in it."

"My mistake." Misunderstood her foot. If that was his idea of a misunderstanding, then she was the Queen of New York. "Next time my life is turned upside down by a deathbed confession, I'll try to make sure the story is more complete."

She tucked her tray under her arm. "Is there anything else? I've got customers to wait on." He wasn't the only one who could be dismissive.

"I'll have a Scotch. Neat."

Great. He planned to stick around. Maybe she would let Jackie have the table. "Anything else?"

"Yes, there is. You forgot this." Reaching into his briefcase, he pulled out a gray envelope. Seeing it, Roxy nearly groaned out loud. "Your mother took so much effort to preserve the collection. Seemed a shame to break up the set."

She felt like an idiot. Figures she'd mess up her grand exit. She never was good at stage directions. "Thank you. But you didn't have to drive all the way here to return it. You could have mailed it back to me."

"No problem at all. I didn't want to risk the envelope being damaged. Besides..."

Roxy had been reaching for the stack, when his hand came down to cover hers. "I figured this would buy me a few more minutes of your time," he finished, his eyes catching hers.

Warmth spread through Roxy's body, starting with her arm and moving upward. Glancing down at the table, she saw his hand still covered hers. The tapered fingers were almost twice the size of hers. If he wanted, he would wrap her hand right up in a strong, tight embrace. Feeling the warmth seeping into her cheeks, she pulled free.

"For what?" she asked, gripping her tray tightly. Squeezing the hard plastic helped chase away the sensation his hand left behind.

"I told you. You left before we could finish our conversation."

"Given what I stuck around for, can you blame me? I'll go get your drink."

"Tsk, tsk, tsk," he said as soon as she'd spun around. "You're going to need a lot thicker skin than that if you want to go after the Sinclairs."

Roxy froze. What did he say?

"That is why you came by to see me, isn't it?" he continued. "Because you want to make a claim against Wentworth Sinclair's estate?"

She was afraid to say yes, in case the other shoe dropped on her head. Slowly she turned around to find the lawyer looking more than a little pleased with himself for having caught her off guard. Was he trying to tell her she had a case after all?

So help him, if he was playing with her....

"Look, here's the deal." He leaned forward, gold cuff links catching the light. "Your case is a long shot. Both parties have passed away, and the only proof you have is a pile of love letters. Not to mention thirty years have gone by. The courts aren't exactly generous when it comes to claims that old. Truth is, scaling Mount Everest would be easier."

"Thanks for the recap." And here she thought there was something to his comment. "If that's what you came all the way over here to tell me, you wasted the gas."

"You're not letting me finish again."

Roxy stopped. Although hearing him out seemed like a waste of time to her. How many times did she need to hear him say her case wasn't good enough for him? "Okay," she said, waiting. "Finish. My case is harder than climbing Mount Everest. What else do you need to tell me?"

A slow smile broke out across his face. A confident smile that stilled everything in her body. "Only that I happen to really enjoy mountain climbing."

CHAPTER TWO

"I'LL, um, go get your drink." Spinning around, Roxy made a beeline to the bar. It was the only response she could think of. Did he say what she thought he said? He was taking her case?

"You look like a truck hit you," Jackie remarked when she reached the bar rail. "What happened? Richie Rich turn out to be a creep?"

If she weren't still in a daze, Roxy would comment on the hopeful expectancy in the other woman's voice. "Not a creep. My lawyer," she corrected.

"I thought you said you didn't have one," Dion said.

"I didn't think I did." She still wasn't sure. She didn't trust her ears. For that matter, she wasn't entirely sure she trusted Mike Templeton. There had to be a catch.

Quickly she looked over her shoulder. There he sat, stiff and formal, arranging what looked like paperwork on the table. He certainly didn't seem the type to lead someone on.

"If you're serious," she said, when her rounds finally brought him back to his table, "then what was all that business about Henry Hudson and not having proof?"

"Had to figure out how loyal you were to your story somehow, didn't I?" he remarked, raising the glass to his lips.

"Un-freaking-believable." It was a *test*. If it weren't such an amazingly bad idea, she'd pour Scotch in his lap. She still might. "Do you have any idea how pis— How upset I was?"

"From the way you stormed out, I could hazard a guess. But that also tipped the scale in your favor. Either you truly believed your story or you were a damn good actress."

She could give him a long list of directors and casting agents who could refute the latter. Still, a *test?* She had half a mind to tell him he could stuff himself regardless of whether he wanted to take on her claim or not. "I can't believe you. Are you like this with everyone who tries to hire you?"

"Only the ones claiming to be heirs to multimillion-dollar fortunes."

Millions? Was he joking? Roxy checked his expression. His face was deadly serious.

Oh, my. She dropped into the seat across from him. "Millions?" she repeated.

"What were you expecting?"

"I don't know." She swiped the hair from her face, trying to focus. "I knew they were rich, but… Wow."

His test was beginning to make a bit of sense. Millions. A tingle ran up her spine.

"There's no guarantee, mind you. Like I said, the courts seldom rule in favor of claims like yours."

Mind still reeling, Roxy nodded.

"Plus, the Sinclairs' lawyers will put up a heck of a fight. This isn't the first time someone's challenged their estate, I'm sure. Nevertheless, if we play our cards right, and there's no reason to believe I won't, we'll both be looking at a nice little payday."

Again, Roxy nodded. She didn't know what else to do. His proclamation had stunned her to silence.

"Yo, Roxy! Table four!" Dion called. "Get your butt in gear."

A few feet away, a trio of women with empty martini glasses were looking in her direction, visibly annoyed.

"You better get to your customers," Mike noted.

He watched with amusement as the waitress half stumbled, half rushed away. Funny how her expression went from annoyed to dazed in literally the blink of an eye. The prospect of money could do that to a person. Made him jump in his car and drive to this place, didn't it?

For a moment he'd been afraid he'd laid it on a little too heavy with that "test" stuff, but she accepted his behavior. All he needed to do now was get her to cooperate with the rest of the case. Shouldn't be too hard. Especially given her alternative.

Leaning back in his chair, he sipped his drink and looked around the bar. As bars went, the Elderion was in the upper-lower half. Below average, but far enough up to avoid being a dive. Both the tables and the clientele had mileage.

Wentworth's letter lay where Roxanne dropped it. He ran his finger along the edge of the gray envelope. The contents had long been committed to memory. *"I can still smell your scent on my skin,"* Wentworth had written for the opening line. College passion. He knew it well. That heady reckless feeling. The blind confidence the days would last forever. Until reality barged in with its expectations and traditions waiting to be fulfilled and impractical dreams had to be shoved aside.

Look at you. We raised you to be better than this, Michael.

A hollow feeling lodged in his stomach. He blamed the surroundings. Ever since walking in to the Elderion, he'd been possessed by the strangest feeling of déjà vu.

Memories of another bar with dim lights and warm beer came floating back. When quality and atmosphere took a backseat to political debates and slow dancing in the dark.

His semester of ill-spent youth. He hadn't thought about those days in years. They'd been jettisoned to the past when he took his first law internship.

A few feet away, his new client—least he hoped she was his new client—negotiated her way through the narrow tables with the grace of a dancer. Amazing she could navigate anything in that scrap of cloth she called a uniform. Without the pink-and-gray blazer for coverage, he had a perfect view of how the spandex skirt molded to her curves. An open invitation to check out the assets. As she bent over, the skirt pulled tighter. Forget invitation, Mike decided, try full-blown neon sign. Feeling an uncomfortable tightness, he shifted his legs. Definitely not what his usual client would wear.

But then, this case wasn't his usual case. In fact, it was everything he'd been taught to avoid—splashy, risky, generating more notoriety than respect. Beggars couldn't be choosers could they? Beat closing his doors and telling his family he wasn't the Templeton they'd groomed him to be. Watching Roxanne dodge the palm of a customer right before it caressed her bottom, he retrieved his pen and made a quick note: smooth out the rough edges.

It was an hour later before Roxanne returned to his table, carrying with her a bottle of water. Mike tried not to stare at her legs as she approached. Given her outfit, it was a Herculean task at best. "You're still here," she said.

"Seemed silly to drive all the way back to the office when I could work here." He'd stacked what little legal work he did have in piles on the desk.

"It's eight o'clock. Most people have stopped working by now."

"Maybe in this place, but I'm not most people." He should know. It'd been drilled into his head enough growing up. "I also figured you'd have questions."

"You're right. I do." She pointed to the empty chair. "Do you mind?"

"Your big bad boss won't care?"

"I'm on my ten."

"Then be my guest. What's your question?"

"Well, first…" She picked at the label on her water bottle, obviously searching for the right words. "Are you sure you weren't kidding? About it being a million-dollar claim? That wasn't another one of your tests, was it?"

Ah, straight to the money. "I told you, I don't kid. Not about case value. Although keep in mind, I'm not making any promises, either. I'm saying there's potential. Nothing more."

"I appreciate the honesty. I don't like being misled."

"Me, neither," he replied. Seemed the hothead had a bit of a cautious streak after all. A good sign.

He watched as she peeled off a strip of label. "So what's the next step?" she asked. "Do I take a DNA test or something?"

If it were so easy. "Easy there, Cowboy. Don't get ahead of yourself. It's a little more complicated. You got any Sinclair DNA lying around?" he asked her.

Immediately her eyes went to the envelope. Cautious *and* quick. "I'm afraid you've watched too many crime shows. Getting anything off letters that old would be a miracle." Besides, he'd already had a similar thought and checked online. "You're going to need a more recent sample."

"How do we get one?"

Now they were getting to the complicated part. "Best

way would be for one of the Sinclair sisters to agree to a test. They are Wentworth's closest living relatives."

"But you said they would put up a fight."

"Doesn't mean we don't ask," he told her. "We give them enough evidence, and they'll have to comply."

"You mean, prove I'm a Sinclair, and they'll let me have proof."

Mike couldn't help smiling. Definitely quick. He liked that. If he had to take a case like this, he preferred to work with a client who understood what they were doing. Made his job easier. "Never fear. We'll make enough noise that they'll have to pay attention. The squeaky wheel and that sort of thing."

Frowning, she tore another strip. Some of the eagerness had left her face. Without it, she looked tired and, dare he say, a bit vulnerable. "You make it sound like I'm out to get them."

"The Sinclairs would argue you are."

"Why? I didn't go looking for this. My mother dropped the story in my lap."

"A story you promptly took to a lawyer to see if you have a claim to his estate."

That silenced her. "I didn't look at it that way." Another strip peeled away. "I'm just trying to make my life better. If this guy—Wentworth Sinclair—was my father, he'd want that, too, wouldn't he?"

Mike had to admit, if the relationship painted in the letter he read carried forward, she might be right. "Which is why we're pursuing the claim. To help you get that better life."

"What if they refuse to listen?"

"Then we'll keep fighting," Mike answered simply. Sooner or later, the Sinclairs would have to pay attention if only to make them disappear. He wasn't kidding about the squeaky wheel; it always yielded some kind of result.

Roxy was looking down at the table. Following her gaze, Mike saw that at some point while talking, he'd once again covered her hand. When had he reached across? When the dimness hit her eyes? That wasn't like him. He always kept an invisible wall between himself and his clients. For good reason. Getting too close led to making mistakes.

He studied the hand beneath his. She had skin the color of eggshells, pale and off-white. There was a small tattoo on the inside of her wrist as well. A yellow butterfly. The wings called out for a thumb to brush across them.

Mike realized he was about to do just that when she pulled her hand free and balled it into a fist. He found himself doing the same.

"Why?" she asked aloud.

Distracted by his reaction to the butterfly, it took a moment for her question to register. "Why what?"

"Why would you fight for me? If it's such a long shot, why are you taking this case?"

Somehow he didn't think she'd appreciate the truth, that he needed the money from this case as badly as she wanted it. "Told you, I like a challenge. As for fighting, I don't believe in quitting. Or losing. So you can be assured, I'll stick around to the bloody end."

"Colorful term."

"I also don't believe in mincing words."

"That so? Never would have guessed from your gentle desk side manner." She smiled as she delivered the comment. Mike fought the urge to smile back, taking a sip of his drink instead.

"You can have hand-holding or you can have results." Unfortunate choice of words given his behavior a moment earlier. "Up to you."

"Results are fine," she replied. "In my book, hand-holding is overrated. Sympathy just leads to a whole lot of unwanted problems."

Add practical to her list of attributes. Maybe this case would go smoother than he thought, in spite of this morning's dramatics. "I agree."

"Still..."

Mike's senses went on alert. Any sentence beginning with the word "still" never ended well. "What is it?"

"Don't get me wrong. I'm not looking for reassurance, but I'm wondering. When you say the word bloody, just how bloody do you mean?"

"The Sinclair legal team won't hold back, if that's what you're asking. They'll have no qualms about digging into your life." Her expression fell, followed quickly by his stomach. She had a skeleton, didn't she? "If you've got secrets, you best start sharing."

"No secrets." She shook her head, a little too vehemently if you asked him.

"Then what?"

"I've got a kid. A little girl. Her name is Steffi."

Wentworth Sinclair's granddaughter. That wasn't what he expected to hear. "No problem," he replied. His enthusiasm started building. Alice and Frances Sinclair would no doubt be very interested in the little girl's existence. "In fact, this might actually make the case—"

"Whoa!" She held up her hand, cutting him off. "I don't want her involved. She's only four years old. She won't understand what's going on."

Mike took a deep breath. "I don't think you understand. The fact that Wentworth might have a granddaughter could go a long way in convincing the sisters to comply with our requests."

She shook her head. "I don't care. I'm not going to have

her being upset. She can't be involved. You'll have to find a different way."

"I don't think—"

"Promise."

What was he going to do? He wanted to tell her she was in no position to issue conditions, that as her lawyer, it was his job to do everything he could to win her case, meaning he was the one who would decide what tactics he could or couldn't use. He also wanted to tell her there was no way he could keep such a promise. Sooner or later the Sinclair sisters would discover the child's existence. Her fiercely determined expression stopped him from saying so. There was no way he'd get her to budge on the issue tonight. Push and he ran the risk of her walking away again.

"Fine." He'd agree to her condition for now, and renegotiate their position later.

"Thank you." Satisfied, she opened her now naked water bottle and took a long drink. "When do we start?"

The spark had returned to her eyes, turning them brilliantly green. She was leaning forward, too, enough to remind him her tank top was extremely low cut. His legal mind definitely did not appreciate the male awareness the sight caused. Definitely had to smooth out the rough edges.

"Soon," he told her. "Very soon."

He stayed the rest of the evening. Nursing his drink and scribbling notes on his yellow legal pad. Damn unnerving it was, too. His existence filled the entire room making it impossible to ignore him. Three times she messed up an order because he distracted her, mistakes Dion made clear he planned to take out of her check.

Why was he sticking around anyway? He'd returned her letter, they'd talked. Shouldn't he be at his uptown apartment, drinking expensive Scotch by a fireplace? Surely he wasn't sticking around for the ambience. No one came to the Elderion for the ambiance.

"Maybe he wants to negotiate payment," Jackie teased. Ever since Roxy had mentioned the fact Mike was working on a legal problem for her the other waitress wouldn't stop with the innuendos.

"Very funny," she shot back, though the comment did make her hair stand on edge. They hadn't talked about payment. How did he expect her to pay for his services?

His presence continued to dog her as she delivered a round to the table next to his. Thank goodness the patrons all ordered bottled beer. She wasn't sure she could handle anything more complicated while standing in such close proximity.

Funny thing was the guy hadn't looked in her direction. Not once, and she'd been checking fairly frequently. Staring she could handle. She got looks every night. So why couldn't she shake Mike Templeton? Why did she feel that same penetrating scrutiny she felt back at his office every time she walked in his line of sight? All night long, it felt like he was right behind her, staring at her soul.

Another thing. He insisted on looking good. By this point in the night, the rest of the men in the place had long shed their jackets and ties. Heck, some were close to shedding their shirts. The room smelled of damp skin and aftershave.

Mike, however, barely looked bothered. His tie remained tightly knotted, and he still wore his suit jacket. Roxy didn't even think there were wrinkles in his shirt. If he was going to stick around, the least he could do was try to blend in with the rest of the drunken businessmen.

"Why are you still here?" she finally asked, when her rounds brought her to his table.

He looked up from the chicken scratches he'd been making on his notepad. "I'd like to think the answer's apparent. I'm working."

"I can see that. Why are you still working?"

She expected him to say something equally obvious such as "I'm not done yet" but he didn't. Instead he got an unusually faraway look in his eye. "I have to."

No, Roxy thought. *She* had to. A guy like Mike Templeton chose to. In the interest of good relations, she kept the difference to herself, and instead tried to decipher the notes in front of her. "Smooth out the rough edges? What does that mean?"

"Part of my overall strategy. I'm still fleshing it out."

"You planning to share it with me?"

"Eventually." The vague answer didn't sit well. Too much like information being kept from her, and she'd had enough of that this month. "Why can't I see now?"

"Because it's not fleshed out yet."

"Uh-huh." Uncertain she believed him, she bounced her tray off her thigh, and tried to see if she could find further explanation hidden in his expression. "In other words, trust you."

"Yes." He paused. "You can do that, can't you?"

Roxy didn't answer. "You want another Scotch?" she asked instead.

"Should I take that as a no?"

"Should I take that as you don't want another drink?" she countered.

"Diet cola. And when the idea is fully formed, you'll know. You don't share your order pad before bringing the drinks do you?"

The two analogies had absolutely nothing to do with one another as far as she could see. "I would if the customer asked. If they didn't like being kept in the dark."

"Fine," he said, giving an exasperated sigh. "Here."

He angled his pad so she could read better. All she saw were a bunch of half sentences and notations she didn't understand.

"Satisfied?" he asked when she turned the notepad around.

Yes. Along with embarrassed. "You have terrible handwriting."

"I wasn't planning on my notes being studied. Are you always this mistrustful?"

"Can you blame me?" she replied. "I just found out my mother lied to me for thirty years."

"Twenty-nine," he corrected, earning a smirk.

"Twenty-nine. Plus, I work here. This place hardly inspires trust."

"What do you mean?"

He wanted examples? "See that table over there?" She pointed to table two where a quartet of tipsy businessmen were laughing and nuzzling with an equally tipsy pair of women. "Half those guys wear wedding bands. So does one of the women.

"You see it all the time," she continued. "Men telling women how beautiful and special they are while the entire time keeping their left hands stuffed in a pocket so no one sees the tan line." Or promising comfort when all they really wanted was a roll in the sack.

"Interesting point," Mike replied. "One difference, though. I'm not one of your bar customers."

No, she thought, looking him over. He wasn't. "I don't know you much better," she pointed out.

"You will."

Something about the way he said those two words made her stomach flutter, and made the already close atmosphere even closer. All evening long, she'd been battling a stirring awareness, and now it threatened to blossom. She didn't like the feeling one bit.

Jackie's innuendos popped into her head.

"How do you expect me to pay out?" she blurted. He frowned, clearly confused, but to her the change in topic made perfect sense. "We never talked, and last time I checked you guys don't work for free. How exactly do you expect to collect payment?"

Realization crested across his face, followed quickly by his mouth drawing into a tight line. "It's called a contingency fee," he said tersely.

"Like those personal injury lawyers that advertise on television? The ones that say you don't have to pay them until you win?"

"Exactly. What else did you expect?"

He already knew, and she felt her skin begin to color. What could she say? She was paranoid. Life made her that way. "I didn't. Why else would I ask?"

"If you don't like that plan, you can pay hourly." He looked around the bar. "If doing so fits your budget."

Doubtful, and he knew that, too. "Your plan is fine."

"Good. Glad you approve."

"Do you still want your diet soda?"

"Please."

Shoot. She'd been hoping he'd say no, so she wouldn't have to visit his table again. "Coming right up. I'll drop it off before I cash out."

"You're done for the evening?" He straightened in his seat at the news.

Roxy nodded. The ability to clock out earlier than other bars was one of the reasons she continued working at the place. She could get home at a decent hour and be awake enough to get up with Steffi.

Reaching for his wallet, Mike pulled out a trio of bills. "This should cover my tab and tip. I'll meet you out front."

"For what?"

"To drive you home of course."

Drive her home. Maybe Jackie's comment wasn't so far off. She fingered the bills, noting his tip was beyond generous for one drink. "What's the catch?"

"No catch."

"Really?" She may have made her share of bad calls, but she wasn't stupid. Uptown lawyers didn't hang out at the Elderion and offer waitresses rides for no reason. She hadn't forgotten what he implied about her mother. "You drive all your clients home in the middle of the night?"

"If they're dressed like that, I do."

What was wrong with the way she was dressed?

"For one thing, you're not," he replied when she asked.

A comment like that was supposed to make her want to get into a car with him? "I'll have you know I've been riding the same bus for years without a single incident."

"Well, aren't you lucky."

"Luck has nothing to do with it. After a while you develop a kind of invisible armor and no one bothers you."

He frowned. "Invisible armor?"

"Street smarts, you know? People see you and realize straight off they can't hassle you. You blend in." It was outsiders like him that had to worry. Unfortunately, from the way he was already packing his things, Roxy had the distinct feeling he wasn't interested in her argument or in taking no for an answer.

What the heck. Wouldn't kill her to ride in a warm car for a change.

"I'll meet you in five," she told him.

Did she really think she was safe riding the bus wearing

that outfit? Watching her sashay off, Mike rolled his eyes. For crying out loud, she wasn't even his type.

In this lifetime anyway. A memory danced on the edge of his mind. Of other late-night bus rides and willing partners. He shook it away.

"You make this commute every night?" he asked when they finally met up. She'd slipped a leather jacket over her uniform. The waist-length jacket covered her bare shoulders, but still left the legs exposed.

"Five nights a week."

They rounded the corner and headed to the pay lot, walking past the bus stop in time to see a drunken patron relieving himself on the wall. Did her invisible armor protect her from that, too? he wondered as the splash narrowly missed his shoe.

"I thought about adding a sixth," Roxy was saying, "but that would mean less time with Steffi. I hardly see her much as it is. She sees more of her babysitter."

"When you win this case, you'll have all the time in the world."

"At this point in my life I'd settle for not having to schlep drinks for a living. I don't care what they say, the smell of stale beer doesn't go away."

"You never thought of doing something else?"

"Oh, sure. I was going to be a doctor but the Elderion was too awesome to give up.

"Sorry," she quickly added. "Couldn't help myself. I could have found a day job, but originally I wanted my days free for auditions."

"Auditions? You're an actress?" A strange emotion stirred inside him. He should be concerned her career aspirations made her more interested in grabbing fifteen minutes of fame than in seeing the case through. Instead the tug felt more like envy. He chalked it up to being in the bar. The night had him thinking of old times and old aspirations.

The driver had brought out his sedan from the back of the lot. As Roxy slid into the passenger seat, her skirt bunched higher, almost to the juncture of her thighs. Mike averted his eyes while she adjusted herself. Yeah, she blended in.

"I'm impressed," he said when he settled into his driver's seat.

"Don't be. It was eight years of nothing."

"Couldn't have been that bad."

"Try worse. Turns out you need one of two things to make it in show business. Talent or cleavage. I was saving up for the latter when I had Steffi."

"So you quit for motherhood."

"Couldn't very well work all night, run around to auditions all day and take care of her, too. Since the whole acting thing wasn't working out anyway, I figured I'd cut my losses and do one thing halfway decently."

"Halfway?"

Her shrug failed to hide her embarrassment. Clearly she hadn't expected him to pick up on the modifier. "The whole 'wish I could spend more time with her' thing. Not that I have a choice, right?"

"No." He stared at the brake lights ahead of him. The city that never sleeps. Even after midnight, gridlock could snag you. "But then a lot of choices aren't really in our control."

"What do you mean?"

This time he was the one who shrugged as a way of covering up. He didn't know what he meant. The words sort of bubbled up on their own. "That a lot of the time life makes the decisions for us."

"You mean like how getting knocked up put my acting

career out of its misery?" Her nonchalant expression was poorly crafted. No wonder she failed as an actress.

"She's why I'm doing all this now," she continued after a beat. "Partly anyway. I want her to have more choices than I can give her now."

This time she wasn't acting. The desperate determination in her voice was very real.

A thought suddenly occurred to him. "What about her father?"

"What about him?"

He'd hit a sore spot. He could feel her stiffen. "Is he still in the picture?"

"No."

Interesting. "Any chance he'll pop back in?"

"No."

"You sure?" Wouldn't be the first time an ex reappeared at the scent of a payday. From his point of view, the fewer complications the better.

"He's not in our lives," she repeated, her voice a little terse.

Her clenched jaw said there was more to the story. "Because he's not…?" He left the end of his sentence hoping she'd fill in the blank.

"Because he's not," she repeated. "Why are you asking anyway? I thought this case was about *my* paternity."

"It's my job to know as many details as possible about my clients."

"Even things that aren't your business?

"Everything about you is my business."

"I don't think so," she scoffed.

This was the second time tonight she'd tried to dictate what he could and couldn't discuss. Time he explained how this relationship would work. Yanking the steering wheel, he cut off the car in the next lane and pulled to the curb. "Let's get a few things straight right now. You came to me asking for help. I can't do that without your cooperation. Your. Full. Cooperation. That means if I need to know what you had for dinner last Saturday night, you need to tell me. Do you understand? Because if you can't, then this—" he waved his hand in the space between them "—isn't going to work.

"Are we clear?" he asked, looking her in the eye. Although the lecture was necessary, she could very well tell him to go to blazes. He held his breath, hoping he hadn't pushed her—and his luck—too far.

From her seat, she glared, her eyes bright in the flash of passing headlights. "Crystal."

"Good. Now I suggest you learn to deal with tough questions, because we've only scratched the surface." They were definitely revisiting her daughter's paternity, too. There was way too much emotion behind her reaction.

They drove the rest of the distance in silence, eventually pulling up in front of a nondescript building, on a street lined with them. Tall towers with squares of light, the kind of buildings his architect brother would call void of personality. At this hour of night, with the green landscaping unlit, Mike thought they had an eerie futuristic quality.

He stole a look at his companion. She hadn't moved since his lecture, her face locked on the view outside the windshield. With the shadows hiding her makeup and her hair tumbling down her back, he was surprised how classical her profile looked. Reminding him of one of those Greek busts in a museum, strong and delicate at the same time. If, that is, the pieces in the museum were gritting their teeth.

Her fingers were already wrapped around the door handle. "Want to wait till I come to a full stop or will slowing down to a crawl be good enough?" he asked her.

"Either will be fine." Her voice was tight to match her jaw. Still upset over his lecture. He added the discussion to his mental revisit list. Thing was getting pretty long. "I'll stop at the front walkway if you don't mind. Road burn never looks good on a client."

Without so much as cracking a smile, she pointed to the crosswalk a few feet ahead. "Here is fine. I'll walk the rest of the way." She pushed open the door the moment the wheels stopped spinning. Eager to get away.

"Roxanne!" Call it guilt or anxiety over his harshness earlier, but he needed to call her back and make sure they were truly on the same page. "Do we understand each other?"

"We do." From her resignation, however, she wasn't happy about it. Never mind, she'd be happy enough with him when they settled her case.

"You still want to proceed then?" he double-checked.

She nodded, again with resignation. "I do."

"I have an opening at nine-thirty tomorrow. I'll see you then."

Resignation quickly switched to surprise. "You want to meet tomorrow?"

"Unless you'd rather meet tonight. We have a lot to go over, and you're my only source of information. Sooner we get started, the better."

Seeing her widening eyes, he added, "Is that a problem?"

"No," she replied. "No problem."

There was, but to her credit, she seemed resolved to solving whatever it was. "I'll see you at nine-thirty."

"Sharp," he added. As if he had anything better to do. "Oh, and Roxanne? You might as well get used to spending time with me. In fact, you could say I'm about to become your new best friend."

"Great." Thrilled, she was not; he could tell by the smirk.

Surprisingly, however, he found the annoyance almost amusing. There was mettle underneath her attitude that would come in handy. Smiling, he watched her walk away, waiting till she disappeared behind the frosted front door before shifting his car into Drive. For the first time in weeks, he looked forward to a new workday. Roxanne O'Brien didn't know it yet, but she'd just become his newest and biggest priority.

He had a feeling both their futures would be better for it.

CHAPTER THREE

ROXY could feel Mike all the way to her front door and this time the sensation had nothing to do with his "presence." He was watching her.

Her new best friend. The idea was beyond laughable. She wasn't entirely sure she even liked the guy with his bossy, arrogant, elegant attitude. Add nosy, too. What business was it of his whether Steffi's father was around or not? *Everything about you is my business.* Recalling the authority in his voice, she got a hot flash. Men who could truly take charge were few and far between in her world. Most of them simply took off.

Bringing her back to Steffi's father. What a nice big bitter circle. She really did have to stop overreacting when people mentioned him. Not every remark was a reference to her bad judgment.

No, those would come later, when the Sinclairs got involved. Maybe chasing down the truth wasn't such a good idea.

Then she thought about Steffi, and her resolve returned.

Mrs. Ortega's apartment was on the third floor. The older woman met her at the door. "She give you any problems?" Roxy asked.

"Nada. Went down during her movie, same as always. She had a busy day. I had all three grandchildren."

"Sounds like a houseful."

Steffi was curled up sound asleep on the sofa, the late-night news acting as a night-light. In her hand she clutched a purple-haired plastic pony. Roxy smiled. Her daughter was in the middle of a pony fascination, the purple-haired animal not having left her hand in a month.

Carefully she scooped her up. The little girl immediately stirred. "Dusty's thirsty," she murmured, half swatting at her amber curls. Roxy wasn't quite sure she was awake.

"We'll get him some water upstairs."

"Okay." The little girl nodded and tucked her head into the crook of Roxy's neck. Her skin smelled of sleep and baby shampoo. Roxy inhaled a noseful and the scent tugged at her heart. Her little angel. Steffi might have started as a mistake, but she was the one decent accomplishment in Roxy's life. She'd do anything not to screw it up.

After making arrangements with Mrs. Ortega for the next morning, she carried Steffi to the elevator. Stepping off onto the eleventh floor, she could hear the screech of a high speed chase playing on a television. Would it be too much to ask for it not to be her apartment?

Yes. Fumbling to balance her keys and her daughter, she opened the door to find the volume blasting. A thin, acne-prone stain wearing an orange-and-blue throwback jersey lay sprawled on the sofa. Roxy cringed. Wayne. When she first decided to take on a roommate, she figured an extra person would allow her to afford a better apartment and Alexis had been one of the few decent applicants who didn't mind living with a four-year-old. Roxy didn't realize till they signed the lease that the woman's loser brother came along with the package. He showed up at all times of the night, offering some lame excuse as to why he needed to sponge off them for the night. If she didn't need Alexis's share of the rent money, she'd kick them both to the curb.

Another reason to hope Mike Templeton was as good as he said. "Can you turn the TV down?" she whispered harshly.

"Why? The kid's asleep."

She shot him a glare. Not for long. "Because you can hear it at the elevator."

"Turn it down, Wayne." Carrying a laundry basket on her hip, his sister, Alexis, came down the hallway. "No one wants to hear that noise."

With a roll of his eyes, Wayne reached for his remote.

Alexis greeted her with a nod and dropped the basket on the dining room table. "Some guy came by looking for you. He find you?"

"Dude wouldn't stop buzzing," Wayne said. "Woke me up."

Poor baby. "Yeah, he found me," she told Alexis.

"New boyfriend?"

"No. Business. He's a lawyer who's going to be helping me with some stuff of my mother's." She flashed back to five minutes earlier, in the close confines of his car. *Better get used to my company. You and I are going to be spending a lot of time together.* Against her will, a low shiver worked its way to the base of her spine. Immediately she kicked herself. You know, Roxy, your outbursts of moral outrage might carry a little more weight if you didn't find the man attractive.

"What kind of business?" Wayne asked. "You getting money?"

"I thought you said your mother didn't leave you anything?" Alexis said. She paused. "Is this about that stuff your mother said?"

"What stuff?" Wayne asked.

Roxy ignored him. In a moment of extreme loneliness and needing someone to talk to, Roxy had shared her mother's last words to her roommate. In fact, it was Alexis who first suggested she might have money coming to her.

"Yeah."

"He going to help you?" Her roommate's eyes became big brown saucers. Roxy swore the pupils were dollar signs. It made her reluctant to answer.

"Maybe."

She could have answered no and it wouldn't matter. Alexis had already boarded the money train and was running at high speed. "Get out. We're talking Kardashian kind of money, right? I read those Sinclairs are loaded."

"We aren't talking any kind of money." She especially wasn't talking money with the two of them. "He said he'd look into things. That's all. I have to put Steffi down before she wakes up."

It was a wonder the little girl hadn't woken up already with all the noise going on. She really must have had a busy day. Knowing her daughter had fun should have been a relief. Instead she felt a stab of guilt. She should have been the one providing the fun, not the elderly grandmother downstairs. The one who read her stories and fed her dinner. So many things she should be doing. What happened if she couldn't? Would she fade into the background like her mother, there but not there, a virtual stranger in a work uniform?

She lay her daughter in the plastic princess bed and pulled the blankets over her. Almost immediately Steffi burrowed into the mattress, Dusty the horse still gripped in her fist. Roxy brushed a curl from her cheek, and marveled at the innocence. Mike Templeton better realize how much she had riding on his ability to climb legal mountains.

* * *

"Tell me everything you can about your mother."

It was the next morning, and Roxy was sitting with her new best friend for their nine-thirty meeting. She half expected another lecture about her overreaction the night before, but he behaved as if it never happened. He even provided breakfast. Muffins and coffee, arranged neatly on his office conference table. Like they were having an indoor picnic.

"Standard client procedure?" she'd asked.

The question earned her an odd, almost evasive look that triggered her curiosity meter. "Figured you could use breakfast," he'd replied when she remarked on it.

Now he sat, legal pad at the ready, asking her about her mother. "There's not much to tell." Her mother had always been an enigma. Thanks to those letters, she was now a total stranger. "She wasn't what you'd call an open book, in case you couldn't guess." More like a locked diary.

"Let's start at the beginning. When did your parents get married?"

"June 18. They eloped."

She watched as he wrote down the date. It was barely legible. How could a man who moved his pen so fluidly have such horrendous penmanship?

"Seven months before you were born."

"Yup. To the day. I always figured I was the reason they got married."

"And you were their only child."

"One and only. I used to wish I had brothers and sisters, though. Being the only one could be lonely sometimes. Now that I think about it, that's probably one of the reasons I became an actress. I did a lot of pretending."

"Trust me, siblings aren't always great to have around," he replied.

"You have brothers and sisters?"

"One of each. And before you ask, I'm the oldest."

She wasn't sure why, but the idea he had a family intrigued her. Were they all as smooth and refined as he was? She pictured a trio of perfection all in navy blue blazers. "Are they lawyers, too?"

"No, I'm the only one."

"Tough act to follow, huh?"

Voice flat, he replied, "So I'm told." Another unreadable expression crossed his face. Sounded like she'd touched a nerve. Sibling rivalry or something else?

She wanted to ask more, but he steered the conversation back to being one-sided. "Your father—the one you grew up with—is he still alive?"

"Looked alive at the funeral."

Like she figured he would, he stopped writing and looked up, just in time to witness the shame creeping into her cheeks. "He took off for Florida when I was little. Guess he figured once he made a legal woman out of my mother, his job was done."

"They're divorced then."

"Good Lord, no. They were Irish Catholic. They stayed married." Instead they lived separate lives in separate states. Chained to one another by a mistake. Her.

Wonder what he'd think when he learned that he might not have had to marry her mother at all.

Mike scribbled on his notepad. "Interesting."

"What is?"

"That neither sought an annulment. If your father knew about Wentworth, he'd certainly have grounds."

"Oh." She popped a piece of muffin into her mouth, swallowing it along with the familiar defensiveness that had risen with the conversation. Her mother's story always cut so close to home. Reminded her too much of choices she did or didn't make. She always wondered which path would have been better. Hers or her mother's?

"Maybe he didn't care," she said, as much to herself as aloud. "I always figured he wanted out as easily as possible. My mother was— I'm not sure what word I'd use."

"Quiet?"

Too simple. "Absent."

"Because she was working?"

"No. I mean, yes, she worked, but absent in a different way." She thought of all the nights she spent alone with her babysitter, nights followed by mornings where her mother would sit wordlessly with coffee and cigarettes while Roxy ate her cereal. "She was there, but not there. Like that guy in the musical, *Chicago.* Mr. Cellophane. Invisible. Only instead of being Roxy's husband, she was Roxy's mother."

She laughed at her own joke before sobering. "I always felt like part of her was missing. Guess there was."

She broke off a piece of muffin, ate it, broke off another. "She must have really loved him."

"Who?"

"Wentworth, obviously." What else would explain the change from the woman described in those letters to the ineffectual, worn-down woman Roxy grew up with? "I have no idea how much she loved my father."

"Enough to marry him."

Roxy gave him a long look. He wasn't serious, was he? "We both know there were a lot of reasons to get married that had nothing to do with being in love. First and foremost the fact she was pregnant."

With another man's child. "Think that's why he left?"

"There's only one person who knows that answer."

"I know."

Looking down, Roxy saw that while talking, she'd broken the rest of her muffin into small pieces. If ever there was a conversation worth avoiding, this was the one. Hey, Dad, I was wondering, did Mom ever mention whether you biologically deserved the title? She wasn't sure which response would be better. Him knowing, meaning yet another person kept the truth from her, or him not knowing. Which meant he really had taken off because he didn't care.

Appetite gone, she rose from the table and walked toward the window. The conference room looked across to the building next door. In one window, she could see the back of a woman as she spoke on the phone. A large potted plant sat in another. If she leaned closer to the glass and looked left, she could just see the street below.

Behind her, she heard the crinkle of leather, and a moment later the air grew warm and thick. Mike stood behind her.

Odd. At work she spent her time weaving in and out of a crowd, bodies often pressing against her. The human swarm didn't feel half as overpowering as the body heat coming from her lawyer. It was like she could feel him breathing.

He didn't say a word. He merely stood there offering silent camaraderie. Feeling him—his presence—Roxy suddenly became acutely aware they were alone and behind closed doors. Why that mattered, she wasn't sure, but it did. Maybe it was the strange urge she had to lean back and let him hold her.

"Are you close to your family?" she asked him.

"I don't see why that's relevant."

Despite not seeing his face, she could easily imagine his raised brow.

"I'm curious," she told him. And talking about her family was depressing. "Besides, I thought we were going to be each other's new best friend. Isn't that what you said last night?"

"An expression. I didn't mean we were going to start getting our nails done and telling each other secrets."

"You have secrets?"

"No." But his answer came out stiff. She'd poked the nerve again.

Turning around, she found him standing far closer than she'd expected. No wonder she'd felt his body heat so keenly. "You don't sound very convincing."

"This meeting is about you. Not me." Again, the words and expression didn't go hand in hand. In this case, the shameful look in his copper eyes belied the stern dictate. Instead of the desired effect, it only made her more curious.

"Do they live in New York?"

"Who?"

"Your parents. Do they live in the city?"

He let out a frustrated breath, catching on that she would keep pressing until he answered. "Part of the year. They're very busy with their careers."

"They're successful like you then."

"Success is taken for granted in my family."

"Kind of like how screwing up is in mine."

"At least you have the choice."

He looked…distressed; she couldn't come up with a better word. She only knew the look didn't suit him.

He was frowning again. Never one to pay much attention to men's mouths, she hadn't noticed before, but he had a great-looking one. Lips not too full, not too thin, with a sharply defined Cupid's bow. They weren't suited for frowning.

She raised her eyes to study the rest of his face and connected with his gaze. In that second, a spark ignited. A feeling she couldn't define but felt all the way to her toes. She found herself mesmerized by the cloudiness in his eyes, the way the brown darkened the copper-colored flecks, making them almost invisible. "You didn't have a choice?"

Her question flipped a switch, and the moment ended. The flecks returned, and he was back once again to lawyer mode. "Don't know. I make a practice of succeeding."

Roxy got the hint. Sharing time had ended. "Let's hope you don't break the streak with my case."

"I don't intend to."

He spoke with savage determination. And yet, in the back of her mind, Roxy found herself wondering exactly who the determination was meant to convince. Her?

Or himself?

CHAPTER FOUR

Dear Fiona,
I can't believe it's only been two days. Feels like two years. You must think I'm crazy writing you again, especially after we talked half the night, but I can't stop thinking about you. This morning in English class, while the professor was going over the syllabus, all I could think of was your voice. I love your accent. I could listen to it for hours. You don't even have to say much. The grocery list would work....

TAKING off his glasses, Mike rubbed his eyes. He'd been reading since Roxanne's departure, hoping to get a feel of Wentworth's state of mind. He found out. The guy had it bad. Four letters into the pile and it was already obvious. Wonder if his parents knew he was infatuated with one of their housekeepers. Did they care? Was he going to find a letter later in the stack telling Fiona goodbye?

He hoped not. It would completely kill his case. Roxanne, too, since she was clearly counting on the money. Couldn't be easy waiting tables and raising a kid on your own. Taking the bus home in a skimpy uniform night after night. He didn't care how invisible she thought she was; when you showed that much leg, you weren't invisible.

Once again, a memory danced around his head. Grace

Reynolds. Wow, he hadn't thought about her in years. How often did they snuggle in the last row of a bus, doing things buses weren't meant for? They almost got caught more than once. The thrill of discovery was half the fun.

Roxanne reminded him of Grace. Or rather of that time. Of course, there was a big difference between an Ivy League philosophy student and a cocktail waitress. Big difference. Must be the acting thing. The idea Roxanne chased her dream. Sure, she failed, but she still chased.

Mike couldn't remember the last time he had a dream. Least one that wasn't ordained from birth and piled heavy with expectations. Except for that one crazy semester. But that had been childish fantasy. He'd let those days go. Why were the memories coming back?

I don't know, Mike. Why did you have those thoughts this morning?

They were definitely not childish fantasies. He didn't know what they were. One second he's talking about his family—which was none of her business—next he's looking in her eyes and thinking about how the light crowned her hair, and noting how her eyes were more a merger of earthy colors rather than simple green.

Things he had no business noticing about a client.

He'd felt this inexplicable pull the moment their eyes met.

Oh, God, listen to him. Who did he think he was, Wentworth Sinclair? His days of sparks and pulls were long gone.

Setting Wentworth's letter aside, he turned his attention to a different pile. The pile he'd been avoiding for days.

When he broke off from Ashby Gannon, everything seemed so straightforward. Templetons make things happen. They go for what they want. Wasn't that what he'd been drilled to do? Failure never entered his mind. After all, he had contacts, a proven reputation. He did all the right research. Created a business plan. Talk about arrogant overconfidence. Business plans and contacts didn't mean squat when the economy was tanking.

The first six months had been all right, but then the referrals dried up as his colleagues began keeping the work in-house. Doing "all right" became a luxury. Last month he didn't clear enough to make expenses. This month looked worse.

Which was why he needed Roxanne's case to succeed—and settle—quickly. If he could keep himself afloat until the Sinclairs made an offer, he might be all right. Otherwise…

We raised you to be better than this.

"I know, Dad," he muttered to the voice in his head. Dear Lord, did he know.

The phone rang, drowning out the thoughts. "Knew you'd be burning the midnight oil," his baby brother, Grant, said when he answered the phone. "No rest for the wicked, huh?"

Or the soon to be bankrupt. "What do you want?"

"Everything's great," Grant replied. "Thanks for asking."

"Precisely why I didn't bother asking. Everything's always going great lately." His brother was high on life at the moment.

"Can't argue with you there," Grant replied. "I'm calling to see what you're doing tomorrow night. Sophie and I thought we could all grab dinner."

Mike stilled. "Tomorrow?"

"Yeah. We thought it'd be great to talk to you in person for a change."

No, it wouldn't. Keeping up appearances was so much easier over the phone. "I can't."

He searched his brain for an excuse, the guilt hitting him before he even got the words out. "The Bar's hosting an event."

His stomach churned at the lie. This was his brother, after all. Family. He shouldn't feel the need to pretend anything with him.

Other than the fact he spent the better part of two years lecturing Grant on living up to his potential. It was getting harder and harder to pretend he had life under control in the face of his brother's newfound happiness. The reminder of his hypocrisy was too loud.

"Another one? I swear, you're a worse workaholic than my Sophie, and we know how bad she can be."

"Not everyone can afford to lounge around," he remarked, eyes falling to the stack of bills."

"I'm sure you can."

If only it were that easy. He opened his mouth to say as much, then quickly shut it. His problems were his; he'd deal with them. "I've already committed to this thing. Bought my ticket."

"Say no more. Heaven forbid you back out on an RSVP."

"Not my fault I believe in keeping my commitments." Nonexistent or otherwise.

"How about next week then?"

Again, Mike paused. The right answer was yes, of course. He had no plans. Couldn't afford them. He washed a hand over his face. "I don't know." He hated putting his brother off. "I just took on this big case and it's going to take up a lot of time…."

"Big case, hey? Anything interesting?"

Mike gave him the short version, causing the man to whistle. "Long-lost heirs. Impressive. Not your usual kind of client."

Definitely not, Mike replied in his head. "I'm branching out."

"Can't wait to hear more."

"Not much more to tell yet. I'm just drafting the initial DNA request this afternoon."

"I meant when we see you on Saturday. You can give us an update."

Closing his eyes, Mike shook his head. He wasn't going to dodge this one. "All right," he said, "I'll come by next Saturday."

"Great. I'll take care of the reservations," Grant answered. "It'll be great to catch up."

"Yeah, it will," Mike replied in a quiet voice.

They spoke a little longer, mostly about Grant's latest architectural project, which was going spectacularly. As he listened, Mike tried to remind himself Grant had floundered for two whole years, and his returning to architecture was to be celebrated. He hated the part of him that twisted with envy. He was happy for him. Truly.

After promising for a second—and third—time he would keep their next date, he hung up. No sooner did the phone line click dead than he found his thoughts right back to Roxanne. When she left this morning, she'd promised to make a phone call of her own. To Florida to ask her father about Wentworth. He didn't envy the task. *Are you close to your parents?* Her question came floating back, along with the note in her voice that made her sound so very small and vulnerable. The memory alone was enough to tug at him. He'd never had a client get to him like this before. Then again, he'd never had a client this important before, either. Grant was right: she wasn't his usual client.

She was way, way more.

"Don't look now, but your lawyer's back."

Hearing Jackie's announcement, Roxy nearly dropped her tray. "Mike's here?" Sure enough, he sat at the same table as before in the same blue blazer as this morning.

Recalling how closely she'd stood to those buttons, Roxy felt a shiver go through her. "What does he want?"

"Better be a drink," Dion replied. "We aren't here so he can set up shop and take the table away from paying customers."

Roxy ignored him. She was too busy watching Mike as he folded his coat over the back of a chair. Why on earth would he drive across town for a second night in a row?

Only one way to find out. Soon as she unloaded the drinks on her tray, she made her way to his table. Just like last night, he was scribbling away on a yellow legal pad. "Is there a problem?"

He looked up, so unsuited for a bar like this it wasn't funny. It caused her breath to catch. "Why would there be a problem?" he asked.

"Because you're here."

"Felt like a Scotch."

An incomplete answer if ever she heard one. "Don't they serve liquor in your neck of the woods?"

"They do, but I like this place. It reminds me of somewhere I used to spend time."

Really? The idea of Mike Templeton anywhere near a bar like the Elderion on a regular basis boggled her mind. She covered her surprise with a shrug. "It's a free country." Though she had to wonder.

"Wait." She paused midturn. "This isn't about my taking the bus home is it? Because I told you already—"

"You take the bus all the time. Don't worry, I got that message loud and clear."

"Good. I hate having to repeat myself."

"Wouldn't want that, would we." He was looking over the rim of his glasses at her. The way the light reflected off the lenses made reading his eyes impossible so she couldn't tell if his tone was sarcastic or not.

"Although I have to ask," he continued. "Would it be so awful if I did bring you home?"

No, her mind immediately answered. Wow, talk about old mistakes rearing their ugly head. As if she'd let anyone take her home again. "I'll go get your Scotch."

"I did come by for a reason."

Ah, she knew there was something. She waited for him to explain.

"I wanted to let you know I plan to submit the DNA request on Monday."

"So soon?" Her heart stopped. The crowd around them receded, drowned out by the wind tunnel sounding in her ears. She hadn't expected things to move so quickly. "I haven't reached my father yet." A sinking sensation erupted in her stomach. Could she still call him her father?

"You'll reach him soon enough. The Sinclairs will reject this request out of hand anyway giving you plenty of time. We're really filing so they know we exist. Once we make our position clear, we can force an offer."

"Offer?" She was confused. "I thought we were asking for a DNA test."

"We are."

He motioned for her to sit down. After glancing over to make sure Dion wasn't paying attention, Roxy complied.

"This is our opening move. They'll react. We'll counteract, and so on, till we get what we want."

"You're talking about the money."

"Exactly."

"Where does the DNA test come in?"

"It doesn't."

"But—" She was lost. "Are you saying there won't be a DNA test?"

Mike looked up from his paperwork. "Not if we accept a settlement offer first."

"Wait a second. Without a test, how will I know for certain whether Wentworth is my father?"

"Does it matter?"

Yes, it mattered. She didn't realize until this moment but it mattered a lot. "Did you think I only wanted the money?"

"Basically, yes."

In other words, his opinion from the other day hadn't changed at all. He still thought her a gold-digging fraud. Worst part of it was she'd gone to him about the money. She had no one to blame for his opinion but herself.

"I've got tables to wait on." She couldn't deal with this right now. Not at work. Blindly she headed into the crowd, colliding with the first body that crossed her path.

"Hey," a nasal-voiced brunette whined. "Watch where you're going."

"Sorry," Roxy muttered.

"Look what you did. You made me spill my drink!"

"I'll get you a new one." More charges against her paycheck.

"Damn right, you're getting me a free drink." Based on the way her words slurred, she didn't need one, either. "And a new blouse. Did you see what you did?" She gave a wobbly wave across her torso. A blue splash, about waist-high, marred the orange silk. "This is designer! Do you know how much it cost?"

Full price or discount? Roxy would bet she didn't pay retail. She knew the woman's type.

Still, the customer was always right. "Send the bill to the guy in the blue blazer," she told the woman. "He's the money man."

The brunette squinted in confusion. "What?"

"Just send us the bill." More charges for Dion to deduct from her paycheck. At this rate, she might as well be working for free. Trying to move on, she attempted to sidestep the woman, but unfortunately, the brunette wasn't ready to let the topic drop. "I want to talk to a manager," she slurred. Came out more like *I wannatalkamanger.* "Someone's going to pay for my blouse."

"Like I said, send us the dry-cleaning bill, and we'll gladly take care of it."

"Dry cleaners? What's a dry cleaner going to do? This shirt's ruined."

Pul-leeze. The stain wasn't that big. Dion would tell the woman the same exact answer. She turned around, planning to head to the bar and get him. The brunette, thinking she was walking away, grabbed her arm. "Don't you walk away from me."

She attempted to yank Roxy around. Stopping short on her heels, Roxy instead stumbled backward, bumping shoulders with the woman and causing more cocktail to splash.

"You stupid idiot!" the woman shrieked. Blue liquid stained her bare arm. "Look at what you did now! How would you like it if I spilled a drink all over you?"

There was maybe a half an inch left in her martini glass. Rearing back, the woman tossed the liquid at Roxy's face. An arm appeared out of nowhere and grabbed Roxy's waist, pulling her safely out of the line of fire.

She didn't need to look to see who the arm belonged to. The way her insides reacted was identification enough.

"Come on, Roxy," Mike murmured in her ear, "let's go get you some air."

"Why are you pulling me away?" she protested as he dragged her toward the front door. "I didn't start the fight."

"No, but I didn't want to take the chance of you sticking around and letting the situation escalate. Last thing we need is an article in the *Daily Post* about you getting into a bar fight."

"News flash, I work in a bar." She yanked her arm free. What did a news article matter anyway?

Oh, right. The lawsuit. He didn't want bad publicity impacting his "settlement."

A blast of cold air hit her, a harsh reminder spring was still a few weeks away. "Here." Before she could say a word, she found herself enveloped in a blue worsted-wool cocoon. Despite her annoyance, she wrapped the blazer around her with gratitude.

"She started it," she muttered.

"Technically you started it when you stormed into the crowd. You've got to stop overreacting to everything I say. Or—" he adjusted the jacket on her shoulders "—at least stop storming off before we're done talking. Do you want to explain what I said this time that was so wrong?"

"Isn't it obvious?"

"Honestly, not really. The other night you talked about wanting to make a better life for your daughter. I assumed you meant financially."

"I did." After all, it was the Sinclair money that would help her help Steffi, not the bloodline. Truth be told, she didn't understand her reaction completely herself except that as soon as he talked about not going through with the DNA test, her blood ran cold. She didn't realize until that moment how badly she wanted—she needed—to know the truth. Needed to know how and why she was brought into this world. If she was created out of love or simply created.

She hugged the jacket tighter. The cloth smelled of bar soap and musk-scented aftershave, exactly how she expected his clothes to smell.

Meanwhile, Mike had moved over to the curb where he stood studying the traffic. Realizing she was seeing him in shirtsleeves for the first time, she took a good look. Without the extra layer he looked different. More exposed, more human. The broadcloth pulled taut across his shoulders and back, revealing a body that was lean and muscular. Bet if she touched him, it would feel like chiseled rock. She doubted a man like him, with so many assets, could understand her desire. "I can't explain why, but knowing makes a difference."

"You know that makes the case a whole lot more difficult," he said.

"I know."

Joining him, she touched his shoulder. "Not knowing for certain would haunt me. I want to be able to tell Steffi where she came from." She wanted to know herself.

"You're the client." He washed a hand across his features. "If you want a DNA test, then we push for a DNA test."

Roxy smiled. She knew his acquiescence had everything to do with her wishes as his client and not for her personally, but at the moment she didn't care. It just felt good to have her wishes heard.

The bar door opened, and Jackie's ponytailed head peered around the corner. "Hey, Rox, you comin' back in or what? We're swamped here."

"I'll be right there," Roxy replied. To Mike, she said, "Your idea of disaster is bad publicity, but mine is getting fired. Bills still need to be paid."

He half nodded in response. "I know what you mean."

Doubtful, but she appreciated the attempt at commiseration. There was another gust of wind and musk teased her nostrils, reminded her that the warmth around her shoulders belonged to him. Reluctantly she moved to shed his jacket.

"Keep it on till you get inside," Mike told her.

"You sure? A drink might come flying in my direction when I walk through the door."

"I'll take my chances," he replied, flashing a smile.

"Thank—" Her answer drifted off as she found herself caught in his coppery eyes. The gentle reassurance swirling in the brown depths caught her breath. All of a sudden her lungs felt too big for her chest, as if some giant balloon had expanded. The air hummed with energy and the sound of their breathing. What happened to the traffic? Surely the world hadn't disappeared leaving only the two of them.

Or had it? The spark, that inexplicable connecting spark from this morning resurrected itself. Her gaze dropped to his mouth. She heard a hitch and realized, without having to look, that his gaze had dropped, too. He was studying her mouth. Did he like what he saw? She did. Her body swayed a little bit closer. Close enough to put them both in a very dangerous position.

CHAPTER FIVE

What are you doing, Templeton? Mike didn't know. In front of him, Roxanne's lips glistened invitingly. He couldn't tear his eyes away. The strong connection he felt this morning had returned, and he was trapped in its pull. Thoughts raced through his head. Wild, crazy thoughts like pressing her against the brick wall and kissing her until their lungs ran out of air. And more.

He didn't have these kinds of thoughts. Not anymore. He certainly shouldn't be having them now.

"This is a mistake." He delivered his verdict in a whisper, part of him wondering if he was speaking quietly on purpose. To avoid hearing his own warning. Roxanne heard, though, and relief filled her face. Clearly she agreed.

Whether the tightness in his gut was relief or disappointment, he refused to say.

He was pretty sure he knew the answer when she looked away and the tightness grew. "I better get inside before Dion has my head," she said in a soft voice. She shrugged off his jacket and handed it to him. "You should take this back," she said. "I can't afford the dry-cleaning bill."

"Yet," he corrected, hoping the teasing would bring back some of the connection.

"Yet," she repeated.

That was another thing. Agreeing to push for the DNA

test. All he did was postpone any settlement offers, delaying payment. He couldn't afford to delay. Like the lady said, you still got to pay the bills.

But listening to her, the way she was trying so hard to keep her voice from quivering, he knew he had to say yes. He wanted her to have her answers.

Why was he suddenly feeling so invested in her results? What happened to the invisible wall between lawyer and client? To focusing on using this case to regain his financial footing? Was nostalgia getting to him?

Or a set of soft red curls, he asked himself, fingers twitching to touch them.

He pulled himself back to business. "Hopefully no one took my paperwork while we were outside talking," he said. "I can see your boss tossing them out so someone else could sit down."

"Me, too," Roxanne replied, rewarding him with a smile. Mike felt a wave of something rolling over him, settling dangerously near his chest. Whatever had him acting out of character—nostalgia or the curls—it was getting stronger.

Maybe instead of worrying about paperwork, he should worry about that instead.

Roxy clicked off her cell phone and let it drop to her lap. Just her luck. Her father had taken off for a fishing trip in the Bahamas, and no one was sure when he would return. So much for getting answers from him. He wasn't even available by cell; she had to leave a message with his lady "friend".

And she'd been worried about blindsiding him so soon after her mother's death. She should have realized. After all, this was the man who, when she told him about being pregnant said, "What do you want me to do?"

Her fingers played with the edge of her phone case. She'd told Mike she'd give him an update after she called. Updating, however, meant talking to each other, which she'd been avoiding doing the past three days. She'd even gone so far as to ignore his phone calls.

"A mistake." His words floated back. Actually they never left. She'd been hearing them loud and clear since he whispered them Friday night. A mistake. Story of her life.

He was right, of course. They had been teetering on the brink of a very bad idea. She had absolutely no business kissing the man, no matter how compassionate he seemed or how drawn she was to him. Seeking reassurance in a man's arms was a dangerous idea with ramifications that lasted a lifetime. She should know. Assuming, of course, things had gone further than a kiss. What made her think he was remotely interested? Why would he be?

Desire and loneliness. The worst combination in the world. Made a person make stupid decisions. Like reaching out for the wrong person or seeking solace in the wrong places. Problem was desire only killed loneliness for a short time. Then the sun came up leaving you to deal with the fallout. She'd learned that lesson the hard way four years ago.

Clearly Mike's resolution saved them both a lot of potential problems. Now if she could only shake the needy, lonely ache in her chest.

A purple-and-white blur danced before her face. Blinking back to earth, she smiled at her little girl, who was making her pony dance through the air.

"Can I have a cookie?" Steffi asked.

"After dinner," Roxy replied. The answer earned her a pout. "If you're really hungry, you can have orange chips." Orange chips were her way of selling sliced carrots as a snack. Sometimes the trick worked; sometimes it didn't.

Today looked to be a hard sell. "Wayne bought potato chips."

"I don't think Wayne would want us touching his things without asking," she replied. Talk about irony. Wayne sure didn't have a problem with touching others' stuff. "We have orange chips. Would you like some?"

"Okay." Enthusiastic, the response was not. "Can Dusty have some, too?"

"Sure." If it would help her daughter eat better. "We'll give him his own bowl so he can share with the other ponies. And," she added, "if you're both good and eat them all up, we can have macaroni and cheese for supper."

"Yay!" Satisfied she'd won something—in her little mind, mac and cheese was boxed gold—her daughter went back to her farm set. A half dozen ponies lay on their sides on the floor in front of the red plastic barn. "The horses are having a sleepover," she explained in an important voice.

"I better get the chips then. They might get hungry."

"Chips, chips, chips," Steffi chanted, pretending the cheer came from the horses.

While she watched her daughter chatter and play, a lump worked its way into Roxy's throat. Today was the way every day should be. Filled with mommy-daughter time and pretend pony games. If it were up to her, Steffi would never go a day unhappy. Or feeling unwanted. She'd wake up every day knowing the world was glad she existed.

If she had one regret in this world it was that Steffi didn't have a father who knew what a joy the little girl was. At the moment her daughter was too young to wonder too much about her dad. Eventually, though, she would, and Roxy would be forced to tell her the truth. Then what?

Hopefully she could at least give her a grandfather.

In her chest, the lonely feeling grew. She squeezed her phone. Go on, call him. You know you want to.

That was the problem. In spite of her avoidance, she wanted to talk with him. Worse, she wanted to feel his body close to hers again, and lose herself in the coppery concern of his eyes. She wanted to carry through on that kiss. So much for hard lessons learned, eh?

The front door buzzed while she was putting the bag of sliced carrots back in the fridge.

"Roxanne?" called the voice on the other end.

Her insides took a pathetic little tumble. She cursed herself. "Mike?" she repeated, as if she really needed to identify him. "What are you doing here?"

"Hoping to talk with you obviously. I've been trying to reach you all day."

"My phone's been off," she lied.

There was a pause. "Oh. May I come up?"

Did she have a choice? She buzzed him in.

Soon as she did, all her mental berating went out the window. Her heart sped up at the prospect of seeing him. Quickly she scanned the apartment. The place looked terrible. Folded laundry sat in a basket in the hall waiting to be put away. Steffi's toys littered the floor—the farm took up a lot of real estate. A half-drunk juice box and bowls of carrots on the floor. Picture books on the couch. How fast could she straighten up? Or did she straighten herself up instead? Change the yoga pants and T-shirt she'd tossed on this morning. And makeup! She wasn't wearing a stitch! She was a bigger mess than the apartment. Get a grip, Roxy. Bad idea, remember?

He knocked. She jumped.

"Mommy, someone's at the door," Steffi announced, not moving from the floor.

"I know, baby." Stupid elevator would be fast for once. Combing her fingers through her hair, she prayed whatever brought him here was important enough to make him oblivious to his surroundings.

Opening the door, she realized instantly it wouldn't matter if he was oblivious or not. No amount of sprucing would make her or the apartment worthy. He'd still outclass the place.

"What's up?" she asked, forcing a casual note into her voice. She could at least act unaffected, right?"

A challenge as he strode inside the same way he entered the bar. Like he owned the place. "I met with Jim Brassard today," he said.

"Who's Jim Brassard?"

"Managing partner at—" He stopped short when he saw Steffi. Her daughter was squatting in front of her farm, staring up at him with Dusty clutched protectively in her fist.

"Baby, this is Michael," Roxy said. "He's a…friend… of Mommy's."

Mike arched a brow at the word friend, but made no correction. "Hello, Steffi."

For a second, Roxy thought he might stick out his hand to go along with his formal greeting. Instead the two of them had a mini stare-off. Steffi won. Mike looked back up at her, with a silent "What now?"

"Mike and I have some business we need to talk about at the table. Can you play with your ponies while we talk?"

Wordlessly Steffi went back to her farm, but not before casting another look in Mike's direction from over her shoulder.

"She looks like you," Mike remarked, shedding his overcoat. He'd given up the winter camel hair in favor of a trench coat that hung unbuttoned over a different shade gray suit. Eyeing the peach-colored shirt, Roxy did her best not to think about the body she glimpsed the other night. Naturally she failed.

"Can I get you some coffee or something?" she asked, still acting unaffected. It felt weird watching him settle in as if this were his home. He so clearly didn't fit.

"We're not at the bar," he replied. "You don't have to serve me." He moved to sit down only to shoot back up. Reaching down, he held up a plastic duck.

Roxy's cheeks warmed. "Sorry. The chair doubles as the farm pond. Steffi, can you come get Mr. Quack Quack? I think he's done swimming."

Wordlessly Steffi trotted over and plucked the critter from Mike's fingers before settling back in front of her farmhouse. Mr. Quack Quack, Roxy noticed, found a home on her lap where he couldn't be touched.

"We don't get a lot of visitors," she whispered to Mike, feeling the need to explain. "Make's her a little shy. So long as you don't mess up her farm animals you should be fine."

"Don't worry. I think the farm is safe."

Seeing he'd settled in and had his briefcase on the table, Roxy switched to business mode. "So you talked to this Jim person," she prodded.

"Jim Brassard from Brassard, Lester. He manages the Sinclair sisters' legal affairs. I remember him from when I was at Ashby Gannon. He's sharp. Very old school, too."

Roxy wasn't sure she liked the term "old school." "What did he say?"

"About what I expected. I presented our evidence and requested a test. He said no."

Roxy's heart sank. He told her to expect a denial, but a part of her still hoped the news would be welcomed with open arms. Foolish, she knew, but wouldn't it have been nice?

The end of the table's veneer edging had come unglued, so she picked at it nervously. "What now?"

"We wait and see," he replied. "I laid some solid groundwork today. Plus, Brassard recognizing me from Ashby Gannon helped. Helped him realize he's not dealing with some ambulance-chasing creep."

"To fight uptown, you gotta go uptown," she mumbled.

"What?"

"Nothing. Something I told myself once."

"Keep in mind," he said, "we've only just started. This was our preliminary salvo. If you want your DNA test, we need to show them we aren't going away.

"You still want to push for the test, right?" he asked.

Roxy looked to the little girl playing nearby. Playing Mike's way—for the money—would ensure her little girl's future. But she deserved to know something about where she came from. "Yes," she answered without doubt. "I want to know. Steffi needs to know her mother wasn't…" She paused, the thought too painful to say aloud. "I want to know."

Returning to playing with the veneer, she kept her eyes more focused on the chipped plastic than on the man across from her. His scrutiny felt more intense than ever. Who knew what looking into his eyes would make her feel. "I—" she heard him start.

Roxy gave in and looked up. "Yes?"

"Never mind. Back to Jim's response. His refusal means we'll need to step things up on our own end."

"How?" Her attention was aroused.

"Legally he can refuse our request until the cows come home. The law is very specific about the amount of time you have to bring a claim against an estate, and you're well past the deadline."

Story of her life. Too little. Too late. "What can we do then?"

He clicked his black lacquer pen. "Way I see things,

our best approach is to mount a two-prong approach. We file the appropriate legal challenges and wait for them to wend their way through court—which could take years, by the way."

"What's the other prong?"

"We increase public pressure. Force the Sinclairs to act in the interest of good public relations."

She waited while he rummaged through his briefcase, coming up with his yellow legal pad. The pages were half-filled by this point and he had to flip several over until he reached a blank sheet. When he did, he folded his hands and leaned forward.

Roxy leaned forward, too. There was a cautiousness to his movements that made her wary. She wanted to make sure she didn't miss a word. "What exactly do you want to do?"

Those coppery eyes sparkled, completely not helping her cause. Making matters worse, he slowly raised the left corner of his mouth, creating a lopsided, sexy smile.

"We talk to the press."

Mike had hoped the fact she'd been an actress would mean Roxanne would be fairly receptive to his idea. He'd hoped wrong. Immediately her attention went to the little girl playing nearby. "Won't talking to the press tick them off?"

"There is a risk," he conceded. "But going public also lets us tell our side of the story."

"You mean mine," she corrected. "*My* side of the story. You're not going to be the one sharing your life history."

"No, I'm not." She was right about that.

He watched her chew the inside of her cheek, an action that turned her mouth into an uneven, yet still amazingly appealing, pout. Without makeup she looked a lot younger than twenty-nine. Sure, there were circles under her eyes from keeping late hours, but the fatigue was offset by a newly acquired innocence. The vulnerability he always sensed lurking had risen to the surface. She looked softer. Sweeter. Dangerous words to use when describing a client, especially when he spent the better part of the past couple of days reminding himself a good lawyer did not pursue his clients. They did not kiss them. And they especially didn't fantasize about taking late-night bus rides and reliving college age exploits.

So of course, when she didn't return his calls, he went across town for a face-to-face meeting so he could battle those thoughts all over again. As if he couldn't be more distracted.

"It's a good strategy." For the case's sake, he forced himself to stay on topic. "Going public prevents them from sweeping you or your request under the rug."

No sale. He could tell by the way her eyes went from mostly green to mottled brown.

Seriously, did he really know her mood based on eye color?

Why was she so against the idea anyhow? She'd wanted to be an actress, for crying out loud. This was her shot to be in the limelight.

There was a rattle of plastic behind him. Her daughter fixing a plastic fence, mumbling something to the plastic purple-and-white pony about not getting lost.

Of course. He bet her reaction went back to their conversation the other night regarding Steffi's father. "You know," he said, "another benefit to talking to the press is that you get to be proactive. You can control the message." He indicated Steffi with a flicker of his eyes.

Picking up on his point immediately, she crossed her arms. "You promised to leave her out of this."

Now her eyes were green. A very angry shade of green.

Her whisper was equally harsh. "I told you I didn't want her involved."

"What I said was I'd do my best." He decided not to point out her wish had been completely unrealistic.

"Well, if this is your best, then you suck." Shoving her chair so hard it nearly tipped over, she marched into the kitchen. From behind the dividing wall, Mike heard the sound of pots and cupboards being slammed about.

Feeling scrutinized, he looked over to find Steffi staring at him with wide, accusing eyes. Great. The kid was mad at him, too. What was he supposed to do?

"Your mother is… Um, that is, she and I…" The girl continued to stare.

Dammit. He'd have an easier time getting through to Roxanne.

"You've got to stop the storming off," he said, joining her in the kitchen. "It makes having a conversation very difficult."

She stood at the kitchen sink filling a saucepan with water. "I promised Steffi macaroni and cheese."

"At this exact moment?"

"Better than making her wait. Not like we had anything more to talk about."

Mike rolled his eyes. "I thought you were past arguing with me about everything I want to do?"

"You thought wrong." She slapped off the faucet and lifted the pan from the sink. The motion caused her T-shirt skimming the waistband of her pants to rise, too, creating yet another invitation to look at her behind. Damn if he wasn't developing a fixation for studying the woman's body.

He fanned his fingers in his hair, tugging the roots as a way of forcing his eyes upward. "Look, I get it. You want to protect your child. But surely you realized you couldn't keep her existence a secret forever. Brassard's investigators would find her in two seconds."

"Of course I didn't think I could keep her a secret."

"Then what?" There was a small space of countertop between the stove and sink. He leaned against it, fingers curling around the Formica lip, and waited while she adjusted the burner. "Is it because you're embarrassed?"

"What? No! How can you even say that? Steffi's the best thing I ever accomplished. I could never be embarrassed of her."

Not of her, maybe. But of something else? Her angry reaction the other night came home to roost. "Is it her father then?"

Roxanne slapped the lid on the saucepan with a clank so loud he wondered if she wanted the water to boil faster or let off steam. "I told you, Steffi's father's out of the picture."

Out, but not forgotten. "Wouldn't be the first time an absentee parent crawled out of the woodwork at the scent of money."

"He wouldn't."

So she said the other night. "You can't be certain."

"Yes, I can. In order to crawl anywhere he'd have to know she exists."

"He doesn't know?"

"No." She'd crossed the room and was manically moving boxes around an upper cabinet. "I couldn't tell him."

Mike couldn't see her face, but he could hear the tension in her voice. She was literally gritting her teeth. "What do you mean you couldn't tell him?" Didn't she mean wouldn't? "Is he dead? Married?"

She laughed at his suggestions, hollow and without humor, but didn't answer. It was like pulling teeth.

"I need to know," he pushed. "If there's any chance

the Sinclairs can dig up the information, then you need to tell me."

"I couldn't tell him because I don't know his last name." She choked on the answer, the words barely getting out. "I'm not a hundred percent sure of his first name, either."

It took a moment for him to process her reply. When he finally did, he was shocked at how viscerally he reacted. His chest burned with anger against the man. "You're saying—"

"I got drunk and knocked up by a total stranger? Yeah, that pretty much sums up the story." She was trying to sound indifferent, as though it was no big deal, and having no luck. Hearing the same in her voice, his anger toward this faceless stranger rose. He hurt for her. If he could take away her embarrassment and shame he would.

His hand barely closed over her shoulder when she shrugged him away. "Like mother like daughter, right?" she said bitterly.

"What happened?" Much as he didn't want to ask, he had to know. For the case, he told himself.

"What do you think happened? I'd had a really lousy day so I went to the lounge to drown my sorrows. This guy offered a shoulder and free drinks. He was gone when I woke up."

Mike balled his fist. What kind of man wouldn't want to be there when she woke up?

"Least I got Steffi out of the deal." Again, she failed at nonchalance. Mike blamed the unshed tears brimming in her eyes.

"She doesn't know obviously. When she asks about her father, I can usually distract her."

Sniffing back the emotion, she reached up with a shaky hand and closed the cabinet door. "Don't know what I'll tell her when she gets older."

Finally the pieces were coming together. "You're afraid she'll learn the truth."

"What if I embarrass her?" she asked in a voice so small it kicked him square in the gut.

Unlikely, given the girl was four years old and could be kept sheltered, but he understood the fear nonetheless. More than she realized. "No one wants to let down the people they love. To think you failed them."

"You must think you picked a real winner of a client."

He had to hold back the urge to cup her chin and force her to meet his eyes. "Actually I think I picked just fine. Way I see it, you're simply a woman who made a mistake. Hardly the first."

"The second in my family alone," she remarked. "Least my mother and Wentworth could say they were in love. I can pretend he would have been happy about the news."

Whereas her other father what? Wasn't?

That's why the DNA test was so important to her. She needed context. A better legacy to give her daughter.

Emotions that had been shoved to the background years before began to unfurl, and in that moment he found himself looking not at a client or even a physically attractive woman, but a person, alone and hurting. He understood her fear. She was afraid of letting her daughter down, because doing so might mean losing her as well.

Yeah, he understood that fear all too well. Suddenly winning her case became doubly important, becoming as much about helping her as it did about saving his own failing hide. He would do anything in his power to make sure she got everything she deserved.

Halfway across the kitchen, he stopped. The strength of his conviction frightened him. She was a client, for goodness' sake. She shouldn't be so damn important. She shouldn't be anything more than the means to an end.

Yet, here he was closing the space between them with the singular thought of taking her in his arms.

"Mommy?" There was the sound of small feet approaching the doorway. Mike immediately stiffened and moved away. Roxy did the same.

Steffi appeared in the doorway. "Dusty and I finished our chips," she announced. "Can we have our macaroni cheese now?"

"Sure, baby," Roxy replied. She still hadn't turned around. Mike saw her swiping at her cheek. "I'm making it right now. How about you go wash your hands, okay?"

"Okay." The little girl shot a look in his direction before turning around. He didn't think four-year-olds had accusing glares, but he'd been wrong. She clearly blamed him for her mother's unusual behavior.

On the stove, the saucepan cover rattled. "Don't know why I bother to tell her to wash her hands," Roxy said, giving a large sniff. "She's going to grab that horse again, and goodness knows how many germs are on that thing."

She was grasping at normalcy, pretending the earlier conversation didn't happen. Needing the reprieve himself, he let her. He returned to his spot next to the stove. "I take it she loves horses."

"What gave you your first clue?" Macaroni cascaded from the box into boiling water. "Right before the holidays I took her to Central Park and she saw the carriages. Since that moment it's been all horses all the time. I'm not sure, but I think she wants to move into that farm."

"Has she been to the stables in the park yet?"

"No. I'd like to, but I'm concerned she'll want to sign up for riding lessons and I'm not sure when I'll be able to afford them. I hate saying 'maybe…we'll see.' Feels like such a cop-out."

"My sister, Nicole, took lessons," he told her. "Did the whole jumping and riding around the circle thing."

"Was she any good? Wait, let me guess." She cast him a look from over her shoulder. "She was excellent."

"Made the junior Olympic team in high school."

"Impressive."

Not really. Not when you stopped to think there hadn't been any other choice but to excel. A hobby's not worth doing, unless done right, his parents always said.

He followed her back to the dining room table and watched as she lay down the plates in a neat triangle. "How about you? What activity did you dominate?" she asked. "Football? Debate team?"

"Swimming. I was fourth in the all-city eight-hundred meter butterfly my senior year."

He didn't tell her how disappointed his parents had been at the results or how much he hated the sport. Mike had actually wanted to take fencing. A late-night swashbuckler movie had him convinced sword fighting would be the best hobby ever. But his father had been on the swim team in college. Besides, he'd been clumsy in fencing class, enthusiastic but uncoordinated, where as the swimming instructor noted he had natural ability. Unable to fit both in his schedule, fencing class got dropped in favor of the sport with more potential.

He probably wouldn't have enjoyed fencing all that much anyway.

"We're ready, Mommy." Steffi returned. As predicted, the purple-and-white pony was clutched firmly in her hand.

"Dusty wash his hands, too?"

"Uh-huh." The little girl nodded and placed her pony next to one of the plates. Then and only then did Mike realize the table was set for three. Roxanne must have noticed, too, because she suddenly became quite interested in tucking her hair behind her ear. "I wasn't thinking. Would you like to stay for dinner?"

"He can't," Steffi piped in. "He didn't eat any orange chips."

Mimicking the stance her mother had held a few minutes earlier, the little girl crossed her arms in front of her chest.

"Mike and I are going to eat ours with dinner," Roxy replied. Then, as if realizing she'd made an assumption again, her cheeks grew pink. "That is, if you want..."

"Sure." After all his thoughts in the kitchen, he'd probably be better off going home, but he needed to finish their conversation about talking to the press. "Although..." He leaned toward her. "Orange chips?"

"Don't worry," Roxanne replied. "You'll be fine."

Considering the fact his hand still twitched to touch her, Mike wondered.

Orange chips, it turned out thankfully, were nothing more than presliced carrots, which Roxanne thoughtfully steamed.

The meal itself was fairly quiet. Still in judgment mode, Steffi kept a close eye on whether or not he ate his carrots. Mike made a point of eating several forkfuls quickly. Wasn't much choice if he wanted to eat his meal without continual scrutiny. The gesture seemed to mollify her, and she soon focused on her own food.

Her mother on the other hand... Out of the corner of his eye, he stole a look at the woman poking at the pasta on her plate. Although the dinner invitation had been her idea, she had been strangely withdrawn since serving the food. Mike couldn't blame her. He felt a little awkward himself, the realizations from the kitchen still churning up his insides.

Across the table, Steffi dipped her pony's nose in the yellow sauce.

"Don't put your toys in your food," Roxanne told her.

"Dusty's drinking the cheese."

"Steffi."

"Okay." She dragged the word out to two syllables before turning her scrutiny back on him. "You're not eating your macaroni."

"I, um…" How did he tell the girl he didn't like her favorite meal? Especially when he already felt dangerously close to her bad side.

Roxanne saved the day. "Stop worrying about what Mike's doing, and focus on your own meal. Do you want some more?"

Mouth slick with bright yellow cheese, Steffi nodded. "Wayne ate two boxes of macaroni cheese."

"Wayne?" Mike asked, perking up.

"My roommate's brother. He's the one who answered the buzzer when you came by the other evening. And when did you see Wayne eat macaroni and cheese?"

"This morning. When you were taking a shower."

Mike remembered Wayne now. Mr. Personality. "He's here in the morning?"

"He's here all the time," Roxanne replied, scraping half her plate's contents onto her daughter's.

"He uses bad words," Steffi piped in.

"Yes, he does, and don't talk with your mouth full. Bad words are the least of his sins," Roxanne told him. "I thought sharing costs with a roommate would be a good idea, but…" She shrugged, letting him fill in the rest of the sentence.

The woman was entirely too hard on herself, Mike decided. Although, Wayne might serve one good purpose.

"That's another reason to go public. Could get you out of this arrangement that much faster."

She sat back in her chair, fork twisting between her fingers. At least she was considering the point. Meant he was making some headway.

Dinner finished. Mike was just standing to help clear the dishes when a key jingled in the lock. The door opened, and a young couple walked in, one a chunky, unnatural blonde, the other a bony punk wearing a zippered sweater and oversize plaid baseball cap. Both zeroed in on him straight away.

The infamous Wayne and his sister he presumed.

Alexis was the first to greet him, coming around to lean against his side of the table. "Hey," she said, flipping her hair over her shoulder.

Meanwhile Wayne made a beeline for the couch where he immediately threw himself down and turned on the television set. The sound of a reality TV argument filled the apartment.

"Ignore him," the roommate—Alexis he remembered her name being—said. "He's ticked off because he lost money."

From the couch Wayne issued an obscene-laden complaint against spring baseball, proving Roxanne's comment about bad language.

"Told you not to bet on them, idiot," Alexis shot back. She smiled and leaned backward a little more. The change in position caused her back to arch, and her breasts, both ample and on display, to thrust upward. "You must be Roxy's lawyer. The one who's going to make her rich."

From the corner of his eye he saw Roxanne wince, and his sympathy went out to her. "You mean, am I trying to help her prove Wentworth Sinclair is her father? Yes, I am."

"And how is that going?" the blonde asked.

"I'm afraid I can't talk about cases with anyone but my clients."

"Not even with your client's roommate?"

"Not even with her."

"How—" she flipped her hair again "—considerate of you."

"It's the law, idiot," Wayne said. "He can't talk about his cases. Don't you watch television?"

"Doesn't mean he can't be considerate, too," Alexis shot back. She smiled. "Right?"

Mike glanced around the table. Still in her chair, Steffi had gone back to watching him, as if waiting for his response. Meanwhile, Roxanne was nowhere to be seen. A noise in the kitchen told him that's where she escaped. Quickly he snatched up his plate and Steffi's now empty one. "Roxanne is waiting for these," he said following suit.

"So that's the infamous Wayne and his sister, hey?"

She stood at the sink, again filling the saucepan, this time with soapy water. "I hate that Sophie is growing up around people like him," she muttered. Him, meaning Wayne. "I can't wait until I can afford to get out of here."

"You know how you can speed up the process," he replied as he set the dirty plates in the sink.

The remark earned him a sigh. "I know."

"Mommy, Wayne wants a beer," Steffi called out from the dining room table. "And can I have a cookie?"

"Absolutely you can have a cookie, baby. Come on in here and I'll give you one." Reaching into the cabinet, she took down a bag of chocolate frosted cookies and took out two.

"Tell Wayne I said he could get his own drinks," she told the girl after handing the treats over.

"Okay, Mommy."

"Honest to God," Roxanne said after Steffi skipped

back into the other room. "Asking a four-year-old to pick him up a drink. What kind of idiot does that?"

Mike waited while Roxanne watched Steffi leave the room. He could sense the wheels turning inside his head. Wayne's sudden appearance had, in a weird way, helped his cause.

"Going to the press," she said. "You really think it'll help?"

"Keep the Sinclairs from burying the case under a mound of legal paperwork."

"And you're sure we can control the message?"

Translation, he was certain they could protect Steffi. "You know what they say. Best defense is a good offense."

"What's the big deal? It's only a beer." Wayne shuffled his way to the fridge, grabbed a can, paused and grabbed a second. "Wasn't like the kid was doing anything."

"Do it," she said as soon as Wayne shuffled back.

Mike tried to keep his enthusiasm at a minimum so he didn't scare her off. "You sure?"

"I'm sure," she said, eyes finding Steffi. "I want to speed this case along."

"Great. I'll start drafting a plan right way. Find a marketing consultant who will be able to help us out." He worked with a good one back at Ashby Gannon. Expensive but good.

Roxanne continued to look off in Steffi's direction. Her hands twisted in the hem of her T-shirt, rolling and unrolling the material. "Hey," he said, catching hold of one. "You made the right call."

The doubt in her eyes as she looked at him stung. "I won't let anything go wrong. I promise."

It frightened him how much he meant his words.

CHAPTER SIX

"SHOOT, shoot, shoot."

"Mommy you're saying bad words."

"I know, baby. I'm sorry. Mom's just really late for an appointment." Really, really late.

It was Saturday morning. Last night Mike showed up at the lounge requesting—make that insisting—she show up to his office this morning. Why he couldn't make the request over the phone she didn't know; he seemed to have this thing for coming by her workplace.

For that matter, she didn't know why she had to show up on a Saturday morning. "We need to get you ready for next week's interview," he'd said. Roxy kinda thought she was ready. They'd spent the whole week working with some fancy consultant he knew who liked picking apart how she pronounced words. "Going with a g, not an a, Miss O'Brien. And don't slouch." If it weren't for Mike and his soothing "You're doing great, Roxanne," she'd have walked out.

Doubt there'd be too much praise being tossed around this morning. She was over a half hour late. Nothing had gone right. First she woke to find Wayne and some complete stranger sleeping the night off in her living room. Then Mrs. Ortega called to say she couldn't babysit forcing her to drag Steffi along. Finally, to top it all off, she missed her scheduled bus meaning she had to hike half a block to the subway station. One more lousy piece of luck and she'd lose it.

"I know, I know, I'm late," she said in a rush when she finally found her way into Mike's office. "This morning has been absolutely—"

The most stunning-looking woman Roxy had ever seen sat on the edge of Mike's desk, Jimmy Choo dangling from her toe. She had blond glossy hair that she wore clipped at the base of her neck and the type of lips women spent thousands of dollars in collagen to achieve. Only hers looked natural. She wore a duster-style sweater and camel hair slacks. Another consultant?

If so, she looked mighty at home around Mike.

Roxy shifted Steffi, who she'd scooped up upon leaving the elevator, from one hip to the other. Mike could have at least warned her there'd be someone joining them so she could have worn something a little better than jeans and a turtleneck.

"Finally!" Mike said. "I was concerned something had happened."

His attention went to Steffi. "Or maybe something did. Hello, Steffi."

Steffi stared.

"Babysitting issues," Roxy explained. "Mrs. Ortega canceled. I didn't have anyone else to watch her."

"No worries. Happens to the best of us," the blonde remarked.

Mike gave the woman a look. "Since when did you grow tolerant of child care issues?"

"Since I became a parent."

"You're not a parent. You're a dog owner," Mike replied.

"She's still a responsibility."

"One you can carry in your purse."

The banter was nauseatingly good-humored. If the woman was another consultant, she was one Mike obviously knew very well. It dawned on Roxy that the blonde was exactly the kind of woman she pictured with Mike, too.

She moved with the same kind of fluid grace, rising to her feet and extending a perfectly manicured hand. "Mike's apparently too busy hassling me about my dog to be polite. I'm Sophie Messina," she said. "It's nice to meet you, Roxanne."

"Sophie is here to help you get ready for your public debut," Mike explained.

Get ready, how? She'd already worked with the media guy. Her skepticism started to kick in. Calling upon what few acting skills she had, Roxy pretended a smile. "Really?"

"Don't worry, I won't push you to do anything drastic," the blonde—Sophie—replied. "Alfredo is going to love your hair by the way."

Roxy narrowed her eyes. "Who's Alfredo?"

"You don't know?" Wearing a frown, Sophie spun around to face Mike. "You did tell her what we were doing today, didn't you?"

"I planned to explain once we were all together."

"Explain once—? You're kidding me."

"Explain what?" Roxy looked at the two of them.

Oh, my God. Smooth out the rough edges. That's what he wrote while in the bar that first night. Part of the overall plan, he'd said. He'd share when he was ready.

He'd been talking about *her* rough edges. "This is a makeover?" she asked them.

Why didn't he come right out and say she wasn't suitable for talking to the press? Too "rough" as it were.

"You son of a—" She caught herself before Steffi heard the next word.

"Roxanne, wait."

"For what? For you to insult me more?"

Forget it.

"What do you mean, insult?"

"When you said this was to prepare for next week's interview, I thought you meant working on my interview skills. Not my appearance."

"I told you you should have said something beforehand," Sophie said, leaning against the desk. "If it were me, I'd be mad, too."

"No one asked your opinion, Sophie," Mike snapped.

"Maybe you should because she's right. What's wrong with the way I look? I've been looking this way for thirty years and it's worked for me just fine."

In the back of her mind, she feared her reaction was over the top as usual. But, dammit, he hurt her feelings. How dare he get his blonde friend to clean her up. She'd thought…

Thought he might think she measured up.

"You misunderstand what I'm trying to do," he said.

"Do I? Because the term makeover sounds pretty clear-cut."

Letting out a long breath, Mike jammed his fingers through his hair. In spite of it being Saturday, he wore a tweed jacket over his lamb's wool sweater. More proof of her inadequacy, Roxy supposed, that she underdressed for a weekend meeting. "Sophie, would you mind taking Steffi to the big conference room and showing her the TV set? I need to talk with Roxanne alone."

To her credit, the blonde silently asked permission before moving. Nodding, Roxy set her daughter on the floor and nudged her toward the door. "It's okay, Steffi. I'll be there in a minute."

"I thought you understood how important it is to put your best foot forward when speaking to the press," Mike said after the door shut.

"Oh, I understand." All too well. "Apparently you don't consider my foot good enough."

"Not true. Your foot is fine."

"Just not good enough to show the world."

"Oh, come on, Roxy, use your head. This isn't about whether or not you look good. It's about selling you as Wentworth Sinclair's daughter. You're an actress. Think of this as playing a role. Roxanne O'Brien, heiress."

"I am Roxanne O'Brien, heiress."

"The public will expect you to look different."

"You mean better." Not like Roxanne O'Brien, cocktail waitress. When was plain old Roxy going to be good enough?

"I mean different," Mike repeated. He stepped forward closing the difference between them until it was no more than a few inches. "They are two vastly difference things, and you know it."

Unfortunately the man had a point. To win over the folks uptown, she had to look like she belonged.

"You still should have told me. You know I don't like secrets."

"I know, but if I told you I risked you not showing up.

"Or having a drink dumped in my lap," he added, offering a slow, charm-laden smile. Roxy decided he was taking up far too much of her personal space than normal. The edge of his tweed blazer abutted her rib cage. Every breath he took caused the wool to gently caress her sweater.

"What about your friend?" she asked. "She doesn't mind doing this?"

"Who, Sophie? Are you kidding? I only had to promise my firstborn. Seriously…" He raised a hand when she opened her mouth to say something. "After she was done lecturing me for blowing her and my brother off for dinner this weekend, she jumped right aboard."

His brother. To her surprise, relief circulated through her.

"So," Mike was saying. Was it her imagination or had he moved another step closer? "Are you on board?"

"What about Steffi? I can't very well take her with me, can I?"

"Now that you say it that might be a problem. I hadn't counted on her showing up."

"I don't suppose—" Roxy shook her head. The idea was ludicrous.

"What?" Mike pressed.

"Well, I was wondering if you'd be, well, if you'd watch Steffi. But then I realized what a bad idea that was."

"It's not bad at all," he replied. "I wasn't going to go on this excursion of yours anyway."

"You weren't?"

"Get in the way of two women and shopping? I'm not sure it's worth the risk. I'd be glad to watch Steffi."

"You?" Him? The two barely spoke to one another. What would they do, spend the afternoon staring at each other? She chewed her lower lip.

"I'm not sure."

"Trust me," Mike said, his voice transforming soft and silky.

Maybe now would be a good idea to remind him about her theory on promises and the men who made and broke them. Or rather it might have been if Mike hadn't moved close enough she could feel his breath on her neck. "Have I lied to you yet?" he asked.

"I—" Roxy had to think. No, he hadn't. There had been misunderstandings and some poor behavior but he never lied. "You promise to help me keep on top of information," she said. "Good, bad or otherwise. Deal?"

The smile gracing his features was so slow and sexy her knees practically buckled. "Everything," Mike reassured her, and darn if his face wasn't so sincere her stomach tumbled a little. To save herself, she stepped backward.

"All right," she said, "let's get this makeup party started."

"Believe me, I had no idea Mike planned to spring today on you like this," Sophie said a short while later. "I thought for sure he'd explain himself. I swear sometimes he's worse than his brother. Grant lives to keep me off balance."

Roxy listened, but didn't answer. She still wasn't happy about this whole makeover project, even if she could see Mike's point. Partly out of anger, partly because she had no idea what the end product would look like.

"I have to admit, though," the blond woman continued, "it was fun watching you give him the what-for."

She held a silver-and-white jacket next to Roxy's face, then shook her head. "You ask me, he needs someone to do that more often. Might loosen him up a little—the man makes me look low-key." A stretch since the woman had already checked her email a dozen times since leaving the office. "Lord knows Grant's been trying to get him to loosen that tie of his for a while."

"I like how formal he looks," Roxy replied.

"No wonder he likes you."

Roxy hated how her stomach somersaulted at Sophie's comment. Same way she hated trying not to relive the moment in his office or any of the other times he'd come close to touching her. Reminding herself theirs was a temporary relationship helped. “Winning this case seems to be important to him.”

“Winning, huh?” A pair of skeptical blue eyes stared at her from over the clothes rack. “That why he practically leaped over his desk when you walked in the door? And offered to watch your daughter while we shopped?”

Another flutter found its way to Roxy’s stomach. “He probably figured we’d get more done without having to entertain a four-year-old.”

“If you say so.”

Roxy said so. For once she planned to use her head rather than blindly acting out. She shook her head at the cashmere blazer Sophie had held up. “Too high a cost.”

“Sometimes you need to break out of your comfort mold,” Sophie replied. “Grant taught me that. In this case, you might find this to be a good investment.”

They were talking about the jacket, right?

“I have to admit,” Sophie continued. “I’ve never seen Mike so invested in a case before. Or maybe it seems that way because we haven’t seen him much. He’s too busy building his super firm.”

“Super firm?” Roxy had to ask.

“It’s what we prefer to call it because he’s always out drumming up business. Grant figures he’s on a quest to create the biggest, bestest law firm in the city. That would certainly make my future in-laws happy.”

Least you have a choice. “Mike mentioned being from a family of high achievers.”

“You can say that again.” Turning around from the rack to the shelves behind her, Sophie began looking through a collection of turtleneck sweaters. “Normally I would agree with the philosophy.”

“But?” Roxy heard the unspoken word quite clearly.

The blonde shrugged. “Something about the Templetons.

They demand a lot of their kids, even as adults. But what do I know? My parents didn't demand a damn thing from me."

"Me, neither."

"I knew I liked you for some reason," Sophie said with a grin.

As Roxy fingered the leather piping that trimmed a red blazer, a sadness settled over her. *Least you had the choice.* Mike's remark kept coming back to her. Was this the nerve she kept hitting with her questions about his family? The one that made him fold into himself whenever the topic came up?

"Funny," Sophie said. "I expected more clutter."

"Where?" Her remark brought Roxy back to the present.

"At Mike's firm. Today was the first time I visited. I was surprised how little clutter there was. My firm went paperless a while back, and we're still buried in the stuff."

"You're surprised Mike is neat?" Picturing her formal-looking attorney, she couldn't imagine anything about him being cluttered.

"Mike, no. The rest of the staff, yes, I mean, I know it's a co-op office space and they share resources, but he must have at least one paralegal or secretary. I can't believe he managed to find one as neat as he is."

She touched Roxy's shoulder. "Ready to try a few outfits on? I can't wait to see how the wrap dress fits. I have a feeling Mike's eyes will bug out of his head when he sees you in it."

Roxy looked to the ground. The remark was meant to be a compliment. Too bad she didn't feel flattered. It only reminded her she was here because Mike thought she needed "smoothing."

"I thought the point was to impress the Sinclairs," she said.

"It is," Sophie replied. "But would it hurt to impress your lawyer, too?"

"No." She only wished she'd been impressive enough from the start.

My Dearest Fiona:
I miss you, too. When you're not with me, it feels as though the life has been sucked right out of the room. You're my sunshine, my light. Outside my window, I can see the last few leaves of fall. A living O. Henry painting. Their color is nothing compared to yours. Because without you the world feels dead. When I get home, I'm going to take you in my arms and...

Nice dream, pal. Mike set Wentworth's letter down. It was the next to last one in the pile. Twenty-eight letters in looking for information that might prove Wentworth and Fiona fathered a child and he hadn't unearthed a thing. Nothing but a rapidly growing unsettled feeling. Almost like a yearning. And memories of his own college affair. One semester. He'd crammed a lifetime in, though, hadn't he? Enough, he'd assumed, to last.

Odd thing was, it wasn't those days or even those people he missed. Grace, for all the feelings she evoked in him, wasn't what had him feeling empty. It was more. A large, indefinable emotion that he couldn't escape. Same way he couldn't shake how whenever he thought of those days now, Grace's fuzzy dark-haired image morphed into a less fuzzy, decided red-haired one.

"You tap your pen a lot."

At the far end of the conference table, Steffi sat munching on carrot slices. She was staring at him with those big eyes of hers.

"Nervous habit," he answered.

"Why are you nervous?"

"I'm wondering why your mom and Sophie aren't back yet, is all." The pair had been gone for almost four hours. What was taking so long? Making matters worse, Sophie refused to answer his last two texts. "You'll have to wait and see" she'd written before signing off.

"Are they lost?" Steffi's eyes got wide and her lower lip started to jut out.

Great. He didn't mean to make the girl worry. "No, no, nothing like that. When I say nervous I mean eager."

"What's eager?"

You dug yourself into a hole on that one. Mike set down his pen. "Eager is a good thing. It means I'm looking forward to seeing your mother again."

"Because you miss her?"

Talk about a loaded question. "Because she was going shopping, and I want to see what she bought."

He was beginning to wonder if asking Sophie to help had been a good idea. Along with having expensive tastes, his brother's girlfriend was used to talking charge. Combine her control freakiness with Roxanne's quick temper and you were talking incendiary. Visions of two strong-willed women coming to verbal blows popped into his head. Wouldn't that be an excellent headline? Would-Be Heiress Throws Left Hook in Salon.

If he wanted to be brutally honest with himself, the more pressing reason he wanted to talk with Roxanne was to make sure she'd truly forgiven him. It wasn't as if he truly meant to keep his plans a secret. He'd merely been concerned how she would react to his suggestion. He figured if he waited till the last minute, the process would go smoother. A bad plan, as it turned out.

Then again, when it came to Roxy, he seemed to travel down Bad Plan road a lot. If he was going to make this so-called media tour work, he needed to remember to keep his priorities straight.

"I miss Mommy," Steffi said as she stuffed a carrot slice in her mouth. "I don't like it when I have babysitters."

"You don't like the lady who watches you?"

He'd just gotten burned by a four-year-old. "Mrs. Ortega smells like cold medicine."

Lucky Mrs. Ortega. Wonder what the girl thought of him.

"I'm sure your mom will be back soon. I know she doesn't like to leave you with babysitters longer than she has to." He got a warm feeling thinking about Roxy's dedication. One of many things he was starting to appreciate. Along with her green eyes and shapely behind and the vulnerability that never seemed far from her surface.

"You like Mommy?"

Steffi's question startled him. How'd the little dickens manage to read his thoughts?

His answer, he realized, had to be well thought out. He didn't want to give the girl the wrong impression. Finally he decided on the very benign. "Your mother is a very nice woman."

"Wayne says she's stuck up."

Wayne was a jerk. He could tell from their first meeting. "Do you think Mommy's stuck up?"

"What?" If he'd been drinking he'd have choked. "No. I don't think she's stuck up at all."

"'Cause you like her?"

Mike sighed. Like Roxanne? Hell, yeah, he liked her. Way too much. "It's complicated," he told the little girl.

Wrong answer.

"What's complicated?" she immediately asked.

"Complicated means hard." For crying out loud, how many more questions was this little girl going to ask? She was worse than opposing counsel. "Do you need more juice?"

She didn't fall for his diversion attempt. "Why is it hard?"

Because she's my client. Because there are rules and ethical considerations. Because she wasn't part of the plan. He had a whole list of reasons, none of which would make sense to a girl her age. Hell, at the moment none of them made sense to him. "Your mommy and I are friends," he told her.

"Oh." Whether she found the answer satisfying or disappointing, Mike couldn't tell. Her attention had returned to the plastic bag of carrots and the hair tumbling in front of her face that rendered her expression invisible. He should be relieved she was no longer asking difficult questions, only he wasn't. He felt bad she'd grown so quiet.

Looking up, he swore the second hand had gone backward. In a few minutes, she would be done with her snack and then what? More television? There wasn't anything on to interest her. He knew because she'd already made that pronouncement before getting out her snack. Too bad she couldn't read well yet. He'd teach her to file.

A spotted white-and-purple pony caught his eye, giving him an idea. *Thank you, Dusty.*

"Did you know there's a merry-go-round carousel a few blocks from here?"

Steffi's jaw dropped midchew. She was staring again. "You interested in going?" he asked.

A spark of excitement lit up her face, but she still didn't answer. At some point Roxy probably told her to never go anywhere without Roxy's permission and he could see that her four-year-old brain was trying to determine a loophole. Her pensive expression looked so much like her mother's he felt a tug in his chest.

Things were definitely becoming complicated if a child's expression could affect him.

Before a decision could be made, they heard the sound of female laughter coming from the hallway.

"Mommy's back!" Steffi jumped from her seat and ran toward the door. Mike followed behind. At this point, he wasn't sure who was happier to see them return. That is, he was eager to see how his investment paid off.

The main office door opened and wow! Mike had to grab hold of the reception desk to keep his balance. The woman walking through the door with Sophie was… Was…

He'd lost his ability to speak. It was as if Alfredo and Sophie had conspired to take Roxy's natural beauty and softness and shove them under a magnifying glass. Her red mane had been tamed into thick, strawberry-blond locks that tumbled about her shoulders. The skinny jeans and sweater were gone, too. Tossed in favor of a black-and-white wraparound dress and cardigan sweater that subtly showed off her curves. The hint of flesh dipping to a V between her breasts was as enticing as any low-cut camisole. And her legs… Discreetly he stole a look at her bottom half.

"You look different, Mommy," Steffi said.

"Think so?" Roxy asked.

"Uh-huh. Your hair is straight."

Her eyes found his, looking for his reaction. Had her skin always looked this luminescent or was it the expertly applied makeup? "You look amazing," he replied.

"Then I guess the transformation is complete."

A shadow flickered across her face, and had he been less distracted, he might have questioned what it meant. As it was, though, he was too busy absorbing the change.

Other than the straight hair and different clothes, she

didn't look *drastically* different. Not when he had a chance to study her. It was like everything good and attractive about her appearance had been given a polish. Gone was the fatigue, in favor of brighter cheeks and eyes. She looked…softer, less worn down. The way she was meant to look had life not kicked her around.

"Exactly how an heiress should look," he said softly. How she deserved to look.

Her lashes were thick half-moons as she looked down. "Thank you." There was an odd tone to her voice he couldn't quite place. But then, his listening skills had taken a backseat in favor of other senses.

Somewhere in the background, a throat cleared.

Finding his senses, Mike looked to Sophie who had positioned herself against the coat closet door, arms folded, like a proud artist displaying her work. "Thank you for your help," he said.

"My pleasure. It was fun having someone to shop with for a change. I was right about Alfredo, too. Soon as he saw her hair, he was in heaven. What'd he call you, his 'Strawberry-haired goddess'?"

Roxanne's voice was no more than a notch above a whisper. "Something like that."

"He never gushes over me like that," Sophie said. "He loved her. Absolutely loved her."

Who wouldn't, Mike caught himself thinking.

"More likely he loved the check you wrote at the end of the appointment." With a smile, Roxanne squatted down so she was eye to eye with Steffi. Not for the first time, Mike was impressed by the way she lit up when talking to the little girl. It was obvious to anyone watching Steffi meant everything to her mother.

"We bought you a present, too." She handed the little

girl a pink polka-dotted gift bag, which Steffi immediately dived into.

Her responding squeal could be heard across the street. "It's a pony sweater!" She held up the purple knit top.

"I thought he looked like Dusty. Don't worry, I paid for it myself," she said to Mike. "So it won't get mixed in with your business expenses."

"I wouldn't have minded," he replied, surprised at how much he meant the statement. He watched Steffi struggling to pull the sweater over her head and decided, again to his surprise, that her enthusiasm would have been worth the cost.

"Would you like some help with that?" Sophie asked. "There's a mirror in the ladies' room so you can see what you look like."

"I'll take her," Roxy said.

"No, you stay and finish your conversation with Mike. The two of us will be fine." Sophie rescued both the sweater and the girl and took her by the hand. "So you like horses?" she asked as she led her away.

"Uh-huh." Steffi chattered all the way to the door and into the hall, where the door shut behind her, muffling her running commentary.

"Guess she liked the sweater," Roxy said as she watched her go.

Something was off, Mike realized all of a sudden. A note missing from her voice. A light from her eyes. No sooner did Steffi disappear behind closed doors than the one illuminating her faded. "What is it?" he heard himself ask.

"Nothing important. Did the two of you have a good afternoon?"

He thought about his and Steffi's conversation. "We survived. I learned she doesn't like her babysitters." As he held out a hand and helped her back to her feet, he explained what she had said about Mrs. Ortega.

"Arthritis rub," Roxy replied. "Has a lot of menthol. Makes for a pretty pungent smell."

"Hopefully she doesn't have an equally distasteful description of my aroma."

"Doubt it. You smell pretty good."

Not as good as you, he said to himself. Seduced by the new Roxanne, he leaned farther into her space and breathed deep. Thank God the makeover process hadn't erased the uniqueness of her scent. Underneath the hair spray, he could still detect the faint odor he found intoxicating. Suddenly the office felt very empty. He still had his hand resting beneath her elbow. Quickly he removed it, fingers tensing in revolt. They wanted to stay in contact, tighten their grip even, and pull her closer.

"I can't get over how different you look," he said.

Emotion passed across her face, unreadable and uncertain. "Different good or different bad?"

Her real question was unspoken, but he understood just the same. As if she could ever look bad, he wanted to say. "Different," he said instead, hoping his failure to deliver a solid verdict would make his point. He scanned her face. "I think it's the lack of curls. I miss them."

"You do?" She looked surprised.

"Yeah." There had been an untamed quality to her curls that appealed to him. This look was far more reined in, far more controlled. He caught a strand between his thumb and index finger, the back of his hand brushing her temple as he did so. Her sharp intake of breath was unmistakable. Searching her face, he saw her eyes were shifting from hazel to dark green. That was one thing the makeover could never change. The ever-changing color of her gaze. So damn gorgeous.

"Mommy! Mommy! I love my new sweater!"

At the sound of Steffi's voice, both of them stepped backward, breaking the closeness and the moment. Though, not before Mike swore he saw another shadow crossing Roxanne's face.

The little girl raced up to them, Sophie trailing behind. "Whoa! Slow down so I can see if it fits," Roxanne said. Immediately the four-year-old skidded to a stop, a reverse one-eighty in speed.

"She's very excited," Sophie said, stating the obvious. Watching her rush to regain control was kind of amusing. Sophie was nothing, if not order obsessed.

"Can I wear my sweater when we go to the library?" Steffi asked. Having endured her mother's inspection, she was, at the moment, spinning airplane circles.

"The library?"

Steffi stopped her running. "To see the carousel," Steffi replied. If four-year-olds were capable of verbal eye rolls, Steffi had just accomplished one. She stated the destination as if it was a fact out of *Encyclopedia Britannica* and they were all foolish for forgetting. "Mike said we could go."

"Did he now?"

"You're kidding me," Sophie drawled.

Roxy looked over, the surprise causing the green in her eyes to deepen. Heated discomfort rolled through him. He grabbed hold of the reception desk again, pretending to lean. "I may have mentioned the carousel in Bryant Park. I told her we could take a ride over there," he said to Sophie.

"Can I wear my sweater?" Steffi asked. "Please, please!"

"Wait," Sophie interrupted. "You were going to go ride a merry-go-round? You."

He should have known Sophie would have a comment. "No need to sound so surprised. It's a nice day…the kid's been cooped up in my office. Why not take her for some fresh air?"

"Because you don't..." She waved off the sentence, going for her handbag instead. "I've got to call Grant. He won't believe this."

Triumphantly she brandished her cell phone before casting a smile in Roxanne's direction. "I'd take him up on it. Who knows when he'll make an offer like this again."

Sophie was a fine one to talk. She probably emptied her in-box while waiting at the salon. In reality, he'd forgotten his offer the second Roxanne returned, but now that Steffi reminded him, the afternoon didn't sound all that awful.

From her expression, Roxy didn't share his enthusiasm. "I don't know, baby," she started to say. "It's getting late and—"

"*Pul-leeze.* One ride?"

"I did promise," Mike said, figuring that would push the odds in his favor.

He figured right. The woman was a pushover in terms of her daughter. "All right," she said, adding a sigh to show she wasn't completely one hundred percent on board. "We'll go. But only one ride. Then we head home."

"Yay!" Steffi clasped her hands.

From his spot near the reception desk, Mike smiled at the mother and daughter team. He wasn't sure if he'd stepped back on Bad Idea road or not, but watching the two of them smiling, he couldn't help feeling like he'd just had a major win.

Now if he could only figure out what the shadow that kept showing up on Roxanne's face meant.

CHAPTER SEVEN

"MERRY-GO-ROUND, merry-go-round."

Steffi singsonged the words under her breath as they waited in line at the ticket stand. Her body bounced with excitement.

Roxy was happy for her. She loved watching her daughter having a good time. She just couldn't believe it was at Mike Templeton's suggestion.

"You really planned to take her here on your own?"

Maybe it was the unseasonably warm weather but the park was crowded with families, in spite it being off-season. Some waited in line to ride the custom-made carousel while more milled around a makeshift stage waiting for the next public event. A sign told people Frogiere the French Frog would be arriving in an hour. Several children carried picture books bearing the same name.

"I admit, I wasn't expecting the park to be this crowded," he replied. "It's a good thing you arrived when you did to save us."

Roxy pretended not to catch his grin. She was still annoyed with him over the whole makeover business. Although taking Steffi to a carousel did thaw her a little.

A hand brushed the back of her legs. Looking over her shoulder, she saw a boy a couple years younger than Steffi weaving his way around his mother's legs letting his fingers drift across everything within reach.

The woman immediately apologized. Roxy saw she was wearing a sweater similar to Sophie's, and sported a loudly large diamond. A second child, a little girl, held her right hand and stole looks at Steffi. Both children looked impeccable.

Self-consciousness washed over her from head to toe. "It's all right," she said. "No harm done."

"That's because we washed off the ice cream before getting in line," the woman said smiling. "This is your daughter's first time on the carousel?"

"Yes, it is."

"Jacob's, too. Though, I try to take Samantha once a month when the weather is decent."

The two women began chatting about entertaining children during the winter. Maybe it was her imagination, but Roxy had to ask herself whether the woman would have chatted with her had she been wearing her old clothes. Possibly not. Certainly felt to her she'd been treated differently since the makeover. People who would never speak to her or show her the slightest bit of deference seemed to be extra friendly all of a sudden.

She wished she knew how she felt about the whole thing.

On one hand, when she first looked in the mirror after Alfredo worked his magic, as he put it, she'd loved what she saw. The woman in the reflection looked sleek and sophisticated. A second later, she grew upset with herself. Wasn't approving of her new look a betrayal? A passive agreement that Mike had been right—she needed smoothing out?

Then there was Mike himself. She definitely didn't imagine his expression when she returned to his office. He hadn't been able to take his eyes off her. And when his hand brushed her skin… Even the memory caused excitement and she absentmindedly pressed a fist to her stomach to prevent the emotion from taking hold. Disappointment quickly followed in its tracks anyway. Because Mike's attraction was for the made-over Roxy. It wasn't any more real or substantive than the makeup and clothes.

What killed her the most was how happy she'd been at his reaction, no matter what the reason. She was becoming way too attached to the man's approval for her own good.

"You're so lucky your husband is willing to go with you. Mine is busy with paperwork."

Roxy whipped her head toward Mike. "Oh, he's not—"

"Making this a regular visit?" Mike answered. "You're right. Did you see those ticket prices? Highway robbery."

"The things we do for our kids, huh?" the woman remarked.

He was reaching into his back pocket for his wallet, but his attention had dropped to the bouncing Steffi. "You can say that again."

He couldn't say it once. Steffi wasn't his kid. "Why did you let that woman think we were married?" Roxy asked once they'd moved from the ticket line to the carousel line.

"Why not? Easier than launching into a long explanation about our relationship."

That was just it. They didn't have a relationship beyond lawyer and client. His pretending otherwise was just another layer of fantasy on a day thick with it.

Though smaller than the one in Central Park, the Bryant Park carousel was bright and cheery with beautiful hand-carved animals. Roxy spotted not only horses but a tiger and a whimsical white rabbit. The sounds of foreign music could be barely made out over the noise of kids and conversation. A sign on the fence said that the song was in French, and that the carousel was based on one in France.

Roxy looked around the crowd. Her ticket line acquaintance with her two children were a few people back. She pushed an empty double stroller while her kids were creeping along the barrier fence, something Steffi and half the other kids were doing as well. The mother saw her and offered a commiserating shrug. In front of her, there was a pair of teenage mothers dressed decidedly non-motherly with their children balanced on their hips. Roxy smiled hello, but got nothing but cold blank stares in return.

A few yards from the gate, Steffi squealed in excitement. "Look! It's Dusty!"

Not quite, but there was a brilliant white horse with gold and red trim. "I want to ride him!"

"You'll have to wait and see, baby. There are other kids in line, too. Someone else might get on him first."

As she pretty much expected, her warning fell on deaf ears. Steffi was too busy showing Dusty his "twin." "Dusty wants to ride him, too." She grinned and held the pony over her head for a better look.

Their turn came and the crowd filed onto the wooden platform, where the other kids immediately started running to snag their favorite animal. Steffi was no different. She took off like a shot for her treasured white stallion only to be beat out by a boy in a green puffy coat.

Instantly her daughter's lower lip jutted out. "Sorry, baby. Let's see if there's another horse." Though she would certainly live with the disappointment, Roxy knew Steffi would be let down if she had to ride a different animal or, heaven forbid, one of the sleighs with bench seats. Unfortunately, as they made their way around the circle, it looked more and more like that would be the case.

Nice to see the new look hadn't changed everything.

"Look!" Steffi pulled at her arm, practically removing it from its socket as they rounded the first turn. Soon enough Roxy saw why, and when she did, her chest grew too full for her body. There stood Mike in all his tweeded splendor, leaning against a second white pony. "I saw there was a mate, and figured while you tried to snag the first one, I'd lock in a backup."

It was stupid, but Roxy wanted to throw her arms around him. "Will this pony work?" she asked Steffi.

The little girl nodded, and Roxy moved to lift her up. "You have to hold on with both hands," she said. "Dusty will have to ride with us, okay?" She put her hand out ready to collect the precious plastic horse.

That's when it happened.

The little girl turned to Mike and held out the toy. The lawyer looked like he'd been struck. He stared at the toy for a couple seconds before gently wrapping his long fingers around its plastic middle. "I'll let him ride with me, okay?"

Her daughter nodded.

The fullness in Roxy's chest tripled. Such a simple exchange, and it made her heart ache. The merry-go-round resumed with a jerk, the calliope playing loudly in the center. She barely heard. Nor did she notice the noise and families crowding around her. All her attention was focused on the man and little girl in her orbit. Standing on this wooden platform, she found herself wishing the fantasy could continue. That Saturday afternoons in the park with carousels and giant story-reading frogs was the norm. Not barroom drunks or Wayne passed out in her living room.

Of course, Mike would tell her that once the Sinclairs recognized her existence, this could be her regular life. She could spoil Steffi rotten with merry-go-rounds and ponies and all the giant frogs she wanted.

Only one problem. She wasn't sure that even then the fantasy would be complete. She had a very bad feeling it could never be complete without a certain tweed-wearing ingredient. But he'll have moved on. To the next case, the next challenge. Why wouldn't he? Underneath it all, she'd still be the same old Roxy. He thought her lacking before; eventually the gloss would wear off and he'd find her lacking again.

When the ride was over and Frogiere had made his appearance, they headed to a small café at the rear of the library. Roxy gazed out over the space and the people milling about. "Twenty-nine years living in New York, and not once have I been in this park. Closest I ever came was walking past it on my way to an audition."

"Don't feel bad. It's my first time, too. Too much else going on during the weekends," he added.

Horseback riding, swimming and all those other accomplishments. How could she forget?

"Though now that I think about it," he said, frowning, "the carousel might not have been here when I was really little. I don't remember. I'll have to ask Grant."

"Oh, that reminds me. Sophie said to tell you this is the last time you're allowed to cancel plans."

After checking over at Steffi, who was engrossed in playing with Dusty, Roxy continued, "She's nice. I feel bad for acting like such a brat in front of her." Rightful reason or not, she had to rein in her reactions.

"I wouldn't worry too much. From the tirade I received from her, she considers everything my fault anyway. She doesn't mince words, that's for certain. Probably why Grant likes her so much."

Which reminded her of another comment she was supposed to pass on. "She also thinks the reason you're avoiding the two of them so much is that you feel like the odd man out."

Mike flipped over his menu. "When did she say that to you?"

"At the salon."

"Well, she's being ridiculous."

"Was she?" Then why was he hiding behind his menu while answering? And he was hiding because he wasn't wearing his glasses and therefore couldn't read the type.

"I couldn't be happier for her and Grant. She's good for him. Really good."

"Then why do you keep canceling?"

"I've been busy," he replied, flipping the two-page menu back to its top page. "I've got a law firm to attend to."

The megafirm Grant thought he was trying to build up. The one without clutter, as Sophie put it. Then again, who was she to judge what an office was supposed to look like? "Are you glad you opened your own practice?"

He set the menu down. "What makes you ask?" His tone was harsher than she expected. Way more than the question warranted.

"No real reason. I've been thinking about choices lately is all. The ones my mother made, the ones I made, and wondered, seeing all the time you have to work at it, if you're sorry you didn't stay at your old firm." She wondered even more now, following his reaction.

Mike sipped his water. He retrieved a fork Steffi dropped on the ground. He placed their orders with the waitress. The one thing he didn't do was give her an answer. When the waitress was gone and he leaned forward in his chair, Roxy thought he might but he asked, "Do you regret quitting acting?"

Was this answering a question with a question some kind of tactic or simply changing the topic?

"Wasn't like I had much to give up." One of them should

answer. "Kind of like asking a punching bag if he misses getting hit."

"Couldn't have been so bad."

"I once got told I was too stiff to point at tile samples in a cable access commercial. Trust me, when I say I was terrible, I was terrible."

"Then why…?"

"Did I try?" She shrugged. "I loved pretending to be someone else." Sort of what you're doing now, a voice in her head said. Ignoring it, she reached over and brushed the curls from Steffi's eyes. "I like to think I ended up with the better end of the bargain, although sometimes I wonder if the next audition would have been *the* audition. The one that pushed me into the big-time. It would have been awesome seeing my name in lights."

Their conversation was interrupted by the waitress bringing their order and Steffi expressing wonder at the slab of chocolate cake put in front of her. Roxy immediately earned a brief pout by cutting the piece into two uneven pieces.

"Success isn't all it's cracked up to be," Mike said once the waitress was out of earshot. "It comes with responsibility." His eyes faded a million miles away. "You're expected to always measure up, be an example to others." His finger traced the rim of his glasses. Sad, deliberate circles. "It's not as easy as it looks."

"You've done all right so far."

So far. His tone was hollow. Was he trying to tell her that while not knowing failure, Mike's life had had costs? What kind? she wondered. How deep did the marks go?

"Do you have regrets?"

He didn't answer right away, automatically giving her what she wanted to know. "Regret implies having a choice."

A cop-out answer. Well acquainted with them she recognized the dodge immediately. Never dodge a dodger. There was regret, the evidence lay in the nerve she so consistently pushed whenever she mentioned his family.

She decided to take a chance and push for more. "Who was she?"

"Who?"

"Your regret. I'm guessing it's either a person or a career choice, and since you said you always wanted to be a lawyer..."

Actually if she remembered, he said he couldn't remember a time when he wasn't planning to be a lawyer, but wording wasn't important. Her shot in the dark worked. "Neither," he replied. "Or maybe the answer would be both."

He carved off a piece of apple tart. "Spring of my junior year my adviser told me I was short humanities credits. The number fell through the cracks while I was trying to get in all my major coursework. Anyway, since it was late in the registration process, the only class I could fit in my schedule was philosophy. I had to spend twelve weeks arguing the meaning of life and existentialism."

"Somehow I have trouble picturing you." Steffi carved a bite off her cake and waited for more. Was his regret that he had to take the class?

Apparently not. "Best semester of my life," he told her. "Our study group used to meet Thursday nights at this dive of a bar on the edge of campus where we'd go for hours, and on weekends we'd crash at one of the member's off campus apartment. Grace Reynolds was her name."

Hearing the wistfulness in his voice, Roxy felt a pang of jealousy. Clearly Grace was the female part of the regret.

"We were going to spend the summer backpacking

around Europe—our grand scheme to study political cultures up close. You wouldn't have recognized me."

Based on the man he just described, Roxy agreed. The life was so far removed from the starched, formal man she'd come to know. "What happened?"

"My parents arrived with word I'd gotten an internship at Ashby Gannon. Backpacking or career." He shrugged and reached for a sugar packet. "I chose career."

But had he wanted to? He was trying to act as if the answer was a given, but she wasn't so sure. "What happened with Grace?" Of all the questions she had, the aftermath of his love affair came out first. She needed to know.

"Pretty much what you'd expect. She went backpacking—I went to work. When I returned to school in the fall she was living with someone else. I was studying for the LSATs. We both moved on with our lives."

But the price had been paid, hadn't it? No wonder she'd felt such a connection that day in his office. She was sensing the loneliness he kept so very carefully hidden. Her chest once again squeezed with emotion. Its force scared the hell out of her and called her closer at the same time.

Ever since she'd hired Mike Templeton, she'd sworn she'd use her head instead of her heart. Heaven help her, doing so just got a lot harder.

It was three hours later when the taxicab pulled in front of her building, and Mike climbed out with a sleepy Steffi propped against his shoulder.

After Bryant Park, they'd gone back to Mike's office where Roxy practiced interview questions.

"You didn't have to ride all the way here with us," she told him when they reached her front door. She would have been content with saying goodbye at the office, but Mike insisted.

"Didn't feel right. You had your hands pretty full." He tipped his head toward the packages draped over his wrist along with Steffi, whose legs were wrapped tightly around his chest.

"But now my hands are empty."

"Good. Then you can fish your key out faster. This little pony is getting heavy."

"I'm not a pony, I'm a girl," Steffi muttered.

A tired girl at that. Fresh air and excitement had worn her out. She would be asleep before her head hit the pillow.

Roxy unlocked the door and pushed open the glass with her foot. The greeting smell of greasy food told her she was back in her world. "I'll take her from here," she told Mike.

"I don't mind carrying her upstairs."

"I know, but your cab's waiting, and if you don't get back, the driver's likely to leave. I don't want you stuck standing on the street corner."

She reached out and lifted Steffi from his arms. The little girl's body was warm with his body heat. Roxy shivered a little at the sudden onslaught.

"Thanks again for the merry-go-round. Steffi had a fantastic time."

He leaned in, his breath cool and welcome against her cheek. "How about her mother? Did she enjoy herself?"

Roxy smiled. "Yeah, she did."

"Good. Especially since it appears I hurt her feelings this morning."

"Let's forget this morning happened." She didn't want to think about shortcomings, or makeovers or what any of it meant. Not after such a wonderful afternoon. She wanted to keep the fantasy going a little longer.

"Consider it forgotten." He stayed in her space, eyes veiled and searching. Dark half-moons marked his cheeks, shadows caused by the security light shining down on his lashes. Roxy watched as his tongue wet his lower lip, leaving a trail of shine. Those same lips opened as though to speak, and for a moment, her heart stopped, thinking it might not be conversation he wanted.

"See you Monday," he whispered. He meant for her interview, but with his breath on her skin and his hand squeezing hers, the words sounded like a promise of more.

"Monday," she repeated.

She watched him wait by the taxi door while she waited for the elevator, indulging in the contentment his concern created.

"Look at you," Alexis said when she and Steffi walked through the door.

Her roommate sat on the couch watching television, wedged between Wayne, of course, and some large Irish-looking guy she didn't recognize. Both men followed her directions with slow, leering looks that turned Roxy's stomach.

"Whatcha do?" her roomate asked. "Rob a store on Fifth Avenue?"

"Yeah. I thought you said you didn't get any money yet," Wayne added.

"It's part of Mike's strategy. For when I talk to the press. He wanted me to look more like an 'heiress.'"

"He bought you all this?" Alexis had wriggled her way out of the space and made her way to the shopping bags Roxy set down on the chair. "There's a ton of clothes in here. I can't even afford to walk by this store. Wish I had me a lawyer."

"Only way you're getting a lawyer is if that fat butt of yours gets arrested," Wayne shot at her. He cocked another leering smile in Roxy's direction. "So what you have to do to pay him back?"

"Nothing. It's a business expense."

He raised a beer can to his lips. "Uh-huh."

"Mike likes Mommy," Steffi chose that moment to volunteer.

"I bet he does, kid," Wayne replied, elbowing his friend. They both snickered.

Roxy wasn't in the mood. Because she'd spent the day with a gentleman, Wayne's antics were more repulsive to her than ever. Just the sound of his voice made her skin crawl.

She also needed to correct her daughter before impressions got out of hand. "Mike and I are working together, baby. Remember all the practicing we did back in his office?"

Again, Wayne and his friend sniggered.

"For when Mommy has her big meeting Monday," she finished pointedly. All these comments were turning what had been a wonderful day into something cheap and dirty sounding.

"What big meeting?" Alexis asked. She was holding a pale blue turtleneck to her chest, as if she had a hope of fitting her frame into it.

"Mike has a friend who writes for the *Daily Press.* She's going to write a story about me."

"That mean you're getting your money soon?"

"I don't know," Roxy replied. Her roommate didn't need to know the interview was supposed to speed up the process.

"I hope it's soon." Setting the turtleneck down, Alexis began rummaging through another bag. "I'm sick of this dump. Hey, next time you go shopping, you got to take me with you. I want to see if they got anything I would wear."

Roxy's insides stilled. It never dawned on her Alexis planned on moving *with* her. They'd never once discussed plans like that. She'd always assumed the move would be her and Steffi. She never stopped to think Alexis would consider herself part of the plan—or one of the beneficiaries of her inheritance.

"I told you," she said, not sure what else she could say, "the clothes were a business expense. I won't be going back."

"Oh." There was no disguising the disappointment in her roommate's voice.

"Ha, ha," Wayne said. "Looks like you're out of luck, sis."

The stranger on her couch finally spoke. "I didn't come here to sit around all night talking to your snotty roommate. We gonna party or what?"

"Mama, he said—"

Roxy cut her daughter off. "I know, baby. Just ignore him."

"Yeah, kid. Just ignore us," Wayne said. He was already on his feet and stretching, T-shirt rising up to show his scrawny white stomach. "You comin', Alexis?"

"PJ's friend's throwing an afterhours party on his roof. You wanna join us?"

PJ, she assumed, was the stranger, and he looked less than thrilled at the idea. *Don't worry, pal. Even if I didn't have a kid, I wouldn't join you.* She nodded toward Steffi.

"Oh, yeah, right. Forgot," Alexis replied. "Later then."

"Yeah, later."

Wayne's voice sounded from behind her. "You know, I buy my women things, too, if you're interested."

"Not in your dreams." She flinched as his hot breath dampened her skin. Disgust ran down her spine and turned her stomach.

He replied by muttering one of the vilest words she'd ever heard.

And just like that, the fantasy of the day disappeared, and she found herself back in reality.

Mike's cell phone buzzed the second the cab door closed. Grant had been calling him all night. He'd been told about the carousel from Sophie and eager to give him a hard time, no doubt. He'd probably keep calling all night.

He fished the phone from his pocket and immediately his insides knotted when he saw the caller ID. "Hi, Dad," he greeted. "You're back in the country. How was your trip?"

A few months ago, his mother had been bitten by the urge to see France and dragged his father on a bucket list tour of the country. Naturally, being his parents, they couldn't simply play tourist and they ended up investing in a vineyard they discovered in Bordeaux. They recently went back to check on their investment.

"Terrific. Looks like the initial batch will be top-notch. They're talking about possible medals at the upcoming festivals."

Of course they were. His parents wouldn't invest in anything less than a winning project.

"And you should see your mother. While we were over there, she made friends with one of the local shopkeepers. The woman's teaching her French cooking. I swear, she's going to be the Julia Child of pastry before we're finished. She's gotten so good we've had to take up running to keep the extra pounds off."

Again, not a surprise. They'd probably be doing triathlons next. Cosponsored by their vineyard and the bakery his mother would no doubt start.

"How are things going with you?"

The dreaded question. "Terrific." The lie flowed off his tongue so easily no one would ever guess his stomach had knotted a second time. "I took on a new case last week. Very exciting."

"I know." He did? "I ran into Jim Brassard at Troika yesterday afternoon. He told me you're representing some woman who's going after the Sinclairs?"

Roxy was right. The phrase was unattractive. "I didn't know you and Jim were friends."

"The Bar Association's a small world, Michael. You know that. Is it true?"

"I represent a client with a claim to the estate, if that's what you mean," he replied, not liking the way he referred to Roxanne as some woman.

"Isn't that a little out of character? Since when do you take on flashy cases?"

You think this is flashy, wait till the press interviews start hitting. "I've always handled estate cases. Haven't you always said it takes all kinds to build a practice?"

"Within reason. I also taught you to adhere to some standards. Please tell me I don't have to worry about you passing your business card out at accidents."

Because he was raised better. Mike rolled his eyes. "This is a good case. The woman has a viable claim."

"I hope so. Don't let us down, Michael. Remember, your reputation doesn't just reflect on you in the legal community. You bear my name."

And, as his namesake, had an obligation to not only uphold the Templeton tradition but surpass it. Mike heard the lecture his entire life. Bought it his entire life as well. Placed the lessons before everything else.

He let his mind drift back to a few moments earlier and the way Roxy's face had shimmered oh-so-temptingly under the fluorescent light. What would dear old Dad say about reputation if he knew his namesake was fantasizing about a client?

Not wanting to lose the fantasy, he clicked off the phone, figuring he could always blame a dropped call. He really wasn't in the mood to listen to his father's reminders about family obligations right now. They could come back to haunt him another time.

Right now he wanted to think about his client.

CHAPTER EIGHT

"WILL you stop fidgeting?" Mike reached over and took the fork from Roxanne's hand before she could tap it against the tablecloth again. "It makes you look nervous."

"I *am* nervous," she shot back.

"Doesn't mean you have to let the whole restaurant know."

They were seated in the dining room of the Landmark. He'd selected the stately hotel because its old-money feel made for a good backdrop. Not to mention, it kept the reporter from seeing how slow work was back at his office.

"Shouldn't you have learned how to pretend in acting school?" he asked her.

"I was a lousy actress, remember?" She'd moved to fiddling with her napkin, smoothing and resmoothing the cloth across her lap.

"I remember." Sadly he also completely understood the nerves. His own stomach was doing the Mexican hat dance. They both had a lot riding on this interview. Done right, and Julie's column would spawn other articles. TV coverage. Enough notoriety the Sinclairs would have to act. Screw up, and the Sinclairs could write her off as another crackpot looking for fifteen minutes of fame.

Lord, but it had to work. Under the table, he felt his own knee start to jiggle. He squeezed his thigh.

"You'll be fine," he told Roxy. Taking a page from his own advice, he refused to let her see his agitation. "Just don't say things like 'I can't believe they charge seventeen dollars for a fruit plate.'"

"But I can't believe it."

"I know." The price didn't exactly sit well with him, either. He was beginning to worry about how much money the case was costing him. Not that he'd say so to Roxy. After all, like everyone else, she saw him as a big, uptown lawyer.

"How much longer before she gets here?" she asked.

Mike checked his watch. She was five minutes late. "Soon. Any minute probably."

"Great." He felt the floor jiggling. It was her knee bouncing now.

"Relax. You remember all the answers we rehearsed, don't you?"

"I do."

"Then you have nothing to worry about."

"And you're sure I look all right?"

"I promise, you look fine." More than fine, actually. To his immense pleasure, her hair was less straight, the curls framing her face while a clasp held the rest at the base of her neck. She wore a pale blue cashmere turtleneck and camel hair slacks, with a brown suede jacket. Around her neck she wore a strand of pearls. Her mother's. A far cry from the woman who'd walked into his office a few weeks earlier.

He couldn't help himself. He had to reach over and give her fingers a reassuring squeeze, regardless of whether Julie walked in. The smile Roxanne beamed at him made the gesture worth it. "Thank you."

Before the moment could go any further he spotted the reporter approaching the dining room. He slipped his hand from Roxy's, trying not to feel the chill the absence of contact brought, and waved her over. "Ready?" he asked, rising.

"Ready as I'll ever be."

Julie greeted him with a kiss on the cheek, then extended her hand. "Roxanne O'Brien? Julie Kinogawa from the *Daily Press.* Mike tells me you've got an interesting story to share."

Mike sat back and watched as Roxy took over and told her story the way they rehearsed it. Plainly and honestly. When she got to the part about Steffi, she didn't flinch, admitting her mistakes with the same brutal frankness she used when telling him. It wasn't easy for her. And it wasn't easy to hear. When Mike saw the telltell brown that signaled her eyes were about to moisten, he felt that overwhelming urge to stop the interview and take her in his arms. He didn't, but dammit, it took a lot of effort. When she finished, he didn't know if Julie bought a word. But he was charmed out of his ever loving mind.

"Oh, my God! I can't believe I got through that without making a complete fool of myself!" They were in the Landmark Lobby, having said goodbye to Julie a few minutes earlier. Roxy wanted to fly, she was so hyped up. The interview couldn't have gone better. Soon as Julie started asking questions, the answers flowed out of her. It was as though she became the part she was supposed to be playing—Roxanne O'Brien, long-lost heiress. Then again, she was Roxanne O'Brien, long-lost heiress, wasn't she? She wanted to giggle, the thought seemed so fantastic.

"I was afraid I'd break down when I started to talk about Steffi, but I kept it together. I think because Julie seemed so understanding. I think she knew why I wanted to keep my daughter out of the spotlight. Is she a mother? Oh, God, listen to me. I'm talking a mile a minute."

Mike laughed. Lord, but she never noticed how lyrical a laugh he had before. Why hadn't she noticed? "It's nice to see you excited," he said.

"Oh, I'm excited all right." Excited like she'd downed a half dozen energy drinks.

Turning to face him, she walked backward, relying on her energy to guide her through the space. "She seemed really interested in what I had to say, don't you think? I mean, like really, really interested." She paused. "Or am I being naive?"

"Well, it wouldn't be the first time a reporter feigned friendliness, then did a hatchet job," Mike said.

Roxy's insides froze. Crap. That would be so like her luck.

"But—" coppery reassurance lit up his eyes "—I don't think this is the case."

"I hope you're right." His approval shouldn't feel so good, but it did. It washed through her like a wave, leaving behind a radiant glow that made her feel like the most special woman alive. "I was afraid I'd screw it up."

"All you had to do was tell the truth. How could you screw that up?"

"You'd be surprised."

"Well, you better get used to telling it. If all goes according to plan, this time next week, you'll be flooded with interview offers from around the city. The Sinclair sisters won't have a choice but to acknowledge your existence."

Acknowledge her existence. Hearing those three words, the magnitude of what was about to happen hit her full-on. For once, luck was breaking her way. Life was breaking her way.

"Oh, my God! This is really happening, isn't it?" With

a giddy squeal that was worthy of Steffi, she spun around on her toes. Finally her mother's dying words were going to actually have a legacy besides confusion. She was going to become an heiress! "I can't believe it!"

"I hate to say I told you so, but..."

"You can say it all you want." Far as Roxy was concerned, he was the fairy godmother who made this all come true. "If it weren't for your ad in the directory, none of this would be happening."

Aw, hell. She felt way too magnanimous for simple words. She flung her arms around his neck. "Thank you for everything," she murmured against his shoulder.

His jacket smelled like him, the invitingly masculine scent wrapping around her as surely as his arms. She pressed her cheek to his lapel. Not for long. A second or two. Just long enough for the moment for the aroma to reach inside her. When she pulled back, his arms stayed locked, keeping her trapped in his cocoon. The rest of the world faded away. Looking up, all Roxy could see was the burned copper of his gaze and that perfect shaped mouth.

Who leaned in first didn't matter. Their mouths collided, the kiss desperate and long overdue. Roxy tightened her grip. She couldn't get enough. Couldn't get close enough. Her body was pressed to the length of him, and she still wanted closer—wanted more—with an intensity that she knew would scare the hell out of her once the moment ended.

When the kiss did break, they stood foreheads pressed together, breathless. Roxy wondered if the earth had tipped over. She felt off balance, shaken. She had to clutch Mike's forearms to keep from falling over. "I—I—"

"That—" Mike sounded as shaken as her. His hands were wrapped around her arms; the blood pulsing in his fingertips, discernible through her sweater.

"That was—"

"Definitely a mistake."

Mike's words struck her, hard, recalling the intensity she'd found so frightening a few seconds before. A mistake. He was right.

"Yes," she said, stepping backward. "It was." Right? There was no reason for his words to sound so disheartening.

"I'm your lawyer. You're a client. It's wrong."

"Right. I mean, of course."

"I mean, it's unethical. It's a violation of my legal oath."

She moved farther away, to a railing near the marble steps. Gripping the cold polished brass helped to cool her thoughts if not her insides. "I understand."

But he seemed intent on adding further arguments anyway. "Plus, now you've talked with the press. If Julie or someone else were to see us…"

"I understand. Really, I do." Despite the hollow feeling in the pit of her stomach. "There's Steffi, too. If she were to think we were…you know…then she might get the wrong impression, and I don't want her getting hurt."

The look passing across his face had to be relief. She refused to think it was anything else because that would only put the thought in her head as well. And she didn't want to think anything but relief. "So we agree."

"One hundred percent," Roxy told him. "I let this morning's excitement get me carried away."

"Me, too." He tried a smile. "Guess we chalk it up to gratitude and adrenaline were a dangerous combination."

"Absolutely. It won't happen again."

"No," he agreed. "It won't."

Good, Roxy thought to herself. Better yet, now that the itch was out of her system, maybe she wouldn't be so strangely drawn to every little thing he did or said. Or want to study every expression that crossed his face.

Maybe the longing his presence produced, and that, at the moment, ached stronger than ever, would fade away as well.

CHAPTER NINE

MIKE slapped the lease notice on his desk with a frustrated sigh. It had been two weeks since Julie's column ran in the *Daily Press. Modern Day Anastasia Wants Answers; To Claim Her Role in Sinclair Legacy.* The *Press* believed in over-the-top headlines. Still, the piece worked. Roxy had been asked for interviews from several radio stations, two local affiliates and a national lifestyle magazine. As expected a few unsolicited pieces ran, too. A couple reporters found their way to the Elderion and one poked around Roxy's apartment building writing about her "dubious" roommates. Roxy's candid rebuttal to that piece ran in Julie's column today. Pieces also appeared.

And yet, despite all this media activity, silence from Jim Brassard and the Sinclairs. Even he was beginning to be concerned. Of course, when Roxy asked, he made a point of dodging the answer. He didn't want to upset her while she was meeting with the media.

Or rather upset her more than he already had. Like it had all week, his blood shot straight to his groin as the memory of their kiss came flooding forward. In fact, *kiss* was far too benign a word. All-out assault on his senses? Better.

He told her they should blame the rush of the moment.

If that was true, then why was his brain still screaming *More! More! More!*

Way to blur the lines, Templeton. He spun around his chair to stare at the building behind him. Fifteen years ago he made a call. Career and expectations first, personal desires and interests second. It was the only way he'd be able to achieve the level of success his family wanted from him, and thus far, it had served him well. Now was not the time to back off.

He swiveled back around, accidentally scattering Wentworth's letters with his arm. Bending over, he retrieved the trio that fell to the floor. In his final letter, Wentworth had been full of promises and decisions. He was coming home and telling his parents he was leaving Harvard and marrying Fiona, damn the consequences. Wonder what would have happened if Wentworth had made the trip home safely? Would he have carried through with his plans?

The question made him think, with more than a little guilt, about Grace. Fifteen years ago, coward that he was, he took the exact opposite track from Wentworth. Chose the route mapped out for him. That he did so easily told him Grace wasn't as great a passion as he remembered. Backing away from Roxanne yesterday had been harder.

Wonder what he'd do if he had to make the same decision today?

He didn't have time to ponder the thought for long. The phone rang. Soon as the caller identified himself, everything else became unimportant.

"Steffi, please. Hurry up and finish your dinner so we can get to Mrs. Ortega's. I have to get to work." High-heeled toe tapping on the carpeting, Roxy gave her daughter a stern look. Why was it kids were always their slowest when you needed them to move quickly?

At the dining room table, Steffi poked her meat loaf with her fork. “I don’t like it,” she said.

“You said you liked it when we had it two nights ago.”

“Now it’s old.”

Roxy took a deep breath. She would not lose her patience. No matter if the clock over the stove told her she had about ten minutes to catch her bus.

Truth was, she couldn’t completely blame her daughter for being cranky. With all these interviews and meetings, she’d had to spend more and more time at the babysitter’s. What was the alternative? Leaving her here to hang with Wayne?

“Can I have more milk?” Steffi asked.

“When you’ve finished your meat loaf.” Nice try, kid, but she was hip to that game; fill up on milk so you were too full to eat. The little girl whined. After giving another quick look at the clock, Roxy squatted so she was at eye level. Her spandex skirt rose distressingly high on her thighs. Since she’d changed up her wardrobe, she found the waitress uniform increasingly uncomfortable. The skirt was too tight and the camisole showed way too much cleavage.

Actually, it was more than the uniform. Simply going to work at the club had become more difficult too. Each day spent meeting with reporters and being treated like she was somebody, made hauling vodka tonics in a pair of high heels worse. It was like she’d finally gotten a tiny glimpse of what the world could possibly become. Except despite the interviews, they still hadn’t heard from the Sinclairs. Mike told her not to worry. Then again, he also never answered her questions about the Sinclairs directly anymore, either, preferring to reassure her instead. His way of avoiding having to give her bad news.

Mike. Thinking of the mind-blowing kiss they shared wasn't doing her mood any favors. All it did was create a hot, needy sensation in the pit of her stomach. It stunk that the worst ideas were always the ones that nagged you.

Steffi still wasn't eating her meat loaf. "Baby, if you don't finish your dinner, you and Dusty won't get any dessert."

"Leave the kid alone. I wouldn't eat that warmed-up stuff, either."

"You're not helping, Alexis," Roxy said.

"Just sayin', I'd take her to that fast food burger place."

"Can we, Mommy?"

"No, Steffi."

"But I want chicken nuggets."

"Stephanie Rose O'Brien, finish your meat loaf."

Still swearing to keep her patience, she followed her roommate into the kitchen. Alexis had been as bad as Steffi lately. Worse ever since the *Daily Press* article appeared, though really Roxy thought the article was only part of a bigger issue.

"By the way," she said, "why didn't you tell me the package from AM America arrived?"

"Excuse me," the heavier woman replied, as she grabbed a bag of cheese curls from the pantry. "I didn't know I was your secretary now."

"You're not," Roxy replied. Her patience at treading lightly was wearing thin. "But I told you I was waiting for it. Would it hurt to say something?"

"Sorry. Must be my susceptible side."

"Disreputable," Roxy said. A correction that earned her an eye roll. "I cleared all that up. Didn't you read Julie's column today?

"You mean your big speech about how people shouldn't judge you because of where you live or who you hang out with?"

"People. I said *people* shouldn't be judged by who they associate with. I was lumping you in with me."

"Gee, thanks. Did your boyfriend suggest you say something like that?"

"Mike isn't my boyfriend." Damn, if she didn't feel an ache clear through to her heart at the mention of his name.

"Whatever."

Oh, for crying out loud. She was getting pretty sick and tired of the comments. Roxy stepped over to the countertop. "What's really bugging you? You've been copping an attitude for two weeks."

"Maybe I don't like being dissed."

"I corrected that in Julie's column."

"Oh, right. You say a few snotty things to your new BFF Julie and that's supposed to make it all better?"

Snotty? It was a correction for crying out loud. She didn't have to do anything. "So what would make it better then?"

Alexis shrugged. "You tell me. You're the one with all the fancy uptown friends now. Why don't you ask your sugar daddy next time he takes you shopping or to one of your fancy lunches?"

Is that what this was all about? Her new wardrobe? Going out to eat?

"Get over yourself," her roommate replied at the suggestion. "All I'm saying is while you're running around with reporters and going to fancy restaurants, Wayne and I are still back here waiting for ours."

"Maybe if Wayne stopped sitting..." Roxy muttered.

Alexis slammed the cabinet door, making Roxy jump.

"I'm getting pretty sick of you trashing my baby brother every time you turn around."

"Then we're even because I'm sick of him living on my couch." She hadn't forgotten the disgusting word he muttered to her the other day. A word his sister had to have heard and said nothing about. "I've told you before I don't like him around Steffi. And you're stupid if you think I don't know what kind of 'business' he's doing in this neighborhood."

"Oh, now you're calling me stupid? Excuse me, but not everyone's lucky enough to have a mother get knocked up by a millionaire.

"But you know that," she added, her mouth full of orange cheese.

Roxy squeezed her fists. "You leave Steffi out of this."

"I wasn't talking about Steffi. I was talking about you, acting like you're all better than us. And don't forget," she said, slicing the air with an orange index finger, "I pay half the rent here. You don't want your kid around my brother, then go live with your boyfriend."

"He's not my—" Roxy didn't have time to argue. She'd deal with this after work. Provided she still had a job. Dion was ticked off at her about reporters, too. "Come on, Steffi. Go get your coat."

"But you said I could have dessert."

"You'll have to have dessert at Mrs. Ortega's. Mommy's really late."

"I don't want to go to Mrs. Ortega's. You promised. I want ice cream!" The four-year-old began to cry, the loud, unreasonable gulps of a tantrum.

Naturally. Roxy lifted the little girl from her chair, wincing as her squirming legs banged her exposed thighs. The pain hurt less than the guilt.

"You promised!" Steffi chanted over and over. She

might as well have been saying "You're the worst mother in the world. I hate you", and even though she knew the world wouldn't end because of one missed dessert, Roxy couldn't help feeling like her daughter was right.

Adding insult to injury, as the door shut behind her and a still crying Steffi, she could hear Wayne and Alexis laughing.

"Well, look who decided to grace us with her presence," Jackie drawled when she finally managed to rush in, twenty minutes late.

So not what she needed right now. "Sorry I'm late, Dion," she said, tying on her apron. "Steffi gave me a hard time about going to the sitter's."

"So glad you could fit us in your schedule," he replied. "I gave Jackie your tables one through four."

"What?" He was cutting down her groups? "Why?"

"Because I needed someone to cover them, and she showed up on time."

Great. Just great. First Steffi, then Alexis, now she'd have to make do with half her tip money. Was the whole world conspiring against her tonight?

"Not like you need the money anyway, seeing how you're an heiress now."

"I'm not an heiress yet." Soon as she said it, Roxy realized how off-putting the comment sounded.

"Reminds me," Dion said. "I caught another one of those reporters poking around, asking the customers questions."

"I'm sorry." The articles that appeared earlier in the week ticked him off. "Least it's free publicity."

"Oh, yeah, the owner's thrilled with the place being called shabby."

"Maybe he'll spring for an upgrade." The place certainly needed it.

The bartender didn't appreciate the suggestion. "Maybe you should get your butt in gear and wait on customers before I give Jackie more of your tables."

Without another word, Roxy grabbed her pad and tray, making sure she moved quick enough that neither Dion nor Jackie saw her eyes getting wet. Why was the whole world so angry with her? She didn't ask for her mother to have an affair with Wentworth Sinclair. Why were they all out to punish her now?

If Mike were here, he'd understand.

Soon as the thought formed in her brain, she froze in her tracks. What the heck? A few weeks ago, her insides ran screaming at the idea of leaning on anyone, let alone him. Now here she was desperate to cry on his shoulder. What the heck happened to her?

Mike happened, that's what. Mike and his coppery, reassuring gaze and his day at the park.

This, she thought, was why kissing him had been a bad idea. Why she agreed with him it couldn't happen again, despite being the most mind-blowing kiss she'd ever had. She was getting too attached, too reliant on the man. Seeing him as more than a lawyer. A useless point since the other day, while standing in the Landmark, he made it quite clear that his being a lawyer came first.

Her first table ordered bottled beer. Same with the second. Dion not only reassigned her tables, but he left her with the ones who weren't going to spend any money. The night was getting better and better. Only one thing would make this disaster complete and that was…

"Hello, Roxy."

Mike was sitting at table eight. Karma really felt like kicking her in the butt today, didn't it?

Definitely. Why else would he look absolutely spectacular, in a beige suit she'd never seen before and a striped shirt? Shadows danced across his cheekbones, creating hollows and highlighting planes. Roxy's insides melted upon sight. Knowing her reaction wasn't merely physical was making it worse. She'd felt her spirits lift as soon as she heard his voice.

Suddenly she realized the problem with Mike wasn't a matter of becoming too attached; she *was* attached. Very, very attached. Oh, man, but she was in trouble, wasn't she?

She tucked nonexistent hair behind her ears. "Fancy meeting you here. Got tired of your office?"

"What can I say? There's something about this place that keeps drawing me back." He smiled, and the rest of the club receded. "You got a minute?"

"Not right now. Dion's upset because I was late. Problem with Steffi."

"Nothing serious, I hope."

Seeing his expression change and become serious did nothing to stop the emotion weaving its way through her. In fact, her heart grew. "No. She's tired of going to the babysitter is all."

"Well, Mrs. Ortega does smell like arthritis rub."

"True." *And you smell like wool and Dial soap and have arms that make a woman feel secure and safe.*

She had to shake these thoughts from her head. They weren't doing either of them any good. "Can you stick around till my break?"

"Of course."

"I'll get you the usual then."

Making her way to the bar, she tried to decide if his sticking around was good or not. For the past couple weeks, since the kiss, they'd managed to keep their dealings businesslike and short, involving a third party as often as possible. But tonight, with her working the crowd and wearing this skimpy outfit, knowing his eyes were going to be on her… Maybe risking Dion's anger was the better decision after all.

She purposely waited until she'd served all her other tables before bringing him his drink. She wasn't sure why, except that having an empty tray made it less likely she'd become distracted and ignore her customers. Make that more distracted. His looming presence would be permanently stuck in the front of her brain from now until her break.

It took like what seemed most of the night, but Dion finally gave her a break. "We'll have to be quick," she told Mike, slipping into the chair across from him. "Dion made it very clear I couldn't take a second more than ten minutes." He wants more, he can meet you at his office, the bartender had snarked.

"Still angry about the articles, huh."

"Everybody's mad," Roxy replied. "Alexis and Wayne are mad, Steffi's mad, Jackie and Dion are mad. They all think I've gone uptown and think I'm too good for them."

"They're right."

Mike's answer surprised her. Wasn't this the same man who insisted on a makeover? "You sure you didn't have a few pops before you got here?" she asked.

"Not a drop. You're better than all this, Roxanne. If the rest of the world can't see that, then the world's full of idiots."

The moisture returned to her eyes forcing her to blink. Dammit. How was she supposed to unattach herself if he was going to behave so nicely?

Along with reaching across the table to brush a tear from her cheek the way he was doing now. His touch was soft and sweet. She had to fight not to lean into his palm.

"Thank you for the pep talk," she said, managing a bit of a smile.

"You're welcome. I have something else that might cheer you up more."

"Really?" She started to ask when she saw his grin. Only one thing would make him smile that wide and look that confident. Her heart stopped beating. "Don't tell me…"

"Jim Brassard called me earlier this evening."

"Are you saying…?"

His wide grin grew wider. "The Sinclair sisters want to meet you."

CHAPTER TEN

IN NEW YORK society circles, Alice and Frances Sinclair were considered eccentric icons. Both twice divorced, they lived together in the Gramercy Park brownstone where they grew up while their children lived in more modern penthouses nearby. Between the two of them, the Sinclair name was part of almost every charitable board in the city.

Roxy's knees shook as they stood in front of the iron gate. "What if they don't like me?" she whispered in Mike's ear.

"You asked the same thing about Julie. Be yourself and everything will be fine."

Roxy wished she shared his confidence, but she couldn't shake the feeling of anxiety crawling along the back of her neck. For all she knew, the Sinclairs wanted to see her so they could tell her to her face to buzz off.

"Remember, you're their family." As usual Mike seemed to read her thoughts and say the words she needed to hear. What would she do when she didn't have him standing by her side anymore?

She couldn't bear to think about it.

A metallic-sounding voice came on the gate speaker to greet them. Mike introduced themselves and a moment later, the gate clicked open.

"Promising sign."

“Unless there are dogs about to run at us.”

“That’s my girl. Mistrustful as ever.”

Because she’d never been this close to good fortune before. Sixty minutes from now she could be…

Dear God, she was too afraid to form the words.

The ornately carved main entrance sat back from the curb, a short cement walkway protecting the sisters from the noise of the street. No more than six feet, it felt like six hundred. Two steps in, Roxy felt a reassuring pressure at the curve of her elbow. “Making sure you don’t trip in those shoes,” he said in a soft voice.

“I’m wearing flats.”

“You still never know.” He gave her elbow a squeeze, sending waves of reassurance up her arm. Roxy felt so cherished in that one moment, she swore her heart grew too big for her heart. *Oh, how she loved this man.*

Before she could argue with herself about her choice of words, they reached the front door and a suited servant opened it. A middle-age woman in a crisp black suit came walking up just behind. “I’m Millicent Webster, the sisters’ secretary,” she greeted, in a polite and formal voice. “They’re waiting for you in the solarium. If you follow me, I’ll take you.”

Roxy wasn’t sure what a solarium was, but she quickly surmised it was another name for sunroom as they were led down a corridor to a large, window-filled room in the rear of the house. When they arrived, they found the two elderly women seated side by side in matching Queen Anne chairs. They were chatting with a gray-haired man sitting on the sofa. The man immediately stood up. “Good afternoon, Mike. Thank you for coming.” He looked straight at Roxy. “And you must be Roxanne O’Brien.”

Roxy cleared her throat. “Yes,” she whispered. Over in

their chairs, the Sinclair sisters were staring intently; she could feel the scrutiny.

The gasp when she walked in didn't help, either.

"I'm Jim Brassard, the Sinclair family attorney. May I introduce Frances and Alice Sinclair."

Frances, the taller of the two motioned for them to take a seat. "We're so glad you could meet with us. Aren't we, Alice?"

"Yes, we are." Alice was a few inches smaller, with bright black eyes that matched her sister's. Both had short-cropped hair and strong features. For the first time Roxy noticed the giant Newfoundland sprawled between the chairs. She just knew there would be dogs. Though this one didn't look too threatening.

"This is Bunty," Frances said, following her line of sight. "He's been with us forever. My second husband bought him as a puppy. Turns out he was the only thing worth salvaging about the relationship. Don't worry. He won't bite. Poor creature hasn't moved fast in years."

Mike chuckled. Roxy managed a wan smile. Her pulse was racing, making breathing, let alone making noise, difficult. Smoothing the front of her slacks, she perched on the edge of the sofa, where Frances had indicated.

"Thank you for being willing to talk with us," she heard Mike say. "I know this must be awkward for you."

"Our family, by nature, is very private," Frances replied. "We aren't one to seek publicity." She cocked her head. "But you already knew that, didn't you, Mr. Templeton."

Roxy looked up in time to see his cheeks blush a sheepish tinge. "I might have heard something to that effect. We weren't trying to embarrass the family, I assure you. Simply get your attention."

"Well, you did. Get our attention," Jim said.

Meanwhile, Alice was still studying her. The probing

made Roxy want to squirm her way behind the sofa cushions. Nervously she tucked her hair behind her ear.

"Alice, stop," Frances snapped, realizing. "You're making the girl uncomfortable."

"I'm sorry. I don't mean to. It's just…that hair and your eyes. I knew as soon as I saw your photograph in the newspaper."

"Knew?" Roxy asked.

"How much you resemble your mother."

They knew her mother. Roxy couldn't believe it.

"We didn't know her name," Frances continued. "Both Alice and I were married and living elsewhere at the time. But she worked for us. As a weekend maid."

"It was the hair," Alice said. "You couldn't forget the hair. Long, strawberry curls. I was so jealous. She had an accent, too, I believe."

"Irish," Roxy supplied. "She came from County Cork as a little girl. I'm confused, though. Are you sure it was my mother? I thought she worked for a hotel."

"She might have. Father let the whole staff go one summer. At the time, we wondered what set him off."

"Then again something was always setting father off," Frances said. "He had a very short temper."

"Finding out his son was involved with one of the staff could certainly anger a man," Mike said.

"I certainly remember how upset Wenty was when he found out. I had stopped by and he was pacing back and forth fuming. Told me he didn't want to talk about it. It was a couple weeks before he left for Cambridge, I believe."

"We didn't talk to him nearly enough that semester," Frances said softly.

"No, we didn't."

Sisterly regret hung in the air. No matter what happened regarding her, she suspected Alice and Frances loved their baby brother, and wanted to do right for him. She looked to her lap, trying to imagine how events unfolded. Her mother, fresh out of high school, coming to work for the Sinclairs, meeting a young Wentworth. The two of them growing closer, then intimate. Powell Sinclair finding out and firing the entire staff.

"You never saw her again after that?" Mike asked.

"Why would we? Shortly after, Wenty left for Cambridge. He was at Harvard. We were both trying to build marriages."

"Fat lot that did," Alice muttered.

And the redhead was nothing more than a former, fired staff member. No reason to follow up. Why indeed? Her mother's failure to talk with the Sinclairs was starting to make sense now. She must have feared what Powell would do.

"Then before we knew it, Wenty died. He should never have been driving so fast."

"He was eager to get home," Jim Brassard said.

"He was rushing home for a reason," Mike told him. He reached into his back pocket and dropped the stack of letters in Roxy's lap. Still looking down, Roxy ran her finger over the velvet ribbon. Mike had told her what Wentworth's final few letters said. His final promises to the woman he loved. She'd given the press a brief overview of the stack's content, but only the broadest of strokes. These pages were the couple's final intimate moments.

"My mother held on to these for thirty years," she told the sisters, holding out the stack.

"Wentworth's final letters," Frances declared. "You mentioned them in your interviews."

The older woman withdrew the top letter. "May we?"

"Please."

Time ticked off on a nearby floor clock. Roxy and Mike waited while the sisters and Jim Brassard read the letters in silence. At some point, a staff member brought in a tea service. Watching the woman set down the tray, Roxy wondered what her mother would think, her sitting as a guest in the solarium thirty years after she got tossed out. Was this what she wanted? *I hope so, Mom.*

She stole a glance to her left. Mike looked right at home. His suit, his bearing—they fit in. No surprise. What did surprise her was how comfortable she felt. This was her father's home. Her family's home. The notion made her smile. Over the rim of his teacup, Mike gave her a wink. Her heart thumped a little harder. Once again, a familiar four-letter word filled her heart. A troublesome four-letter word if true. Love wasn't on the agenda. Not with a man who considered kissing her a mistake.

Examining her feelings for her lawyer, though, would have to wait. Having read enough, the sisters set the letters down and offered a pair of polite coughs.

"Wentworth was always dramatic," Alice remarked. "Whatever his interest, he threw himself in with a passion for as long as he was involved."

"I think his relationship with Roxanne's mother was more than a casual interest," Mike said.

"Oh, I have no doubt they were in love and that he intended to issue an ultimatum to our father," Frances said.

"He was always issuing ultimatums," Alice added. "It was part of his passionate nature. Once, when he discovered our father was investing in a Japanese venture, he went on a hunger strike. Said he wouldn't eat until he had proof the company wasn't involved in harming dolphins."

Her older sister nodded and reverently slid the letter back into the envelope. "That was one of his more over-the-top demonstrations."

Roxy listened to them in disbelief. They weren't seriously equating his love affair with her mother with dolphin-safe fishing? "Forgive me, but those letters—"

"Oh, I know," Alice cut her off. "They are amazingly detailed."

"To say the least," Jim Brassard muttered. "You weren't kidding, Mike."

"And, I have no doubt that he believed every word at the time," Frances said. "Whether he was serious about his threats is something we'll never know."

"He gave up the hunger strike after thirty-six hours," Alice said in a soft voice.

"Still." Frances squared her shoulders. "Fact remains that when he wrote these letters, he was in love, and I think, given your story, your mother loved him. If there were consequences to their love affair, it's our responsibility to see to them."

"Are you saying what I think you're saying?" Mike asked.

Roxy held her breath for the answer. If she heard right, Frances and Alice were willing to… No, she wouldn't believe until she heard the words straight from one of the sister's mouths.

"The Sinclairs place a high value on responsibility and on family. If our brother fathered a child, then that child is part of our family. We won't turn our backs on her existence."

Oh, my goodness, she was saying what Roxy thought she said.

"The question is," the woman continued, showing marks of the shrewdness that made her father a scion of business. "What are your motives, Miss O'Brien?"

"I want the truth." Roxy had been thinking about this for a while now. "More than anything, I want to know the truth. I want to know who I am."

Both women smiled and gave slight nods of their heads. Her answer apparently pleased them. “That’s what we’d like as well,” Frances replied. “We’ll be glad to cooperate with your DNA test, Miss O’Brien.”

Pop! Champagne foamed up and down the side of the bottle. Roxy laughed as Mike held it up to keep it from running onto his desk. “Not my neatest opening,” he said. “But what’s the point of splurging on champagne if you can’t be messy?”

“Good point.”

They picked up the bottle on the way back from Gramercy Park, feeling the need to cap off the meeting with a celebration. Tomorrow they would go to a local lab so Roxy could have her cheek swabbed for DNA. If lucky, they’d have the results within a week.

Best part of everything had been the sisters themselves. After they agreed to the test, the pair shared with her the family photo albums. She saw pictures of Wentworth as a child and as he looked a few months before he died. Call her crazy, but she could see a little of Steffi in his face. Around the jaw and the chin.

She watched Mike pour champagne into the two ceramic mugs on his desk. “Pretty big drinks,” she said, noting they were three-quarters full.

“Big celebrations call for big drinks,” he replied, handing her one. “Why, you got somewhere to be?”

Actually she did. Work. “I’m supposed to be at the Lounge in—” She looked at her watch. Shoot! Was it really that late? “I was supposed to be at work fifteen minutes ago.”

In a flash, Mike set down his cup, and was on his feet. “I’ll drive you.”

“It’s okay.”

"You sure?"

"There's no need." She'd only be rushing to a job that no longer existed. Dion made it very clear at the end of last night's shift, he wouldn't tolerate any more missed time. "I'm pretty sure I'm now unemployed."

"I'm sorry."

"Yeah, me, too." Surprised her how casual she sounded. You'd think she'd be more upset about becoming unemployed. She simply couldn't work up the angst right now.

"What about Steffi? Do we need to get her?"

"She's at Mrs. Ortega's till midnight, and given Alexis's mood lately, it's the best place for her. The less time we're in the apartment, the better."

"Still giving you a hard time, hey?"

"Worse this morning than last night. I didn't dare tell her about our meeting."

She sighed. When Alexis first moved in, the relationship seemed like it had such potential. "I can't wait to get Steffi out of that environment."

"If things go well, you'll be able to move anywhere you'd like," he said, handing her a cup. "To positive DNA tests."

Roxy clinked her mug against his. "To scaling Mt. Everest barefoot. And having a kick-ass attorney."

She took a sip and grimaced at the dry flavor. Guess it was an acquired taste.

Mike set down his drink.

"I wouldn't start patting ourselves on the back too soon. We passed a big hurdle getting them to agree to the DNA test, but we haven't scaled the peak yet. After the results are in, we still have to prove you deserve a share of the estate. I know the sisters said they wanted to do right by their brother's family, but Jim Brassard is going to do whatever he can to protect their assets. He can make it a hell of a fight if he wants to."

"But I've got you." Roxy wasn't worried. She had faith Mike would succeed. He'd gotten her this far, hadn't he?"

Imagine that. Roxy O'Brien having faith. Who'd have thought that a month ago. She took another drink, this time finding the champagne a little more appealing.

"What?" she asked, catching him watching. There was so much tender curiosity in his eyes. Shivers danced along her skin, matching the bubbles in her cup.

"You look very pensive all of a sudden," he said.

"I was thinking how much things can change in a month. Four weeks ago I stormed out of this office thinking you were a condescending, arrogant jerk."

"And now?"

Now I can't imagine a day without you in it. "Now I'm sitting here drinking champagne." To punctuate her point, she took a sip. "I'm glad I left one of my letters behind."

"Me, too."

Coming around to her side of the desk, he sat down next to her. His hip brushed against hers causing the air between them to crackle. Roxy thought about shifting, but the contact felt too nice. She liked the warmth spreading though her body.

"I have a confession to make," he said.

"What's that?"

"I would have tracked you down anyway. I wanted the case."

For the moment, Roxy pretended he didn't say the second line, and focused on him tracking her down. "Well, if this is going to be honesty time, I suppose I owe you an apology."

"You mean for something other than thinking I was arrogant and condescending?"

"Yes," she replied, bumping his shoulder. Wow, had she really already drank half her cup? The stuff grew on you. "When you said you would win this case, you told me you never said anything you couldn't back up. I didn't believe you."

"You might want to hold off on that. Like I said, we haven't won yet."

"But I was wrong to doubt you, your abilities." She stared at the bubbles rising from the golden liquid and popping, creating tiny little sprays in her mug. "Your sincerity. Your confidence. I shouldn't have.

"To Mike Templeton," she said, raising her glass. "The winner he said he was."

"Don't."

What'd she say? He stood up, taking his warmth and his contact with him as he headed to the picture window. The air grew cold. "I thought you wanted me to believe in you."

"Believe your case had a chance, yes. But—" He looked out to some place far away. "I'm not a winner, Roxy."

"Don't be silly." Of course he was. He'd been a winner his whole life. He told her so. "We won today, didn't we?"

He opened his mouth to protest, but she waved it off. He could talk about waiting until the case was over and all that, but as far as she was concerned, he had won today. He'd won her faith.

And maybe a little more? Maybe her heart?

She slipped off the desk, surprised when the floor swayed a little. Stupid floor.

For the third time today, she wondered if her feelings ran deeper than simple gratitude. "Third time's a charm, isn't it?" a voice in her head asked. Possibly. Romance so wasn't on her agenda. He was the wrong man, the wrong person to fall for. And yet, here she was.

She joined him at the window. Between the night outside, and the fluorescent office lights, his face was cast in shadows. He looked sad. Regretful. Slipping in front of him, she sat on the window heater. "What's with the modesty all of a sudden?"

"Speaking the truth is all," he replied. "I don't like to take credit for something that isn't my accomplishment."

"Whose accomplishment is it?"

He blinked, and looked at her with surprise. "Yours, of course. If you win, if you prove you're a Sinclair and get your share of the inheritance, you'll be the reason why."

"Well, sure." She took another long drink. Silly man. "It's my DNA. Still, I couldn't have done anything without you. Don't sell yourself short, Counselor." She giggled the last word because the bubbles chose that moment to tickle her nose.

"I am a good lawyer, aren't I?"

He said it like discovering a new fact. "Okay," he said, "how about we agree we did this together. To us."

She watched as he tipped back his drink. "We make a good team, Roxanne O'Brien," he said, topping off his mug.

At the word team, Roxy's heart did a little dance. "You shouldn't say stuff like that unless you mean it," she told him.

"What makes you think I don't?"

Because if she believed him, she'd fall completely under his spell, that's why. As it was, she'd already dropped three-quarters of the way, maybe more.

God, but she felt so good being here with him.

He was topping off her mug again. She didn't mind. The mellow, happy feeling in her limbs felt amazing. She wanted the whole world to feel the same way. The man standing next to her most of all.

"Do you ever loosen your tie?" she asked, swaying toward him.

He laughed. Such an attractive laugh, thought Roxy, taking another drink. Her cup was emptying way too fast, and her head suddenly felt very heavy. So heavy she had to rest her forehead on his chest. Mike's fingers threaded through her hair.

"That's better," she murmured.

"You've had too much champagne," he said. The unnatural lilt in his voice made her giggle.

"S'your fault. Told you the cup was filled too high." She tried looking up and the room shifted. "I probably should have had something to eat."

"Probably," he replied with a broad smile. With one hand still cradling the back of her head, he used his other to lift his mug and take a long drink. "Same here."

Wow, but he smiled pretty. Could men's smiles be pretty? Never mind, his was. "You haven't answered my question. Do you ever loosen your tie?"

"Haven't since college," he said, giving another one of those adorable laughs. "Got to dress like a Templeton, you know. Can't be seen looking like a bum. Might reflect badly on the family name." Another sip and he leaned in close. "Want to know a secret?"

"Sure." He could tell her anything in that sexy whisper. "What?"

"Sometimes I take my tie off at the end of the day."

"What do you do with it?"

"Depends." He grinned, his eyes shiny like two copper pennies. "On whether or not I've got company."

Oh, my. Roxy's insides turned hot and needy. "It's the end of the day now," she whispered. "And I'm company."

"So you are."

She touched the Windsor knot at his neck. Mike was

right about the alcohol. Her fingers felt thick and clumsy as she undid the silk. Every fumble had her brushing the underside of his chin and caressing his throat. Finally she tugged the cloth loose. “There,” she said with a smile. “You’re loosened.”

“Better?”

“Much.” Her smile turned serious as another question came to mind. “Do you really regret kissing me the other day?”

“I never said I regretted it.”

“Yes, you did.”

“No. I said kissing you was a *mistake.*”

“Isn’t that the same thing?” Suddenly it was incredibly important for her to know the truth.

“No. A mistake says I shouldn’t have done it. Regret implies I was sorry, and I’m not sorry in the least.”

Awareness pulsed deep inside her, a low, throbbing need to feel his touch again. Slowly she let her fingers slide from the knot in his tie to the plains of his chest. His hard, chiseled chest. When she reached his heart, her palm flattened and she could feel his heartbeat reaching her through the cloth. The need intensified knowing the rapid beat was because of her. “Would it be a mistake to kiss me again?” she asked, searching his face.

Black eyes, their pupils blown so wide from desire, searched back. Their heat bore into her. “Yes,” he whispered.

Yet he didn’t move. “Because I’m your client?”

“No. Because you’re tipsy.” He cradled her face, his thumbs fanning warm arcs across her cheek. “A gentleman doesn’t take advantage of a woman who’s been drinking.”

He smoothed her eyebrows. “No matter how beautiful and tempting she is.”

Roxy leaned closer. "What if I kissed you? Would that be a mistake, too?"

A thrill passed through her seeing his Adam's apple bob hard in his throat. He nodded. "Yes."

"Would you regret it?"

"Question is, would you?"

"Guess we'll have to see, won't we?" Pulling herself on her tiptoes, she pressed her lips to his. The kiss was softer, slower than last time. Roxy's eyes fluttered closed. She concentrated on the feel of Mike's mouth on hers, his taste, the texture of his lips as they massaged hers. She was right; his mouth was perfect. She heard a soft moan escape his throat, and felt his hand cup the back of her skull. Fingers tangled in her hair, angling her face upward. Her lips parted, and for a moment, the kiss became more intimate, a dance of tongues.

The soft caress of his breath on his cheek signaled the dance's end.

"Do you regret that?" she asked, coming down to earth.

He shook his head. "Not one second."

"Good. Because neither do I." If anything, tonight felt right. So very, very right. "What would you do then, if I kissed you a second time?"

"Oh, now, that could be a problem."

"Why?"

Lips, soft and eager, nibbled her jawline. "Because I can't guarantee I'll be able to stop at a simple kiss." To prove his point, he slid his hands down to her bottom and pulled her close so she could feel his arousal.

Smiling, Roxy hooked one leg around his calves and merged their bodies even closer. "Who says I want you to?"

CHAPTER ELEVEN

"For goodness' sake, Michael, you really need to check your voice mail. This is my third message in three days. What on earth are you thinking running around doing press interviews with that woman? You are a lawyer, not a—"

Mike switched off the phone midmessage. The woman buttoning her slacks was far more interesting. "Those looked better on the floor," he said with a lazy smile.

Roxanne smiled back. "Wouldn't that make a pretty headline. *Heiress Caught Commuting with Her Pants Down.*"

"I don't know about a headline, but it would definitely make a pretty sight." He ran his hand along the inner thigh he now had intimate knowledge of until she slapped it away.

"Listen to you. The guy who thought my work skirt was too short."

"It was. Doesn't mean I didn't like what I saw." He frowned. "Why are you talking like you're taking the bus?"

"Well, Mr. Half a Bottle of Champagne, I don't think you're capable of driving, do you?"

"Stay here, then." He pulled her into a deep kiss, grinning when her arms found their way around his neck. "I love how you smell," he murmured, burying his face in the crook of her neck. "I could smell you all night. And taste, and…" He kissed the hollow below her collarbone and was rewarded with a whimper.

Maybe they should take the bus, find an empty back-seat….

"I have to go," she said when he finally let her up for air. "I told Mrs. Ortega I'd pick up Steffi at midnight."

"Blast Mrs. Ortega." Much as he wanted to argue the point, he knew she was right. They couldn't leave Steffi at the sitter's indefinitely. Eventually this little celebratory rendezvous would have to end. "Let me put on my shirt and I'll get us a cab."

"Us?" She pulled back. "You know you can't stay, right? I can't have Steffi waking up and getting the wrong impression."

He could argue that, given the environment Roxy and her daughter lived in, his sleeping over was the least detrimental, but he wouldn't. He respected Roxy's protectiveness.

However, she never said he couldn't see her first thing in the morning.

"Breakfast?" she said when he told her.

"When I come get you for the DNA test. I'll bring muffins. Then, after the test is over, if Steffi's still at preschool and there's time…" He ran an index finger down the front of her shirt and hooked the waistband of her pants.

"I'll keep my fingers crossed the lab's running on time," Roxy said.

Catching the mischievous glint in her eyes, Mike couldn't help himself. He kissed her again. Deep and hard.

"Down, Counselor," Roxy teased. "Save it for tomorrow.

"By the way," she added, tossing him his shirt, "make sure you bring extra muffins."

"For what?" *Please don't say Wayne and Alexis.*

To his immense pleasure, she didn't. She did, however, give him a quick peck on the cheek. "To keep up your strength, of course."

She slipped out of his arms.

Was he wrong? Mike asked himself while waiting by his reception desk for Roxy to return from the washroom. In the back of his mind, he knew he was supposed to feel guilty. She was a client for crying out loud. How many times over the past few weeks had he reminded himself of the ethical and professional repercussions or lectured himself he had a job to do and that his personal desires meant nothing. Because they'd never mattered before.

Except for tonight. Tonight he'd wanted and he'd taken—for three hours he'd taken—and damn if he wasn't glad. For the first time in a very long time, Mike felt one hundred percent alive.

Was this how Wentworth felt when he was with Fiona? No wonder the guy was planning to fight.

"Ready?

Roxanne stood at the lobby door, her hair still wild from their lovemaking. "Sorry to keep you waiting," she said.

Looking at her, Mike's heart hitched. Amazing how easily tides could turn. A little over a month ago he sat on the edge of failure and judging Roxanne for being rough around the edges. Four and a half weeks later, she was on the cusp of becoming Manhattan's latest socialite and his future was set.

No wonder he felt alive.

He moved toward her, slipping an arm around her waist to lead her toward the door. "No need to apologize," he told her. "You were worth the wait."

"What's a lab tree?" From her perch on top of the counter, Steffi drank her juice from a plastic cup while Roxy moved around the kitchen looking for her coffee mug.

"Laboratory," she corrected. Where was the darn thing? She'd had it a minute ago. "It's a place where people go to get their blood tested."

"Are you sick?"

"Oh, no, baby, I'm not sick." She'd never felt better. To remind herself, she stretched her arms over her head, reveling in the burn of sore muscles from the night before. A soft sigh escaped her lips.

This was the train of thought that caused her to misplace her coffee in the first place.

"Your mama's taking a test to prove she's better than the rest of us." Alexis ambled in, still wearing her nightshirt, and took two mugs from the cabinet.

"Are you better than me?" Steffi asked.

"No one's better than anybody," Roxy replied. "Alexis is making a joke."

From behind the refrigerator door, her roommate coughed. Roxy ignored her. No one was going to ruin her mood, not Alexis. Not even Wayne. In a short while, Mike would be here. Together they'd drop Steffi off at the preschool, go to the lab for her DNA test, and hopefully, if there was time, come back to repeat last night.

For the first time in her life, things were perfect. And, in a few days, when the test results returned, life would become better! She and Steffi would have a full-fledged family tree and the money to build a brand-new life.

She found her coffee. On the dining room table. Cold, but Roxy drank it anyway. Or rather she started to. The phone stopped her.

"Mommy, your phone's ringing." Steffi pointed to the cell on the counter.

Alexis, who'd been standing right next to the phone, looked down and shrugged. "I wouldn't want to mess up one of your interviews," she sneered.

"Never mind, I've got it." Resisting the temptation to get in a snark contest, Roxy simply crossed the room and picked it up. The caller ID said Unknown, but the area code looked familiar.

"Hello?"

"Christina said you're trying to reach me. Said it was important."

Her father. Her other father, that is. Talk about timing. "Yeah, Dad, I wanted to talk to you. It's about Mom."

"There a problem? I thought she had insurance to bury her."

"She did. This is about something else." Taking a deep breath, she asked the multimillion-dollar question. "Did you ever hear of a man named Wentworth Sinclair?"

Mike drove straight to Roxanne's apartment from his. He'd be early but who cared? Early meant a few extra minutes to say hello. The thought made his body wake up better than any alarm clock.

Fortune continued to smile on him as he snagged a parking spot right in front of the building and stepped onto the sidewalk the same time an elderly man exited the building.

"Someone's getting breakfast delivered," the man said as he held open the front door. He nodded at the wax pastry bag and tray of coffee.

"You can say that again." Mike grinned.

To his surprise, it took three rounds of knocking for Roxanne to open the door. He'd have thought she'd be awake by now, this lab appointment being the apex of everything she wanted. Then again, she did earn the right to be a little tired after last night.

His fist was about to start round four when he finally heard the scrape and jingle of security locks. A second later, Roxanne's face appeared in the doorway. And Mike's insides froze.

One look at the pale skin, the colorless lips, the puffy red eyes, told him she'd been crying. "What's wrong?" he asked, dropping the coffee and muffins on the table. "Is it Steffi?"

"Steffi's fine." She wiped at her cheeks. "My father called."

"Oh, I'm so sorry." He didn't know what else to say. Her distress made sense now. "I wish I'd been here earlier. He didn't take the news well."

"Actually he took the news fine," she said with a sniff. "In fact he knew all about Wentworth and my mom."

What? He did? "And he never said anything after all this time?"

Roxy shook her head. "Didn't see the point. He also told me not to bother taking the test. Because there's absolutely no way I can be Wentworth's daughter."

CHAPTER TWELVE

HE DIDN'T believe her.

"What are you talking about?" he asked, his face the picture of confusion. "Of course you're Wentworth's daughter. The sisters said as much."

"The sisters were wrong. Wentworth died before my mother got pregnant."

"How can you be so certain?"

"Because—" Over on the couch, Steffi sat watching her pony show. Oblivious to the drama playing out around her. Wanting to keep her world undisturbed, Roxy led Mike to the kitchen, where they could talk out of earshot. Her cell phone lay on the counter where she'd dropped it. Right next to the burn mark on the Formica where Wayne left a hot sauce pan and a half-finished cup of coffee. This was her reality. She should have known.

"My father explained everything." Succumbing to the unbearable heaviness that gripped her body, she slumped against the counter. Every last lousy word of their conversation had been cemented in her memory. *You ain't no Sinclair. That was just your mother's wishful thinking.* "Turns out I was born early. The real due date was too far out for me to be Wentworth's."

"Due dates can be fudged."

"Incompetent cervixes can't. Apparently the doctor

warned my mother she could go early if she didn't stay off her feet, and she kept working anyway." Why she ignored the doctor's advice, her father didn't say. Maybe they'd been pressed for money or she wanted out of the house.

Or maybe she'd wanted to go early so she could pretend. Keep the fantasy going. "Who knows what went on in that head of hers," her father had said. "She never was all there."

Hearing him speak so bluntly about something so important hurt almost as much as the story itself. Apparently, according to her father, he and her mother met in a local bar, about three weeks after Wentworth's accident. Her mother had been upset. Drinking. He bought her a drink to calm her nerves, and then a second. Next thing they were getting it on in the backseat of his Dodge Dart.

"That's exactly how my father put it, too. Getting it on." She gave a mirthless bark. "Me and my mom, two peas in a pod. Only difference is my dad lived in the same neighborhood, so when my mom found out she was knocked up, she gave him a call. Good Irish Catholic boy that he was, my dad married her."

So much for being the child of some great, unfinished love affair. She was exactly who she always thought she was. A big, unwelcome, unwanted mistake. "My father hadn't left because Fiona still loved Wentworth. He left because he didn't love us enough to stick around."

Roxy dropped her head. All her big plans, her hopes for the future. Killed by a fifteen-minute phone call and a "Sorry, kiddo, I thought you knew."

What a joke. Her gullibility made her sick to her stomach.

Mike was pacing the length of the kitchen. She watched his shoes, thinking how out of place they looked against the scuffed beige flooring. Another reminder of reality.

"This can't be happening," he was saying. His muttered words mirrored the voice in her head. "Everything was so damn certain yesterday. What the hell happened?"

"Reality happened," she murmured in reply.

A wash of his hand over his features, his voice steeled. "No need to panic. Not yet. Your father could still have his dates wrong."

If only. "He doesn't."

He stopped his pacing. "You don't know that."

"I know my luck." Why should her paternity be any different from the other bad choices and failures in her life? What on earth made her think she could possibly be an heiress?

Looking back, she realized her gut had been shooting her warning signs for weeks, telling her she was getting in so deep, but she'd been too seduced by the idea of being a Sinclair she'd ignored them.

Who was she kidding? She believed her mother's story because she *wanted* to. All these years she'd wondered what it was she did to make her parents check out. She'd grasped at her mother's love affair because the truth hurt too much. Now truth wanted to make her pay by hammering itself home. *Mistake, mistake, mistake.*

The word repeated in her head as she played with the hem of her sweater set. Her *heiress costume,* she amended bitterly. "I should have known. I failed as an actress, as a daughter, as a mother…"

Steffi. What did she have to offer her daughter now? No inheritance. No father. She didn't even have her crappy job. All she had was this lousy apartment, a world filled with lowlifes like Wayne and a family history of drunken pickups. How long before her daughter started seeing her as the mistake she was, too?

Nausea rose in her throat. She rushed to the sink, making it seconds before losing her morning coffee. Heave after acidic heave burned her throat. Mike tried to rub small soothing circles on her back, but she shoved him away. To the other side of the room. Where she couldn't see the pity that had to be in his coppery eyes. Add him to her list of mistakes. He thought he'd made love to an heiress last night. Instead he got the premakeover Roxy. The one who couldn't measure up. Why would he want her now?

"It's over." She stared at the sink drain, watching the water wash away the mess. If only she could wash the fallout from this past month as easily.

"No. It's not over. Not yet."

He was pacing again, Roxy could hear his heels hitting the linoleum. "I'll go to Florida and interview your father myself. I should have in the first place. And your mother's medical records. We'll track them down. Maybe her doctor's still alive."

"Why? What's the use? Still going to be the same outcome."

"You don't know that."

Oh, but she did. "Face it, Mike, it's a lost cause."

"So, what? That's it? You're just going to quit?"

"What else am I supposed to do?

"You can keep fighting."

"Why? So I can make a bigger fool out of myself? Hope the Sinclairs give me some money to go away?"

"Why not? A lot better than hiding in your apartment playing the victim."

Playing the vict— Roxy whirled around. "What the hell is that supposed to mean?"

"Exactly what it sounds like."

"I am not playing anything." As if he would understand anyway. When had life ever kicked him in the teeth?

"Oh, no? Sure sounds it to me. One little phone call and you're ready to quit."

"As opposed to what? Fighting a lost cause so I can get bought off? That wasn't why I did this."

"Wasn't it?"

And so it came back to her being a fortune hunter. After all they'd shared. *After she gave him her heart.* Anger ripped through her. "You know it wasn't," she hissed. It took everything not to slap his face. "I wanted to know the truth."

"You're right. I'm sorry." The apology would carry more weight if she couldn't see the wheels turning in his head. Formulating the next line of attack.

It came with a milder voice. "All I meant was you came to me wanting to give Steffi a better life. You still can."

By basically coercing a payout. "I can't," she told him. If she did lose her daughter's respect when she got older, she could at least keep some ability to look herself in the mirror.

Mike shook his head. "I can't let you quit. This case is way too important."

"Haven't you been listening? There is no case!"

"There has to be."

The ferocity with which he shouted the words shocked her. She knew he wasn't used to losing, but this… This was over-the-top. You'd think karma had played the joke on him instead of her. Surely she wasn't that important to him.

"Sorry," she told him. "Guess you'll have to win with another client."

"There is no other client."

What? She stared at him.

Mike ran a hand over his features. "I don't have any other clients," he repeated. "You're it."

"But, I don't understand. Your ad, the uptown offices…"

"Teetering on the brink of extinction." His fierceness turned sheepish. "You of all people should know things aren't always what they appear to be."

You'd think there'd be more clutter. Sophie's observation had been right. There was no clutter because there was no business.

Except for her. Her and her multimillion-dollar payday. A huge emptiness formed in the center of her chest. Roxy cut off his argument. She wasn't going to believe him anyway. No wonder he treated her like such an important client. Hanging around the bar. Doting on her.

Making love to her.

"That's all this was to you, wasn't it? A case. A way to salvage your business."

He started. Shock? Or guilt. "No. I mean, maybe things started out that way but..."

She didn't want to hear another argument. Here she thought last night meant something more, something deeper. That he felt the same emotions. But no, while she'd been making love, he'd been keeping his prized client happy.

Chalk up another bad choice.

For the first time since answering the door, she looked him straight in the eye.

"I think you should leave."

"Leave?" He looked genuinely surprised. "I'm not leaving you."

"Yeah, you are." He should be pleased. For once she wasn't the one walking away; she was making him do it. "What's that saying, fool me once, fool me twice? I'm not going to let you stick around so I can get fooled a third time."

Pushing her way past him, she marched to the front

door and flung it open. "Your job here is finished, Mr. Templeton."

Mike stared at her long and hard. "Don't do this, Roxy."

"Too late, I already have."

Took another couple of beats, but he finally got the message and walked away.

"Mommy?" From her place on the couch, Steffi broke the silence as soon as the door shut. "Mike didn't say goodbye."

Roxy kept her face to the wood, watching the lock swim in front of her eyes. "No, baby, he didn't."

Then again, she expected as much.

Damn, damn, damn!

The obscenity was the only word Mike was capable of forming. He chanted it the entire drive to his office, screaming it once or twice in the empty interior, hoping maybe, just maybe, he could make some sense of what happened in Roxy's apartment.

He had nothing.

Roxy couldn't be quitting. There was still plenty to fight. Until they had definitive, actual proof she had a case…

But no, she'd rather give up. Accept failure. He kicked over a potted plant. Dammit! Why did her father have to call this morning of all mornings? Why couldn't the miserable bastard stay missing a little while longer?

Fine. If Roxy didn't want to pursue her claim, that was her business. He didn't need her or her case. He'd figure out another way to save his firm. He was a Templeton for crying out loud. He wasn't born to fail.

His toe kicked a scrap of cloth on the way to his desk. Bending down he found his tie from last night, tangled around the wheels of one of his guest chairs. Pain shot through him, starting deep in his stomach and exploding in vast emptiness across his chest. Letting out a groan, he squeezed the silk in his fist against the rising tide of memories. Images. Feelings. This was why you didn't get involved with clients. Because they made a man start believing in long-discarded emotions again. Made him think he was a winner again.

It's over. Roxy's words hit him hard. Did she know how much she ended with those two words? It was over.

He'd failed. His eyes dropped to the tie. In more ways than he thought possible.

"That's it? You left?"

"She told me to, Grant. What was I supposed to do? Fight her?"

From the disappointed looks his brother and Sophie were shooting him from across the living room, fight was exactly what they expected.

He bristled defensively. "I don't need a client who's going to fight me every step of the way."

Sophie folded her arms, jostling the Yorkshire terrier sleeping on her lap. "Referring to Roxanne as a client? Really?"

"She was a client. What should I call her?"

"I don't know. You tell me." Challenge glittered in her blue eyes.

Mike broke the stare. They didn't know he'd slept with Roxy. Some things were none of their business.

Besides, he was trying not to think about the night they spent together. Every time he did, his chest hurt.

"I feel bad for her," Grant said. "First her mother turns her world upside down, then her father turns it the other way. And on top of everything she loses her job?"

"Terrible," Sophie agreed. "Have you tried calling her?" she asked Mike.

Had he tried calling her? "I just finished saying the woman wants nothing to do with me."

"I know what you said. But have you called her?"

Damn her. She had a whiff of the truth and she wouldn't give up. "Half a dozen times," he replied, looking to his glass of Scotch. "She's blocked my number."

"Ouch. I'm sorry."

He shrugged, feigning indifference, hoping Sophie would drop the subject. "It is what it is. Can't be helped."

"You've got it bad, don't you?"

It was Grant, not Sophie. At his brother's question, Mike looked up. "What are you talking about?"

"You and your 'client'." He quoted the word with his fingers. "She's a lot more isn't she?"

"Don't be—" He stopped. What was the sense in protesting? They'd only keep hammering until he gave up the truth. Roxanne was more. A lot more. He could barely sit in his office without picturing her there with him. Laughing. Brushing the hair from her face. The other night, he actually drove himself to the Elderion, with some foolish notion that the lounge would dredge up older memories. Stupid. Nostalgia didn't have a chance against Roxanne. He didn't even make it to his regular table before her absence slammed into him like a truck and he had to go home.

"How'd you know?" he asked.

"Personal experience," his brother replied. "I've used the nonchalant act myself. Back before Sophie and I got our act together."

"I also told him how attentive you were the other weekend," Sophie added. "Unless you stare at all your clients like a lovesick puppy."

"No, just Roxanne." He took a drink. It had been a mistake, he wanted to add, but he couldn't. Nothing about Roxanne was a mistake. Not her history, not her annoying habit of overreacting and certainly not her. Grant and Sophie were right. He had it bad. Head over heels kind of bad.

"Doesn't matter," he said, moving to their fireplace. His chest was hurting again. He realized now the ache came from a place far deeper than his body. "She told me I didn't belong in her world."

"I'm not surprised," Grant replied.

"Gee, thanks."

"Seriously. No offense, but if I were her, you'd be the last person I'd want to see, too."

His brother appeared at his shoulder. "Here she is, feeling like the world kicked her in the teeth. A guy like you would only highlight the problems."

"What do you mean, a guy like me?"

"You know what I mean, Golden Boy. I'm sure she feels lousy enough about life without her polar opposite around to remind her how low she is."

"You're saying I made her feel inferior?"

"Not on purpose. But having grown up with you, I can say it's not always easy living with Mom and Dad's clone."

If only they knew....

He was more concerned with Roxanne right now. Had he really made her feel like less of a person? The thought made him sick. "I never meant to—"

No, you only insisted she have a makeover so she'd fit in better. Made her feel less than acceptable as she was.

He slapped his glass on the mantel. "God, I'm such a hypocrite."

"I wouldn't go that far," Grant said.

"I would. I have no right making anyone feel inadequate." He stared at his empty glass, how the diamonds on the cut crystal were perfectly uniformed except for one. "Especially now," he said in a quiet voice.

"What are you talking about?"

Taking a deep breath, Mike told them the whole story. About how the firm was failing and how the money from Roxanne's case was his last hope for keeping it afloat.

When he finished, Grant simply said, "Wow."

"I knew there wasn't enough paper clutter," Sophie said. "Green office, my foot."

"I'm surprised you didn't catch on sooner," Mike told her.

The relief he hoped he would feel upon confession didn't materialize. Instead all he felt was embarrassed for not saying anything sooner. Thinking of Roxanne having to share her story over and over, he developed new respect. Took real strength to raise a child on her own, no family, no real money. When he first met her, he'd recognized the mettle in her. If only she saw it herself. Maybe they'd still be talking.

"Do Mom and Dad know?" Grant was asking.

He shook his head. "Are you kidding? Like you said, I'm the Golden Boy. The one who's supposed to do everything right." The freakin' Templeton namesake. "I was giving them what they expected." Same way he always did.

"The curse of Templeton expectations rides again."

"Excuse me?" Looking to his brother, he saw the younger man had grown intensely interested in the label on his beer bottle. "The family emphasis on super success. Screwed us all up. I got a fear of success…you developed a fear of failure. Wonder what Nicole ended up with."

"Maybe she lucked out."

"Maybe." Grant pulled a strip off the label and rolled it between his fingers. "You do realize of course, that closing shop isn't the end of the world."

"For you, maybe. I'm the one who's supposed to be better than all the rest."

"That's why you pushed Roxanne's case so hard."

"I couldn't afford to have the case drag out for years in court." The tactic worked, he had to admit that. Just not the way he intended.

"The day she told me about her father, I was shocked. I..." Remembering that final conversation, he winced. "I focused more on the case than her."

"No wonder she threw you out."

"No wonder indeed."

"What are you going to do now?" Sophie asked.

"What do I do now?" He'd messed up his career and his relationship with Roxanne. Failure wasn't a place he was used to operating from. He was lost.

"You could try talking with her," Sophie said.

"I told you, I already have. She wants nothing to do with me."

A hand clapped on his shoulder. Grant. "If you want, I can share with you a valuable piece of advice I got last summer. Something you said to me in fact."

Valuable advice? From him? "I have to hear this pearl of wisdom. What is it?"

"When's the last time a Templeton didn't go after what he wanted?"

CHAPTER THIRTEEN

"Look, Mommy. The animals made a merry-go-round!"

Roxy drew her attention away from the message on her cell phone only to wince at the plastic toys arranged in a circle on the living room floor. "That's nice. Are they having fun?"

"Uh-huh. I liked the merry-go-round we went to. Can we go back there?"

"What's wrong with the one in Central Park?"

Steffi looked up from making the horses dance. "This one has the rabbit," she said matter-of-factly.

"Oh."

"So can we go?"

Go to Bryant Park. Took her twenty-nine years to get to the place, and now it would be forever tainted with memories.

"We'll see," she said to Steffi. She hated saying no outright when she had no logical reason to give the four-year-old. What was she supposed to say? No, baby, I can't because thinking about the carousel makes Mommy cry? "Maybe someday."

"Okay. Can Mike come?"

A knife twisted in her chest. "I don't think we'll see Mike anymore."

"Why not?"

"Because we're not working together anymore. We're all done with our business."

"Why?"

Roxy sighed. Because Grandma's big deathbed confession turned out to be a deathbed fantasy, and then Mommy and Mike said some hurtful things to each other and Mommy sent Mike away, but that's okay because he would have left eventually anyway and she wanted to keep her heart from breaking. Except she didn't move fast enough and her heart ached anyway.

How was she supposed to explain that to a four-year-old?

As luck would have it, she didn't have to because someone knocked on the door. "I don't want to go see Mrs. Ortega," Steffi immediately started whining.

"We aren't going to Mrs. Ortega's," Roxy told her. "It's probably Priti from next door looking to borrow something."

But it wasn't Priti. It was Wayne. His shoulder rubbed against her as he pushed his way in. "We got any beer left?" he asked, strolling to the kitchen.

"We don't have anything," she replied sharply. "Alexis's not here. She's out with PJ." PJ, along with Wayne, had become a fixture in the apartment this week, meaning she now had two freeloaders living there. And annoying as that was, Roxy couldn't say a blessed thing. A little fact Alexis took great pleasure in. Along with all the other misfortunes that had befallen Steffi.

He came back into view, a can in each hand. "I hate cans," he said. "We gotta get more bottles."

Tell it to someone who cares. "I told you, Alexis isn't here. Wait a moment. How'd you get in the building anyway?"

"I had some business to take care of."

Business. She could imagine. "Well, you don't have any business here, so why don't you take off?"

"Relax." Wayne held up his arms. "I'm not here to cause trouble. I came by to see you. Thought maybe you might need some company."

The idea repulsed her beyond repulsion. "No, thanks. Steffi and I are fine by ourselves."

"Now don't go being like that. I know your lawyer man up and dumped you cause you ain't getting money."

"Mike didn't dump me." If anything, she dumped him, not that Wayne would believe her. "There was nothing to dump since we weren't having that kind of relationship."

"What kind of relationship is that?" Wayne suddenly appeared next to her shoulder, his breath sour from beer.

"Professional." Why was she even entertaining the guy's questions? Oh, right, because of Alexis. That reason was starting to wear thin.

Wayne smiled. "I can do professional," he said in a low voice that was supposed to sound sexy. "I can do anything you want. Like I told you. I treat my women real good. What do you say?" To illustrate his point, he ran an index finger down her arm. Roxy choked back the bile in her throat. Instead she looked over at Steffi, who was watching the entire exchange with her eyes as wide as saucers. "Steffi, baby, how about you take Dusty and go down to your room and play for a few minutes?"

As if hearing his name made her worry something would happen, the little girl grabbed her purple-and-white friend. "What about the merry-go-round?" she asked.

"Let's give the animals a break and I'll bring them in a few minutes, okay? Now please be a good girl and go to your room."

"Yeah, kid," Wayne echoed, winking in Roxy's direction. "Beat it."

The little girl rose to her feet, but wavered. Roxy gave her a nod and a smile to let her know everything would be all right. It worked, and eventually the child toddled to her bedroom and shut the door.

Roxy waited until she heard the click before whirling around and slapping Wayne's hand away. "Don't you ever talk to me or my daughter like that again, do you hear?"

The nineteen-year-old responded with a click of his piercing against his teeth. "Alexis ain't going to like you talking to me that way."

That was it. This blight of a human being had been darkening her doorstep long enough. Suggesting she would sleep with him because she hit hard times? She may have sunk low, but she would never sink that low. Ever.

She jabbed her index finger into his shoulder. "Look here, you little wannabe punk, I don't care whose baby brother you are. You so much as look at me or my little girl, and I will squeeze your private parts so hard you'll be singing soprano. Do you understand? Not one single look. Now take your beer and get out of my apartment."

Alexis would definitely not like this, but frankly she didn't care. There was only so much a woman should put up with.

Openly ignoring her threat, Wayne looked her up and down. "What if I don't want to leave?" he asked, stepping closer.

Roxy grabbed her cell phone, which thankfully, she still had in her pocket. "Then I'll call the police," she told him. "We'll see how your parole officer feels about you getting arrested. Especially since you were doing business." She pushed the first button. "Nine."

"Alexis's going to be ticked."

"I don't care. The only reason I'm giving you a countdown at all is because of Alexis." If she had actual proof of his "business," she wouldn't even give him that courtesy. She'd have his skinny butt hauled back to prison in a second. "One," she said.

"All right, all right," he said before she could repeat the last number. "Don't get all wigged out."

"You don't know wigged out, pal. Now get out."

"Uppity..." He muttered the second word but Roxy could guess it. The same oath he used before. This time he curled his lip in distaste.

"You think you're so much better than us because you did a few TV interviews and some dude bought you some fancy clothes," he said, "but I got news for you. You ain't all that."

"Maybe not," Roxy replied. "But I'm still better than you."

And she was better than this life.

"I don't like Wayne," Steffi told her when Roxy tucked her in bed a little while later. "He's mean."

Out of the mouths of babes... Roxy smoothed the sheets around her chest. "I think he is, too, but don't you worry. I won't let him bother you anymore."

"Is that why we're hiding in the bedroom? Because he's mean?"

"We're in the bedroom," Roxy said, "because it's bedtime." And yes, because she was afraid he might decide to come back, and the bedroom door had workable locks. "We can have a slumber party."

"Like the ponies?"

"Exactly."

Steffi snuggled in against her pillow, a little red-haired angel. She was a great kid, yet untouched by the Waynes in this world. So far, Roxy'd been able to keep them at bay. She intended to keep doing so. Tomorrow morning, she'd start looking for a new job and a new apartment. Maybe some place out of the city, where Steffi could have a yard. After all, when she started this Sinclair heiress business, hadn't it been to give her daughter a better life? If Wayne's little visit did anything, it told her she could sit around licking her wounds, mourning the losses she'd never get back or she could get off her duff and give her daughter the life she deserved. She chose the latter.

"I like Mike better," Steffi said, her eyes starting to blink with sleep. "He's nicer."

Speaking of losses she'd never get back. "Yes, he is. He's very nice."

"Do you like him?"

She a lot more than liked him. When he walked out, he took her heart with him. "It's complicated, baby."

"Complicated means hard. Mike told me."

"Mike's right."

"He said the same thing when I asked if he liked you."

Smart guy, thought Roxy. Notice he didn't come straight out and say yes, either.

"I don't think it is."

"What is?" She missed what her daughter was trying to say.

Steffi yawned. "Hard. Unless the person doesn't like you back. But you and Mike like each other so—" she yawned again "—I don't think it's hard."

Roxy didn't know how to respond to that. How could she explain to a four-year-old that feelings weren't so black and white? There were other issues that made relationships complicated, such as being able to look the man she loved in the eye. Or look at herself.

"I love you, Mommy," Steffi said.

Heart overflowing, Roxy kissed her forehead. "I love you, too. Sweet dreams."

Giving her one last kiss, she turned out the light and laid down on her bed. For the first time since talking to her father, she felt a surge of positivity. Standing up to Wayne made her feel stronger. In control. A little bit like…

Like she had when she was doing the interviews.

At the time, she said she felt like a different person was giving those interviews. Some woman she didn't know. Capable. Confident.

Could it be that woman was still there? She certainly showed up to tell off Wayne.

Better than staying in your apartment playing victim. Mike's words came back. She'd been hurt and angry when he said them, and retaliated in kind. But now she wondered. Did she have a choice?

"Mommy?" Steffi's voice reached out through the darkness. She hoped the little girl was simply restless, and not stressed out about Wayne or other problems.

"Yes, baby?"

"I hope liking Mike stops being hard. So you won't be so sad."

Roxy felt the ache before it had fully formed. The slow winding pang of loss. "That'd be nice."

"Maybe if we took him to the merry-go-round, you could like him again. You smiled a lot that day."

"Yes, I did." How could she not? It'd been a magical day.

"Mike smiled a lot, too. We should go to the merry-go-round again." Having voiced her decision, she gave a satisfied sigh. Roxy heard the rustle of sheets and, a few seconds later, the slow, steady sound of breathing.

Could it really be so simple? Were all these obstacles things she made up? Put in her own way? Mike accused her of playing the victim. That's certainly what she'd been doing these past couple days.

She rolled on her side. In some ways, that's what her

mother did, too. She clung to her love for Wentworth so strongly, she faded away from everyone else. At least Wentworth was willing to act and make something happen. He died planning to take a stand against his father. In his mind, loving someone wasn't so complicated.

Okay, she thought folding her arms behind her head. Maybe she wasn't a Sinclair by blood. Didn't mean she couldn't steal a little of Wentworth's determination.

Without thinking, she reached for her cell phone that lay on the nightstand. Mike's text was still on the screen, undeleted, waiting for her. *You were not a mistake,* he'd written. Her case? Her? Both? The words, coupled with her newfound control couldn't help but give her hope.

When did a Templeton not go after what he wanted?

Mike remembered all too well when he posted the same question to his brother. Circumstances were different. Grant and Sophie were simply being proud and stubborn. All they needed was for one of them to make the first move. In his case, he'd tried to talk to Roxanne, and she refused.

Who could blame her? She'd been hurting and he was worried about what? A law practice? Letting down his family?

Wentworth Sinclair would be ashamed.

He slapped a file in the large cardboard box. The downside of being a small law practice was that when it came time to move, you had to do the actual moving. There were no administrative staff members or clerks to help you out.

Just as well, thought Mike as he assembled another file storage box. He wasn't fit for the company of others anyway.

Wentworth's letters lay in a stack nearby. He ran his finger over the black scrawl. Six times. Six times he'd called and not so much as a voice mail. In the end, he settled for sending her a text message, hoping the apology would help.

"So it's true."

Judge Michael Templeton, Jr. wore a Burberry trench coat and his salt-and-pepper hair was combed back, emphasizing his handsome, time-sharpened features. He entered the room as though the office was his own and sat down, opting for Mike's desk chair over one of the guest seats. "When Jim Brassard told me you inquired about a position, I thought for sure he misunderstood. What's going on?"

Mike dropped another file in the box. "Isn't it obvious?" he said. "I'm closing up shop."

"I meant why are you closing your practice? You didn't mention anything. I thought you enjoyed being your own boss."

"I also enjoy eating."

Based on the way he stiffened, his father didn't appreciate the sharp comeback. "Is that your way of saying business is a little slow?"

Mike chuckled at his father's adjective. "A little," he replied. "You may not have noticed, but we're in an economic downturn."

"If business is slow, then get out there and double your efforts. Beat the bushes for business. You don't throw in the towel, Michael. That's not how we do things."

How we do things. The phrase set Mike's teeth on edge. God, but he was so tired of hearing how "they" were raised. How he was supposed to be.

"Do you remember when you first started swimming and you couldn't keep up with the rest of your squad?" his father asked.

"What I remember is being two years younger." His father convinced the coach he needed the challenge.

"Exactly. But you dug in and by the end of the year you were beating those boys."

Of course he dug in. He was eight years old and his father was dragging him to a swimming pool every weekend for extra practice. Pushing him every step of the way till his times improved. And Mike obeyed. To win his approval. To make his father proud. On and on the cycle went. Go higher. Be better. Be the best. So many expectations, his shoulders hurt.

"We didn't raise you to be a quitter, Michael. When I was your age, I already had a thriving practice with two associates. Did I have tough times, sure, but I worked for my success. I thought we raised you the same way."

Oh, they did, all right. His father raised him to be a mirror image. The perfect namesake. "What if I don't want it?" he asked aloud.

"What are you talking about? Of course you want it. We talked about this last year. How you'd done all you could at Ashby Gannon, and should be stepping out on your own."

We discussed. *You should.* Not once did they discuss what Mike wanted. God, wasn't it time he stopped being a puppet and grew up?

"People change their minds," he told his father. "Maybe I don't want this—" he waved his arm around the room "—anymore. Maybe I want something else."

"You've wanted to be a lawyer since you were eight years old, Michael."

"Did I? Because I remember at eight years old I wanted to be a pirate." He slapped the file he was holding on the table. "In fact, that's the last time I remember wanting anything that wasn't shaped or picked for me." Until six nights ago, with Roxanne. Holding her was all his idea. Best one he'd ever had, too. "The only reason I said I wanted to be a lawyer was because that's what you were, and like any eight-year-old, I wanted to be like my father. I had no idea you would decide 'like' meant mirror image."

His father scoffed. "I did no such thing."

"Didn't you? Swimming. The debate club. Your alma maters. What was all that about then, if not to repeat your past glories?"

"To help you be the best you could be. For heaven's sake, Michael, you make it sound like we put a gun to your head."

"No gun, just a whole lot of expectations."

"If you're saying we pushed you, yes. We wanted the best for you."

"You didn't want the best." Roxanne wanted the best. She was willing to do anything, including the one thing she feared the most—losing her daughter's respect to give Steffi a better life. "You wanted us to *be* the best. Always. Because God forbid we reflect badly on the family."

"That is not true!" his father bellowed, an uncharacteristic tone of voice for him and a sign Mike had hit a nerve dead-on. He pushed further.

"If so, then why are you here?"

"Because Jim Brassard told me—"

"Told you I was closing up shop and you were afraid he was telling the truth. Well, guess what, he was. I failed. I opened my own law practice, crashed and burned. Deal with it."

Soon as Mike said the words, a thousand pounds lifted from his shoulders. He'd done it. He'd failed and the world didn't end.

Not that you could tell from the look on his father's face. Disappointment marked every line.

"Fine," the elder Templeton said. "You're closing your firm, and it's my fault. Happy?"

Mike shook his head. His father truly didn't understand,

did he? None of this was about him. Took Mike till just this moment to realize his succeeding or failing was all his. Same with the choices he made. "Why does it have to involve you at all, Dad? Sometimes bad luck happens."

He could tell his father wasn't convinced. Maybe never would be. For the first time, Mike realized there was nothing he could do about what his father thought. "So what do you plan to do? Go back to Ashby Gannon or Brassard's firm?"

"Maybe. I don't know." The uncertainty had a liberating feel. Suddenly the world was wide-open.

There was one thing he did want. Or rather, two. Question was, did they want him?

Only one way to know for sure. Forgetting all about his father and packing, Mike grabbed the stack of letters off his desk. Wentworth would be proud.

"Where are you going?" his father called after him.

"What a Templeton's supposed to do," he replied, grinning. More for himself and the world than to the man seated at his desk.

"I'm going after what I want."

First thing he'd do when he got to Roxanne's would be to apologize and ask for another chance. She'd have to talk with him eventually, right? If necessary, he'd camp out in her hallway and accost her when she stepped outside. Whatever he needed to do.

He made it as far as the lobby before his mind started playing tricks on him. Getting off the elevator he swore he saw Steffi coming through the revolving door.

"Mike!" The figment waved brightly. "Look, Mommy, it's Mike."

His wishful eyes traveled to the woman behind her. It really was Roxanne. Dressed in a pair of faded jeans and the pale blue turtleneck, she'd never looked lovelier. When she saw him, she offered a tremulous smile.

Mike's pulse skipped a couple beats. He stopped dead. "Hey!" he said.

Silence filled the gap as he struggled with what to say next, hindered by the Manhattan-size lump lodged in his throat. "I was on my way to your apartment," he finally managed to say.

"You were? Why?"

To kiss you senseless. "To return your mother's letters," he said. As if it would prove his point, he held up his briefcase.

"Oh," she replied.

Was that disappointment he caught flickering across her face? He was afraid to hope. "Why are you…?"

"Same thing."

"Oh." His heart dropped. Guess it wasn't disappointment after all.

"Where's your tie?" Steffi asked.

"My what? Oh, my tie." Automatically his hand went to the collar of his T-shirt. "I didn't wear one today. I didn't want it to get dirty while I was packing."

Roxanne frowned, hearing his answer. "Packing?" she asked. "Are you going somewhere?"

"Eventually. I hope. I'm closing my practice."

"Why?" Perhaps she didn't realize, but she rushed toward him a few steps. "Is something—? Did something—?"

Mike saved her the trouble of searching for the right question and explained. When he finished, she looked down at her shoes. "The money from my case. You needed it to stay afloat."

He always said she was quick. "I needed the case for a lot of reasons," he told her. "Notoriety, money."

"Then if I hadn't…"

"You aren't to blame for anything." He refused to pile on guilt when she had enough issues on her shoulders. "This was my doing, one hundred percent. I took the case for all the wrong reasons. That's why, when you dropped the lawsuit, I acted like such a jerk."

"You were worried."

"Not worried. Afraid." Taking a deep breath, he said aloud the truth he'd kept to himself for a long time. "I was afraid of what would happen when I failed."

"Because you never had a choice," she said quietly.

"Exactly." She understood. "I thought I'd be letting everybody down."

"And now?"

"Now I'm thinking the only person I've failed all these years is myself. Plus you."

She shook her head. "You never failed me."

He didn't? Giving in to his longing to be closer, he stepped forward, hoping when he drew near, she wouldn't back away. "I've been taking a good long look at how I see success," he said. He thought about his father, still upstairs. "Some of it in the past few minutes in fact."

"What did you decide?"

"That I need to reexamine my personal definition of success and failure. See, I've spent a good portion of my life chasing one and fearing the other. Turns out I never really knew either till I met this woman who managed to be both sweet and graceful at the same time, in spite of all the stuff life tossed her."

Of course, she'd argue that she's not very successful at all.

"That so?"

"Uh-huh." He lucked out. She didn't back away. He continued closing the gap. "In fact," he said, "she'd argue she's a complete failure, even though that couldn't be further from the truth.

"She's very feisty," he said with a smile. "Before you showed up, I was debating about going to her apartment and camping out on her doorstep till she spoke to me."

"You were going to sleep on the steps?" Steffi asked. "Do you have a sleeping bag?"

Leave it to a four-year-old to ask the important questions. "I was hoping it wouldn't come to that, but if your mother wouldn't talk to me, I would have."

"Mommy's the woman?"

Mike nodded.

"But we came here because Mommy wanted to talk to you."

He wasn't sure if he should let the hope that lodged in his chest grow or not. He decided to take a chance. "What did you want to talk with me about?"

Roxy blinked back her tears. She'd rehearsed this scene in her head a dozen times last night, but none of her versions involved Mike saying such beautiful things or his looking so breathtakingly casual. She spent all night arguing back and forth with herself over coming here. Did she take a chance and trust the sincerity that always glowed in his eyes or did she give up like her mother?

"Did you mean it?" she asked him. "What you said in your text?"

He nodded. "Every word. You were definitely not a mistake."

Relief whooshed from her lungs. Five words. Six if you added the new word, definitely. Five words that meant everything. She felt them wrap around her heart, unlocking the feelings inside and telling her that yes, this choice was worth making.

"Funny, but I had to do some reevaluating, too," she told him. "Seems this guy I know told me I was playing victim, letting all the 'stuff' life threw me convince me I'm not worthy of anything better."

"He was wrong."

"Wait!" She touched her fingers to his lips. "He was right. I was crying 'poor me,' but not anymore."

"What made you change your mind?"

She smiled, thinking of the letters in his briefcase. "My mother. I didn't want to be like her. I didn't want to find myself lying on my deathbed pining for the man I couldn't have. Especially when I had the power to get him back."

Strong arms wrapped around her waist, drawing her close. "You never lost him," he whispered.

Roxy's heart soared. "I'm so very glad," she whispered back. Rising on tiptoes, she brought her mouth to his. "I have a question. What would you have done if the successful woman didn't listen to you?"

"I would have looked her in the eye and told her I was grateful for every second I knew her. That nothing we shared was a mistake."

His words reached deep into her soul, healing its wounds. Telling her she'd made the right choice.

"And then," he said, fingers tangling in her hair, "I would have kissed her till she realized I'm crazy about her. I have been since the minute she stormed out of my office in a huff."

"Sounds perfect," Roxy whispered, her voice catching on the tears. "Because I'm pretty sure she's crazy about you, too."

In the end, it wasn't the words that convinced her, but the emotion that glowed from his eyes while he spoke. Looking deep into them, she saw love, compassion and the coppery-brown sincerity that captured her heart. For the first time, seeing them mixed together didn't frighten her, either. If anything, they made her feel more successful than she'd ever felt in her life. Because she loved and was loved.

"Just in case, though..." She touched his cheek. "You should probably kiss her senseless anyway."

"My pleasure," Mike replied. Slipping an arm around her waist, he pulled her close, his lips speaking a truth all their own. Only a small tug on her sweater stopped the moment.

"Does this mean Mike's going to come with us to the merry-go-round?" Steffi asked.

Mike laughed and scooped the little girl into his arms. "Absolutely, my little pony! There is nothing I want to do more right now." He smiled at Roxy over the little girl's head.

And Roxy, smiling back, believed every word.

* * * * *